NB

# MY LOST DAUGHTER

FORGE BOOKS BY
NANCY TAYLOR ROSENBERG

The Cheater
My Lost Daughter

# My Lost
# Daughter

## NANCY TAYLOR ROSENBERG

A TOM DOHERTY ASSOCIATES BOOK    NEW YORK

MY LOST DAUGHTER

Copyright © 2010 by NTR Literary Inventions, Inc.

A Forge Book
Published by Tom Doherty Associates, LLC
175 Fifth Avenue
New York, NY 10010

www.tor-forge.com

Forge® is a registered trademark of Tom Doherty Associates, LLC.

ISBN 978-0-7653-1903-6

First Edition: September 2010

Printed in the United States of America

0  9  8  7  6  5  4  3  2  1

# MY LOST DAUGHTER

# PROLOGUE

Death was approaching. Rodents and other small creatures scurried as the dry leaves crinkled and the tall weeds were forcefully pushed aside.

Few people ever visited the area because the trees and brush were dense, and a chemical plant a few miles away had long ago polluted the water. From the road above, the shoreline was invisible. The area was also surrounded by a tall wire fence, the gate secured by a heavy padlock.

Two men climbed down the steep embankment to the lake. Earlier, one of the men had used a bolt cutter to gain access. They stood side by side at the water's edge, the only light from the full moon and the scattering of stars above them.

After several minutes of silence had passed, the taller of the two men asked, "Are you absolutely certain this is what you want?"

"Completely, you know that."

"What are you expecting to happen when it's over?"

"I'll be dead and my family will collect on my insurance."

"That's not what I mean," the taller man said. "What do you believe happens to a person when they die?"

"I'd like to believe I'll be reborn into a healthy body without the limitations I've had in this one. But I know that's bullshit."

"You must believe. None of us could go through this if we didn't believe in an afterlife. You took a vow, remember?"

His face twisted in frustration. "Okay, I believe."

"You could live many more years the way you are now," the taller man commented. "Your body is in good shape."

"It's my mind that's the problem." The shorter man became agitated. "Look, we've gone over this a hundred times. I can't live like this anymore. I don't care what happens. I want to die. That's my happy ending. I've fought this too long. I want it to be over."

"Your family will miss you."

"No," the shorter man answered. "My family will be relieved. I'm an embarrassment to them. I know they love me. I also know they'll be better off without me." He wiped his sweaty palms on his pants. "Can't we get this over with?"

"You can walk away now and no one will ever know about tonight. There's no disgrace in bowing out."

"Please, you promised it would be quick and that you wouldn't try to talk me out of it." He reached out and grabbed the taller man's arm. "Give me the gun, damn it. I'll do it myself."

The tension was so thick, it was palpable. This was the part the taller man enjoyed the most and he wanted to savor it, learn from it. A courageous man stood before him. How many men could stare death in the face and invite it to take him? And this man, whether he realized it or not, was prepared to meet the ultimate test, self-sacrifice. Even knowing these things, he couldn't stop himself from salivating over the terrified look in his eyes, watching as the man's determination was undermined by confusion and doubt. There was no greater suspense. No book, no movie, no TV show could compare with it. The question hung heavy in the night air.

Would he stay or would he go?

The other thing he loved was the intimacy, the dirty deeds people told him, things they had held back from their closest friends and relatives. In their final moments, he became their confessor. "You know what happens if you shoot yourself?" he told the smaller man. "Your death will be classified as a suicide and your family won't collect on your life insurance. From what you've told me, you didn't take out the policy until last year. Most insurance companies have a two-year clause when it comes to suicide." He extended his hand with the gun in it. "If that's what you want, go ahead and shoot yourself."

"Fool!" the man shouted, his anger fueled by fear. "You know that's not what I want. The only reason I'm doing this is to pay my family back for what I've put them through. Two years ago, I almost strangled my son while I was psychotic. My wife covered for me or I would still be in prison. My son never forgave me. Even today, he hates me." He paused, too emotional to continue. At last, he said, "Kill me now or I'll get someone else to do it."

The taller man had to stifle a laugh. Where would he find someone to kill him and for free, no less? The man should be grateful. Most people would be too afraid. Going to prison was the least of their fears. Knowing they would have to reconcile what they had done with their creator was a far greater deterrent. When it came to crunch time, everyone believed.

"My own time is coming soon, my friend." He moved closer to the man and lowered his voice to a whisper. "When I touch your shoulder, turn around and drop your head until your chin almost touches your chest. This is the best way. You'll die instantly and there'll be no pain."

They linked eyes in silence. The man who would soon be dead was drenched in sweat and visibly trembling. The taller man knew it was wrong to make him suffer any longer. He softly touched his shoulder and the man turned his back and bent his head down to his chest, standing perfectly still. He was saying something under his breath, more than likely praying. The taller man eased his finger off the trigger to give him a few more seconds of life.

As soon as the man stopped mumbling, he raised the gun, bracing it with his free hand as he took aim. "I'll see you on the other side."

A loud explosion pierced the silence. The bullet seared its way into the back of the shorter man's head. He loved the sound of a dead body striking the ground. It reminded him of a tree falling in the wilderness; only tonight there was someone to hear it, bear witness to it. And it had been perfect because there was no wind, no traffic, and no barking dogs to interfere with his hearing.

As his friend's bloody and lifeless body remained on the ground, the man used a small flashlight to search around. As soon as he found what he was looking for, he picked it up and placed it in his pocket. He then shoved the gun in the back of his jeans, wiped his prints off the flashlight, and tossed it in the bushes. After taking another final look to be certain he hadn't missed anything, he zipped up his jacket and climbed back up the hill.

# ONE

Once the jury was seated and the defendant was led in and placed at the counsel table beside the defense attorney, the bailiff stepped to the front of the courtroom. "All rise," Leonard Davis announced. "Division Forty-seven of the Superior Court of Ventura County is now in session, the Honorable Lillian Forrester presiding."

A tall, slender redhead entered through the back door of the courtroom, ascending the three steps to the bench in a swirl of black robes. Lily's hair was one of her most distinctive features, and she wore it long, an inch or so past her shoulders. Today, however, she'd swept it into a ponytail at the base of her neck. Wispy tendrils had already escaped onto her forehead and neck. Her skin was pale with a scattering of freckles across her nose and cheeks. She was a striking woman, with a natural, fresh look and delicate features.

Lily knew the prosecution of criminals was a cat and mouse game. The majority of cases never made their way to trial. If every case required the time and resources of a jury trial, the criminal justice system would collapse. Even in the most gruesome homicides, a plea agreement was the preferable way to put a case to rest.

But plea agreements in cases of this magnitude weren't normally offered right away. The system was similar to a boa constrictor. The longer it squeezed a criminal, the more information would pop out and the more willing a defendant would be to accept whatever sentence was offered. This was particularly true when the alternative was death.

The courtroom was packed and noisy. Lily had forbidden the proceedings to be televised, so members of the media filled most of the seats. Reporters were scribbling on notepads or creeping down the aisles with their cameras in hand to snap photos. The case was sensational, the kind that turned murderers into celebrities. The defendant, Noelle Lynn Reynolds, had been a popular local girl, a former cheerleader and prom queen at Ventura High. The petite blonde with the round face and dove gray eyes didn't look much older than her high school yearbook photos, although she was only a few months shy of her twenty-third birthday. The last thing she looked like was a cold-blooded murderer, a woman so callous she would kill her own child in order to enjoy a carefree existence.

Gone were the plunging necklines and bare midriff Reynolds had so proudly displayed in the various nightclubs, bars, and beaches she'd frequented in the weeks following her two-year-old son's disappearance. She was dressed in a dowdy polyester suit, her large breast implants squashed inside the beige fabric of her jacket. Her hair was slicked back from her face and she wore no makeup. The flamboyant party girl had been intentionally disguised for the benefit of the jury.

Lily's eyes came to rest on Clinton Silverstein, a district attorney she had known and worked with since the beginning of her career. One of the judges was retiring and Clinton was hoping to get his slot. This case could be a deciding factor, and in Lily's opinion, the prosecutor had already made a poor decision. The State was asking for the death penalty. Lily felt it was highly unlikely that a middle-class Ventura jury would send a young woman like Noelle Reynolds to her death, regardless of the unspeakable crime she'd committed.

Lily had called Silverstein into her chambers on several occasions, attempting to get him to reconsider. In a case of this magnitude, prosecutors generally filed numerous counts such as second-degree murder, or even manslaughter, along with other crimes that were considered lesser or included, meaning if the jury decided guilt in one count, they couldn't find the defendant guilty of the others. The benefit of this type of filing is that it gives the jury an alternative other than acquittal. Pleading special circumstances, which justified the death penalty, was also used to pressure the defendant into accepting a plea agreement.

Silverstein wanted justice, though, and had given little thought to offering Reynolds a deal. An adorable little boy had died terrified and alone at the hands of the one person in the world who should have loved and protected him. The prosecutor argued that an attractive, young, and manipulative woman such as Noelle Reynolds would do well in prison, even if she had killed a child. If she'd been a man, another inmate might have sought revenge, as even criminals looked down on people who victimized children. Women weren't as violent as male offenders, though, nor were they as willing to throw their future away to make certain a fellow inmate received the ultimate punishment.

Tragically, Noelle Reynolds wouldn't be the only woman in prison for murdering her child. When women killed, they generally murdered individuals they had once loved—husbands, boyfriends, parents, or children.

In most instances, in exchange for their guilty plea and the money they would save the state by not taking the case to trial, the defendant would be offered life without the possibility of parole, or twenty-five years to life in the state prison. In an indeterminate term, such as twenty-five to life, the defendant would be eligible for parole in approximately twelve years.

After spending months studying autopsy photos of a lifeless toddler whose decomposing body had been stuffed in a garbage bag and tossed into the ocean, Silverstein had turned the case into a personal vendetta. What Noelle Reynolds hadn't realized was that bodies that ended up in the ocean in Ventura always washed ashore at the sewage plant in Oxnard, adding another disgusting element to an already heinous crime.

Lily let her eyes slowly drift over to the defense attorney. Richard Fowler was a former lover, and she'd given thought to asking Judge Hennessey, the presiding judge, to assign someone else when she learned Fowler was representing Noelle Reynolds. But the case was important and she didn't believe there was a conflict of interest. The Ventura justice community was tight and everyone knew each other. They not only knew each other, they had sex, married, and divorced each other.

Lily hadn't seen Fowler in years and was shocked at how much he had aged. Of course, the fact that she was engaged to Christopher Rendell, a brilliant, handsome judge who was several years younger than Fowler, played a prominent role in purging any lingering attraction she might have for the attorney.

Her eyes narrowed, however, as she checked out the young blonde serving as Fowler's co-counsel, wondering if she was the woman he'd married several years ago. Good lord, she thought, the girl didn't look older than twenty-five. Talk about robbing the cradle. But regardless of the gray hairs and the lines around his mouth and eyes, Richard Fowler was still a good-looking and desirable man.

Accepting the court file from the hands of her clerk, Susan Martin, Lily's penetrating gaze swept over the room. "*People vs. Noelle Lynn Reynolds,* case number A367428912—a violation of Section 187 of the California Penal Code, Murder in the First Degree." Special circumstances had also been pled, but would be decided in a separate penalty stage of the trial once the defendant was convicted. And she would be convicted. The evidence was overwhelming.

Lily repositioned the skinny black microphone closer to her mouth, and then looked over at the prosecutor. "Mr. Silverstein, are you ready to present your opening statement?"

"Yes, Your Honor," he answered, pushing himself to his feet. A short, overweight man in his late forties, he ran his hands through his bushy brown hair. "Ladies and gentlemen, the people will prove to you that Noelle Reynolds willfully and intentionally, with malice aforethought, murdered her two-year-old son, Brandon Lewis Reynolds." He paused, letting the weight of his words sink in. "What kind of mother could do this to her own child? What led up to such a depraved act? Let me paint you a picture of such an individual.

"Noelle Reynolds lived a life of privilege. Her father was a doctor and earned enough money to give his only daughter whatever she desired. At sixteen, he bought her a Porsche and gave her an American Express card with no spending limit. And as we all know, privilege can lead to popularity. Noelle was captain of her cheerleading team, as well as prom queen at Ventura High. Her grades were exemplary, enough so that she gained admittance to UCLA."

He walked over to the jury rail. "But something went wrong, and it went wrong fast. Noelle failed almost every class. Noelle's roommate at UCLA will testify during the course of this trial that Noelle paid her to do her work assignments. Having others do her work was a lifelong habit for the defendant. Another witness will testify how she bleached her hair to look more like Noelle, and took the SATs for her, the only reason Noelle was accepted to UCLA. Earlier classmates will testify as to how they were consistently paid by Noelle to do her work and steal answers to exams." He spun around and faced the defendant, pointing an accusing finger at her. "Noelle Reynolds, the woman sitting comfortably before you in an air-conditioned courtroom after leaving her precious toddler to suffocate in the trunk of her car, has lied her way through life and lived off the backs of others. But the one thing she wanted, she couldn't have. She wanted Mark Stringer, a fellow student at UCLA. She wanted him so desperately that she set out to get pregnant with his child with the belief that he would marry her. When she didn't immediately get pregnant by Stringer, the defendant went on a promiscuous binge, sleeping with an untold number of men until she accomplished her goal. What Noelle didn't know, and even Mark Stringer himself wasn't aware of at that time, was that he was physically unable to father a child. Mr. Stringer was sterile.

"For the first time in her life, Noelle tasted failure and rejection. And she now had a baby to care for when she had never cared for anyone or anything other than herself. As her lies began to unravel and her gravy train came to a screeching halt, the defendant began to plot ways she could rid herself of what she saw as a liability— her own flesh and blood, her son, little Brandon Reynolds."

As Silverstein walked back to the counsel table, his face frozen into hard lines, he stopped and stood beside a large poster-size photograph of Brandon, propped up on an easel. The boy had white blond hair and enormous blue eyes, and there was a happy smile on his young face. "Does this look like a liability to you, something to be shoved in a garbage bag and left to float in the frigid waters of the ocean until his tiny ravaged body ended up in a place his murderous mother believed he belonged—floating among human waste at the Oxnard sewage plant? I don't think so."

Several of the female jurors had tears streaming down their faces and even a few of the men found it hard to remain dry-eyed in the face of such depravity. At the counsel table, Silverstein leaned down to quickly confer with his co-counsel, Beth Sanders, a forty-ish woman with brown hair and a masculine jawline. "When the defendant ran home to her father, believing he would take care of her problems as he'd always done in the past, Dr. Reynolds became furious and refused to let his daughter and her new baby live in his home. He also cut the defendant off financially, forcing her to get a job to support herself and little Brandon. Ms. Reynolds begged her friends in Ventura to help her, but by now, they all had responsibilities of their own."

Many judges actually went to sleep on the bench, especially during this stage of the proceedings. Prior to a case reaching Lily's courtroom, a preliminary hearing was held in the municipal court. A preliminary hearing was similar to a mini trial without a jury. At the conclusion, the municipal court judge decided if the defendant should be held to answer in superior court. Of course, Lily had

already read through the court reporter's transcript on the preliminary hearing, so she was all too familiar with the facts of the case.
She had never fallen asleep but her thoughts occasionally wandered,
and having Richard Fowler only a few feet away was hugely distracting. She tried not to look at him, but she was only human and as
hard as she fought, she couldn't stop herself from remembering
the first time they had made love.

The district attorney's office had been having a party. She generally didn't go to these affairs, but it had been her birthday and no
one had remembered except her mother. Her husband hadn't remembered. Her daughter hadn't remembered. If her mother hadn't
sent her a card, even Lily would have forgotten. But she would never
forget that night. She had experienced pleasure she never knew existed, went on to end her marriage to Shana's father, and had set
a chain of events in motion that had possibly led a rapist to her
doorstep and turned her into a killer.

SPRING, 1993
VENTURA, CALIFORNIA

The Elephant Bar was filled to capacity with suits, both the male and female versions.
Since the completion of the new government center complex, the legal community had
claimed the bar as their own. The atmosphere was straight out of Casablanca,
circa 1993, with whitewashed walls, ceiling fans, and a black piano player who played
when no one could hear and everyone was too preoccupied to listen. But deals were cut
here daily, plea bargains and under-the-table transactions, the days of a person's life
dealt out like so many playing cards. Attorneys would brag about settling a case in
Division 69; everyone knew that meant over drinks at the Elephant Bar.

Clinton Silverstein and Marshall Duffy, both district attorneys, were standing at
a table near the front door. It was one of those high tables with no stools, the kind
used by establishments like the Elephant Bar to cram more bodies into a small space.
Silverstein was running his finger around the glass rim of his gin and tonic while
Duffy poured beer from a pitcher. Duffy was black and handsome, dressed in a stylishly tailored pin-striped suit and a crisp white shirt and tie. He towered over the
short, stocky Silverstein. "You're a righteous nutcase, you know," he said, "even if I
do call you a friend."

"I'm a nutcase. Well, at least I don't wear tinted contacts. Do you know how weird those things make you look?" Silverstein stepped back from the table, loosening his tie and smiling at the other man.

Duffy tipped his glass and let the beer slide down his throat before responding. "My baby blues. Women love them. As long as they get me laid, I'm wearing them. So what's the big deal with this transfer? I thought you put in for it."

"Before, I put in before, back when Fowler was still running the unit. I'm sick of the misdemeanor division. Shit, if I have to handle another DWI, I'm gonna hang myself from a tree with a beer bottle stuck up my ass."

"So you don't. You got the transfer. What have you got against Forrester? She can't be all that bad. Nice little ass. Reminds me of my wife's." Duffy stepped back and almost toppled a plastic palm tree.

"I don't care what she looks like. I just know she's one tense lady. What she needs is a good tranquilizer, a good fuck, or both. That's what I think. She's going to run that unit with an iron fist."

"Sounds like the pot calling the kettle black, my man." Duffy's eyes turned toward the door. "Take a big slug of that drink, Clinty. Your new boss just arrived.

"Lily," Duffy called to her. "Over here."

The bar was dark and smoky, and Lily's eyes were still adjusting from the sunlight outside. She followed the voice. "Hello, Marshall. Looks like the party started without me." She was anxious, scanning the room. From the looks of it, the entire agency and half the private attorneys in the area were here.

"Hey, we're all waiting for you. You're one of the guests of honor tonight. What're you drinking?"

She started to order her usual glass of white wine and then changed her mind. "I guess a margarita, with salt." As Duffy flagged the waitress, she added impulsively, "Order me a shot of Patrón." Might as well do it right, she decided. This is what the men did when they had a bad day, came over here and got smashed. It appeared to work for them. Maybe it would work for her. Today had been a rough one, and the new job assignment was weighing heavily on her mind.

"Whoa there, I'm impressed. Clinton and I were just talking about you. He's been telling me how excited he is about working with you."

"Guess he's not that excited. He just walked away." Lily laughed, but it wasn't really funny. Attorneys like Silverstein presented another problem she had to contend with, one brought on by the promotion. Now she had to supervise other attorneys, some with far more experience and much larger egos. It wasn't going to be easy. She could use a good stiff drink.

Duffy turned his head to the side, surprised. Clinton was standing a few tables over talking to Richard Fowler, Lily's predecessor.

Lily tried to look into Duffy's translucent blue eyes, but her gaze was drawn to Fowler. "You transferred into homicide, took my slot, right?" Her eyes burned into Fowler's back, willing him to turn around. Instead of bending down and placing her briefcase and purse on the floor, she dropped them with a loud thud. The noise was lost in the bar and Fowler still didn't turn around. Her face felt flushed. "Where's the waitress?" she asked Duffy, thinking she'd change her order to a glass of wine. She didn't want Fowler to see her tossing down shots of tequila like a rock star. It was too late. Duffy had already given the girl the order.

"Guess you can call me a victim of the big Butler shuffle," Duffy said, placing his elbows on the table.

His words drifted past her and once again her thoughts turned to Fowler. For the past two weeks he'd been working with her, coaching her to make the shift in supervisors as smooth as possible. He was tall, maybe six-five, with the lean, hard body of a runner. His hair and eyes were dark, a sharp contrast against his fair skin. He moved his long body and long legs without sound wherever he went, fluid and relaxed like a large cat ready to pounce on unsuspecting prey. He moved the way Lily wanted to move. And he moved Lily.

He finally saw her and headed in her direction. When the waitress appeared with the drinks, Fowler lifted the margarita off the tray, glancing at Lily. She nodded. Then he saw the shot glass and again looked at her. "Yours?" he asked.

"No . . . yes . . . I . . ." She blushed. She was stammering like a fool. Fowler did that to her. "It's been one of those days. Thought I'd try to drown it."

Setting both glasses on the table, he slid in close to her, in front of Duffy, who presently waved good-bye. A cloud of Fowler's cologne drifted to her nostrils, a hint of lime. For the past two weeks she'd been inhaling it, even found it lingering on her clothes like cigarette smoke when she was forced to work closely with a smoker.

"Shots, huh?" he said with a smile that lifted only one corner of his mouth. "Was it really that bad of a week?"

"No, you've been great, Richard. I mentioned the sentencing I had today, didn't

I? You know, the sweetheart who thinks human life is comparable to a Timex watch."

"You mean, 'takes a licking'? Well, it's kinda cute, isn't it? The guy might become a stand-up comic when he gets out."

The defendant they were talking about had pumped six bullets into a stranger in a public park. When the police asked him why he'd kept shooting when the victim was obviously dead, the killer told the cops, "He took a licking and kept on ticking."

"That's the problem," Lily said. "That someone can commit a murder and be back on the streets to do it again in a few years. It makes me sick. It's just something you don't get used to, no matter how many times you see it." She spotted the waitress and bent down to get her purse, turning her back and digging for her money. "Let me buy you a drink."

"The waitress is gone. Next time, if you insist."

He was so close now that their hips were touching. Lily downed the shooter of tequila with one swallow and chased it with the margarita, licking the salt off her lips. The closer he stood to her, the more flustered she became. She was talking like a rookie DA, like she'd never prosecuted a homicide before.

"Do you remember the last party we were both at? I do," he said. "You were wearing this white backless dress and your hair was down, all the way down your back. You looked terrific."

"The last party was a barbecue at Dennis O'Connor's, and that was over five years ago. If my memory serves me right, you were wearing jeans and a blue sweater."

Their eyes met and he refused to look away, searching there, prying where he didn't belong. The tequila was still burning her throat and she felt uncomfortable. She took her cold glass and pressed it against her cheek. "I have to make a phone call. Watch my briefcase, okay?" She turned to head to the back of the bar, and then tossed over her shoulder with a smile, "And, Richard, I've never in my life owned a white backless dress."

There were a lot of things Lily had never done, far more significant than not wearing a backless sundress to a party. One of them was having an affair. Although John had accused her of cheating on him for years, Lily had remained faithful despite the accusations and the complete disappearance of sex in their marriage.

Elbowing her way through the people, she spotted District Attorney Paul Butler on his way to the door. He was a short, serious man in his midfifties who seldom mingled with those who worked beneath him. "Paul," she said, "I didn't see you earlier or I would have come over. I guess your secretary informed you of our conference tomorrow on the Lopez/McDonald matter." The tequila had hit Lily hard on an empty stomach. She willed herself to remain sober, carefully articulating her words.

"Oh, yes," he said with a blank look in his eyes. "Refresh me."

"Double homicide, teenagers, lovers . . . the boy was beaten and bludgeoned, the girl raped and mutilated. Five suspects in custody, all Hispanic—probably gang related." It was front-page and sensational, both kids honor students, college bound. "You asked for the conference yourself, Paul. The case was assigned to me prior to the promotion, and I've already done the workup. Don't you remember?" She tried to sound nonchalant, not wanting to emphasize the fact that he was uninformed on a case of this magnitude.

Butler looked down and coughed. "The budget is due this week and the mayor is all over me."

As he walked past her, she reached out and took his hand, then moved even closer, violating his personal space. "I just want to tell you how much I appreciate the promotion. I know you had others to consider."

Even in the dim light of the bar, she could see his face turning beet red in embarrassment. She was standing far too close, a bad habit resulting from vanity, refusing to wear her glasses outside of the office. She looked down at the top of his head and saw how thin his hair was, something she'd never noticed before. He stepped back as if he knew.

"Certainly, certainly," he said. "Well, I guess we'll discuss this Lopez/McDonald case tomorrow."

As he started to pass, he was pushed into her, against her chest, her breasts. The terrified look in his eyes almost caused her to laugh. Did he actually believe she was flirting with him? How ludicrous. If she was going to flirt with anyone, it sure wouldn't be Butler. She leaned against the brass rail of the bar and watched him scurry away on his short little legs, musing on a world where a genuine expression of gratitude was so rare that it raised suspicion. Maybe Butler wasn't even aware he'd promoted her. Perhaps his assistant just picked her name out of a hat.

No, she rationalized, impossible. He had called Fowler into his office on a rampage and demoted him, offering Lily his position a few hours later. Fowler was still a supervisor, but over the municipal court division, a clear step down. The story went that he'd become enraged over a lenient sentence on a particularly vicious sex crime and had stormed into Judge Raymond Fisher's chambers without announcement, all the way into his private bathroom, where he had found the forty-year-old judge snorting lines of cocaine out of a small bullet-looking device. This was one of the reasons Lily wanted a position on the bench. Like oil in water, some of the slimiest had risen to the top and floated there, untouchable, their shifting shadow spreading and darkening all the lives beneath them. Judge Fisher got caught snorting cocaine; Fowler got demoted. That sounded like a fair and impartial decision.

At the back of the bar, Lily spotted the phone outside the ladies' room. She thought it was the ladies' room, but she couldn't read the African name. She'd been there many times but never drinking Patrón tequila. With the alcohol flooding her bloodstream, the floor moved and swayed like a ship at sea. Searching for the little stick figure of a woman with a skirt and finding none, she decided what the hell, barging through the door. She almost ran over Carol Abrams.

"Lily," the petite blonde said, "congratulations on the promotion. That really was quite a coup."

She patted Lily on both shoulders with dainty hands and bright pink manicured nails. The movement caused her blunt-cut, shiny hair to swing forward, and Lily watched, mesmerized, as it fell back to the exact same position, every hair perfectly aligned. Pushing an unruly strand off her forehead, Lily spotted the chipped paint on her own fingernails and quickly dropped her hands to her side.

"I won't say I didn't want that promotion. No, I won't deny it. But I'm glad that at least it was you and not some idiot that will sit in his office all day and make paper airplanes. You know what I mean?"

Lily went into a stall and shut the door, carefully pulling the latch. Carol Abrams might follow her inside or open the door to continue the conversation while Lily sat there with her panty hose stuck around her thighs. Brilliant and never tiring, Abrams was an asset to any department. In court, she simply wore them down: judges, juries, defense attorneys, every last one of them.

"I don't know how you feel about Fowler, but I don't mind saying I'm glad to see him go. I mean, he clearly knows the law but recently he's lost all semblance of self-control. Everyone knows you don't go after a judge like a madman. My God, I think he's suffering from burnout. You know what I mean?" She stopped and took an audible breath, preparing to continue.

"Carol, I'd prefer we talk about this tomorrow." Just as Lily flushed the toilet, she realized she didn't want to leave until Abrams had left and wished she hadn't flushed. She had an urge to tell her off to her face, open the door and tell her Fowler knew more about the law than she would ever know in her hyperactive life, but she didn't need enemies.

She opened the door and the woman was gone. Thank God for small favors. Seeing her bedraggled face in the mirror, she removed the bobby pins out of the loose knot and brushed her red hair. She reapplied her lipstick, tried to resmudge her eye shadow, and headed to the phone to call her twelve-year-old daughter.

"Shana, it's me."

"Hold on, Mom, let me put Charlotte on hold."

Lily thought it was insane for a child her age to have a private line as well as call-waiting, but her father . . .

"MOM, I'm on the other line." Shana was screaming at her the way people did on the Jerry Springer Show.

Lily opened her eyes wide and stepped back from the phone. Shana was getting more sarcastic every day. Lily remembered what it was like to go through puberty, and she was trying her best to let it slide, thinking it was just an adolescent phase. "Are you doing your homework or just talking on the phone, sweetie? Where's your dad?"

"Charlotte's helping me on the phone and Dad's asleep on the sofa."

Lily pictured him there as he was every evening, the dishes piled in the sink, the television blasting, stretched out on the sofa snoring. He worked for the government in employee relations and got home every day at four-thirty. The year before, his hours had been cut and he now not only got home early, he didn't work at all on Tuesdays and Thursdays. Rather than get another job to substitute for the income he had lost, John just fiddled around the house or fell asleep in front of the TV. This was one of the reasons she had begun staying late at the office. With John sacked out in front of the television and Shana in her room on the phone every night with the door closed, there wasn't a compelling reason to go home. "Tell him I'm tied up in a meeting and will be home in a few hours."

"Tell him yourself."

"I love you," Lily whispered, hearing the phone click as Shana went back to the other line. She saw her adorable face in her mind and tried to match it to her tone of voice. Her own child, her precious little girl, was becoming rude and obnoxious. She'd just hung up on her. Only a few years ago, Shana would sit on the floor in front of Lily for hours, enthralled at every word that came out of her mouth, her face bright and beaming. Now she was talking to her like a dog and hanging up on her. If Lily had spoken that way to her father, she would have been slapped to the floor. But John said those days were over, that children had a right to talk back. And Shana adored her father.

Lily started to call John and then decided against it. She'd say something to him about Shana talking on the phone and not studying; she couldn't stop herself. She could only be what she had already become. John would hang up and march to Shana's room, telling her that her mother said she had to get off the phone, but it was okay because he wouldn't tell on her. He might even add that her mother said she had to clean her room. That would go over great. If that didn't make Shana despise her, he could also remind her that her mother once said she'd have to become a waitress because she'd never study hard enough to get into college. One of those off-the-wall comments a parent makes to prove a point to the other parent, her remark wasn't something to repeat to a child. But John repeated it and said a lot of other things that were outright lies.

He was a brilliant manipulator, Lily thought as she walked back into the noisy bar, straightening her skirt and pushing up her bra. He should have been a defense attorney. No, he'd make a perfect divorce lawyer.

Back at the table, she saw a fresh margarita, a new shooter, and Richard Fowler. She slid the shot glass away and took a sip of her margarita, letting her hair fall seductively over one corner of her eye while she drank in Fowler from his shoes to the top of his head. She was looking at a determined man, a man of conviction, a warrior, not the type of man who needed to fight with a child as his shield. Nor was he a man who could be happy with a mediocre government job where his hours had been cut to only twenty a week and his wife carried the weight of the family while he puttered around in the kitchen. He wasn't a wimp like John.

Silverstein's New York accent rang out from the adjoining table, where he was throwing popcorn in his mouth and trying to talk at the same time. He was complaining about some case, four out of five kernels ending up on his clothes or the floor. Duffy had apparently gone home.

"Your hair looks great," Richard told her. "I had no idea it was still so long. You never wear it down at the office." He reached out and touched a strand, twirling it between his fingers.

"Not too professional. I don't know why I don't cut it. Guess I'm trying to hold on to my youth or something." She was breathless. He was so close.

Fowler's fingers disappeared from her hair. Lily wanted to reach for his hand and put it back, feel the electricity again, feel his fingers on her face, her skin, but the moment was shattered. From across the room, they both saw Lawrence Bodenham, a private defense attorney. He honed in on Lily and headed in her direction. The new rage with those in private practice was to wear their hair long, almost shoulder-length, and Bodenham's curled at the bottom. Reaching the table, he extended his hand.

"Lawrence Bodenham," he said. "You're Lily Forrester, right?"

"Right," she said, really feeling the tequila now, wishing the man would leave and she could think of something brilliant and seductive to say to Fowler, particularly now that she'd had a few drinks and was feeling the false courage of alcohol. She made no move to shake Bodenham's hand and he withdrew it.

"I'm representing Daniel Duthoy on that 288 matter, and I've been having some problems with Carol Abrams regarding discovery."

The case was only vaguely familiar to Lily. Richard evidently knew it well and turned to face the attorney with a look of disgust. The crime he had mentioned was sodomy and the victim was a ten-year-old boy, the defendant a pillar of the community—a Big Brother.

"Remember me?" Richard snapped. "If you have any problems, Bodenham, just tell it to the judge. Or why don't you call Butler up at home from the phone in your Porsche? He loves guys like you who pull down over a million a year defending these good folks who like to butt-fuck little boys."

Bodenham stepped back a safe distance before responding. "I hear you're back assigning drunk driving and petty thefts to new DAs who don't know their ass from a hole in the ground. Good career move, Fowler." As soon as the words left his mouth, the attorney disappeared into the crowd.

Richard pushed back from the table, slapping it with his palm. "That about makes an evening for me. See you around, kiddo."

Lily caught his coattail, stopping him. "You've had too much to drink, Richard. Let me drive you." She was standing with her purse and briefcase, ready.

For the first time that evening, he smiled broadly, flashing perfect white teeth. "Come on, then. If you want to save me, now's the time. But if you think I'm going to let a drunk like you drive me, you're crazy. You never bought me that drink, so now you can buy me a cup of coffee."

A short time later, they were sitting in a booth at Denny's, two blocks from the

Elephant Bar, sipping black coffee and eating cheeseburgers. They were laughing and getting sober. Lily finished her burger and turned to Richard. "So tell me exactly what happened with Judge Fisher."

"I found the little bastard snorting cocaine. Not much more to tell than that."

"But how did he have the gall to call Butler and complain? Wasn't he the least bit concerned?"

"Hell no, he just told Butler that he didn't want to see my face anywhere near his court again." Richard dabbed at his mouth with his napkin. "I did happen to go up and down the hall and tell a few people that Fisher was having a little party and that they better hurry if they wanted to do some rails of the cleanest-cut coke around."

"What's wrong with you?" Lily said, laughing. "Do you have a death wish or something? I thought you and Butler were on great terms, that he thought you could do no wrong. Why didn't he back you up?"

"Oh, Butler's a good man. He believed me. He's just a pussy. His theory is when the dirt flies, all of us end up buried in it. I actually think he felt bad about the whole thing. When all is said and done, I'll probably end up taking his job."

Lily brushed her hair off her face. The waitress came with the check, and Lily grabbed it and threw a twenty down on the table. "I don't know how I'm going to handle this new job. Isn't it hard to become involved in the cases and then have to rely on someone else to try them?"

"That's what supervision is all about. If you can't trust people or feel you have to track every single proceeding in that unit, you'll lose your mind. Don't nag and don't be a babysitter, Lily, or you'll fall into the age-old stereotype of the woman manager."

Lily stared into space, digesting his advice.

Outside in the cool air, he stood beside her. "I'll walk you to your car. Where did you park?"

In her mind she saw herself already walking through the door of her ranch house. The first thing she saw every day was the backyard. "I parked at the courthouse," she said, looking straight in front of her. John had decided to adjust the sprinkler system about six months ago and had dug up the entire backyard. He'd planted one side with sod, leaving the other side dirt after he couldn't figure out how to get the sprinklers working.

"My car is at the bar. I'll drive you," Richard told her. "You shouldn't be walking around alone at night."

"Thanks." On weekends, John would sit in a lawn chair and sun himself on the grass side as if the dirt side didn't exist. No matter how many times she told him it irritated her and how ridiculous it looked, he made no attempt to change it. She didn't want to go home. She didn't want to be the primary decision maker, the disciplinarian, the strong one. She wanted to laugh and feel pleasure, feel attractive and physically desirable. She wanted to believe a birthday was a cause for celebration.

They walked in silence. She'd have to settle for the moment. Soon it would be gone and she'd be at home in bed with John. After all these years of abstinence and John's accusations that she was fooling around on the side—for the first time she wished it was true. And it could only be with the man walking beside her, the same man she called forth in her fantasies. But he was married and there was no reason to believe he was physically attracted to her. If John was no longer interested in her sexually, why would another man want her? She was no longer desirable. She might as well accept it. She'd accepted everything else about her life.

He unlocked the passenger side door of his white BMW and tossed what looked like his gym clothes into the backseat. In the driver's seat, he put the key in the ignition, then dropped his hands in his lap and turned to her. He reached across and kissed her fully on the mouth, his hands buried in her thick hair. His face with day-old stubble scratched her sensitive skin but she didn't notice.

"Come home with me," he whispered. "Please, I want you."

"But . . ." Lily thought of his wife and teenage son, the fact that she should go home; that she might want it now and regret it later. His lips were there again as he worked his way to her neck and gently bit on her ear. His hands on her back pressed her against him.

She was flooded with warmth, pushing herself closer into his body, her flesh alive with nerve endings. Everything washed away: the job, John, Shana, her birthday, her upbringing, her caution.

"Please," he said, lifting her chin and forcing her to look into his eyes. "No one is there if that's what you're thinking. And no one is coming home tonight." He took her hand and placed it on the crotch of his pants, on his erection. She let it stay there as he kissed her again.

She was a normal woman with normal desires. Richard wasn't going to use her as a receptacle, as John would say. He was the repairman, the doctor, the magician. He was going to plug her back into the wall outlet and turn on the lights. She wasn't broken. She'd just been placed on the shelf.

"Drive," she said, "and fast. Drive fast."

An hour later, they were standing at the plate-glass window in his living room, looking out over the city lights of Ventura. He was nude; she was wrapped in a large bath sheet. The house was in the foothills, contemporary, with high ceilings and an open, airy feeling. Her jacket, her shoes, her bra and hose were scattered across the room. They had never made it to the bedroom.

Once in the house, she had stripped her clothes off almost ahead of him, and they had stood there facing each other a foot apart, both their arms at their sides.

"I always knew your body would look like this," he told her.

"What does it look like?"

"Lush. It looks like mounds of strawberry yogurt. I want to taste it."

They made love on the sofa, their feet sticking off one end, arms and legs everywhere. It was the only piece of furniture in the room. With his long, sinewy arms he held her upper body down and buried his head between her legs. He lingered there even when she protested and sighed and cried out, "No. No. No."

She finally could take it no longer and dragged him up by his hair and forced him to switch places with her, and with her hair spread over the hard muscles of his stomach, she took him in her mouth, hungry for the taste and smell of him, the feel of him. "Oh, God," he cried, "God."

She crawled on top of him and straddled him, riding him like a horse, pushed up on her arms, tossing her hair, leaning down to kiss him and then throwing her head back again. This was her fantasy. She was living her dream. She imagined she was on a great white horse, galloping over huge hurdles and streams, heading for the white light of pleasure. Finding it, she collapsed on his chest, sweating, satiated. He rolled her off onto the floor and turned her around, taking her from behind, holding her buttocks in his hands and slamming against her until he exploded and fell on top of her, his warm, heavy breath in her ear.

"Jesus," he said, "did I hurt you?"

"Hardly," she said. "Did I hurt you?"

He lifted her wet hair and kissed the back of her neck tenderly. "I don't think you can call that pain."

Suddenly embarrassed, she broke free, sat up with her knees drawn and her arms wrapped around them. Already feelings of guilt were fluttering in the pit of her stomach, but a quick look at Richard made them disappear. She had finally met John's accusations and suspicions. And it had been easy, too easy. And it had been good enough to want much more. Her body was screaming at her, begging her, demanding more. Perhaps she could actually feed this desire, this need. She could go on wanting Richard until he ignored her and disappointed her and no longer cared if she walked alone at night. This is what it must feel like when two people met each other on an even level, shared similar points of view. She let her eyes drift down in mock coyness; a smile playing at the corners of her lips. Her behavior had been shocking, wanton, thrilling. Throughout the world, people felt this good all the time, at every second in every day. Getting a divorce was not a crime punishable by death. She could feel this way again.

They showered together in the master bathroom. Passing the bed, she saw it was unmade and the room was strewn with clothes and newspapers and glasses sitting on tables without coasters. In the shower, they rubbed soap all over each other's bodies. He dumped half a bottle of shampoo on her head and it dripped down into her eyes. "Get me a towel," she said, laughing and listening to the delightful sound bounce off the tiled walls, amazed that it had been manufactured inside her. "You've blinded me." She took the little soap, greatly used, and made him turn around and rubbed it between the two muscular cheeks of his ass, like she'd done to her daughter when she was a baby. He jumped and told her to stop, but she knew he loved it. Outside the shower, he wanted to comb her pubic hair so some of the hairs would be there in the morning. She couldn't believe it, but she let him. It tickled. He commented on the fact that she was a real redhead, causing her to take one of his nipples and twist it hard. "Because you doubted me," and because she just wanted to, had always wanted to do something like that. Afterward, he gave her the only clean towel and walked naked, dripping water onto the carpet, to the living room, where they now stood and talked.

He moved behind her and put his arms around her. "Do you want something to drink? I don't have any tequila, but I can find something else."

Her head ached at the mere mention of tequila. "No, thanks, I have to go, you know, and soon." She had already decided that his wife no longer lived there. She wanted it to be true so badly that she couldn't ask. "I hate to do this to you, but you realize you're going to have to drive me back to my car."

"I don't mind, Lily," he said, his voice reflecting the beginning of a letdown. "But do we have to end it so soon? Can't we just stay here a minute and relish it?" He held her face in both of his hands. "This was much more than just an office fuck and you know it."

She sighed deeply. "I know."

Lily picked her clothes up off the floor and put them back on. She turned away from him when she hooked her bra in the front and turned it around, shaking her breasts into the cups. She put on her blouse first and then her panties. They were plain white comfortable panties, and she was ashamed they were not French-cut lace.

He was still looking out at the city as he spoke. "My wife left me for someone else, Lily. While I was at work, she came with a moving van and moved most of the furniture out."

"I'm sorry, Richard. Did you love her?"

"Sure, I loved her. I lived with her for seventeen years. I don't even know where she is now. She's here in the city somewhere, but she doesn't want me to know where. Our son is with her."

"Do you know the man?" Lily asked, curious about the whole thing, wondering how she could want him so badly while someone who had lived with him for seventeen years no longer wanted him at all.

"It's not a man, Lily. My wife left me for a woman."

"How is your son handling this?"

"Greg doesn't know and I would never tell him. He just thinks the woman is her roommate." His face was bathed in shadows. He was facing Lily now, but he quickly turned back to the window. "I mean, I don't believe he knows."

"You might be surprised, Rich. Kids know a lot more than we think. He may know and have already accepted it. He is living with his mother, right?"

"He's a strange kid, off in his own world." He glanced at Lily over his shoulder and saw that she was dressed and waiting. "Greg used to be an honor student and now he's a surfer. Instead of studying, the kid surfs. He'll be lucky to get into a junior college. I always dreamed he'd be an attorney, that maybe someday we'd have our own law practice. Dreams . . . things don't always turn out the way you planned them."

She saw his need to talk but knew she had to go. "Can we talk in the car? I wish I could stay and we could talk more, but I am married. It's not a good marriage," she paused, "obviously, or I wouldn't be here with you. It may end soon, for all I know, but I don't want it to end badly. Can you understand that?"

"Just give me a minute. I'll get dressed."

At the government center complex, she leaned against the car as he kissed her. "Why do you park here? Don't you know they can see you from the jail?"

"Well," she said, nuzzling him and softly biting his ear, "maybe I might be able to park underground one day."

"Where the judges park?"

"What do you think?"

"I think there's a good possibility if that's what you want. Do you know I recommended you for my replacement?"

She didn't and was pleased. "Thanks, and that was before tonight." She smiled, unlocking the door to her Honda. She started the ignition and waved and then stuck her head out the window. "To be continued, huh?"

"Right," he said, "to be continued."

# TWO

"I thought you might want this," Lily's clerk said, placing a cup of black coffee on her console.

"Thanks, Susie, you're a godsend." Lily quickly returned her full attention back to Clinton Silverstein. She was embarrassed that her clerk thought she'd been asleep on the bench. When the pain in her back became unbearable, she had no choice but to take pain pills and if she didn't keep herself oiled with coffee, she sometimes became drowsy. She hadn't been asleep, however. Part of her brain was listening while another part was reliving the memory of that first night with Richard Fowler.

The attorney caught her eye again and she turned away in embarrassment, wondering what he would do if he knew what she'd been thinking. Her sexual awakening had been tainted only a short time later when she and Shana were raped, and it had taken years for her to regain the ability to experience the kind of pleasure she had that night.

Her relationship with Fowler had ended years ago, and it had ended unpleasantly. It was sad, because they had been coming together as a family. Shana had grown close to his son, Greg. They were both only children and Shana thought of Greg as an older brother. She wondered if they still kept in touch with each other.

Whatever love Lily had held for Richard was long dead. She was even miffed that he'd agreed to represent Noelle Reynolds. Since the girl was virtually penniless, she knew he must be defending her for the publicity. It was sad to see a once great attorney sink to that level. Of course, Dr. Reynolds might have finally managed to get his hand out of his pocket, particularly now that his daughter's life was on the line.

Focusing on Silverstein's opening statement, she liked the direction he was taking, depicting the defendant as a spoiled rich girl who'd cheated and lied her way through life. Since Reynolds had no prior criminal record, which was considered a mitigating factor, the prosecutor had to make certain he established significant circumstances in aggravation or the death penalty would never fly.

"The people will produce irrefutable evidence," Silverstein continued, his voice elevating, "that the defendant attempted to kill Brandon months before she locked him in the trunk of her car and left him to die. To prove how callous the defendant is, we will produce numerous photographs of her posing for seductive photographs at various nightclubs in Los Angeles around the time of her son's death."

Everyone had seen these pictures. The media had relied heavily on them to sensationalize the case. They were clearly damaging as they showed Reynolds smiling and partying directly following her son's disappearance. The photos had also ruled out any possibility the defense might have of establishing that the boy's death was accidental. The images depicted almost everything there was to see of Noelle Reynolds's body, but what they didn't show was the face and actions of a grieving mother, the one thing that might have kept Reynolds from receiving the death penalty. According to the judicial council rules, a defendant's failure to show remorse for his or her actions was considered an aggravating factor.

"The coroner's report states that little Brandon's body remained in the trunk of his mother's car for a minimum of three weeks."

Silverstein removed a handkerchief from his pocket and blotted the perspiration off his forehead. "What mother could be so calculating and cruel that she could drive around for three weeks with the corpse of her deceased child decomposing in the trunk of her Taurus? As inhuman as it sounds, the trunk had become Noelle Reynolds's babysitter, more than likely for some time prior to Brandon's demise. We know this because numerous sedatives were found in Ms. Reynolds's medicine cabinet, many of which were found in Brandon's tissues during autopsy. Noelle Reynolds drugged her son so she could drink and party with her friends, but with full knowledge that her actions could cause his death.

"We will also show you an emergency room report from August of last year when Dr. Reynolds took his grandson to the hospital because he was having trouble swallowing. The defendant told her father that the boy had accidentally eaten Ajax. I've been told by physicians that even if a child gets into an abrasive substance such as Comet or Ajax, they only consume a minute amount because it burns the sensitive tissues in their mouth and throat. The autopsy reports indicated that Brandon's esophagus was scarred, which indicates a sizable amount of Ajax was more than likely fed to him. The coroner also found traces of arsenic in Brandon's tissues, so it's obvious the monster that sits before you had been actively experimenting with different ways to murder her child."

An audible gasp came from the courtroom and several members of the media scrambled toward the back door. Although Fowler knew what had just been described through discovery motions, the police and DA's office had managed to keep the Ajax and arsenic information out of the hands of the media, and all the reporters wanted to be the first to break the story.

A good prosecutor seldom released their most damning evidence during their opening statement, preferring to leave it for a later stage in the trial when their case might be lagging. Determined to convince the jury that Noelle Reynolds was guilty, Silverstein had placed all his cards on the table before he even called his first witness.

A commotion arose in the rear of the courtroom as the reporters tried to push their way past one another. One thing led to another and a female was knocked to the ground. A man beside her grabbed another male around the neck, and a full-fledged fight broke out.

Lily pounded her gavel. "Order!" she shouted, furious. Her bailiff raced to the back of the room and her clerk called for more officers. "I demand you come to order this minute! Anyone who isn't in their seats or out of this courtroom immediately will spend the night in jail."

QUANTICO, VIRGINIA

Special Agent Mary Stevens was working at her desk in the BAU (Behavioral Analysis Unit) of the FBI when John Adams, her SAC (Special Agent in Charge), called and asked her to report to his office.

The BAU was housed at the FBI Academy in Quantico, Virginia. A former homicide detective in Ventura, Mary had been recruited by the Bureau when she'd attended the National Academy Program, a tough twelve-week residential training course for upper-level law enforcement officers from around the world. After a year at the Bureau's headquarters in Washington, she was hired by John Adams. Adams had been a close friend of her deceased father and was chief of the elite analysis and profiling unit. Most people knew it as the Behavior Science Unit, which still existed as part of the academy program but no longer consulted with police agencies in the apprehension and profiling of serial criminals.

Mary considered the use of acronyms inside the FBI to be unnecessary and excessive. Most police departments had stopped using the ten-code system for better clarification and officer safety. When an officer had been shot, was under fire, or found himself in foot pursuit of an armed suspect, a few seconds could cost him his life. Taking the time to remember the correct code was too dangerous. If the officer made a mistake, he could end up with a tow truck instead of an ambulance.

The ten-code system was developed in 1937 and expanded in 1974 under the belief that it allowed for brevity and standardization of radio traffic. She suspected the Bureau's extensive use of acronyms traced back to J. Edgar Hoover's paranoid need for secrecy. Boys loved their decoder rings.

She picked up a large file and headed down the corridor leading to Adams's office, her heels clicking on the linoleum floor. One of her present assignments was to investigative a fairly new phenomenon surfacing in the United States—suicide clubs. Organizations of this nature had existed in Europe and Asia for years, particularly in Japan, where suicide was embedded in the country's culture. In Japan, the clubs were referred to as suicide circles. One club in Russia had more than twenty thousand members.

Mary caught a whiff of cologne just as fellow agent, Genna Weir, stepped up beside her. Weir and Mary were the only females in the unit, and had quickly formed a friendship. Weir was forty-two, stood five-seven, and was in peak physical condition. The lines in her face and the shadows under her eyes made her look closer to fifty. Dealing with the most depraved and violent criminals in the world took its toll. A steely-eyed brunette with superb reasoning abilities, Weir was highly respected within the unit and the Bureau.

"What's up with you and Brooks? Are you guys taking the post in California? I'd do anything to get out of this hellhole. I grew up in Florida and anything less than sixty degrees feels like a meat locker."

"We haven't heard back yet," Mary told her, hedging on the truth. She had requested the transfer months ago but Adams refused to approve it, claiming he couldn't afford to lose her. "There's also a problem with Brooks's mother."

Weir tilted her head to one side, a mischievous smile on her face. "Oh, I remember. You guys had some crazy plan to get your mothers to share an apartment. What were you thinking? I knew that would never happen. Old women hate each other."

"It's not an apartment, Genna. They're going to live in my house and it's really nice. Both of our mothers are at the stage in life where they can't live alone anymore. My mother stopped driving last year, so she gets extremely lonely. Brooks's mother is in the same condition. Rather than put them in a retirement home, which they would loathe, Brooks and I are going to hire someone to take care of them at home so they can maintain a degree of independence. Of course, this person will be able to drive them places, so they won't be stuck in the house all the time."

"I thought your house was rented."

"The lease is up and Brooks wants us to buy a new place together in Ventura. Of course, the first thing we have to do is secure the assignment."

"You'll be scratching the paint off the walls." Weir chuckled. "The most serious crimes you'll handle will be a few bank robberies. You might get lucky and pick up a kidnapping or a drug deal. Regardless, that's a far cry from profiling serial killers."

Suicide clubs had also popped up on various social networking sites, such as MySpace, Meetup, Facebook, and Twitter. The clubs were cleverly disguised, however, and as soon as law enforcement managed to take down one, twenty more would pop up.

Mary entered her boss's office and sat down in a chair in front of his desk. As usual, Adams was on the phone and he waved her away. She stood and walked over to the wall where crime scene photos of ongoing cases were posted. Truly a wall of horror, grotesque images of corpses in different poses and in various stages of decomposition stared back at her. They had a sexual predator on the loose in Chicago. The UNSUB (Unidentified Subject) had recently escalated from rape and sodomy to murder. She saw the blood-splattered body of a girl who appeared to be around five and quickly turned away. Mary refused to work cases where the victims were children. Genna Weir had two kids and had no trouble tracking down child killers.

Mary had been fascinated by death since she was a teenager. Her father had been a police officer in Los Angeles and she used to go to his office and peek at his files. She could thumb through au-

topsy photos as if she were flipping through the pages of a magazine in a doctor's office, but seeing a tiny body that had been bru-
talized was more than she could handle. Brooks said her sensitivity
to wrongs committed against children proved that she'd be a wonderful mother. Mary wasn't sure she wanted to bring a child into
the world knowing the monsters that prowled the streets.

Her father, Harold Stevens, had risen to the rank of deputy chief
at the LAPD before he'd been gunned down by an armed robber at
a Quick Mart ten years ago. Her breath still caught in her throat
when she thought about it. All he had done was stop after work to
buy a bottle of wine for her mother. One of the reasons Adams
had recruited her was the hope that she might possess her father's
intuition. According to Adams and the other vets who served in
the same platoon as her father, he possessed a sixth sense and could
spot friend or foe only seconds after making visual contact. His
special talent had failed on the one day it really mattered, the day
he died.

Adams concluded his phone call and leaned back in his chair.
"Sit down, Stevens. I hear you have some news on those unusual
homicides."

Mary returned to her seat, opening the file and balancing it on
her knees. "The lab finally confirmed that the same gun was used in
the Connelly case in Dallas, the Thomason case in Houston, as well
as the San Francisco area cases, Madison and Sherman. The ones in
California are the most recent. Maybe our UNSUB didn't like the
heat in Texas." She despised the use of UNSUB. Police departments
used only one word—suspect.

"Are you saying we may have another serial killer at work?"

"That's my thinking, sir."

He stared at a spot over her head. "It's brilliant, don't you see?
Our UNSUB has found a way to indulge his bloodlust, and at the
same time, reduce his chances of apprehension. The victims were
suicidal, right?"

"All four of them," Mary told him. "Two of the men even served
time in mental hospitals following attempted suicides. You can see

why the local police didn't believe they were legitimate homicides. If the medical examiner in San Francisco hadn't handled the autopsies on both the Sherman and Madison cases, he would have ruled the deaths suicides."

"Have we linked the gun to any other deaths, suicides or otherwise?"

"Not yet." Mary swallowed hard. "I want you to hear something. Around the world, over a million people kill themselves every year and another ten to twenty million attempt suicide and don't succeed. In the United States alone, there were forty-five-thousand suicides last year."

"Jesus Christ! Finding out which ones were homicides will be impossible. The FSRTC is already backed up to China."

Adams was referring to the Forensic Science Research and Training Center, which was internationally renowned for the development of new methodologies in forensic science and was the primary means for transferring new concepts, techniques, and procedures to forensic science and law enforcement communities. It was the starship of the Bureau. More than a million examinations were conducted every year.

"We don't have the time or resources for such a monumental task, Stevens," Adams told her. "Do what you can with the four cases we know about and forget the rest. Los Angeles has asked for our assistance in profiling a serial rapist. I'll have the files sent to you so you can review them in time for the team meeting tomorrow." He slipped his glasses on and began reading some material on his desk, his way of letting Mary know she was dismissed.

Since the FBI dealt with intentional acts of violence, Mary wasn't surprised Adams wasn't aware of the statistics on suicides. But she was certain a killer was preying on individuals who had given up on life, some of the most vulnerable people in society. "With all due respect, sir, we can't walk away from this. Our UNSUB is maniacal and insatiable. He's discovered a minefield of willing victims and he's going to keep killing until we find a way to stop him."

Adams looked up, a somewhat annoyed expression on his face. "And how do you propose we stop him, Stevens?"

She adjusted her position in the chair. "The first thing is to shut down the suicide clubs. I think the Bureau should also issue a directive to all medical examiners to be on the lookout for any homicides or suicides that appear even slightly suspicious."

"You want us to tell them to do their jobs. The law requires an autopsy be performed on any death unless the deceased was under the direct care of a physician."

Mary leaned forward in her seat. "You just said the FSRTC was backed up with cases. The same is true in the majority of medical examiners' offices. Suicides are low priority. Medical examiners spend a fraction of time on them compared to the rest of the deaths they investigate."

"I doubt if you'll find a medical examiner who will agree with that statement."

Mary stood and walked to the edge of his desk. "Let's talk turkey, chief. A person no one cares about arrives at the morgue with their wrists slit, and the coroner ends up rubber-stamping them a suicide. All I'm suggesting is we alert them to what we've discovered in these four cases."

Adams rubbed a spot near his eyebrow. "The suicide clubs are your best chance of finding the killer, but I'll give thought to issuing a directive of some kind."

Mary was relieved that she'd talked him out of assigning her another case. She paced in front of his desk. "I found out how most of the suicide clubs operate. It's a fairly simple system. When a person signs up, they're placed at the bottom of a list. They then have to assist the suicide of the person on the top. The decision as to manner and place of death is left to the two individuals involved."

"What ages are we talking about?"

"The suicide rate has historically been the highest among teenagers. Last year the number of suicides in the United States skyrocketed. In addition, we're seeing far more adults. I assume this is due to the economy. People have lost their jobs, their homes, and their savings. That's a bitter pill to swallow for even the most well-balanced individuals." He was nodding his head, a sign that she had his full attention. "There's another possibility to consider, one I think you'll find interesting. We may not have an actual serial killer per se, but someone along the lines of a hired gun."

"You mean a professional assassin?"

"Possibly," she said, clearing her throat. "But I'm not sure this person is a professional. He could be a friend, a relative, or a member of a suicide club. In my opinion, this also relates back to the economy. If a person arranges for someone to kill him, his dependants can collect on his life insurance. This could be the reason suicide clubs have grown in popularity. These people want their death to look like a homicide, or some type of accidental shooting, anything but suicide."

Adams's face fell. "It's a sad world we're living in today."

"Amen to that one," she told him, falling silent.

"Did the four individuals you mentioned have life insurance?"

"All of them. Even that is suspicious, don't you see? The majority of homicide victims aren't that well heeled. When they are, we usually have a good idea who killed them and nine times out of ten the motive is greed. As for the average person, these are hard times and life insurance isn't necessary for survival. If you're struggling financially, what bill do you pay first, your life insurance premium or your mortgage?" She stopped pacing and placed her palms on top of his desk. "Should I try to infiltrate some of the clubs in the areas we know the UNSUB has been recently active?"

"Absolutely not." Adams thought of her like a daughter and had a tendency to be overly protective. "Get some of the field agents to handle it. I need you here running the show."

Mary stood and walked to the door, then turned back around. "Have you given any more thought to me taking the post in Ventura?"

"You just talked me into issuing a Bureau directive about your case," he said, scowling. "Now you want to abandon everything and move back to Ventura. You're driving me crazy, Stevens. I don't want to lose you. You're just getting your feet wet here, but you're good. Give it some time and I'll try to get Brooks transferred into BAU."

Mary let out a long sigh, her back stiffening. "You said that a year ago when we got married. For Brooks to get a position in BAU, someone has to quit, retire, or die. Everyone on the team seems to be in good health. As for retiring, you're the only one who's anywhere near retirement age. Bulldog McIntyre certainly isn't going to quit. He lives for this job, and so does Genna Weir, Mark Conrad, Pete Cook, and the rest."

Adams looked exasperated. "Settle down, Mary."

"Everyone wants to work in BAU. It's one of the most coveted positions in the Bureau." He was holding his ground. She had to pull out all the stops. "Please, Uncle John, I finally found a man I can love. I can't help it if he's assigned to another city. There are two openings in Ventura right now. You know how rare that is? If Brooks and I don't hurry, they'll be taken."

"I'll consider it."

"You're being unfair," Mary argued. "You want me here so you can look after me. Dad saved your life, so you feel like you owe him. There are agents with twice as much experience who've had transfer requests for BAU on file for years. My father would want me to be happy, to give my mother a chance to see her grandchild. Mom isn't getting any younger, Uncle John. She stopped driving last year, and she's reaching the age where she can't live alone any longer. Brooks and I have a place for her in Ventura."

Adams looked beaten. "You know I don't like you to call me Uncle John when we're at work. We went over the rules when I hired you."

She pinned him with her eyes. "If you can't do this for me, do it for my father."

"Fine," he said, tossing his hands in the air. "If that's what you really want, I'll put through the damn paperwork."

Mary rushed over and kissed him on the cheek. "Thank you! You made my day."

"Oh yeah, well, you ruined mine."

"Come on, Uncle John," she said, ruffling his hair. "It's not like we're never going to see each other again. I'll come and visit you and you can come to . . ." His position within the Bureau was so vital, he hadn't taken a vacation in years. A tear crept down her face and she quickly brushed it away with her finger. Since she'd arrived at Quantico, he'd been like a father and it was hard to let go. She'd already lost one father. "I'll find a way for us to see each other, I promise. We can videoconference. I know you won't be able to come to Ventura, so Brooks and I will come to you. We'll bring the baby to see you for sure."

"You're pregnant already. Christ, what is this guy, a jackrabbit?"

"I'm not pregnant right now," Mary told him, "but I might be as soon as I start sleeping in the same bed as my husband."

Adams brushed her away. His door was open and she knew he was afraid one of the other agents would walk by and see them. "Who's going to handle the case?"

"I will." Mary moved an appropriate distance away. "I'm sure my new SAC won't mind. There's not much going on in Ventura, so I should have plenty of free time on my hands."

He arched an eyebrow. "Aren't you being overconfident?"

"Maybe," Mary said, smiling. She started to tell him that her new SAC would be her husband, but knew she couldn't. Because she'd kept her maiden name, most people at the Bureau wouldn't be aware she and Brooks were married. She intended to keep it that way for as long as possible. If she did get pregnant, she would retire anyway. "I'll let you know if I have a problem."

Without looking up, Adams grumbled, "Get back to work, Stevens. Until your papers come through, your ass still belongs to me."

# THREE

The commotion in the courtroom finally died down and Lily looked over at Silverstein. "You may continue, counselor."

"On the night of Brandon's death," Silverstein stated, lowering his voice so the jurors had to listen more carefully, "the Santa Ana winds had blown in and the temperature was in the mid to high eighties. This wasn't the case inside the trunk of the car, where little Brandon was confined. Inside the trunk, the temperature was a scalding hundred and twenty degrees. Try to imagine the terror of a two-year-old in the pitch black of the trunk, gasping for breath and hopelessly screaming for help until he finally succumbed to hyperthermia. The cruelty inflicted on this child is second only to the evil inside the mind of the woman who gave birth to him."

Silverstein was now establishing circumstances in aggravation. Lily looked over at him, wanting him to know that she was about to interrupt him. As soon as he got the hint and stopped speaking, she addressed the court. "Ladies and gentlemen, this court will recess for fifteen minutes. We will resume promptly at eleven o'clock." She tapped her gavel once and quickly exited the courtroom.

Shana was now in her final year at Stanford Law. Lily had been calling her for weeks and had not heard back. In the past, she would have thought nothing of it. Stanford was a difficult school and her daughter spent almost every waking moment on her studies. Any remaining time was reserved for her boyfriend.

Shana despised Lily's second husband, Bryce, and had seldom visited her mother because of him. But now it was more than Bryce. Lily and her daughter had suffered a horrifying ordeal in Ventura. A man broke into Lily's home and raped both her and her daughter at knifepoint. Shana had been twelve at the time and sixteen years had now passed, but no one genuinely recovered from this kind of trauma. Even Lily had moved to Santa Barbara for a number of years to put the memories from Ventura behind her, renting a home there and working as a prosecutor. When she was offered a judgeship in Ventura, it was impossible to resist, especially since Shana was about to complete her law degree and go out into the world. She had hoped that her daughter would eventually come to the same conclusion she had—that it wasn't the city but the crime, and that running away solved nothing. Eventually Shana had to face her demons or she would never defeat them, a fact Lily knew all too well.

John and Lily had been divorced for seven years when he was murdered, an event that appeared to have taken a greater emotional toll on Shana than the rape. It didn't matter to Shana that her father had become an alcoholic and could no longer support himself. She still adored him and demanded to live with him in Los Angeles, where she briefly attended UCLA. Alone and dejected, Lily had married Bryce and then later divorced him when she discovered he'd been cheating since the onset of their marriage. She was now living with Christopher Rendell, a handsome, intelligent, and charming judge. She had also purchased a new house on the beach, which she was certain Shana would love as it was nowhere near where they'd lived when they were attacked.

Since Chris had asked her to marry him, Lily had repeatedly requested that Shana come to Ventura to meet him. Her daughter also seemed to be serious about a young man she'd dated for several years, but she had consistently reneged on her promises to bring him to Ventura to meet Lily. Shana didn't even spend summers in Ventura. She had refused to live in the dorm at college, so Lily had rented her an apartment in Palo Alto, near where the university was located. Shana stayed there year-round.

Lily's concern for Shana was deepening. Several years back, a parent could find out what their kid was up to by talking to their roommate. But today, students didn't install phones in their dormitories or apartments. Instead, they relied on cell phones.

As she headed down the back corridor leading to her chambers, she saw Chris standing in the doorway and picked up her pace. After all the hell she'd been through in her life, Lily had finally found genuine love and happiness. She grabbed his hand and led him past her assistant, taking him into her office and closing the door.

"The damn media," she told him. "I should have forbidden them in the courtroom. Silverstein caused the problem, though, the over-eager little shit."

"What happened?"

"I'll tell you at lunch. I need to make some phone calls right now." She looked him up and down. "You have a lot of free time lately. Slow calendar?"

"Today's light," he said. "Yesterday was a bitch, though." He wrapped his long arms around her and pulled her tightly against his body. A moment later, he parted her robe and slid his hand underneath her skirt. "I hope I'm more important than these calls you need to make. Fifteen minutes is a lot of time." He smiled, his eyes filled with lust. "God, I want you. I've had an erection all morning. I feel like a teenager."

Lily's fiancé was a six-foot-five blond Adonis with a rock-hard body and a gentle soul. Until his wife's and daughter's deaths, he'd been a devout Mormon. Before Lily, the only woman he'd ever had sex with was his wife, and even then, his experience was limited. Obviously, he was playing catch-up and Lily was doing her best to keep up with him. Although she loved his enthusiasm, working together in the same building made her too available to his impulses.

All her life she had aspired to become a judge. As much as she loved Chris, she couldn't allow him to jeopardize her career. The presiding judge didn't like her and would jump at the chance to unseat her. Judge Hennessey believed a person who'd been a victim of a violent rape was unable to rule objectively on sex crimes. Lily had received her appointment while Hennessey was recovering from a massive heart attack, or she wouldn't be a judge today.

To qualify for a judgeship, a person had to be an attorney for five years. Chris was the wunderkind of the judicial system, having been appointed to the bench at twenty-six. Now in his mid-forties, he had graduated at the top of his class at Harvard Law at the age of eighteen. He had accepted the position in Ventura because he wanted to leave Salt Lake City, where he had been a prosecutor. As he told it, only a few months after his wife and daughter were killed, the church elders began pushing him to remarry one of the church's widows.

Chris was nuzzling her neck. "I want you."

"Well, you can't have me here," Lily told him, trying to wiggle out of his arms. She thought about Richard Fowler and how much he'd aged, wondering if people said the same about her. Richard had awakened her sexuality, only to have it traumatized a short time later.

She sighed when Chris began stroking the spot between her legs. It was as if his fingers possessed some type of electric charge. As soon as he touched her, she became aroused. She asked herself if her heightened sensitivity had anything to do with working so closely with Richard. They'd once had sex in an interview room at the DA's office. After the rapes, sex had been difficult so she wasn't the only one making up for lost time.

Before she knew it, Chris had turned her around and leaned her over the desk. He pushed her skirt up around her waist, and they made love until Lily moaned in pleasure. A few moments later, Chris did the same. It was quick but it was good, and all thoughts of Richard were vanquished.

"I can't believe we just did that," Lily told him, standing and repairing her clothing. "I'm not sure the door is even locked. Jeannie could have walked in on us, for God's sake. You have to control yourself, Chris."

His handsome face stretched into a smile. "You didn't put up a lot of resistance."

"No, I didn't." Lily laughed. Chris had it right when he said he felt like a teenager again. She felt the same and it was exhilarating. She captured his face in her hands. "That's because I love you. I love everything about you. We just can't do this here at the courthouse. People will think we're depraved." She kissed him on the lips and then headed for the door, knowing she didn't have time now to call Shana.

Chris followed her and before she turned the doorknob, she whispered, "I'm going to fuck you silly tonight. I guarantee you won't have to worry about controlling your erections tomorrow."

"Oh, really," he said, laughing.

"For sure." Lily flung the door open and saw Jeannie staring down at her desk. Ah, she thought, the woman might not have been able to see them, but she probably heard enough to figure out what they'd been doing. Jeanne was a dedicated assistant. Lily didn't expect her to tell anyone what her boss and Judge Rendell had been doing behind closed doors. She didn't really care as long as it didn't get back to Judge Hennessey. She wished the old goat would croak and put everyone out of their misery.

Chris stepped around Lily and slipped out of the room, a somber expression on his face, probably trying to convince Jeannie that they'd been consulting on a complex legal issue. Lily was about to follow him when Jeannie started talking.

"Don't you want your messages, Judge Forrester?"

"I'll look at them when we break for lunch."

Chris was waiting for her in the hallway, his back pressed to the wall. "You can't have sex with me without a kiss." He chuckled, reaching out for her. "I feel used."

"I kissed you," Lily said, her eyes darting up and down the hall to make certain no one was around. "I have to pee and now I don't have time. You owe me."

"I'm sorry," he told her, a hangdog look on his face. "You're not mad at me, are you?"

"No, I'm just in a hurry." How could she be mad at him, she thought as she strode toward the courtroom. He'd chased the demons away and made her feel whole again. With Bryce, they were always lurking in the shadows. Only one thing troubled her. She had to tell Chris the truth before they got married.

There was a reason Lily had no problem imposing the death penalty. No one with her past could feel otherwise. She had personally executed a man she believed had raped her and her daughter. Not only that, she had gotten away with it.

Even though Chris had distanced himself from his strict Mormon upbringing, he was one of the most ethical men she'd ever known. He might report her to the authorities and she could end up facing a murder charge. No matter what the risk, however, she had to tell him. She hadn't told Bryce and their marriage had disintegrated. But she hadn't really loved Bryce. She'd married him because she needed him; she was terrified of being alone.

She refused to enter into another relationship built on lies. Chris would understand a mother wanting revenge against the man who had brutally raped her twelve-year-old daughter at knifepoint while she looked on, powerless to stop him. But could he accept her actually killing someone? Chris had told her he'd given thought to seeking revenge against the truck driver who had caused the deaths of his wife and daughter, which gave her hope. But thinking about killing someone wasn't the same as actually doing it.

The real test would come when Lily told him she'd killed the wrong man.

# FOUR

At the noon break, Lily finally managed to get through to her daughter. "Why haven't you returned my calls? I've been worried sick about you."

"Why? Don't you have a new boyfriend to entertain you?"

"Yes, I do, Shana, and I'd like you to meet him. I can book you a flight for this weekend. If you want, I'll even buy a ticket for Brett. We'll all be together. It'll be fun. The new house is right on the beach." Lily heard her sniffing and suspected she'd been crying. "What's wrong, honey?"

"Brett dumped me."

"When did this happen?"

"Three weeks ago."

"Why didn't you tell me? You know I'm always here for you. Why did you break up? Did you have a fight?"

"He was dating someone else behind my back. She's a bitch, Mom. I don't know what he sees in her. She's at least twenty pounds overweight and has the brain of an insect. She doesn't even go to Stanford. She's a junior at Berkeley, probably majoring in palm reading or some other asinine subject."

Lily was at a loss for words. She waited to see if Shana would continue the conversation. When she didn't, she told her, "There's plenty of fish in the sea. You're beautiful, kind, and intelligent. You'll have no problem finding another guy. My bet is you'll find someone much better than Brett. Things like this happen for a reason. I thought Bryce and I would be together forever and look what a jerk he turned out to be." Lily's former husband had become an alcoholic. When she had discovered that he was routinely unfaithful, the marriage had ended.

"It's more than just the idiot girl, Mom. Brett thinks I have too much baggage."

"Are you going on a trip?"

"You've been spending too much time in the courtroom, Mom," Shana told her. "He's referring to emotional baggage. He says I'm too uptight when we have sex. I can't help it, you know? Sometimes I'm fine, but other times I panic. I've tried so hard to forget everything." She began sobbing. "My roommate bailed on me so I'm alone now. A girl in my apartment building was raped last month, and the police haven't made an arrest yet. I keep thinking I'm going to be next. I haven't slept in weeks."

"Oh, baby," Lily said, her heart breaking. "I understand how you must feel but you can't live in fear. You need to keep your mind occupied. Doesn't your work keep you busy? Why don't you have one of your friends stay with you for a while? You know, until you find another roommate."

"I don't want to be a lawyer."

Lily felt like she'd been punched in the stomach. "When did you make this decision?"

"I don't want to prosecute criminals. Why do I have to be the one to put them away? They might come after me when they get out of prison. Marco Curazon came after me and killed my father. What if they hurt my children to get back at me?"

"What happened with Curazon was a one in a million instance, and you don't have to be a prosecutor. Most of the defendants forget all about you when they get to prison."

"One in a million, huh? You don't have any statistics. You just made that up."

"Things like that very rarely occur, Shana. You can't be afraid of everything. If you do, Curazon will have won. Is that what you want?"

"I won't even make a decent living if I become a county prosecutor. Look at you, you're a fucking judge and you don't make that much money. I've worked too hard to make shit."

Lily was crushed that her daughter wanted to abandon her dream of becoming a prosecutor. She hoped she would change her mind when she got over the breakup. Everyone got overwhelmed now and then. And Shana had been seeing this guy for a long time. She sounded so agitated and frightened. Lily had no choice but to take her seriously. She had been somewhat aloof since she'd entered law school, but she had seemed strong and confident whenever she spoke to her or when she managed to get the time to visit her. "You don't have to practice criminal law, Shana. You could go into domestic or corporate law. There are dozens of avenues you could pursue."

"I've been in college for six years. You treat me like I'm still a kid. I'm twenty-eight, Mother. I should already have a career, a husband, maybe a kid. I can't even support myself."

"It's not your fault that you got a late start. A lot of things happened, honey."

"You don't understand," Shana told her. "I'm tired of staying up all night studying. Law is boring. I hate it and I hate living in this stupid town. I feel like I've been stuck here my entire life. I don't have any friends. The law school's full of arrogant assholes and everyone is younger than me. They think they're hot shit because they got into Stanford. It's not Harvard or Yale, you know."

"Stanford is ranked third in the nation, Shana," Lily reminded her. "I couldn't afford to go to a top-ranked school. I had to work and take care of you."

"You, you, you." Her voice became loud and abrasive. "Everything is always about you. The only reason I'm here is to please you. Just because you went into law, you decided I should, too. No one ever thinks about what I want."

"You only have a few months left." Lily's hands were shaking. How could she talk this way? Shana had wanted be a prosecutor ever since the rapes, believing she could make a difference and keep dangerous criminals off the street. Lily had spent a fortune on her education, even taking money from her pension, which had been greatly reduced the previous year when the stock market crashed. Judges made good money, but she didn't have much left after she paid for Shana's expenses. And the girl never seemed to have enough money and was constantly asking for more. Lily gave in because she didn't want to get into an argument. "Can't you stick it out, honey? You're so close."

"You still don't understand!" Shana yelled. "Even if I manage to graduate, I still have to pass the bar. Do you know how many people fail? Can you imagine going to school for all these years and then not being able to pass a stupid test? I met a guy who'd failed the bar five times. He's working as a bartender now. I'll kill myself if that happens. You know I choke at tests. I always have."

Lily loved her daughter with all her heart, but she had turned into what people today referred to as an "energy vampire." Five minutes into a conversation and Lily was completely drained, and that was when nothing was wrong. Right now she was so exhausted, she felt like cancelling the afternoon session and going home. "Shana, darling," she said, propping her head up with her hand, "Ventura has a number of excellent review programs geared specifically to passing the exam. So you spend some extra time preparing. What's the big deal? I was in one of those programs and it helped me tremendously."

"Don't placate me, Mother. You passed the bar the first time and scored in the top ten percent of the nation. Shit, don't you know what an accomplishment that was? I can't even begin to compete with you. I inherited your looks, not your intellect. Dad would have never let this happen to me. You just can't admit that you have a daughter that isn't as smart as you."

Both Lily's lines were lit and blinking. She looked at the clock and saw it was past time for her to return to the courtroom. If Hennessey found out she'd held a fully staffed courtroom waiting, he would carve her a new asshole. She punched the button for the intercom and told Jeannie to advise the clerk that she was running late due to an emergency. When she returned to the line, Shana was still speaking.

". . . You never told me the California bar exam is one of the hardest in the nation. They have an exclusionary bar. That means that rather than merely trying to screen out people who're incompetent, the exam is used to regulate the number of lawyers in the state. Other states have shorter and easier bar exams because they don't have the large number of attorneys California has." Shana stopped speaking and sucked in oxygen. "Why didn't you send me to school in Oklahoma or something? Then I would at least have a chance. But no, you wanted me to fail. Dad said you liked it when people screwed up because it made you feel even more superior."

Lily felt like crawling out of the office on bloody knees. According to her daughter and her deceased husband, she was responsible for everything that went wrong in the family. John had even blamed her for the rapes. But John was dead, and Lily had done everything in her power to establish a good relationship with Shana. Every time she thought the past was behind her, it came back to smack her in the face. "I'm coming up there. We'll sort things out and get you back on track. I can't come until tomorrow night because I'm in trial."

"You're always in trial. Don't worry about me, Mom. I'll be fine."

Lily heard the phone click and knew Shana had hung up. Chris stuck his head in the door to her private office with a downcast look on his face. They were supposed to have had lunch at Joe's Bar and Grill a few blocks from the courthouse. When she'd finally got through to Shana, Lily had told him to go without her and she'd meet him as soon as she finished. "I'm sorry," she told him, a line of perspiration across her forehead. "I'm late and they're waiting."

He placed a sack on her desk. "I brought you a sandwich. You've got to eat, Lily. You're already too thin."

"I'm five-ten, Chris," she said, shoving her arms into her robe. "I've been thin all my life. It has something to do with my metabolism. Thanks for the sandwich. I'll eat it at the afternoon break."

Lily jogged down the corridor to Division Forty-seven, her black robe flapping like a cape. By the time she raced up the steps to the bench, she was out of breath and panting. She took a few deep breaths to calm herself, and then called the court to order. Once Clinton Silverstein concluded his opening statement, Lily turned to Fowler. "You may begin your opening statement, counselor."

Fowler stood and faced the jury. "Ladies and gentlemen, we have been brought together today because a tragedy has occurred. An innocent, unsuspecting child was the victim of a senseless act that was undeserved. You or I could just as easily have been involved in the situation leading up to the events that brought us here today. But there is a second tragedy in this case. My client, who has attended our school system and is the daughter of a highly respected member of our community, stands here today before you wrongfully accused of this crime. Try to imagine, if you will, what it feels like to be falsely accused of the kinds of things the prosecution wants us to consider. How would you react? What the prosecution has failed to tell you is that part of this case is based on junk science. Sure, my client's DNA was found inside the trunk of the car where the prosecutor claims she intentionally left her beloved child's body. This is her car, so her DNA is naturally present throughout the vehicle.

"Do you think for a moment that Dr. Reynolds, an esteemed member of the medical community for over thirty years, would not have made provisions for his grandson's care if he had any suspicions whatsoever that the child was being abused by his daughter? Certainly, there were ill feelings between Noelle and her father during the course of her lifetime." Fowler paused and chuckled. "Who can say they got along perfectly with their parents? My father served in the marines and would have let me rot in a jail cell if I broke the law, let alone abused a child. Like Dr. Reynolds, he was a stern parent who laid down the rules and expected me to follow them.

"I know your heart is breaking for the unfortunate victim in this case, but that should not be convincing to you or any other group of reasonable people. Ladies and gentlemen, we cannot bring the poor, unfortunate victim back to tell you what happened. My client would, if she only could, have the truth exposed. Nor should we depend on the kinds of unreliable testimony and shoddy police work you will see exposed in the State's case. Please keep asking yourself the hard questions, and remember there's always another side to every story. As you listen to the prosecution's case, remind yourself that they will not tell you the whole story. It's not their job to do that. They have invested too much of the State's resources already in the misdirected investigation and charging of my client, and it's too late for them to admit they're wrong. My client will be the first to admit she's far from being a perfect person, but hasn't every one of us made a mistake we later regretted?

"Ladies and gentlemen," Fowler said, summing up, "promise me you'll listen to the whole story, and prevent another tragedy from occurring—the wrongful conviction of an innocent person."

Once Fowler sat down, Lily said into her microphone, "This court is adjourned until tomorrow morning at nine o'clock." For a while, she just sat there, staring blankly out over the courtroom. When the attorneys began packing up their litigation cases, she finally exited the bench.

Chris drove his own car three days a week so he could work out at their health club. She peeked into his chambers, but both he and his assistant had already left. Heading back to her own chambers and finding Jeannie gone as well, she glanced at her watch and saw that it was six-thirty. She never ran this late, but her mind had been all over the place today.

Taking the elevator to the garage, where her Volvo was parked, she got in the car and took off. She suddenly realized why her thoughts had kept turning to Shana during Silverstein's opening statement. Her daughter possessed some of the same personality traits as Noelle Reynolds, not that she would ever commit an act of violence. John had spoiled her, turning her into a demanding brat. His failure to discipline their daughter was one of the reasons their marriage had failed. He always made Lily the bad guy, placing an irreparable strain on her relationship with Shana. The most despicable part was he had done it intentionally.

Hitting a wall of traffic, Lily's mind spun back in time and she began driving on autopilot. She had just been made supervisor of the sex crimes division. The crimes they handled were so horrific and the caseload so backlogged, Lily was forced to work fifteen-hour days, leaving little time to be with her family. One of the reasons she had given in to Richard's sexual advances at work was there was simply no other time to see him.

One particular day would stick in her memory forever. John coached Shana's softball team and she was pitching that day. Lily was held over at work and then got stuck in rush-hour traffic. By the time she arrived at the community center playing field, the game was almost over.

1993
VENTURA, CALIFORNIA

Lily's heels sank into the soft dirt as she walked to a position behind the plate and laced her fingers through the wire fence. Shana was pitching and she made eye contact as her right arm moved back for the pitch. The other parents in the bleachers wore down-filled jackets and sipped steaming coffee from Styrofoam cups. Lily wrapped her arms around herself in an attempt to stay warm.

Her daughter was charismatic, the only way to describe the type of popularity she'd been blessed with since the first grade. A ball of energy, beauty, and quick wit, she'd been the most adorable little girl Lily had ever seen. And she'd been Lily's life. Up until the last few years, no matter what was going on in her career, Lily saw her entire universe spinning around Shana. Her daughter had been the one who'd convinced her that there was goodness in the world, real goodness. She had taught Lily how to smile, laugh, and cry tears of joy. She was slipping away now, growing up, changing into a woman. She didn't need Lily anymore. She had her father to meet her every need. Whereas Lily had always been John's baby, Shana was now all he cared about.

The problems with Shana were more than just the oedipal phase of puberty. John was turning her own daughter against her for reasons she couldn't understand. Was it because she'd told him she wanted to become a judge? John had always dreamed of her entering private practice where she would "make a ton of money" and he could retire and spend his time managing their investments. A position on the bench might be prestigious, but the salary was only a notch above what she presently earned as a prosecutor. John didn't understand. He told Lily she was a fool, insisting that she wanted the judgeship for the power alone, simply to feed her ego.

Shana had been only a few months old when Lily decided to enter law school. The decision was major as she was working as an admitting clerk at a local hospital and John was employed at a personnel agency, where his salary fluctuated from month to month. The only way they could afford to get by was for Lily to continue working. John encouraged her desire to become an attorney, continually talking about all the money she would make and how they would never have to pinch pennies again. "You go to law school, and I'll open my own personnel agency. We'll have it made." Lily worked the graveyard shift and attended classes during the day, leaving Shana with the babysitter only during the hours she was in class. The remainder of the day and evening, prior to the start of her shift at the hospital, Lily carried her daughter around with her, chatting with the baby as if she were an adult.

Lily remembered the exact moment Shana started to talk. It wasn't remarkable, she only said "da da" like all babies, but in no time she started chattering away. All the words Lily had said to her seemed to pop back out like magic. The more the child talked, the more Lily talked to her, until Shana developed a fairly extensive vocabulary. People would ask her name and Shana would smile and say, "Plaintiff." Thinking she had said "plain tough," they would roar with laughter. Shana would clap, giggle, and say it again.

Lily had never once spanked her. She read every book she could get on parenting. "We don't bite children," she'd tell her, "but we can bite an apple."

Although Lily slept only a few hours a day, napping when Shana napped and nodding off at work during the early morning hours, she was happy. She had no time to worry about her relationship with John. Her grueling schedule left little time for anyone other than her daughter. Oddly, John didn't seem to mind. He'd stopped having sex with Lily not long after Shana was born. Lily had tried to rekindle that part of their life but had not had much success.

She accepted a position with the district attorney's office as soon as Shana entered kindergarten. Every morning Lily would make her lunch and walk her to school before work. Shana's classmates and teachers adored her. She knew how to share, loved to make other children and adults laugh, and looked as if she'd stepped out of a Disney movie with her freckled face and carrot-colored hair.

In a way, those first words, "plain tough," also applied to little Shana. Lily had raised her to fear nothing, wanting her to be able to protect herself against anyone and anything that came her way. Just as she had taught Shana how to share and be kind to others, she'd taught her to be strong, brave, and mature. "When I'm not here," Lily would tell her, "or your daddy's not here, if anything bad ever happens, then you must believe you're a grown-up and do exactly what a grown-up would do. Believe you can do it because you can." Shana would always blink her eyes and smile when Lily made her speech. She looked for occasions when she could prove herself to her mother, knowing it would make Lily smile with approval. With Lily's encouragement she climbed trees, played ball, would stomp on a spider rather than scream, and once punched a neighbor's dog in the nose when it growled at her. Afterward, she ran home and leapt into her mother's arms, bursting with pride. To John and Lily, she was the golden child, the magic child.

As the years went by and the magic persisted, Shana learned to see it and use it for the power it afforded her. Seeking to bask in her light, her friends would do her homework, give her money, and let her wear their new clothes, many times before they'd even had a chance to wear them.

Shana had started to change around her tenth birthday. John's influence grew stronger, and the girl began snapping at her parents. She also developed quite a temper. Lily refused to tolerate it, but John undermined Lily's attempts to discipline her and allowed Shana to order him around like a servant. The fissure between them as parents widened.

Lily tried to talk to her, use the old psychology tricks, but nothing worked. Finally she sat down with her when John was gone and had a serious discussion about her behavior. "You just don't understand," the girl told her. "All day long I have to smile and be nice to everyone. Sometimes when I get home I can't control it any longer."

Shana had to defend her turf as the most popular girl in her school. Other girls would get envious and make up stories about her. Like a politician seeking reelection, Shana would take polls, recruit more followers, and make certain her constituents would vote for her. On one occasion a girl punched her in the face after school, and Shana slugged her so hard she almost broke her hand. When she was expelled for fighting, Lily told her to give it up. But it was a hard thing to give up, this being on top. Like Lily, Shana was tenacious and driven to control the world around her.

Last month Shana had come home in a particularly nasty mood and Lily had broached the subject again. "Most people have a few good friends in life that they enjoy. Why do you need the entire school? Why is it so important that everyone likes you?"

"You don't understand," Shana said. "It's not like that at all. They need me."

Lily shook her head, incredulous. "That's absurd, honey. They don't need you. What are you saying?" Then she'd given it more thought. "Are you saying someone has to be a leader, and that if that person isn't you, it will be someone else?"

"Yeah, that's it," Shana told her. "See, Mom, I don't smoke, use drugs, or listen to bad music. And I certainly don't go all the way with boys. I get good grades— pretty good, anyway—and I give kids advice and listen to their problems. Girls get into fights with other girls and I get them to make up."

So that's the story, Lily had thought. It sounded like her reasons for being a district attorney and aspiring to be a judge. She held the reins to her life and had taught her daughter to do the same.

The short brunette at bat swung and connected; the parents in the stands screamed as she raced the short distance to first base. The next batter hit the ball as well, but was tagged at first base. The game was over and Shana's team had won.

The girls moved toward the dugout, the majority getting as close to Shana as possible. Postgame activity had changed since the year before. Instead of going for the cookies and sodas the team mother provided, a number of girls were taking out brushes and lip gloss from their purses.

John infiltrated the group, putting both hands around Shana's waist and lifting her into the air. "I'm so proud of you, pumpkin." They both saw Lily a few feet away and smiled. They weren't smiling at her, though. Lily knew they were flaunting their closeness, showing her that this was their private moment, one they didn't care to share. Placing Shana back on the ground, John stared straight at Lily and draped his arm around Shana's shoulders, walking with her the short distance to the dugout, pulling her close, glancing back to see if Lily was still watching, the other girls crowding around John now as well as Shana. Lily winced, locking her fingers on the wire fence. They both looked away.

A short time later, John headed in her direction, stopping to pick up a few bats on the way. The baseball cap made thick crevices appear in his forehead. At forty-seven, he was eleven years older than Lily, and his hair was thinning to the point where more scalp showed than hair. He was still an attractive man, however, with a robust body and a bright smile, displaying rows of even white teeth in his tan and muscular face. At the moment, his expression wasn't pleasant, nor was it the adoring look reserved for his daughter.

"Made it, huh?" he said, tipping his baseball cap back on his head. "Pried yourself away to catch the last five minutes of the game. You sure you're not missing something at the office? You don't want your family to get in the way of your big ambition to be a judge."

"That was uncalled for," Lily said, looking around to see if anyone was within earshot. "I'll take Shana home in my car." She turned and plodded through the dirt in the direction of the dugout.

Shana's face was flushed with excitement. She stood almost a head above the other girls. Her long red hair had more golden tones in it than Lily's, and she wore it in a ponytail pulled through the back of her baseball cap. Her wide-set eyes were such a deep shade of sapphire that they almost matched the navy blue lettering on her uniform. High pronounced cheekbones gave her face an ethereal, elegant quality far beyond her years. With the right makeup, clothes, and photographer, Lily thought, Shana's face could be on the cover of next month's Glamour magazine.

One girl followed as Shana broke away and headed for the car. "Oh, this is my Mom. Mom, this is Sally. Call me in thirty minutes," Shana told her. Once they were home, the phone would ring in her room all evening, each girl calling at the preselected time.

Sally stood there with her mouth gaping. "You look so much alike. I can't believe it."

Shana got into the car and slammed the door, her eyes cutting to her mother with resentment. Lily felt her heart sink. Shana had always been so proud that they resembled each other. She used to tell Lily how all her friends thought her mother was so pretty. Lily remembered how she'd gaze up at her and ask if she'd be that tall when she grew up. The past week, Shana had screamed at her that she was a giraffe, the tallest girl in school, and ended the tirade by saying it was Lily's fault.

Lily tried to start a conversation. "That was a great job of pitching out there. Sorry I didn't get to see more of the game. I rushed but the traffic . . ." Shana stared straight ahead, refusing to answer. It was going to be one of those days. "How was school?"

"Fine."

"Do you have much homework?"

"Done."

"Want to go roller-skating with me Saturday?"

"I practice softball every day and have gym class. I don't need any more exercise."

"How about the mall? Do you want to go to the mall?"

"I thought I was grounded." She shot Lily another look full of animosity. "Can Charlotte and Sally go?"

"No, I want to spend time with you alone. I don't want to spend time with Charlotte and Sally. Besides, where is my top you loaned to Charlotte without my permission?"

"Don't worry. You'll get your precious top back. I just forgot. Will you chill out, Mom?" With this last statement, her voice went high and shrill. Then something changed and she turned to her mother with a sweet smile and a sugar-coated voice. "I need a new outfit. There's a dance in the gym next week and we're all going."

Here we go again, Lily thought, acid bubbling back in her throat. In desperation she'd recently found herself doing something she despised. She'd bought Shana things in the past year or so just to get that one little smile. As a parent, she was on a seesaw. One day she tried to uphold her long-standing rules and restrictions. Then the next time she broke all her own rules. To compete with John she had to play a new game, his game. His game was to give Shana anything she wanted. "I just bought you a bunch of new clothes two weeks ago, Shana. Can't you wear one of those to the dance?"

"MOM . . . I've already worn them to school. I don't want to wear them to the dance."

"We'll see," Lily told her, pacifying.

Shana stared out the passenger window.

"So, what else is going on? Any gossip?"

"I started my period today."

Lily was excited and it showed. Shana rolled her eyes. This was something strictly feminine, something they could share. They could go home and lock themselves in the bedroom and talk, rekindle the bond they'd had before John had turned Shana away. "I knew you'd start any day now. Didn't I tell you that I started at your age? That's why you've been so snippy and emotional. I was, too. It's perfectly normal. Do you have cramps? How do you feel? We'll stop at the drugstore. What are you wearing now?"

"Dad already got me some pads today."

Lily's knuckles turned white on the steering wheel. She took her foot off the gas and the car came to an abrupt standstill in the suburban traffic. Cars honked and then passed. She turned to face her daughter. "You could have called me at work and told me. Why didn't you? Why are you shutting me out of your life?" She had to hear the words. Like a masochist, she sought the pain.

"Dad said you were too busy and that you'd get mad if I bothered you."

The words "Dad already got me some pads today" were ringing in Lily's ears. Now they were joined by "Dad said you were too busy." In the act of not sharing that one historically female moment, the rite of passage, and the fact that Shana could go to her father without embarrassment, her daughter had destroyed her. They drove home in silence.

# FIVE

Lily and Christopher Rendell were sitting on the balcony of her new home, finishing off a bottle of Merlot. The salty sea air made it seem colder than it actually was, and they were both bundled up in their terry cloth bathrobes.

The two-bedroom house wasn't very large, but it was only a short walk to the sand and Lily loved it. The balcony was elevated to protect the house from high surfs or they could have simply walked out their back door. Erected twenty years ago, the house had a spacious kitchen, two wood-burning fireplaces, and a comfortable room with a high ceiling that served as both the living room and family room. There was no dining room, but a marble-topped bar ran the length of the kitchen and Lily had managed to squeeze in a table large enough for four people.

The Realtor told Lily that the former owners had a home in Beverly Hills and only used this house once or twice a month. The recession seemed to have impacted the rich as well as the average person, and Lily was more than happy to relieve them of the responsibility for their beach house.

Lily had just taken a shower and her red hair hung to her shoulders in wet ringlets. Before the recession, she could have never afforded a place on the water. Of course, the price of housing in Ventura was only a fraction of what it was in other beach communities.

The city had grown up around the historic San Buenaventura Mission, founded in 1782. On one side were miles of sandy beaches, along with multimillion-dollar homes with boat slips. The rest of the city had sprawled upward into the foothills, where many of the residents had panoramic views of the ocean. Unlike Santa Barbara, a similar city approximately twenty miles north, Ventura hadn't developed into a playground for the rich and famous. New shops and restaurants had slowly appeared throughout the years, but most things had stayed the same. Lily thought there was a tired feeling to Ventura, as if a dusty bubble had been placed over it, trapping it twenty years in the past. The nearby farming communities didn't help, especially with all the avocado fields. The Spanish influence was still present, yet it hadn't been cultivated as it had in Santa Barbara, where lovely mission-style homes and buildings had been built to harmonize with meticulously renovated existing structures.

Chris leaned over his knees. "Why don't you let me go up north with you?"

"I don't think that would be a good idea," Lily told him, chewing on a ragged cuticle. Chris was everything she'd ever wanted—intelligent, empathetic, and romantic. Unlike Bryce, she felt confident he would be faithful and be an excellent stepfather to Shana. When he'd asked Lily to marry him three months ago, she'd been thrilled but hesitant. They decided to live together before they made their final decision, so Chris moved into Lily's new beach house and rented out his own home for six months.

Chris was a municipal court judge. Cases didn't make their way to the superior court unless they were felonies. Everything else was handled in the municipal court, which they referred to as the "Zoo" because of the constant chaos. Chris could resolve twenty cases in one day, while the crimes Lily adjudicated could take months. Plea agreements or negotiated settlements, as they now called them, were a superior court judge's only salvation. Without them, Lily's calendar would become hopelessly backlogged.

All Lily could think about was Shana. She had booked a flight to San Francisco for tomorrow evening, knowing she would have to recess court early in order to get to LAX. Friday night traffic on the 405 Freeway was a nightmare and completely unpredictable. No matter how much travel time a person allotted, they could still miss their plane.

Going anywhere during a trial of this magnitude was risky. If she didn't get back for some reason, Judge Hennessey could have her censured. A judge walking out on a murder trial, especially one that involved the death penalty, was tantamount to professional suicide. According to the Standards of Judicial Administration, to enable the just and efficient resolution of cases, the judge, not the lawyers or litigants, was responsible for controlling the pace of litigation. A strong judicial commitment was essential to reducing delay and, once achieved, maintaining a current docket.

The proceedings leading to trial in a capital case were sometimes more time consuming than the actual trial. If Shana's problems turned out to be more serious than Lily anticipated, a replacement judge would have to start over from day one. If there was too long of a delay, the defense could ask for a mistrial under the grounds that their client had been denied due process.

In addition, once a case fell under Lily's jurisdiction, she was to make every possible attempt to encourage the parties to settle or enter into a plea agreement. Silverstein's determination to make certain Noelle Reynolds received the death penalty had made that impossible. At the end of the day, it wasn't justice that ruled. Moving the calendar was the name of the game.

"Did you hear me, Lily?" Chris said. "I've already analyzed my docket and I'm certain I can resolve everything by early afternoon. Then I can go with you."

"I want you and Shana to have a good relationship," Lily told him. "She's not herself right now." She picked up her portable phone and pushed the auto dial, disconnecting when she reached the voice mail on Shana's cell phone. "I wish I didn't have to wait until tomorrow night. Not being able to reach her is driving me crazy. Should I call the police and ask them to send an officer to the apartment to check on her?"

"You talked to her yesterday," he rationalized. "I'm sure she's fine. She might get mad if the police turn up on her doorstep. Are you worried she might hurt herself?"

Lily took a deep breath and then exhaled. "Maybe."

"From what you've told me, it sounded like she was just venting. You probably caught her at a bad time. Her boyfriend left her for another girl. She's also at that age where she thinks she should be married, so that makes this breakup more upsetting." He paused and took a sip of his wine. "As far as wanting to drop out of school, she's obviously suffering from burnout. Stanford is a tough university. I predict that by the time you get there, though, the picture will have already changed."

Lily cut her eyes to him. "I don't understand why she won't talk to me."

"She did talk to you."

"I mean now, Chris. She knows I'm worried. She could at least answer her phone."

"She's probably out with her friends."

"All she has is a cell phone," Lily explained. "She takes it with her everywhere she goes."

"Maybe she forgot to charge it." He paused, thinking. "Has she ever tried to hurt herself?"

"Not to my knowledge." Just the thought made Lily cringe. She and Shana had gone through so much together. When you'd fought for your life against a violent criminal, the thought of killing yourself seemed almost sacrilegious.

Lily had been amazed at her daughter's resiliency. She had overcome the horror of that night and managed to become strong again, going on to chart a course for her life and sticking to it all these years. Why was she giving up? She wasn't a quitter. Something was wrong.

"She was so hostile yesterday," Lily said, trailing her finger around the rim of her wineglass. "We had problems getting along when she was a kid. Her father turned her against me. I think John thought it was a way to keep me from divorcing him. He knew Shana would pick him instead of me because he spoiled her and let her do anything she wanted. He was right, you know. Do you know how terrible I felt knowing my own child didn't want to live with me?"

"Only a weak and insecure man would do something like that, Lily," Chris told her. "No matter what happens, you never undermine the woman who gave birth to your child. It happens all the time in divorce cases and it turns my stomach. In most instances, it's the women who use the children to humiliate their husbands in custody battles. Think about what that says about Shana's father."

"After the rapes, we became close, but it didn't last. I wanted to send Shana to Stanford, but she gave it up to go to UCLA and live with her father."

"Why didn't she like Bryce?"

"There was something about him that Shana just couldn't tolerate," Lily told him. "They squabbled and picked at each other like kids. Later I decided that she might have been a better judge of character than I was."

"I doubt that, Lily."

"Anyway, when she started calling less this past year, I just assumed it was because she was spending all her free time with Brett."

"She probably was."

Lily went on as if she hadn't heard him. "I offered to come up there on numerous occasions but Shana always said she was too busy with her studies. Last year was difficult for me, too. Bryce and I divorced and you know all the things that happened in the mess that followed. My God, that horrible woman almost killed me, and you think I'm a good judge of character?"

Chris refilled Lily's wineglass. "Your daughter went through a terrible ordeal. If she handled that without becoming suicidal, it's highly unlikely she is now. She didn't say anything along those lines, did she?"

Lily was too restless to remain seated. She walked over to the railing and stared out over the ocean, watching as a man and woman walked hand in hand along the edge of the water. The fog had rolled in and she couldn't see much beyond the shore, but the sound of the waves had a calming effect on her. Chris got up and joined her, placing his arm around her waist. "She said something about killing herself if she didn't pass the bar."

Chris laughed. "I doubt if she meant it as anything other than a figure of speech. I think I said something along the same lines. Everyone does. You're under so much pressure. And the California bar exam is a bitch. Even I failed the first time. Talk about panicked. I'd never failed anything in my life."

Lily was surprised. "But didn't you graduate at the top of your class?"

"Yeah, but I was just a kid, remember? Besides, I'm not as smart as everyone thinks. I have a great memory, that's all. I memorize everything. If I haven't seen it before or the question is arranged differently, I'm lost."

"I don't believe you. You're just saying that so I'll feel better about Shana. I might understand you having problems with the exam, though, because you were so young. How many people graduate Harvard Law at eighteen? Good Lord, Chris, you're a genius. You can't play dumb with me because I know better."

They both fell silent for a while. "They say victims of violent crimes," he said, "particularly sex offenses, find the events resurfacing later in life. Maybe that's what's happening with Shana."

Lily turned around and faced him, resting her back against the railing. "I don't believe in repressed memory. Whether you realize it or not, that's what you're talking about. When something terrible happens, even if you're a kid, you don't forget it and then suddenly remember it years later. That's just nonsense the shrinks invented."

"But there've been dozens of court cases. Men and women have been sentenced to prison on the basis of repressed memory. Some of it has to be legitimate, don't you think?"

Lily was hard-nosed on certain issues. "Maybe one in a thousand is real. If a child was victimized before the age of five, he might not remember, but if he doesn't remember, he simply doesn't remember. What happens in a lot of those cases is a woman gets depressed because her marriage is failing or she can't accept that she's getting older. Her kids might be leaving home, or she believes her husband is having an affair. She goes for counseling and before she knows it, the psychologist has convinced her she was molested as a child and that's the cause of all her problems." She held up a finger. "Don't forget, a lot of these shrinks use hypnotism. People are highly suggestible when they're under hypnosis. Look what happened in the McMartin preschool case. Those people went through hell and the whole thing was totally fabricated."

"Interesting." He placed his hands inside the pockets of his robe. "I never realized you were such a skeptic, Lily. You would have made a good scientist. In the scientific community, if it can't be proven, it doesn't exist."

Before they had started dating, Lily recalled Chris telling her he planned to remain a judge for a few years and then quit to study theoretical physics. "By the way, when are you going to resign and start studying physics at Cal Tech?"

"Probably never," he said. "I found something better to play with than numbers."

"Really? What?"

He smiled seductively. "You."

She reached over and squeezed his ass. "You're turning into a sex maniac."

"It's getting cold out here." He wrapped his arms around his chest. "Let's go inside and snuggle under the covers."

The wind was blowing hard now and she didn't hear him. When one thing went wrong, Lily expected everything else to collapse around her. Too many bad things had happened in her lifetime. She'd made too many mistakes, deceived too many people, sinned in the worst way possible. How did she know Chris wouldn't leave her as soon as she told him the truth? Maybe the best thing to do was to end it now. But she couldn't end it. She loved him too much. She loved waking up beside him every morning, feeling the warmth of his body, knowing she would see him at work and go home with him that night. She was a pessimist, though, and he was an optimist. It worked wonderfully for her, but she sometimes worried about him.

As a Catholic, Lily knew exactly where she was going when she died. And she knew Hell existed because she'd been there. All she could hope for was to somehow escape Hell and sneak into purgatory. Then after ten thousand years, she might make her way to Heaven. She certainly wasn't helping herself by enjoining Chris in her nightmare. It was bad enough that she had to look over her shoulder, never knowing if someone would crawl out of the woodwork and turn her life upside down. If she really loved Chris, and she did, how could she put him in such a position? From what she knew, he had lived a pristine life. In addition, he'd already suffered through the loss of his wife and daughter. He might have given thought to killing the truck driver who'd caused the accident, but he hadn't followed through. "Are you sure you want to do the whole marriage thing? We could live together and be mad, passionate lovers."

"Of course I want to marry you," he told her. "When you love someone, that's what you do. I want to take care of you for the rest of your life, grow old with you, die with you, and share everything I have with you. It's a commitment issue, knowing that someone has made a vow before God."

Her eyes filled with tears. She turned back around so he wouldn't notice. If she could just keep him a little while longer, bask in the love and happiness he gave her. "I'm not sure when I'll be ready," she told him, a slight tremor in her voice. "Shana needs me right now, Chris. She has to be my first priority. And I want her to be here if we get married. Since things didn't work out with Bryce, it's important that we come together as a family. Shana needs that, you know, particularly since she lost her father."

He grabbed her and spun her around. "I don't mind waiting, Lily. I want to help you with Shana any way I can. And we will be a family, I promise. All you have to do is trust me, give things a chance. I'm looking forward to being a stepfather to Shana. I'm certain we'll get along famously."

She glanced through the open door to the coffee table where Chris had placed pictures of his wife and daughter. It was almost like a shrine, a shrine to another life. Although she didn't want to tell him, it was too soon for him to remarry. She saw him sitting there every evening and staring at the faces of his wife and daughter. When she'd first started seeing him, his daughter's clothes and toys were scattered all over his bedroom as if he were waiting for her to walk back into the room. "I love you, Chris, but do we really need to be legally entangled? Marriage and divorce have become almost synonymous to me. Don't you think you should give it more thought? Why would you want to marry a two-time loser?"

His handsome face spread in a confident smile. "It's not your fault you didn't meet me sooner." He tugged on her hand. "Let's go to bed. If you don't want to make love, we can just cuddle."

Her dark mood lifted. How could she be depressed with a wonderful man like this at her side? Lily slipped her hands inside his robe, feeling his muscular chest. "You owe me for that quickie yesterday. I want the full treatment tonight."

He got behind her and playfully pushed her through the balcony door and down the hall to the bedroom, kicking the door shut with his foot. Lily started to break away to make certain the balcony door was locked, but convinced herself that there was nothing to worry about as long as Chris was with her. Then she realized why Shana might be falling apart. The poor girl was alone with no one to protect her. Lily would have to find a way to change that, and she would have to do it immediately, even if it meant destroying her career.

# SIX

As soon as Lily's plane landed in San Francisco at eight o'clock, she called Shana's cell phone and got her voice mail again. "It's me," she said, excited. "I should be there in about forty-five minutes to an hour. Call me back as soon as you get this. I'll—"

Before she could say anything else, a recorded voice said her message was being deleted. Shana's mailbox must still be full, which made her concern intensify. Shana lived and breathed by her cell phone. Lily didn't even know how to make a cell phone delete messages before a person stopped speaking. Of course, there was one way, and it was hurtful, especially since Lily hadn't done anything to cause her daughter to be angry with her. Shana must be screening her calls and manually deleting her mother's messages the moment she saw her number appear.

Lily decided her daughter was having a flashback all right, but it had nothing to do with her being raped. She was reverting back to the spoiled brat she'd been when her father was alive, believing the world revolved around her and ignoring anyone who wouldn't give her what she wanted.

Was this all just a ploy to get Lily to cough up more money?

Shana had been living beyond her means for almost a year now, and not by a small sum. Last month alone, Lily had given her an extra thousand. She hadn't realized she had given Shana so much until her accountant had prepared her taxes. Like John, Lily had developed a habit of never saying no to her daughter. She couldn't stand it when Shana was upset or unhappy.

Then Lily remembered Shana telling her that a girl in her apartment complex had been raped and the suspect was still outstanding. With Shana's history, something like that could cause her to unravel. She went to the Dollar Rent A Car counter, walking off with the keys to a Dodge Caliber. She'd never heard of it, but it drove fairly well. Shana had a Mustang convertible but she hadn't offered to pick her up.

Lily didn't really mind because she enjoyed the scenery. She was particularly fond of driving through this area at night. She loved the way the lights streamed through the towering trees. Palo Alto was similar to an urban forest, surrounded by majestic, ancient redwoods. She hadn't been up here since last year. She chastised herself for not coming more often, but her new position had become all-consuming.

Shana's apartment was located in a three-story structure built out of wood and stone. Lily climbed the stairs to the third floor. Knowing the apartment didn't have a doorbell, she knocked. When no one answered, she pounded on the door with her fists. "Shana, are you in there? It's me, Mom."

She leaned against the door and listened, detecting faint noises inside the apartment. She didn't care what people thought, she had to see if her daughter was all right. As she kicked the door as hard as she could, a young girl walked by, giving her a suspicious glance. At last, she heard Shana's voice.

"Knock it off. I'm coming, for God's sake." She cracked the door and peered out at Lily, then closed it again to undo the chain. Wearing an oversized Stanford sweatshirt and baggy black sweatpants, Shana acted surprised. "Mom," she said. "I thought you said you were coming Friday."

"Today is Friday." She handed Shana her overnight bag. The drive to L.A. had taken her almost two hours, and the plane she flew on was so small, her knees were practically on her chest. Everything combined had caused her back to crash. She had several herniated disks and needed surgery, but she couldn't take off work. "Why aren't you answering your phone? I've been frantic."

"My cell was disconnected yesterday. I called and left word on your answering machine at work this morning, but I guess you'd already left."

"But your phone rang." Lily knew she was lying because Jeannie answered her calls and any messages that came in went to her machine. Jeannie would never forget to tell her her daughter had called.

"The cell phone company gives you a few days to pay up before they disconnect your service. I guess that's supposed to save you from embarrassment. I went to the coffee shop to call you."

"Is that so?" Another lie, Lily told herself, certain cell phone companies merely discontinued the service. A regular phone company occasionally allowed outgoing calls to be made when a customer didn't pay their bill, but Shana didn't have a landline. The phone companies were required to do it by law so a person would have access to emergency services.

How could Shana get behind on her bills with all the money Lily had been sending her? When she was under pressure from a big trial like she was now, she merely gave in to Shana's demands rather than get into an argument. She had believed Shana was mature enough to pay her own bills, but she'd obviously been wrong.

Lily smiled warmly and then pulled her daughter into her arms. "I'm here, sweetheart. That's all that matters." The apartment was the most depressing hovel Lily had ever seen. All the curtains were drawn, and the kitchen and small living room were littered with fast-food wrappers, old leaky paper cups where ants were congregating, and piles of dirty laundry.

Shana walked over and flopped down in a beanbag chair with a torn and dirty cushion, turning her eyes to the television. The picture was snowy with static. On top was a pair of rabbit ears. "I didn't have the money to pay the cable bill. I found these in the trash the other day. The cable company's charges are outrageous, so I decided I didn't need it. Brett told me that since the networks were broadcasting in HD now that I could pick them up without cable. He was wrong, of course, but it doesn't matter. I don't have time to watch TV."

"But you're watching it now?"

"Yeah," Shana said. "I'm watching *Dracula*, the one with Gary Oldman. It's pretty good. Want me to tell you about it?"

Lily walked over and pressed the off button on the television. "No, Shana. I didn't come all this way to discuss vampires. When did you stop going to classes?"

"I don't know. A few weeks ago, I guess."

Lily placed her hands on her hips. "This place is a disaster. The least you can do is clean up after yourself." She started picking up the fast-food sacks. "You have ants. You'll have to notify the apartment manager so they can exterminate. If you don't do something fast, all your neighbors will have ants."

"I haven't felt like cleaning lately. What do you care, anyway? You don't live here."

"Don't forget who pays the bills." Lily stuffed the trash into an overflowing container in the kitchen, and then returned to sit on the sofa. Her back was throbbing so badly now, she couldn't get comfortable. She looked in her purse for her pain pills and came up empty-handed. In her rush to get to the airport, she had forgotten to pack them.

An acrid odor assaulted her nostrils. Her nose led her to the ashtray on the coffee table. She picked through the cigarette butts until she pulled out a marijuana cigarette, her stomach tightening into knots. "I can't believe you're smoking dope," she said, her voice elevating. "No wonder you're having trouble with your studies."

"I don't smoke, Mom," Shana said. "Julie must have left it there before she moved out. She only smoked it every once in a while to relax. Everyone smokes pot. This is Santa Clara County, remember?

The police seized ninety-six hundred marijuana plants from Mount Madonna Park the other day. You can get high just from breathing the air around here. I think Julie had a prescription for it. The doctor gave it to her instead of tranquilizers."

Lily crushed the joint in her palm. Drugs were expensive, which could be the reason Shana was having trouble paying her bills. Shana turned the television back on and stared at the screen as if she had forgotten her mother was there, her long legs sprawled out in front of her.

"You're going home with me," Lily told her. "I'm not taking no for an answer." Still Shana didn't answer. Leaving the room to use the bathroom, she flushed the joint down the toilet. She had to get her daughter out of here, even if it was only for a few days. She was depressed over the situation with the boyfriend. A change of scenery would do her good.

Shana had been in counseling when she was younger, then stopped when she had entered college. Her father's death had been painful, but he'd been dead for years now. If Lily had suspected anything was even slightly amiss, she would have arranged for Shana to see someone here. Outside of the money, there hadn't been any signs she was having problems.

She started to rifle through Shana's bathroom cabinets and then stopped herself. Regardless of what was going on, she refused to invade her daughter's privacy.

When she returned to the other room, Lily headed straight for the TV, this time yanking the plug out of the wall. "First thing in the morning, we'll sit down and figure out what we're going to do about your situation." She paused, brushing a strand of hair behind one ear. "Chris has asked me to marry him. I want you to meet him. I'm certain you'll like him. He's a wonderful man, Shana."

"Right, Mom. I think I've heard that before. Wasn't Bryce a wonderful man, too?"

"Everyone makes mistakes. I'm sorry about you and Brett. You'll find someone else. Just give it some time."

Shana stared at her, a bitter look on her face. "Why are men so attracted to you? You're not that young anymore and you certainly don't dress for shit. Dad still loved you even after he divorced you for cheating. I don't know about Bryce, but he married you. Now you have some new guy in love with you. Every guy I've ever dated has dumped me. My mother has a better love life than I do. You know how that makes me feel?"

Shana had dark circles under her eyes, and her face appeared gaunt and pale. Outside of fast-food restaurants, Lily suspected she hadn't left the apartment since Brett had broken off their relationship three weeks ago. While she was cleaning up, she'd looked inside some of the fast-food sacks and noticed that only a few bites of the food had been eaten. But there was something else Lily sensed—fear. She patted the sofa. "Just give me a pillow and I'll sleep here tonight."

"You can sleep in Julie's room. I haven't changed the sheets, but I don't think you'll catch anything. Compared to me, she was immaculate."

"The sofa is fine. I want us to catch the first plane out tomorrow morning."

Shana shot her a steely look. "I'm not going to Ventura."

"I insist," Lily said in a more forceful tone. "I want you to see Dr. Randolph. You can try to catch up on your reading while you're at home, then you'll be ready to go back to class when you come back. We're only talking about a few days, Shana. Sometimes that's all it takes to put things back into perspective. You told me you were afraid because of—"

"How many times do I have to tell you? I'm not going to fucking Ventura." Shana was shouting and then she got up and paced around the small room, a look on her face that reminded Lily of panthers in cages at the zoo. In the blink of an eye, her mood changed dramatically. The muscles in her face softened and she looked at Lily and smiled as if she had just received some sort of secret message. "Brett's going to come back to me. As soon as he figures out how stupid that girl is, he'll beg me to take him back. So what if he fooled around with someone else? It's not like he loves her or anything. She's just a fuck, that's all. I'll forgive him. I don't have a choice. We're getting married as soon as he passes the bar. We've already found the place we want to get married. It's a beautiful Catholic church in San Francisco. Brett's even going to convert for me. He was raised an Episcopalian and it's not that different from Catholicism."

As Shana paced, beads of perspiration popped out on Lily's forehead and upper lip. One minute she hated everything and everyone and the next she was planning a wedding to a man who no longer wanted her. Other things had changed as well. In the past Shana had never used profanity and she'd always been firmly grounded to reality. Something in her daughter's mind had changed. Her personality seemed to have fractured. A psychiatrist would probably classify it as a psychotic break, and Lily knew something like that was serious. Some people never recovered. She couldn't let that happen to her daughter. "When was the last time you spoke to Brett?"

"I don't know. Two weeks, maybe three."

"He might not come back, Shana. I don't want you to get your hopes up. If he hasn't called you in three weeks . . ."

"You don't want me to be happy, do you?" she shouted, her mood becoming hostile again. "You've never wanted me to be happy. Everything was great in my life until you and Dad divorced and you rented that awful house. All you had to do was keep the family together until I graduated from high school, but you were too hot for that stupid DA. What was his name?"

Lily remained silent, hurt by her daughter's accusations.

"Richard Fowler. Now I remember. At least one guy dumped you. You divorced Dad and wrecked all of our lives for a guy who only wanted you for his fuck buddy." She stared at her mother in disgust. "I'm going to take a shower. Listen for the door in case Brett comes, but don't open it for anyone else. They still haven't caught that disgusting rapist. Thank God he didn't kill her." Her eyes darted around the room. "At night I stay on the couch. I drink a ton of coffee so I won't fall asleep. I don't really need that much

sleep. I can get by with less than two hours a night. Some nights I
don't sleep at all and look at me, I'm perfectly fine."

She stuck her hand inside one of the pillows in the sofa and
pulled out a large hammer. "I bought this to defend myself if
someone picks the lock or tries to kick in the door." She scrunched
her face up and made a rapid downward motion with the hammer.
"If I can hit him over the head, I'm pretty sure he won't be able to
rape me. I might even be able to kill the piece of shit."

"Aren't you overreacting, Shana?" Lily said, leaning forward so
she could massage her aching back. "There's no reason to believe
this man might come here and rape you. Think about it, honey. It
was probably an isolated incident. The suspect must have fled by
now. He'd be a fool to hang around here. Palo Alto is a small town
and he'd be risking apprehension."

"Overreacting," Shana snarled. "A rape occurs on a college
campus every twenty-four hours. I have to protect myself, especially since Brett isn't here and Julie moved out."

"Why did she move out?"

"She got kicked out because of her grades."

"Have you advertised for another roommate?"

"Why should I? I already told you I'm going to quit school and
get a job. Brett doesn't want me to work after we get married. He
wants me to stay at home and take care of our children. His mother
worked when he was a kid and he never saw her. I didn't see you
very much when I was young. I don't want our children to have
that kind of life."

"Listen to what you're saying, Shana," Lily said, wincing in
pain. Her daughter's words were so hurtful, she felt as if there
were a dozen gaping wounds on her body. Tension also intensified
her pain as the muscles in her back contracted and pressed against
the herniated disks. "Why would you quit school and throw away
all you've worked for to please a man who's cheated on you and
doesn't seem to want you anymore? You're not making sense, honey.
And you can't go without sleep. To be honest, I think you're suf-

fering from sleep deprivation. Whether you realize it or not, sleep deprivation is a serious condition."

"I love him." Shana tossed her arms around, even more agitated. "What do you know about love? You didn't love my dad and you didn't love Bryce. You use men up and throw them away. Brett and I have something special. He worships me. He wants me to be the mother of his children. He's going to take care of me, make certain I'm safe. His father owns a huge law firm in Los Angeles and he's going to make Brett a partner. He's even going to buy us a house."

Lily was beginning to panic. Her daughter was clearly irrational and the look in her eyes was frightening. She was either already psychotic or she was teetering on the brink. There was no doubt she needed immediate treatment. She would have to find someone local. The problem was it was so late, and tomorrow was Saturday. Most psychologists didn't keep their offices open on weekends. Finding someone who would see a new patient right away wasn't feasible. The only thing she could think of was to take her to a mental health clinic. She didn't believe an emergency room would dispense the kind of medicine her daughter needed. Every university had some kind of student clinic, but she didn't want something like that in Shana's records. "Do you have a phone book? I need to call the airlines."

"I'm not going. You'll be wasting your money if you buy me a ticket."

"You don't have to come with me. I just need to call and confirm my flight for tomorrow. Will you at least let me buy you a decent meal?" She glanced around the room. "You'll get sick if you keep eating junk food."

"Fine," Shana said, picking the hammer up from the coffee table and handing it to her. "I'll go to dinner with you if you promise not to talk about me going to Ventura anymore. I think the phone book is on top of the refrigerator. If you can't find it, just look up the number on my computer. I'll take my shower now. Talking to you makes me feel dirty."

The bathroom was in the hallway. Once Shana went inside and closed the door, Lily darted into her bedroom and sat down at her desk. Books were stacked on the floor, along with piles of paper. She typed in "mental health" on Shana's computer and found a listing of private hospitals in the San Francisco area. Most of them were for alcohol and drug rehab, but she didn't care. All she needed was someone to prescribe medication. If Shana could get some sleep, she might be able to get over the hump by Sunday night when Lily had to leave. She was an adult so she couldn't force her to come back to Ventura with her.

Lily found a hospital named Whitehall that was located on the outskirts of San Francisco. From the picture, she believed she had passed it on her way to Palo Alto and it looked like a nice place. Quickly entering the phone number and address into her cell phone, she returned to the living room to wait for Shana.

"I think I got all the rats out of my hair." Shana was dressed in a pair of blue slacks that looked several sizes too large for her and a heavy white wool sweater.

She was a beautiful woman, Lily thought, far more attractive than herself. Her hair had more gold tones in it, although she'd inherited her mother's natural curl. They both hated their hair because it was perpetually frizzy and hard to manage. Shana's body was more curvaceous than Lily's and her legs were long and shapely. Lily's legs were pasty white toothpicks. She used to work out every morning, but lately she hadn't had the energy and her back pain was too severe. But right now, Shana's looks meant nothing. If she acted like this around other people, they would turn around and run the other way.

Lily stood and smiled. "Are we ready?"

"Yeah, I just need to get my cell phone."

Shana didn't realize what she had said. If the phone didn't work, why would she want to take it with her? She had been avoiding Lily's calls, plain and simple. Why? What had she done? She gave her everything she asked for. She was obviously sick. Nothing else made sense.

They finally made it out of the apartment. Lily knew Shana would refuse to go if she knew where they were headed. It was late now, past ten, and it seemed far more important to get help rather than to buy her a meal she more than likely wouldn't eat.

Approximately thirty minutes later, she pulled into the driveway of the hospital and parked. There was no sign on the building and only six cars in the parking lot, which she assumed belonged to the staff. The exterior of the hospital resembled an old Southern mansion, which was probably why they had named it Whitehall. There were balconies and ivy growing up walls near the entrance.

"I've never been to this restaurant," Shana told her, staring up at the large white structure. "What kind of food do they serve?"

Lily's nerves were frazzled. She wished she'd had time to call the hospital and explain the situation but if Shana had overheard her, she would have refused to leave the apartment. "Let's go see, okay?"

The lobby resembled a hotel, which made Lily's story that it was a restaurant more believable. "Why don't you have a seat while I see if they'll take us without a reservation?"

"There's no one there, Mom. Maybe they're closed."

Lily ignored her and walked up to the counter. She saw a phone on the counter and picked it up. When a female voice answered, she cupped her hands around her mouth and spoke in a hushed tone. "My daughter needs help and I don't know where else to take her. I tricked her into coming here. She thinks this is a restaurant."

"Don't worry," the woman said, "we'll take care of her. Stay there and I'll come right out."

A middle-aged woman dressed in business attire appeared, glancing at Lily and then over at Shana as if she wasn't sure which one of them had the problem. Lily hurried across the room, leaving Shana on the sofa.

"Michelle Newman," the woman said. "I'm one of the hospital administrators. It might be better if you stepped outside for a while. As soon as we take her back, you can return and wait here in the lobby. The interview process usually takes about an hour."

"But you don't even know what's wrong with her."

"We're professionals, Ms. . . ."

"Forrester . . . Lily Forrester. I don't want her admitted. She just needs some type of medication to calm her down and help her sleep. She's depressed and she hasn't been sleeping." Shana was glaring at her. Lily knew she had to do something fast.

"We'll call you in to discuss our assessment of your daughter as soon as we conclude the interview. All I need is her name, date of birth, and her insurance information."

Lily provided her with the information. "Okay, I'll leave. She's not going to be a happy camper. She spent some time in a mental hospital years ago and hated it." The woman's interest intensified. "Nothing was actually wrong with her. I mean, she doesn't suffer from a mental disorder. She was basically stressed out, which might be what's happening now. She attends law school over at the university."

Shana was gesturing for her. Lily held up a palm to let her know she should wait. "Your ad said you deal mostly with drug and alcohol problems. Is that correct?"

"We treat a wide variety of illnesses and addictions. Shana is in good hands, Ms. Forrester. Whitehall is one of the finest hospitals of its kind in California."

A large man with bulging muscles came out, dressed in a striped polo shirt and tan slacks, a bored expression on his face.

Lily started inching her way toward the door when Shana stood to follow her. The man came up behind her and grabbed her by the arm.

"Get your hands off of me!" Shana shouted, trying to jerk away. "Mom, what kind of place is this? Why are you leaving? What's going on?"

"Everything will be fine, honey. This is a hospital and they're going to help you."

Shana started kicking and screaming. "Why are you doing this to me? Are you punishing me because I didn't answer your stupid calls? I just haven't been in the mood to talk to anyone." She paused and gulped in air, red-faced and furious. "This is a damn mental institution, isn't it? You're the one who's insane, not me. I fucking hate you."

Lily felt oddly calm. She walked out of the hospital and didn't look back. She heard another string of profanity just as she stepped outside into the cold night air.

She sat down on the steps of the hospital, wishing that she still smoked cigarettes. Here she was amidst all this natural beauty, and all she felt was a blinding sense of failure. The scent of burning wood filled the air. The sky was clear and the moon was full. Shana hadn't meant the ugly things she had said, she told herself. Once she got some rest, she would be fine.

Lily also knew the use of illegal drugs was escalating among high-achieving young people such as doctors, mathematicians, and physicists, people a person would never conceive of as drug abusers. The competition was so fierce today and the workload was so heavy that they sometimes resorted to drugs just to stay awake. But she'd never considered law school to be that difficult. Maybe Shana wasn't as intelligent as she thought. Here was another area that reminded her of Noelle Reynolds. She had skated along for years before the truth came out.

Most people's finances were in such terrible shape, they couldn't afford to send their children to an expensive university like Stanford. Parents who had saved for years in order to provide their children with an education woke up one morning last year to find it all gone.

Lily was fortunate because she had a steady income, but knowing that the presiding judge wanted her gone kept her constantly on edge. If she made any mistake whatsoever, Hennessey would fire her. There were far too many attorneys in California and setting up a private practice was expensive and time consuming. Her expertise was in criminal law, which would make it hard for her to earn a living as a defense attorney. The majority of criminals were indigent.

She reached the Dodge rental car and slipped into the driver's seat. She gave thought to climbing into the backseat to take a nap, but she was too anxious to sleep. Maybe she'd done the wrong thing by bringing Shana to this place. She always seemed to do the wrong thing when it came to her daughter. Shana had made that perfectly clear tonight.

Lily struggled to keep from going back inside and taking Shana home. If she wasn't in trial, she could stay in Palo Alto and take care of her, get to the bottom of things. Her career had always interfered with her life, especially when it came to her daughter. But she had to support herself. There was the expense of the new house and providing for Shana's education, which seemed to grow more costly every month.

What was she doing with all that money? Lily asked herself. She hadn't bought new furniture and Lily hadn't seen any shopping bags from clothing stores. It had to be drugs. She thought of gambling. Although gambling wasn't legal in California, there were Internet gaming sites and a person could get in just as much trouble as they could inside a real casino.

Then another thought passed through Lily's mind. Shana could have become pregnant and undergone an abortion. But even that wouldn't explain the kind of money she claimed she needed every month. She could have been arrested for DWI, which would have cost a bundle. Her father had developed a problem with alcohol and it had landed him in serious trouble.

Merely thinking of the things John had done made Lily furious. While driving under the influence one night, John had struck a pedestrian in Los Angeles, leaving the poor man to die alone on the street. After their divorce, he had quit his government job to become a real estate agent, a job he wasn't cut out for. A person who made their living in sales had to work hard and John had been habitually lazy. He had also been stupid in many ways. While bending over to check the injured man, he had dropped his wallet. The police had tracked him down the next day and arrested him for vehicular manslaughter. It didn't help that it had been his second DWI.

And who did her ex-husband call to post his bail and hire an attorney to represent him? He had called Lily, of course. When she refused to give him money, he had cut a deal with the DA, telling them that Lily had killed Bobby Hernandez. In exchange for his information, John received a reduced sentence in the hit-and-run.

Lily had been relieved when the police had showed up on her doorstep, grateful that the nightmare would finally be over. Precious Shana had saved her, though, marching into the DA's office without her mother's knowledge and claiming she was the one who had shot Hernandez. The DA knew she was covering for her mother. The crime was far too sophisticated to have been committed by a young girl. Shana didn't even have a driver's license. Lily would probably still be in prison if Marco Curazon, the man who'd actually raped them, had not been apprehended a short time later.

Shana had shown courage and self-sacrifice in doing what she had done. After Curazon was arrested, Lily had been forced to come up with something to explain Shana's strange behavior. The only thing that made sense was telling them that she had suffered a breakdown. To make sure their story was credible Shana had agreed to spend a week inside a mental hospital in Ventura.

As Lily thought about it, she came to the realization that it wasn't long after the stint in the hospital that Shana started to resent her again. Desperate to talk to someone, she called Chris to tell him what was going on.

"Why in God's name did you take her to a mental hospital? Was she really in that bad a shape?"

"She wasn't rational and she hadn't been sleeping or taking care of herself. I can't explain it, Chris, but she needed immediate treatment. Her place was a mess and I found marijuana. Not much, I admit, but Shana has never used drugs before." She paused and took a breath. "They're not going to keep her, Chris. All I want them to do is give her some medicine so she can sleep. They're evaluating her now."

"I don't know what to say, honey. I've never met the girl. Do what you feel is right."

"Chris, there's something we have to talk about when I get back."

"What?"

"I did something terrible. That's why I was trying to talk you out of marrying me."

"Listen, we've all done things we regret. I want us to start off fresh, make it a new beginning for both of us. The past doesn't matter. It's our future that matters, and I know it's going to be wonderful."

"But you don't understand. I committed a crime, Chris."

"How long ago was this?"

"Sixteen years ago."

"Forget it, Lily. I don't want to hear it. Whatever you did, you did. I know you well enough to know you must have had a good reason. Nothing is going to stop me from loving you. I told you that from the beginning."

Lily was too worried about Shana to continue. When she got back, she would write him a letter. But a letter could fall into the wrong hands, and she wasn't prepared to go to prison right now. She had tried to confess from the beginning, but ironically, no one had wanted to listen. This horrible thing was trapped inside her and she knew she would never be free of it. Maybe if the truth finally came out, she could put it behind her.

But not now, not when Shana needed her. Her daughter's well-being was the reason Detective Cunningham had refused to arrest her, but shortly after, he'd quit the Ventura PD and moved to Omaha, where he had grown up. Lily wasn't the only one who had to live with this secret. Shana had suffered as well, and for all she knew, keeping something like this inside for so many years could be one of the reasons she had skidded off track.

"Try to get some sleep tonight," Chris said. "Call me first thing in the morning. I already miss you and you've only been gone for one day."

"I miss you, too."

Lily understood what was happening to Shana because it had happened to her. She couldn't remember how it had begun, but she knew exactly how it had ended, just as she knew the remark-

able man who had saved her. The only thing she'd never understand was why.

1993
VENTURA, CALIFORNIA

"Station One, Two-Boy," the dispatcher said over the police radio. "Robbery just occurred at White's Market, Alameda and Fourth. Suspects are two males armed with
nine-millimeters, last seen EB on Third in a brown Nova, unknown license. Clerk has
been shot. Ambulance and rescue en route. Code three."

Cunningham was only a few blocks from the scene. A patrol unit had been dis-
patched, but his eyes scanned the vehicles as he flew past them. All he could see was the
face of Lily Forrester. He reached over and turned the radio off. Why had she called
him and told him she had shot Bobby Hernandez? Why hadn't she left well enough
alone? He had no evidence now that Manny was dead; she was almost in the clear. It
was such a stupid thing to do, exactly the type of thing a woman would do: confess
when they'd almost walked away without a hitch. She had committed the perfect
crime, and then she had dissolved into a sniveling female answering some inner need to
do the moral, ethical thing. Anger rose inside him, acid bubbled like a witch's cauldron
inside his stomach.

"There are no ethics anymore," he said. "Presidents commit crimes and lie, preach-
ers steal and fornicate, parents murder their children, and children murder their parents." That morning he'd read an article about a fire captain charged with twelve counts
of arson. On the next page was a piece on an LAPD detective who had conspired to commit murder for hire. Sitting at a desk right next to him, carrying a gun and wearing a
badge, was a man he was certain was a cold-blooded murderer. Where would it all stop?
How much lower could society sink?

His eyes searched the streets in front of him, took in the houses and faceless individuals milling about. "Get back in your homes, assholes!" he yelled at them. "If you
don't, someone will shoot you just for the thrill of it. Bolt the doors. Hide under your
beds. Can't you see this is a war zone? Don't you know half the people walking around
have more firepower in their pockets than the cops?"

He passed under the freeway and sped down Victoria Boulevard, where the government center was housed. "Cops, police officers, lawmen," he uttered in disgust. He
slowed down and searched the street signs, then made a quick right, the big car fish-
tailing. In one of the driveways, a teenage girl was getting inside a car. "Call a cop

and he just might rape you, little girl. Or maybe he'll club your boyfriend to death because he's had a rotten day. See, no one sane wants to be a cop anymore, and there's no such animal as a lawman."

Now he was climbing into the foothills, searching for the address Lily had given him. It was dark as pitch. He couldn't read the numbers. Suddenly he saw a red Honda and slammed on the brakes. The house was dark. Cutting the engine, he sat perfectly still and listened. It was too dark and too quiet. His nose twitched and he thought he could smell death.

"No!" he cried, slapping both hands on the steering wheel, imagining what he was going to find inside that house: strands of red hair stuck to the walls and ceilings, sweet little freckles scattered like dust in the air, Lily's mouth sucking on the same shotgun she had used to blow Hernandez away. Then he would have to make the notifications, tell her precious little girl, already ravaged and violated.

He held his breath as he approached the front door, which was standing open. All he could hear was his own heart tapping out a staccato beat. Then he saw her in the shadows. Lily was on the floor, leaning against the wall, motionless. He thought the worst. His eyes searched for blood, a shotgun, or a handgun. But when he reached out with an icy finger to touch the pulse point on her neck, his finger rose and fell with life.

"Lily," he said, shaking her gently, falling to his knees. For reasons he couldn't explain, he engulfed her in his arms and crushed her to his chest.

"Daddy," she whispered, the word muffled, her voice that of a child.

"It's going to be okay. I'm here. It's going to be okay." He held her and rocked her, repeating the words again and again. She had lost contact with reality, was in the midst of a psychotic break. She had fallen through the crack, but he had been there to catch her. He recalled his childhood love—the circus and the trapeze artists. He remembered how he had looked up in awe as a beautiful young woman in a shiny costume had flown through the air. Just when he thought she would fall, an upside-down man with muscular arms caught her and held her until they both reached the perch and dismounted, their arms in the air in triumph.

He grabbed Lily's arms and shook her more forcefully. "It's Bruce, Bruce Cunningham. Lily, do you hear me? Say my name. Say it. Say Bruce."

"Bruce," she said, repeating the sound like a parrot.

He let go of her and she fell back against the wall, her eyes still closed and her body rigid. Running his hand along the wall, he found the light switch and flooded the room with light. Then he bent down and slapped her across the face. Her eyes sprang open. "Fight," he ordered her, "fight for your life. It's Bruce Cunningham, Detective Bruce Cunningham. Look at me."

There it was. He saw it: recognition, realization, reality. She was back. He had caught her in his strong hands, and he was swinging her through the air to the perch.

"I killed Bobby Hernandez," she said. "I thought he raped my daughter. I was certain he had raped my daughter. I shot him in cold blood."

"Where are you, Lily?"

"I'm in Ventura, at my new house."

"What's the president's name?"

"George Bush," she said. "Why are you asking me this stuff?"

She didn't even remember where she had been or where she'd been heading, to the ground without a net. He picked a towel off the floor and went to the kitchen and soaked it in water from the tap. Then he stood over her and dropped it into her lap. "Wash your face. You'll feel better," he said tenderly, a father to a child. She buried her face in the towel and after a few minutes had passed, looked up at him with those big blue eyes, the freckles intact, still dotting her nose and pale cheeks.

"You slapped me."

"Yeah, let's get out of here."

"Are you going to cuff me?"

Pushing herself to her feet, she faced him, and a wave of emotion washed over him. One arm moved underneath her knees as he collected her in his arms. Still holding her, he carried her to the car and placed her in the front seat. He touched his lips to her forehead and tried to speak, but words had left him. Her head fell back against the seat.

Leaving the car door open, he ran down the steps and into the house. He grabbed her jacket, her purse, turned the lights off, closed the door, and ran back up the steps. He noted no shortness of breath. His body moved like that of a conditioned athlete, not a middle-aged, overweight detective.

Entering the car on the driver's side, he reached over and fastened her seat belt, then pulled the door closed. "Hold on."

In seconds they were on the flats and the speedometer was inching its way to seventy, then eighty, then ninety. The windows were down and the cold night air beat against their faces. The roar of the big engine assaulted their ears. He reached for the mike, flicked the radio on, and yelled, "Station One, Unit Six-five-four!"

"Six-five-four, go ahead."

"Where's the victim of the two-eleven, the robbery at White's Market?"

"Community Presbyterian, but it looks like a DOA."

"I'm en route." He glanced at Lily and then back at the road. The steering wheel was vibrating in his hands. He dropped the microphone on the seat between them.

They didn't speak for the remainder of the drive. Lily's eyes were wide and her hands were braced against the dash. The car skidded to a stop in the parking lot of the hospital.

"Come with me," he said, throwing the car door open and then leaning in toward her. "Don't say anything. Don't do anything. Just stay beside me."

He crossed the parking lot in great, long strides. Lily was running in her high heels to keep up with him. The automatic doors to the ER opened, and glaring lights struck their eyes. Cunningham flashed his badge and kept walking, the nurse pointing to one of the examining rooms. On the table was a young man who appeared to be from India or Pakistan, uncovered and still. His shirt was ripped open but his chest was unmarked except for red circular spots where they had probably placed the paddles to shock his heart. One side of his head and face were completely gone, unrecognizable as anything but bloody tissue, hamburger meat.

The room was empty except for the three of them. Lily reached for the man's cold hand, gently touching the thin gold band around his finger. Tears welled up in her eyes and she looked with an unspoken plea at Cunningham. He jerked his head toward the door. She followed him out and down the hall. He kept walking through corridors, turning down one hall and then another, until he finally stopped and faced her. They were alone in what appeared to be a section of the hospital under construction or restoration.

"What you saw back there was a product of a Bobby Hernandez. Do you understand?"

There was a black intensity in his eyes and she had to look away. Another person spoke with her voice, mouthed the words through her lips. "Yes," she answered, "I understand."

"The world doesn't need him, the Bobby Hernandezes. You stepped on a cockroach. There are thousands more. They're in all the cabinets, under all the sinks, crawling under every stinking toilet."

He stopped and his shoulders fell, his years reappeared, the lines sank in his face, his stomach bulged over his pants. His face was flushed; perspiration dampened his forehead. His large chest expanded and contracted.

"What happened between us back there didn't happen. What you said to me on the phone you didn't say." He shoved his hand into his pocket and pulled out a twenty dollar bill. Prying her fingers open, he pressed it there, and then closed them with his fleshy hand. "You're going to get in a cab and go back to your life. You're going to forget this night ever happened. If you see me tomorrow or the next day, all you're going to say is, 'Hi, Bruce. How you doing, Bruce,' and you're going to fight the fight and build a new life for you and your daughter."

"But you can't do this!" Lily exclaimed, her voice high and shrill, her body trembling. "You can't listen to me confess to a homicide and then walk away. What about the law?" She started waving her hands around excitedly, her eyes wild again with hysteria. He jerked his head behind him. There was no one around. They were still alone.

Cunningham grabbed both of her hands with his own and pinned them against the wall, his face inches from hers, his breath as hot and heavy as a blowtorch. "I am the law. Do you hear me? I'm the one who lives and breathes it, not the judges on their high benches too far away from it to even smell it. I'm the one who gets shot at, the one who has to inhale the rotting flesh of the society we live in. I'm the one who comes when people call, when they're robbed or beaten or raped. I have every right to make this decision, every right."

Beads of sweat fell from his forehead like salty rain onto Lily's upturned face. "Justice," he said, spitting out the word. "How can the interest of justice be served by trying you for avenging your child, by locking you up, by leaving your daughter so badly damaged that she'll never recover?" He suddenly released his hold on Lily and stepped back. Her arms fell to her sides. "There is a God, lady, and He lives down here in the gutter with the likes of me."

With that, the big man turned his back and started walking down the hall, his scuffed and worn black shoes clanking across the linoleum, the cheap fabric of his suit pulling tightly against his back and broad shoulders. Lily's eyes watched him until he turned the corner and disappeared.

# SEVEN

Their dark-skinned bodies glistened in the flickering candlelight. Mary had one of her long legs tossed over her husband's. "So what do you think?"

"It was fantastic."

"I was talking about my house."

"The house is great, too," Brooks said. "And the weather here is phenomenal. Do you know how cold it is in Texas right now? And we won't need air-conditioning in the summer. We'll shave several hundred bucks off our electric bill."

"I asked you about my house, not the weather. You men are all the same. As soon as you get off, you become brain dead. Do you think Thelma and Rita will be happy here?"

"The house is super and the neighborhood seems safe. There's plenty of living space and an extra bedroom for the housekeeper. If they don't kill each other, everything should work out fine."

Mary got up to go to the bathroom. They had flown in for the weekend to start looking at real estate. She jumped into the shower and then returned and stretched out beside him to put on her moisturizer. "I own this house outright, Brooks. Maybe we should live here and rent a place for Thelma and Rita. You mentioned saving money. Housing is expensive in California. A house like this would sell for six hundred thousand dollars, and that's in a lousy housing market."

Brooks propped several pillows behind his head. "Real estate is at an all-time low right now. We can steal a great house and use it as an investment." He fell serious. "I thought we agreed that I was going to handle the finances."

"I know," Mary told him. "But we also talked about having a baby. If I stop working, we might have trouble making ends meet. A live-in housekeeper is expensive. I know women are having babies late in life today, but they say it's better for a woman to have a child before she's forty. Sperm gets old, too, and there's a greater chance that something might be wrong with the baby. You'll be forty in three years."

"And you'll be forty in four. We'll have a kid by then." He craned his head around to look in her eyes. "You don't want to get pregnant now, do you? I thought you weren't even a hundred percent sure you wanted children."

Mary smiled. "I've changed my mind. Our genes are too good not to replicate."

"Replicate?"

"My degree was in biochemistry, remember?"

Mary heard her cell phone ringing and reached over to snatch it off the nightstand. She carried another phone for personal calls, so she knew it was Bureau business. She hadn't told Adams or anyone else she was going away for the weekend. Brooks had flown commercial and Mary had hitched a ride on a navy jet headed to Port Hueneme, a city not far from Ventura. "Special Agent Stevens."

"This is Agent Charles Pittman. We've never met but I'm presently assigned to the Ventura field office. From what I've heard, you're going to be my replacement."

"How did you know I was in Ventura?"

"I didn't," Pittman told her. "Did you come to get a feel for the area?"

"Not exactly. I have a home here. Before I joined the Bureau, I worked homicide at Ventura PD."

"Great, then you're already ahead of the game. I was transferred from Portland so I started out with a blank slate. Anyway, the PD is presently working a possible homicide that I thought might interest you. You were mentioned as a contact person in the Bureau directive we received last night regarding suspicious homicides. The male victim was wearing a catheter so he may be a paraplegic. The directive stated that you were looking for homicides that might actually be suicides."

Mary was pleased Adams had honored her request and sent out a directive. A paraplegic had a reason to kill himself, and her voice rose in excitement. "Was there a suicide note?"

"If there was, I doubt they'd be working it as a homicide."

"How long ago was the body discovered?"

"The Ventura County Sheriff's Department arrived on the scene about an hour ago. The crime occurred in an area called the Rincon."

"Has the coroner's office already picked up the body?"

"Not yet," Pittman told her. "The sheriff tried to kiss it off to the PD. The body was found in a wooded area across from the beach. From what I understand, the SO and the PD spent the past hour arguing over which agency had jurisdiction."

"I know the Rincon. It's county, so the SO has jurisdiction. Are you going to meet us at the crime scene?"

"My partner and I are busy finishing off the paperwork on our human trafficking case."

Human trafficking, Mary thought, surprised. She might not have to claw the paint off the walls after all. "Thanks for the information," she said, disconnecting.

When she turned around, Brooks had already thrown on a pair of slacks and was reaching for his shirt off the back of the chair. "You don't need to go with me, honey," Mary told him. "Stay here and get some rest. The only reason I'm going is I think it might be related to the peculiar deaths I'm investigating."

Brooks smiled. "I don't want to stay here by myself. Once we take over the post here, there'll only be the two of us. We may not have a chance to work together that often. One of us will have to stay behind and cover the office." His eyes feasted on her naked body. "I was thinking about having another go at you but I guess you better get out of your birthday suit. We'll be leaving in ten minutes."

"We're not official yet," Mary said. "No one in the Bureau even knows we're in Ventura."

"Someone knows or they wouldn't have called you. What's the problem, anyway?" He tossed her jeans to her. "We're still FBI agents."

In slightly less than ten minutes, they were speeding down the 101 Freeway toward Rincon Beach. She glanced out the passenger window, happy to be home again. "Look at the waves, Brooks, they're huge. Maybe we should learn to surf."

"You learn to surf. I'm scared to death of the ocean."

"But you know how to swim, don't you?"

"Not really," he told her. "I grew up in Detroit. My childhood didn't include swimming pools. Mom used to hose us down in the summer. I was even afraid of that. I'm just spooked when it comes to water. Maybe I drowned in another lifetime."

They stopped when they saw the string of police cars and emergency vehicles parked along the access road to the freeway. Mary was wearing her favorite red shirt. When she'd worked homicide in Ventura, she'd called it her "murder shirt." She made a habit of wearing it when she responded to homicides. The color made it easier to find her in a crowd.

Brooks and Mary hung their FBI badges on strings around their necks, then started stopping people and asking them who was in charge. "Oh, that would be Sheriff Earl Mathis," a young deputy told them, pointing to an area up the hill that was surrounded by officers. "He's up there where the body was found. He's a big man, so you won't have any trouble finding him."

"Are you thinking what I'm thinking?" Mary asked Brooks as they hiked up the hill.

"Who found the body, right?"

"The beach is on the other side of the highway. Like I said, I'm familiar with this area and there's nothing up here but trees and scrub brush. I can't think of anyone who'd want to go up there outside of the killer. Keep your eyes peeled. He could still be here, hiding among the officers."

Mary saw a large man barking orders and assumed he was Sheriff Mathis. "I'm Special Agent Mary Stevens and this is Special Agent Brooks East." She extended her hand and Mathis shook it, his grip so strong he almost crushed her fingers. "Can you tell us what happened here tonight, Sheriff?"

Mathis was a tall, heavyset man with a stomach that exploded over the top of his khaki-colored uniform pants. He reeked of cigarette smoke, and a pack of Marlboros was protruding from the pocket in his shirt. Tipping his cowboy hat back on his head, he scowled at them. "What're you feds doing up here?"

Mary cut her eyes to Brooks. Since she was the one who'd wanted to come, he shook his head to let her know he wasn't going to carry the ball for her. "Well, Sheriff Mathis, Agent East and I have been assigned to take over the Ventura field office. We're not settled in yet, but we thought it might be nice to meet some of the local law enforcement. I never thought we'd get to meet the actual sheriff, though." She peered up at him and smiled sweetly. "We've heard so much about you, Sheriff Mathis. It's an honor to meet you, sir."

"Bullshit," he blurted out, his hands on his hips. "You FBI people sure know how to weasel your way into our business." He tossed Mary a plastic bag containing the standard white jumpsuit, a paper hat, and a pair of booties. "Suit up and I'll let you take a look at the body. Then you can scoot on out and let us do our job."

There was only one jumpsuit in the plastic bag. She moved several feet away and turned her back to the sheriff. Exchanging a tense glance with Brooks, she whispered, "Should I ask for another suit for you?"

"I wouldn't push it. Just wait and see what happens."

They climbed up the hill through the dense scrub brush. Once they reached the area where the body was located, Mathis yelled out to his people. "Make some room, guys. The feds are in the mood to look at dead guys."

The stench of rotting flesh permeated the air. Mosquitoes and flies swarmed around them. Mary looked for Brooks but he'd disappeared into the crowd of police officers. A portable spotlight illuminated the area. It appeared that the forensics team had just arrived as several of the techs were still changing into their white jumpsuits while the others were setting up a table to place the evidence on. She dropped down on her knees to get a better look at the body.

The victim, a white male, was facedown in the dirt with a large, gaping wound at the base of his neck, where the spinal cord was located. Ironic, she thought. If he was a paraplegic, an injury to his spinal cord was what had most likely caused his paralysis.

Mary pulled her camera out of her pocket and began snapping pictures. A heavyset man was taking samples from the body and she assumed he was one of the county's pathologists. "Have you established time of death yet?"

The man squinted at her before he saw her FBI badge dangling from her neck. "Best guess for now is he's been here at least a week. I pulled some well-developed insects from inside the wound."

Mary knew a week could end up being far longer. "I heard he was wearing a catheter bag. Is that true?"

"Yes, I believe he was a paraplegic. His legs looked atrophied, but his arms are fairly muscular." He paused and stared at her. "Anything I tell you is off the record, understand?"

"I understand," Mary told him. "I'm an FBI agent, not a reporter." She got up and went to find Sheriff Mathis.

"Who discovered the body?"

"Couple of local kids," he said, coughing. "They climbed up here to shoot cars with their paint guns."

"Did you find a vehicle?"

"Nope."

"What about the murder weapon?"

"Nope, unless the little buggers who found the body stole it. I shipped them off to juvie. I've got my deputies searching for the gun and spent casings, but so far, we haven't found anything. The terrain makes things difficult. We could scratch around up here for a month and end up with nothing more than a shitload of mosquito bites. As to the murder weapon, the killer either took it with him or walked across the street and tossed it into the ocean. Tomorrow, I'll get some men over there to see if it washed up on the beach. Something heavy like a gun usually sinks and we never see the damn thing again."

Mary didn't want to tell him how important the murder weapon was to her investigation. If the killer was the same UNSUB she was looking for, she doubted if he'd left the gun at the scene, particularly since he had already used it to kill four other people.

Purchasing a weapon was risky for a multiple murderer. He more than likely bought it on the street or stole it. One of the things NRA members failed to realize was the fact that most crimes were committed with weapons people purchased to protect themselves.

When the medical examiner left to get a cup of coffee from a pot someone had set up inside a van, Mary found a pair of latex gloves in the pocket of her jumpsuit and slipped them on. The victim was wearing a lightweight tan jacket. She bent down and went through the pockets, but there was nothing there. Then she opened the front of the jumpsuit and reached into her jeans for her pocketknife. She looked around to make certain no one was watching and quickly slit the seams in the victim's jacket, reaching inside and pulling out a folded-over piece of paper. The paper was flimsy so rather than take a chance of ripping it, she unbuttoned her shirt and slipped it inside her red blouse.

Mary had learned about opening the seams of clothing from her grandmother, who used to sew her jewelry and other valuables inside old coats she bought from the Salvation Army. When she passed away, the family had no idea where her valuables were until the funeral home called and told them they'd found a diamond ring sewn inside the seam of the coat she'd been wearing when she dropped dead from a fatal heart attack.

Through the years, Mary had found that any and all orifices were potential hiding places. A homeless woman had died and when she was examined at the morgue, they found hundreds of dollar bills stuffed inside pockets of skin she had carved into her body.

"What happened to you?" Mary found Brooks leaning against the car and staring out at the ocean.

"The smell," Brooks said. "I haven't handled a lot of homicides. I usually bring some camphor with me. I don't even have a handkerchief. Besides, the mosquitoes were eating me alive."

"Wait a minute," she joked. "You can't swim and you can't tolerate the smell of dead bodies. Maybe I should be the SAC instead of you?"

"I have seniority," he said, playfully swatting her ass. "Did you find anything worthwhile?"

"I'd rather talk inside the car."

Mary slid into the passenger seat, turning on the interior lights and carefully unfolding the paper she had stashed inside her blouse. "It's a will," she said, scanning the handwritten document. "I can't read the sentences where the crease was, but it's dated January eighth. That's only a week ago. The signature is James C. Washburn and it's been notarized. Washburn left everything he owned to his wife and children. This is a codicil to a will he made ten years ago."

"Then he must have committed suicide," Brooks said, peering over her shoulder at the document. "How many people make out a new will a week before they get themselves murdered?"

"Some people have premonitions regarding their death. Either that or he was involved in some sort of dangerous activity such as drug dealing. They should check out the area to see if there are any marijuana plants, even though I don't see how he could have attended to them without help."

"Could the gunshot wound be self-inflicted?"

"Possibly," Mary said, "but highly unlikely. Not many people have arms long enough to shoot themselves in the back of the head. No, someone shot him but I believe he may have hired him to do it. We need to check his finances, see if he recently withdrew a large sum of money. If he's in financial trouble, we'll have another motive in addition to his not wanting to continue his life as a paraplegic. The person I want to talk to is the man he hired to kill him. Let's go home so I can make notes of everything I saw out here tonight."

"Aren't you going to return the will?"

Mary already had her camera out and was snapping photos of the handwritten document. "The victim obviously wanted someone to find this or he wouldn't have sewn it inside the lining of his jacket."

"Maybe he didn't want the police to find it," Brooks told her. "That is, unless he was murdered and simply carried the thing around in his jacket. Let's say he did hire someone to kill him. He must have assumed that once the authorities concluded their investigation, they would turn his belongings over to his next of kin. Admittedly, that's a risky way to handle it. The jacket has to have blood on it. His wife might toss it or donate it to some kind of charity."

"I don't think it happened that way."

Brooks scratched his chin, thinking. "If the deceased had wanted the crime to be classified as a homicide so his family could collect on his life insurance, why would he leave a will behind, particularly one that was sewn inside his clothing? The sheriff's office might not have found it, and the original will would remain in place."

Mary's eyes widened. "The wife knew about it, don't you see? Washburn told her exactly where to find it. Because of the insurance money, the last thing he wanted was his death to look like a suicide. What I don't understand is why he needed a new will."

"And if he wanted his wife to have it, why didn't he just give it to her? Maybe he remarried after he made out the first will and it didn't work out. His first wife may have refused to see him."

"Why would he even have the thing in his possession if he knew he was coming up here to die?" Mary turned off the overhead lights and they sat there in silence, both of them deep in thought. "Now that I think of it, the coroner's office generally goes through the clothes and sends them back to the family when they're finished with the autopsy."

Brooks turned to her. "You need to take the will back where you found it before someone accuses you of tampering with evidence."

"I'm not sure I trust the sheriff's office. Mathis strikes me as an idiot, and I wasn't impressed with the medical examiner." She waved the flimsy piece of paper around without thinking. Brooks reached out and stopped her before it fell apart. "I think I'm going to keep it. This could be our most valuable piece of evidence. Maybe the wife is working with the UNSUB and she hired him to kill her husband. The will could even be phony. Let's face it, there's a lot of work involved in taking care of a paraplegic. Or, perhaps Washburn was living with a girlfriend and she dumped him. He could have left everything to this woman and then changed his mind, deciding he wanted his wife and children to have it. For all we know, his caretaker may have abused him."

Except for the moonlight reflecting off the ocean, it was dark inside their rental car. Brooks reached over and pulled Mary to him, kissing her on the mouth. "Take back the evidence and I'll give you a ride you'll never forget."

"Now you're bribing me with sex?" Mary tossed back, not amused. "That's sexual harassment, Brooks. You're my SAC, remember? I could report you."

He gripped the steering wheel with both hands. "I'm also your husband. I order you to take back the will. I can't allow you to steal evidence. Something like this could ruin both of our careers."

"Four people are already dead," Mary shot out, turning sideways in the seat. "And there's good reason to believe Washburn is the fifth victim. Don't forget, the last two were killed in the San Francisco area, which isn't that far from here."

"You have the photographs," Brooks argued. "We can send them to the lab and have them enhanced."

Mary pouted, holding the paper behind her back so he couldn't take it away from her. "I want to know what it says in the spot where it was folded. We may need the actual document to discern it. There may also be fingerprints, even DNA. We can't lift prints or test for DNA off a snapshot."

"I refuse to allow you to tamper with evidence!" Brooks shouted, the game over. "Now hike your pretty little legs back up there and put the document back where you found it. Once we establish a firm connection to these other homicides, we'll gain access to all the evidence."

Mary was annoyed but she kept her mouth closed and got out of the car, slamming the door behind her. She'd never realized that Brooks was such a stickler for Bureau rules. Then again, this was the first time they had ever worked together. Unlike her husband, she did whatever she felt might lead to the capture of a dangerous criminal. If the FBI sacked her, so be it. She'd never wanted to be a cop in the first place.

In a way, what she had said to Brooks about her being the SAC instead of him was true. She knew the area, and outside of Mathis, who must have recently been elected, she was familiar with the top law enforcement personnel, as well as the DAs and judges. Brooks was a fish out of water, a fish who was too frightened to even learn how to swim.

Mary had learned two things tonight. James Washburn had been shot in the same exact place as the four other victims, and working with her husband could make or break their marriage. Genna Weir had been wrong. Taking over the Ventura office would most assuredly not be boring.

# EIGHT

Lily was still waiting in her car. It seemed like hours had passed but it had only been thirty minutes. She started to go back and wait inside the hospital lobby and then changed her mind. She never had time to herself, particularly since Chris had moved in.

She felt as if her life was going in circles. Everything seemed to lead back to that one awful night. John had been right when he'd blamed her for the rapes. Part of the problem stemmed from the new government center complex. The jail and the courthouse were connected via an underground tunnel, and inmates could look out the windows and watch the same people who'd put them behind bars get in and out of their cars every day. No one had thought of the danger involved until it was too late.

1993
VENTURA, CALIFORNIA

Lily had spent a fortune decorating Shana's room and buying her new clothes to fill up her closet, hopeful that she would change her mind about living with her father. She had stayed late at the office to deal with one of Clinton Silverstein's cases. A man named Bobby Hernandez had allegedly raped a woman the police believed was a prostitute, beating her to within an inch of her life and then tossing her out of his van in the middle of nowhere. The men in the DA's office had made fun of the victim because she weighed over two hundred pounds and her face was so swollen from the assault she resembled a sumo wrestler. Lily had been livid, but since the victim's injuries had been photographed, her partially clothed pictures had been passed around the office.

When a prostitute cried rape, many times it was what law enforcement officers referred to as "failure to pay," meaning the john had engaged in sex with the woman and then refused to pay her. The prostitute then went to the police and claimed she was raped, the john paid rather than spend time in the slammer, and the alleged victim changed her mind about pressing charges. Silverstein was convinced this is what had occurred and tried to weasel out of prosecuting the case. That afternoon, the victim had failed to appear in court for the preliminary hearing. Silverstein had marched into Lily's office, angry that he'd wasted his time and demanding that she sign a release for Bobby Hernandez, the man who had allegedly raped and beaten the prostitute.

Lily was outraged when she saw the extent of the woman's injuries. She not only believed it was a legitimate crime but that the defendant's real intention had been to kill her. But without the victim's testimony, the State had no case. As strong as she felt about the danger Bobby Hernandez posed to the community, she knew they had no choice but to go forth with Silverstein's request to close the case and release Hernandez. When they were slammed, the jail sometimes took days to process the paperwork. She decided to put through the release orders but to take the case file home with her, hoping she could find a way to hold Hernandez until the victim surfaced.

Shana had already gone to bed when Lily glanced at the bedroom clock and saw it was almost eleven. She started to retrieve her briefcase from the living room to review the Hernandez case, but she couldn't muster up the energy. Instead, she removed her clothes and climbed under the covers. She then realized that she hadn't checked to see if the doors were locked, a chore John used to handle. With her terry cloth bathrobe wrapped loosely around her, she padded barefoot in the dark, deciding to check the kitchen door first.

Lily had rented the house from a judge and it was located in a wonderful neighborhood, only a few blocks away from Ventura College and a ten-minute drive to the courthouse. She loved the fact that the neighborhood was so quiet—no racing cars, no barking dogs, just blissful silence.

Entering the kitchen, she saw the drapes billowing in the slight breeze, being

sucked through the open sliding glass door. She chastised herself for not locking it earlier. As she pushed the drapes aside and began pulling the door in the track, a funny
feeling came over her, a sense of something amiss. Holding her breath in order to hear
better, she heard a squeak, like the sound a basketball player's sneakers made on the
court.

It all happened at once: the noise behind her, her heart beating so fast it hurt, her robe
pushed up from the floor over her face and head with lightning speed. As she struggled to
scream and free herself, her feet slid out from under her but she didn't fall. She was being
carried in a suffocating embrace. What must be an arm was placed directly over her
mouth. Trying to sink her teeth into it, she bit a mouth of terry cloth instead. She was
nude from the waist down and felt the cold night air against her lower body. Her bladder
emptied, splashing against the tile floor.

She tried to move her arms, but they were trapped across her chest inside the robe.
Kicking out furiously, her foot connected with what must be a kitchen chair, and it
screeched across the floor, landing with a loud thud against the wall.

The backs of her calves and her feet were burning; she realized she was being
dragged down the hall—toward where her daughter slept. "Shana!" she tried to scream.
"Please God, not Shana." The only sound she emitted was a muffled, inhuman groan of
agony coming from her stomach through her vocal cords to her nasal passages. Her
mouth would not move. Her feet struck something—the wall? No longer kicking—
no longer struggling, she was praying: "As I walk through the Valley of Death . . ."
She couldn't remember the words. Not Shana, not her child. She had to protect her
child.

"Mom." She heard her voice, first questioning and childlike and then the terror of
her sickening high-pitched scream reverberated in Lily's head. She heard something
heavy crash into the wall, body against body, the sound heard on a football field when
the players collided. He had her. He had her daughter. He had them both.

In another moment they were on the bed in Lily's bedroom. When he removed his
arm, the robe fell away and she could see him in the light from the bathroom. Shana
was next to her and he was over them both. Light reflected off the steel of the knife he
held only inches from Lily's throat. His other hand was on Shana's neck. Lily grabbed
his arm, and with the abnormal strength of terror, almost succeeded in twisting it
backward, turning the knife toward him, seeing in her mind the blade entering his
body where his heart beat. But he was too strong and with eyes wild with excitement,
darting back and forth, his tongue protruding from his mouth, he forced the blade

sideways into her open mouth, the sharp edges nicking the tender edges of her lips. She bit down on the blade with her teeth, her tongue touching something crusty and vile.

"Taste it," he said, a look of pleasure on his face. "It's her blood. Lick it with your tongue. Lick a whore's blood, a cheating fucking whore's blood."

Removing the knife from Lily's mouth and placing it back at her throat, he moved his other hand from Shana's neck and shoved her gown up, exposing her budding breasts and her new panties. Shana desperately tried to push the gown down to cover herself, turning pleading eyes to Lily. "No," she cried. "Stop him, Mommy. Please make him stop." He thrust his fingers around her neck. She choked and gurgling sounds came from her throat; a trickle of saliva ran from the corner of her mouth. Her eyes were glazed.

"Be calm, Shana. Don't fight. Do what he says. Everything is going to be okay. Please, baby, listen to me." Lily's voice was forced control. "Let her go and I'll give you the best fuck you've ever had. I'll do anything."

"That's it, Momma. You tell her, tell her how fucking good it is. Tell her you want it." His guttural words were uttered through clenched teeth. He had one knee between Shana's legs, forcing them open, and the other knee between Lily's, touching her genitals. "Unzip me," he ordered Shana.

Shana's horror-filled eyes again made contact with her mother's. "Do it, Shana," she said, watching while her child's thin, trembling arm reached out for his crotch, unable to grasp the small end of the zipper. He raised his body up somewhat but the crusty knife remained at Lily's throat.

"Do it for her, Momma." He shifted the knife to his other hand and positioned the tip on Shana's navel. "Teach her how to take care of a man."

Lily had to distract him, somehow get him away from Shana, and find a way to get the knife. Quickly unzipping him and removing his penis, she placed it in her mouth, the ragged edges of the zipper scraping her face. She smelled urine and putrid body odor, but he was becoming erect and moaning, throwing his head back, moving the knife away from Shana's body. He grabbed a handful of her hair and jerked her head back, then fell on top of Lily, looking straight into her eyes and relishing the fear he saw reflected there. Something small and cold struck her chest. It was a gold cross with a crucified Christ dangling from his neck.

Suddenly he thrust himself up. "No, I want her, Momma. I don't want a fucking old redheaded whore." Once again he expertly tossed the knife from one hand to the other before he placed it again at Lily's throat. "Watch, Momma, watch or I'll gut her."

With one vicious yank Shana's underpants were torn off and tossed aside. Her body bounced up on the bed and then fell under the weight of him. He forced himself inside her and Shana screamed in pain. Lily had never felt so powerless in her life. There was no God. She knew it now. No reason to pray. She wished that he'd just cut her throat and end it all.

"Oh, Mommy. Oh, Mommy," Shana gasped.

Lily found her hand beside her and squeezed it tightly, finding it cold and clammy. "Hold on, baby. Close your eyes and make believe you're far away. Hold on."

A loud siren wailed in the street somewhere. He jumped off Shana and sprang from the bed. "The neighbors heard and called the police," Lily said, the sound of the siren growing nearer. "They're going to shoot you, kill you." He was directly under the light emanating from the bathroom, his red sweatshirt and face completely outlined and visible as he frantically tried to zip his jeans. Lily sat up in the bed and screamed, in raw panic and fury, "If they don't shoot you, I'll kill you myself!" The siren was blaring now, only a few blocks away. In seconds, he was gone.

She held her daughter tightly in her arms, stroking her hair and whispering in her ear. "It's over, baby. He's gone. No one is going to hurt you ever again. It's over." The shrill of the siren was becoming distant, fading from earshot. No one had called the police. Their agony had gone unnoticed.

Time stood still as she rocked her daughter and listened to her pitiful, wracking sobs. A million things were racing through her mind. Two or three times she tried to wrench herself away to call the police. Shana was holding on so desperately that she stopped. He was long gone by now, lost in the night. Every sordid detail replayed itself in her mind. A hard ball of rage was forming in her stomach and spewing bile into her mouth.

"Shana, darling, I'm going to get up now, but I'll be right back. I'm going to get a washcloth for you from the bathroom, and then I'm going to call the police and your father." Lily inched away and pulled her robe back over her shoulders, tying the sash loosely around her waist. The rage was somehow calming her, moving her around like a machine with a great churning engine.

"No!" Shana yelled in a voice Lily had never heard. "You can't tell Dad what he did to me." She reached out and grabbed the edge of Lily's robe, causing it to fall open and expose her nakedness. She quickly retied it again. "You can't tell anyone."

The face and voice was that of a child, but the eyes were a woman's. She would never be a child again, never see the world as a safe place without fear. Lily placed a hand to her mouth, biting her knuckles to stifle a scream welling up inside of her. "We must call the police. We must call Daddy."

"No!" Shana shouted again. "I think I'm going to be sick."

Shana ran to the bathroom, vomiting on the floor before she got to the commode. Lily dropped to the floor with her, wiping her face with cold towels. She went to the medicine cabinet and found the bottle of Valium a doctor had recently prescribed for her insomnia. Her hands were shaking as she poured out two pills, one for her and one for Shana. "Take this," she said, handing her the pill with a paper cup of water. "It will relax you."

Shana swallowed the pill, watching with wide eyes as her mother tossed one into her own mouth. She let Lily help her back to the bed. Once again, she held her in her arms.

"We're going to call Daddy and then we're going to leave this house and take you home. I won't call the police, but we're going to tell Daddy. We have no choice, Shana."

Lily knew exactly what she would be subjecting her daughter to if she reported the crime. The police would stay for hours, forcing them to relive the nightmare, making every detail live forever in their minds. Next would be the hospital and the medical-legal exam. They would probe Shana's ravaged body; comb her pubic hairs looking for evidence. They would swab their mouths. If they apprehended him, months of testimony and court appearances would consume their lives. Shana would have to sit on the witness stand and repeat the awful details of this night to a room full of strangers. She would have to re-hearse her testimony with the prosecutor like lines in a play. In that room, breathing the same air, he would also sit. Then the ordeal would become known.

The most despicable thought of all, a truth that Lily alone was far too aware of, was the fact that after all they'd suffered, would suffer, while the nightmares were still the sweating, waking, screaming kind, before they could even begin to resume normal life, he would be free. The term for rape was eight years, out in four. He would even re-ceive credit for time served during and prior to the trial so that by the time he was on the bus to freedom, his countdown to freedom could amount to a measly three years. No, she thought, he could receive a consecutive sentence for the oral copulation, amounting to a few more years. It was not enough. It could never be enough. And she felt certain he had committed other vicious crimes. She recalled the taste of dried, old blood on the knife, and knew he could have murdered someone. This crime was a murder of sorts, the annihilation of innocence.

She also had to consider her career, her life's work, and the reality that although she could prosecute rape cases, she could never try them without bias if she became a superior court judge. Thought by thought, she was getting further away from reporting the crimes to the authorities.

His face kept reappearing before her, and somewhere in the far reaches of her mind, she knew she had seen him before. Her memory of the attack crowded out the past, and she was no longer able to distinguish reality from imagination. But his face . . .

The drug had taken effect and Shana had calmed down somewhat. Moving slowly away, Lily called John on the bedside phone. He was in a deep sleep when she awoke him; he stated a muffled and annoyed "Hello" as if he was expecting a wrong number.

"John, you have to come over here." She spoke quietly but rapidly. "Something has happened."

"Jesus, Lily, what time is it? Is Shana sick?"

"We're both okay, just come now. Don't ask any questions until you get here. Shana's sitting right beside me." Her voice started to crack. She didn't know how much longer she could maintain her composure. "Please come, John. We need you."

She hung up and looked at the clock—only one in the morning, a mere two hours to destroy their lives and rob her and Shana of the happiness they were finally finding in each other. Her thoughts turned to John and what this would do to him. Shana was his life, his shining star, his pampered and sheltered baby girl. When she was born, John had shoved Lily away and centered all his affections on his daughter: holding her, stroking her, kissing her when he no longer kissed his wife. Starting to tremble, Lily hugged herself. She had to be strong.

It seemed like only minutes had passed before John arrived. Time had been standing still, hanging over them like a dark storm cloud, refusing to move, the unleashed downpour contained and waiting. John appeared in the doorway to the bedroom and immediately began shouting. "What in the hell is going on here? The front door is wide open." His tone was accusing, demanding, and it was vented at Lily. "Tell me what happened here tonight."

Shana's muscles had begun to relax in Lily's arms. "Daddy," she said, hearing his voice and crying out to him. "Oh, Daddy." He ran to the edge of the bed and Lily released her. As John engulfed her in his arms, she pressed her body to his chest, sobbing.

He looked at Lily, his dark eyes full of fury, but in their depths, fear was rising. "What happened? Tell me why Shana is crying!"

"Shana, Daddy and I are going to the other room and talk," Lily said softly. "You'll hear us and know we're there. We'll only be a few feet away." She got up and motioned for John to follow.

The Valium had calmed her somewhat and she told John what had transpired. It was an unemotional recitation of facts. If she allowed one tear to fall, the floodgates would open. He leaned over and touched the small cuts at the side of her mouth, but it was not a gesture of concern. It was more like a reflex, confirmation that the things she was telling him were real. His eyes clearly said she was responsible, regardless of what reason predicated. She should have found the strength to stop him. That's how he saw her—invincible. Then he sobbed, his masculine body wracked with pain, that unfamiliar and pitiful sound that signified a grown man crying like a child. He was quite simply heartbroken. His sorrow left no room for rage.

"Well, do you want to call the police? You're her father and I can't make that decision without you. It's not irreversible. We can always file a report later if we change our minds." As she spoke, her eyes darted to the kitchen, wondering about evidence.

"No, I agree with you," John told her. "It would only make things worse for her." Tears were streaming down his face and he wiped them away with the back of his hand. "Would they catch the bastard if we reported it?"

"How the hell do I know, John? No one knows. We don't even have a vehicle description." Lily cursed herself for not running after him, for staying with Shana. "Maybe we're doing the wrong thing by not bringing in the authorities. God, I just don't know." Lily's mind was muddled and crazed. Something inside her was diving, sinking, twisting. She had to stop it, had to somehow rewind the tape and erase it. John's voice sounded distant.

"I want to take Shana home, take her away from this place." His voice was a choked whisper. "I just want to take care of my child."

"I know," she said. "And she's our child, not yours. Don't you think I want to take care of her? I don't want her to suffer. I couldn't stop this. I tried, but I can stop it now. I gave her a sedative. Let's bundle her up and take her home. I'll pack a bag and follow you."

After they wrapped Shana in a blanket, John led her to the door. Shana turned back and her eyes found her mother's. "You go home and go to sleep. Daddy will sleep on the floor next to you." Lily embraced her. "I'll be there in the morning when you wake up."

"Will he come back?"

"No, Shana, he'll never come back. I'll move out of this house tomorrow. We'll never come back here again. In time, we'll both forget this night ever happened."

Once they had gone, Lily hurriedly started throwing things in a small duffel bag. The house was dead quiet again, that ominous stillness like before. The memory of the attacker's face in the last few minutes before he'd left kept flashing in her mind, and each time she dropped what she was doing and stood there, frozen in thought, trying to put her finger on what it was that she associated with his face. Suddenly the face appeared, but not as she remembered it. It appeared in a mug shot.

She ran to the living room, tripping and falling on the edge of her robe, soggy and reeking from Shana's vomit. From her position on the floor, she saw her briefcase and crawled toward it. Her fingers trembled as she dialed the combination lock. On the third try, it clicked open. She threw all the files on the floor and searched for the one she knew contained the photo. Papers went flying across the carpet.

The mug shot was in her hands. He was the same man who'd attempted to rape the prostitute; Silverstein's case that she had dismissed today. Photographed with that smug smile. They must have released him at the time she left the building, giving him back his original clothes with the rest of his property. He was wearing the same red sweatshirt and a gold crucifix. He must have followed her from the complex. She rapidly sorted through the pages in the file until she found the police report.

There was no doubt in her mind as she studied the hated image in her hands. No doubt at all. It was him.

Her breath was coming fast now, catching and rattling in her throat. Whatever effects the Valium had were gone. Adrenaline was pumping through her veins. She rapidly sorted through the pages of the file to the police report. There it was—his address. His home was listed as 254 S. Third Street, in Oxnard. His name was Bobby Hernandez and although he was Hispanic, he had listed his place of birth as Fresno. Lily tore the sheet with his address on it and placed it in the pocket of her robe. She went to the bedroom and threw on a pair of jeans and a sweater, transferring the address to the jeans. Next she dug in the back of her closet and found her fur-lined winter hiking boots and a blue knit ski cap. She placed it on her head and stuffed her hair inside it.

In the garage, behind a stack of boxes, was her father's shotgun, a twelve-gauge Browning semiautomatic, the one he had used to hunt deer. In the stillness of the garage, as her hands touched the barrel of the gun, Lily felt his presence beside her and heard his voice. "Good shot, Lily girl," he would say on the Saturday afternoons when he had taken her to shoot tin cans lined up on a tree stump.

Spotting the small box containing the green slugs, she again heard his voice, right there next to her, clear and distinct. "These are called rifle slugs, Lily girl." She loaded them into the chamber and crammed several more into the tight pocket of her jeans. "These will make a hole big enough to throw a cat through."

As she left the garage, shotgun muzzle down in her arms, her footsteps echoed even when she had left the concrete flooring and was walking on carpet. She felt heavy, rooted to the ground with resolve, walking in another dimension, no longer alone in her body. The phone rang like a shrill bell, invasive, unwelcome, but a signal to begin. It was John.

"Shana's asleep. I'm worried about you. Are you coming over?"

"I'll be there in a few hours. Don't worry. I can't sleep now anyway. I want to calm down and take a bath. He's not coming back here tonight. Just worry about Shana." Do what you do best, she thought without contempt, accepting her role, and I'll do what has to be done.

She started to lock the front door and leave and then she thought of something and returned to the kitchen. Rummaging through the drawers, her fingers seized a black Magic Marker, the one she had used to label the moving boxes. She shoved it in her pocket and left.

The moon was out, the night clear. A streetlight reflected half moons of light on the manicured yards. She crouched at the rear of her car and began marking the license plate. The plate read FPO322. With the marker she altered it to EBO822. It was a small change, but it was the best she could do. She threw the shotgun in the backseat, thought of covering it, and then decided it didn't matter. The rage was an unseen inferno, burning all around her. She kept seeing him over Shana, the knife at her navel, his body heaving on top of her precious child.

She drove toward Oxnard. The streets were quiet. She rolled the window down and let the night air blow in her face. As she passed the farming area of Oxnard, the smell of fertilizer reminded her of his rancid odor. She tasted his vile penis in her mouth and spat out the window. The edges of her lips stung from the razor-sharp nicks of the knife.

The thought of where that knife had been and the dried matter she had tasted made her force the thought from her mind to keep from vomiting.

Slowly she drove down the dark streets, passing from one streetlight to another, one stop sign and another traffic signal, changing from green to yellow and back again. In her mind they were like runway lights illuminating her descent into Hell. Cars sped past her now and then. Inside were couples coming home from parties, dates, bars; lovers crawling out of beds and returning to other beds.

She was trying to formulate a plan. It didn't take her long to find the house. The street was a major thoroughfare in Oxnard and she simply followed the numbers. The area was called Colonia. She knew it well, for it was infested with drug dealing and crime. His house was one in a row of tiny stucco dwellings. Across the street was a vacant lot. The yard was overgrown with weeds, dry and crackling from lack of water. In the driveway there was a dusty black older-model Plymouth and a Ford pickup. The vehicle used in the rape and kidnap had been a van and there was no van.

Like a burglar she cased the area, noting that the nearest streetlight was a block away on the corner. She had driven here with intent, her loaded shotgun in the backseat, but with no definitive plan. She knew she couldn't enter his house and shoot him. That would be suicide. And she had no way of knowing for certain that he was actually inside. There was only one way: wait for him to come out. It could be broad daylight with dozens of people milling about. Some of these homes had five or six families living together.

Turning back toward the field she had passed earlier, she steered the car onto a dirt road, pressing down on the accelerator and flooring it. The car had been washed only a few days before. It was now absorbing the dust she was churning up with her tires. She parked by the road, with crops planted as far as she could see on either side. Taking the shotgun from the backseat, she pointed into the fields and fired it. The blast shattered the stillness of the night and the butt of the gun smashed into her shoulder. Her father had been dead for ten years. She wanted to be certain her weapon of death would perform. Quickly throwing it into the backseat, she spun out and headed back onto the main road.

By her actions she had caused this to happen to her daughter. It had started with the night she had slept with Richard, a married woman out fucking around while her child and husband were home. But no, John had not been home. He had been lurking in the shadows, spying on her, waiting to catch her at something he had repeatedly accused her of dozens of times through the years.

The darkness was slowly changing into the overcast gray of a southern California morning. She could hear birds in the nearby trees as she passed the parkway leading to Oxnard. Here and there, the world was awakening.

Slowly guiding the Honda onto his street, she saw a dark green van parked at the curb, its rear doors open. Her eyes turned at once to the shotgun in the backseat while her pulse raced and her stomach churned. Eyes back to the street, she saw no movement. A television placed on an open window, the words in Spanish. Pulling to the curb, hands locked and sweating on the cool steering wheel, she let go long enough to wipe them on her denim-clad thighs before she reached for the shotgun and transferred it to the front seat, the muzzle pointed at the floorboard.

When a dog barked somewhere, she jumped and took her foot off the brake. The car was still in drive, engine running, and it jerked forward.

After staring so hard at the front of his house that her vision had blurred, she saw a distinct flash of red. She floored the Honda and covered the distance between the houses in seconds. Slamming both feet on the brake, she threw the gearshift into park without thinking and grabbed the shotgun. The sound of the barrel as it struck the hood of her car was earsplitting in the morning silence. He was exiting the house, halfway down the curb, headed toward his van. He saw her and stopped abruptly, planting both his feet firmly on the ground. On his face was a look of shock and confusion.

Inside that moment, reason flickered behind the eyes she lowered to the sight, coursed inside the finger on the trigger, a pinpoint of light before blindness. Her body moved back inches, but the light was gone, the sight a framed portrait of red fabric pulsating with the beat of his heart.

She fired.

The impact knocked him off his feet. His hands and legs flew in the air. The explosion reverberated inside her head. A gaping hole appeared in the center of the red sweatshirt, spewing forth blood. She was drowning in a frothy sea of red blood: Shana's blood, virginal blood, sacrificial blood. Her throat constricted, mucus dripped from her nose, and once again the alien, detached finger squeezed the trigger. The shot hit near his shoulder, severing his arm.

Her knees buckled beneath her. The shotgun fell butt first to the ground. The muzzle came to rest under the soft flesh of her chin, stopping her. Moving her head, she vomited chunks of chicken onto the black asphalt, seeing pieces of flesh boiling.

She pulled herself into the open door of the car, her arms locked around the shotgun. Everything was moving, shaking, bleeding. She saw objects flying through the air, trapping her inside the core of horror.

Move, she ordered her body, still frozen. Move. She grabbed the steering wheel, releasing the shotgun. Don't look. Drive. Her foot responded and the car surged forward. The intersection was there in a second. Turn. Breathe. Turn. Drive. She had not killed a human being. Turn. Drive. Turn. The sun was up, but she saw only a dark tunnel in front of her. She knew she was in Hell and there was no way out. "Please God," she prayed. "In the name of the Father, the Son, and the Holy Ghost, show me the way out."

# NINE

FRIDAY, JANUARY 15
SAN FRANCISCO, CALIFORNIA

Lily awakened from the past with a start, her clothes soaked with perspiration as the horror of that morning slowly receded. She glanced at her watch and saw that she'd been in the car for almost two hours. Why hadn't they come to get her? She jumped out and rushed toward the front of the hospital. Once she was inside, she headed to the counter where the phone was located and picked up the receiver. Michelle Newman answered. "I was waiting in my car. I must have fallen asleep. What's going on with my daughter?"

"Shana has serious problems, Ms. Forrester. Have a seat and I'll come out and speak to you."

Lily didn't feel like having a seat. She walked around in circles until the woman appeared through the side door carrying a clipboard. "What kind of serious problems?"

Newman gestured toward the seating area and Lily followed, taking a seat in one of the chairs while the hospital administrator sat across from her on the sofa. "Shana is heavily addicted to narcotics, Ms. Forrester. She admitted using methamphetamine on a daily basis, as well as marijuana and cocaine."

Lily's hand flew to her chest. "No, I don't believe you. She's never used drugs in her life. She hates drugs. She even told me tonight that she wasn't using anything."

"I'm sorry, I'm sure this must be a shock to you, but we have to do what's best for your daughter now. If Shana continues to use, she'll die. We're talking months, maybe even weeks."

"This is ridiculous," Lily shot out. "You're sensationalizing everything, trying to scare me. Shana isn't going to die in a matter of months or weeks. She's a healthy young woman. She's been under stress, that's all. She broke up with her boyfriend, and she's had trouble sleeping. I told you that when I brought her in here."

Newman fixed her with an icy gaze. "Shana has open sores on her arms and torso. Her system is so polluted with drugs, they're seeping out of her pores. This particular drug is poison, Ms. Forrester. Your daughter is dying."

"That's it," she said, standing. "Go get Shana. I'm taking her home. She doesn't have sores on her body. Don't you think I'd know if my daughter was addicted to hard-core narcotics? She's in her last year of law school at Stanford. Her grades have always been excellent."

"Was she wearing long sleeves when you saw her?" Newman reached into her pocket and pulled out a small photograph and then handed it to Lily so she could see.

Lily began to sob hysterically as she stared at the image. Shana was dressed in her bra and panties and her body was covered in open sores. Some were obviously infected as they were oozing puss. She was skin and bones; she couldn't weigh more than ninety pounds.

"God, no!" she wailed, the sound magnified by the tiled floors. "This is my fault for not coming to see her more often. And the money . . . she must have been using it to buy drugs. My baby, my poor baby . . . she was dealing with this all alone."

The woman handed Lily some tissues and waited for her to calm down. "Our assessment team suggests your daughter be placed in our inpatient drug rehabilitation program. The minimum stay is six weeks, but we strongly recommend that she stay for a period of three to six months." Newman paused to let her words sink in. "I know that sounds like an extraordinarily long period of time, but like I said, the drug your daughter is addicted to is extremely dangerous, much more so than marijuana, heroin, cocaine, or even crack."

"I know that."

Michelle continued, "Health conditions associated with meth abuse include memory loss, aggression, violence, psychotic behavior, heart damage, neurological damage, weight loss, rapid tooth decay, meningitis, paranoia, delusions, hallucinations, severe headaches, skin sensations, compulsive picking, skin infections, muscle tissue breakdown, kidney failure, and increased occurrence of communicable diseases such as HIV, AIDS, and hepatitis."

Lily compressed in the chair, feeling as if someone had dropped a safe on her head.

"If Shana is released too soon, there's a ninety percent chance that she'll begin using again. Once she goes through detox, we'll work on restoring her health. The next step is for one of our staff psychiatrists to find out what led to her addiction. Now, do you have any questions?"

Lily had recovered her composure, but was still reeling in disbelief. If what Michelle Newman was telling her was true, Shana could kiss law school good-bye, and Lily might as well have tossed all the money she had spent on her education in the trash. Why would Shana confide in *this* woman, a complete stranger? "Are you telling me that my daughter walked into your office and simply told you she was a drug addict? I find that hard to believe."

"I'm sure you do," Newman told her. "You don't understand why Shana didn't tell you? Am I right?"

"Not exactly," Lily told her. "I'm not an idiot, Ms. Newman. I—"

"Call me Michelle."

"Fine, Michelle, but I would appreciate it if you didn't interrupt me in the future." Lily brushed a strand of hair off her face. "Now I've forgotten what I was saying."

Michelle folded her hands in her lap.

"I acknowledge that telling me would be difficult. That is, if what you say is true. But now that the cat's out of the bag, so to speak, I'd like to speak to my daughter directly. It might make it easier for me to accept this coming from her mouth instead of yours."

"I'm afraid that's not possible."

"What do you mean?"

"Shana signed a voluntary commitment order. She also gave us explicit instructions that she not be contacted by you or anyone else during the initial stage of her therapy." She paused and waited for Lily's reaction. "Your daughter is an adult, Ms. Forrester. Her insurance will cover her treatment here at Whitehall, so there's no reason for you to be involved. Now, if you will excuse me, I have other matters to attend to." She stood to leave.

"Don't you dare walk away from me!" Lily shot out. "I know my daughter and she would never sign herself into a place like this. I demand to see the commitment papers."

"Certainly," she said, removing a piece of paper from her clipboard. "Is that your daughter's signature?"

Lily's hands trembled on the paper. There was no doubt it was Shana's signature. She stood and her fingers involuntarily opened, the document floating on a pocket of air to the floor. Ignoring Michelle Newman, she walked toward the front door and exited the hospital.

Dr. Charles Morrow shuffled across the dark parking lot of Clearwater General Hospital. A reflection of light in his shiny black leather shoes caught his attention and he looked up at the sky. Among the scattering of stars was the full moon and he gazed at it with longing. Where he should be right now was behind his telescope unlocking the mysteries of the universe. As a young man, his dream was to become an astrophysicist. But his mother was convinced he would become the next Sigmund Freud. By the time the initials M.D. appeared beside his name, his mother was dead. Just as well, he thought. In the world of psychiatry, he was no more than a name in the yellow pages.

In every respect, Morrow was a failure. His wife had left him, obtaining a court order prohibiting him from seeing his son. He was teetering on the brink of financial ruin. Even his nest egg had disappeared.

His most profitable enterprise was the thirty thousand shares of stock he held in Whitehall, a privately owned and operated psychiatric hospital located fifteen miles from Clearwater General. The place had been a gold mine until someone alleged they were picking up drunks and homeless people off the streets in New York and depositing them in Whitehall. Every year they would send a few employees to Manhattan in the early winter months, where they canvassed homeless people who would qualify for Medicare or SSI and enticed them with postcards of sunny beaches in California. Once the attorney general established clear proof of such activities, the government would stop picking up the tab.

Employers and insurers all over the country were trying to rein in health care costs and were becoming more vigilant in rooting out fraudulent and inept providers. HMOs had become Whitehall's worst nightmare.

The heydays were over.

A hospital in Los Angeles, which had been operating along the same lines as Whitehall, had recently made the press for sending out security guards to pick up insured patients from their homes and transport them to their facility. Whitehall was not quite as blatant. They didn't go to people's homes, nor did they try to coerce other patients into coughing up the names of their drinking or drug buddies who had insurance with the right kind of benefits. Whitehall caught most of their cases from emergency rooms. Being in the right place at the right time was the name of the game.

Because Morrow had to see patients at Whitehall during the day, he searched for potential patients at night. This was the sixth hospital he'd visited tonight. He was bone tired and thus far had nothing to show for his efforts.

The automatic doors swung open. The three nurses and the intern standing at the nursing station turned their heads in his direction.

At this hour the staff was eager for a serious case, possibly an accident victim or a coronary. The time went faster that way.

Recognizing Dr. Morrow, the three nurses returned to their charts. At five-nine, the psychiatrist was a thin, edgy man in his midforties. His dark framed glasses needed to be adjusted to fit his face, as they always seemed to rest precariously on the tip of his nose. His limp brown hair fell several inches below his ears, and his normal mode of dress consisted of a white dress shirt and black slacks, the case for his cell phone clipped to his belt.

Morrow was about to give up when a haggard-looking young intern walked up and pointed to the supply room. Once they were both inside with the door shut, the intern began speaking. "You're just the man I've been looking for, Morrow," Harvey Beckman said, smiling. "I've got the perfect situation for you. It's going to cost you more than the usual five hundred, though."

"You know how it works, Harvey," Morrow told him, shoving his glasses back on his nose. "You don't get paid until the patient is admitted and the insurance benefits are verified. The last guy you referred was good for only two weeks and about twenty percent of our charges. We had to sue him for the balance."

"This is the real deal," the intern insisted. "We're talking Blue Cross PPO. Not only that, take a look at what we found in this broad's purse." He reached under a stack of linens and pulled out a black bag. "We could open our own jewelry store."

"Christ!" Morrow exclaimed, his brows furrowing as he stared at the numerous pieces of what appeared to be expensive jewelry resting in a pile of tissue paper. "Why are you hiding her purse in the supply room? Get one of the nurses to lock it up with the rest of the patient's property. We're not thieves, Beckman. You want to end up in prison?"

"I wasn't suggesting we steal anything," he answered, closing the purse and placing it on a shelf. "I just wanted you to know that this lady is worth some serious money."

"Give me a rundown."

"Came in by ambulance around nine o'clock last night complaining of chest pains. EKG was normal. Her blood work isn't back yet. At first, we thought it was an overdose. Come here, look at this." Beckman reached behind him and retrieved a plastic bag, dumping the contents onto the shelf. "We found these when we were looking for her insurance card. Let's see, we've got empty bottles of Percodan, codeine, and Darvon. Regular little drugstore here. Guess she faked the chest pains to get more narcotics."

A look of pleasure spread across Morrow's face. Things were looking up. "Anything else?" he asked as they left the supply room.

"Everything you need, my man," Beckman continued, glancing toward one of the examination rooms. "She even came strolling out with her ass hanging out of her hospital gown. I put a guard on her door to keep her from leaving."

Just then, a voice rang out and Morrow turned toward the sound. Beckman laughed. "That's your gold mine. If I hear 'Amazing Grace' one more time, I'm going to gag her. Reminds me of all those boring Sundays I spent in church when I was a kid. Take her, Charley. She's all yours." He slapped the woman's file into the psychiatrist's hands as he walked away. "Don't forget my money. I expect to be paid by the end of the week. Oh, I forgot, she claims her husband is a billionaire, so if you get to keep her longer than the usual six months, you owe me at least a grand. It's double for double, my man."

Morrow took a seat at one of the nursing stations to complete the paperwork. Perfect. Empty pill bottles, bizarre and erratic behavior. Singing hymns was bizarre enough for his needs, and since the divorce, his needs were substantial. What he needed was money. The intercom came on. Morrow heard a woman's voice pleading for a nurse. A slender, blond RN leaned over from the other side of the counter. "Dr. Beckman instructed us not to enter the patient's room until he had a chance to consult with you," she told him, a concerned look on her face. "I feel sorry for her. Maybe we should at least give her something to sleep."

"The woman's psychotic," Morrow said, tapping his pen on the counter. "For all we know, she could be dangerous. How can we give her medication until the lab reports come back and we determine what medications she's already taken? You don't want to overdose her, do you?" He paused, scribbling instructions in a chart. "I'll have someone pick up Mrs. Hopkins and transport her to Whitehall by nine tomorrow morning."

"Fine," the nurse said. "Doesn't the patient have to sign a voluntary commitment order before you can move her? She's conscious and outside of being somewhat bedraggled and scared when the ambulance brought her in, she seems perfectly normal."

"Are you a psychiatrist?" Morrow snapped, outraged that the nurse would question him. "You do your job and I'll do mine. Are we clear?" Although there were a number of interns at Clearwater who provided him with referrals, most of the nursing staff was unaware that anything irregular was going on.

The blond nurse dropped her head and walked away. Morrow thumbed through the patient's chart. His cell phone rang and he saw that it was Whitehall. "Dr. Morrow."

Michelle Newman said, "We have a new patient."

"How long do we have?"

"Her insurance covers up to six months of inpatient treatment."

"Excellent." Morrow started adding dollar signs in his head.

"Oh, and I used the picture this time. I'm getting pretty good with Photoshop."

"Good work, Michelle. You may meet your monthly quota after all."

# TEN

The woman with the brown curly hair who looked like a bank teller told Shana that she had to sign a release of liability before the hospital could discharge her since in their professional opinion, she should be admitted. Shana was so furious and exhausted from fighting the muscled goon, she would have signed anything. After she scribbled her name on the form, the woman left, leaving her in the room alone.

Shana got up and tried the door, finding it locked. "Shit, damn, fuck!" she yelled, kicking the door as hard as she could until her feet began throbbing.

Her mother couldn't have her committed. She was an adult, for God's sake. Why would she want her to be in this place anyway? All she'd talked about was her graduating from Stanford with a law degree. If she didn't get back to her studies, everything would be ruined. She'd flunk out and have to find another school that would accept her. Then the Stanford diploma she had worked so hard for wouldn't be on the wall of her law office.

Her mother had completely lost it this time. Yeah, Shana was up-set about breaking up with Brett but she knew she'd meet someone else eventually. Having a boyfriend was a huge distraction. She had to tell them what she was doing every minute of the day. And there were all those ridiculous text messages. "How you doing, baby?" or "I can't get your boobs off my mind today." Brett was the jealous kind and became paranoid even when she went out with her girlfriends. All he thought about was sex, sex, and more sex. She enjoyed having orgasms but sometimes guys were so inept and self-centered, she was seldom satisfied. Her vibrator never failed her.

She just hated being dumped. Ever since she could remember, she'd been the most popular girl at school. Although she knew what to say and do to get people to like her, somewhere deep in her sub-conscious, anyone with a penis was a potential rapist. Brett made her watch porno movies, which she despised. Almost all of them contained scenes that were degrading to women. In reality, the whole porno industry was degrading to women. Did men really believe girls wanted them to come on their face? And what girl really wanted a guy to fuck her asshole? Then there was the proverbial threesome, every man's fantasy. At least Brett hadn't pushed for that, although he had mentioned it on several occasions, mostly just before they had sex.

Men were disgusting pigs. Why did she even want one? Because it was normal and she didn't want to spend her life alone. Some-one had to wash the car and carry heavy things, and two incomes were mandatory today if you wanted a good life.

Where in the hell was the woman?

Since there was nothing else to do, she crawled into the bed and entered into the only kind of sleep she got lately. Her eyes would close to slits and she could faintly hear sounds, but she wasn't really asleep and she wasn't truly awake. She called it twilight sleep.

When she came to hours later, only inches away loomed the strangest-looking face she had ever seen. "My name is Peggy." The woman's voice sounded as if it had been recorded on worn-out tape, or like a children's toy in need of a new battery. The toy she remembered was called a See 'n Say. Her mother gave her one for

Christmas one year. When she turned it to the picture of a particular animal and pulled the string, she heard the sound the animal
made. She repeated the woman's name in her mind: Peggy. Then
she knew the sound that would come out: the sound of a pig. She
looked up again and saw two huge nostrils set in a mound of putrid pink flesh.

Miss Piggy spoke: "Welcome to Whitehall."

Lily drove back to Shana's apartment in a daze. Once she was inside, she started tearing the place apart, looking for Shana's drug
stash. She took a broom and shoved it underneath the beds, both
in Shana's room and the one her former roommate had used. The
only thing she found was a bra and a shoe.

She then shoved the mattresses off the beds onto the floor, but
there was nothing there. Shana's drawers were a mess and she desperately needed new underwear. With the kind of money she'd
been sending her, she could buy a lingerie store.

Tears streamed from her eyes. Had Shana committed herself
just to spite her, knowing she was ruining any chances she had
of graduating with her class? Why did she hate her? All she'd ever
done was love her and try to protect her, give her a decent life.

It might have been the wrong thing to do, but Lily had killed
Bobby Hernandez so he would never be able to hurt Shana again.
She didn't expect Shana to appreciate it, and in reality, knowing
her mother had committed such an act might be one of her unresolved conflicts.

But Lily knew a person under the influence of narcotics wasn't
rational, and as far as love went, the only thing an addict loved was
the drug they were using.

There were numerous ways to use meth. A person could snort
it, smoke it, or inject it. Shana had always hated needles so she assumed she either snorted or smoked it. If she smoked it, though,
where was her pipe?

She went through the apartment and ran her palms over all the
hard services, then brought anything that even vaguely resembled a

powdery or crystal substance to her mouth, forcing herself to taste it. All she got was an icky taste and a mouthful of dust. She found a bottle of mouthwash in Shana's bathroom, gargled, and then returned to her task.

Lily finally collapsed shortly after two o'clock, curling up on the sofa in the living room. She stared at the pile of stuff she'd dug out of the seat cushions: four hair clips, three empty condom wrappers, part of a mold-covered cheeseburger, five dead cockroaches, two paper clips, one ballpoint pen, an empty beer can, and a few rubber bands. No drug paraphernalia and no drugs.

Of course, Shana knew Lily was coming, even though she had pretended to have forgotten. But Lily also knew her daughter, and cleaning had never been her strong suit. She would have missed something, maybe not something as major as a syringe or a pipe, yet some evidence of drug use would have been left inside the apartment.

A short time later, Lily sat up on the sofa, too restless to sleep. Shana must have been doing drugs somewhere else, and her best guess was Brett's apartment. That might be why she'd been so frazzled. She was probably going through withdrawals and decided if she had to detox, she might as well do it in a hospital, where they could give her something to help her get through it.

Brett must have been Shana's drug source, the little prick. No wonder she never brought him home to meet her mother. Then when they broke up, Shana was hung out to dry. As hard as it was to accept, everything she had seen tonight fit the profile of a meth user: Shana's manic behavior, her rapid mood changes, the inability to sleep, her unrealistic expectations about her relationship with Brett, even her desire to distance herself from Stanford and Lily.

She started to check Shana's computer to see if she could find an address for Brett, but she stopped herself. No one had forced Shana to use drugs, and having her boyfriend's address might tempt Lily into paying him a visit. The last time she had paid a visit to someone who'd hurt Shana, it had ended in disaster. But had it really?

Bobby Hernandez had been involved in the McDonald/Lopez case, the brutal murder of the two Ventura high school students, the same case Lily had been prosecuting when she was transferred from homicide and made supervisor over the sex crimes division. A tree limb had been shoved up the girl's vagina, and the gang had played target practice by shooting off the poor girl's nipples. The crime itself was the embodiment of evil.

The only way Lily had been able to reconcile herself to what she had done was to perceive it as an act of divine intervention. Hernandez had deserved to die, but the police had not placed him as one of the murderers. If she had not killed him, even if she'd done so for the wrong reasons, he would have escaped punishment and gone on to kill again. Hernandez had also killed the prostitute, so he had taken at least three lives. How many people he had actually killed they would never know.

Lily believed in evil. No one in her position could believe otherwise. Hearing about a crime on TV or over the Internet wasn't the same as prosecuting or adjudicating it. Mothers killed their children, children killed their parents, husbands killed wives, and wives murdered their husbands. More frequently than in the past, otherwise decent individuals suddenly went on killing sprees that took the lives of untold numbers of innocent people for no reason except madness and sheer evil.

Inside every person was a door, Lily believed. Most people, by means of their upbringing and basic morality, tried to keep this door closed to anything even moderately evil. It was one of the reasons human beings frequented churches and temples, to surround themselves with people who shared their beliefs in a higher power and as a form of protection against the evil entities that sought to tempt them. Lily knew her Catholic upbringing had helped to shape her viewpoints, but she also believed a person who willfully put narcotics into their system opened the door to evil. Sadly, that person was now her daughter.

The first thing to know was who and what it was you were fighting, and Lily knew this particular adversary far too well. Marco

Curazon had defeated her and hurt Shana beyond belief. He had not only defiled her, he had robbed her of the person she loved the most in the world—her father.

Lily began to dive into the past, remembering one of her last conversations with Shana's father before Marco Curazon murdered him in the garage of his L.A. condo. As hard as she tried, Lily had not shed a single tear. Yes, he had fathered her child, but he had done horrible things in the weeks leading up to his death.

How had a man who'd once coached Little League fallen so far down in life, particularly with a daughter who worshipped him? And how could Marco Curazon, a man who'd been convicted of two counts of aggravated rape, be back on the street after serving only seven years in prison? Shana had been terrified and righteously so, as Curazon had managed to track her down, fully intending to rape her again. While in prison, many sex offenders became even more fixated on their victims. By a stroke of fate, Curazon had not found her precious daughter.

2000<br>
SANTA BARBARA, CALIFORNIA

"I'm in jail."

Lily had picked up the phone in her office, expecting to hear Shana's voice. She had left several messages on her machine that morning, but Shana had yet to return her call. "John?" she said. His voice was so strained, it took time before she recognized it.

"You have to help me. They just arraigned me."

Lily's adrenaline surged. "Where's Shana?"

"I guess she's in school."

"Good Lord," she said, "why didn't you speak to her? She called me last night in a panic. She was certain Marco Curazon was stalking her. That's why I called the police."

"You don't understand," John said, knowing she thought the police had mistaken him for Shana's prowler. "I went out to get ice cream. When I got back to the duplex, the police were already leaving. The man Shana saw must have been a neighbor.

Please, Lily, she's okay. I was arrested later. I don't know . . . I think, it was around midnight."

"But Shana doesn't know you're in jail."

"She was asleep. She's been under so much stress lately, I didn't want to upset her. I thought the police would release me last night after they booked me. I had no idea they were going to arrest me and haul me into court this morning."

When Lily had learned he was drinking again, she'd feared another arrest for drunk driving. A DWI wasn't a lightweight offense these days, and John already had a prior conviction. "How high was your blood alcohol?"

"They didn't arrest me for drunk driving."

"Oh," Lily said, dismayed. "Then what . . ."

"Vehicular manslaughter."

She almost choked on her own saliva. "You killed someone?"

"Maybe I didn't do anything," he shot back. "Maybe I was just standing outside having a nightcap. You should talk. What happened to that guy? You know . . . what was his name? Hernandez, right?"

The receiver dropped out of Lily's hands.

"Is something wrong?" Lily's assistant was standing quietly in the doorway. As she tiptoed into the room, her concern for her boss intensified. "Are you sick?"

"I-I'm . . ." Lily tilted her head toward the woman's voice, but she couldn't force the words out of her mouth.

"Your ex-husband is on the phone. He says it's urgent . . . that he got disconnected during an important phone conversation. If you don't want to speak to him, I can . . ."

"No," Lily said, frantically snatching the phone off the floor. Hearing only a dial tone, she gave her assistant a blank stare.

"Mr. Forrester is on the other line."

"Thanks," she said, waving her out of the room.

John was accusing, desperate. "You hung up on me. They don't allow you fifteen phone calls, you know. This is a damn jail, Lily! I called you for help."

"I didn't hang up on you," she said, knowing she had to defuse the situation immediately. "A judge called me regarding a case I'm handling. All I did was put you on hold until I answered his question."

"Don't shovel that shit at me," John barked. "You're just stalling, trying to show me what a big shot you are, that even judges come running to you. I don't care who the hell calls you. If you know what's good for you, you'll get your ass down here."

Lily's right leg was jumping up and down. She had to place her hand on it to hold it in place. Was Bobby Hernandez stalking her from the grave? Until a person took a life, they could never understand the gravity of that action. She was forever tied to a dead man. Some nights she paced until dawn, feeling as if she were handcuffed to the rotting corpse of Bobby Hernandez.

"Didn't you hear me?" John yelled. "How many times do I have to tell you? I'm in the Los Angeles County Jail."

"I understand you're in jail. Exactly where are you in the jail? Are you in booking? Are you in an interview room? I'm trying to determine if anyone can hear what you're saying."

The line fell silent. A short time later, a garbled male voice rang out in the background. "The only person who can hear me is this weirdo standing beside me. I think he's from Iran."

"You're using a pay phone, then?" Lily was suspicious because Santa Barbara was long distance and John had not called her collect.

"First the cops interrogate me, now you," he told her. "Trust me, this guy doesn't speak English. Even if he did, he wouldn't know what we're talking about."

Lily lowered her voice. "Why would you bring up Bobby Hernandez?"

"Because I know the truth. Shana and I both know you killed that man. You killed him because you weren't wearing your glasses and mistook him for the rapist. You laid in wait for him and then blew him away. That's premeditated murder."

Lily's muscles locked into place. "Bobby Hernandez was a murderer. He was on his way to becoming a serial killer."

"That's not the point."

"That's precisely the point," Lily said, slamming her fist down on her desk. "Hernandez developed a taste for killing. He decided it was more exciting than taking drugs and robbing people. He killed Peter McDonald and Carmen Lopez with his gangster buddies. They bashed the boy's head in, raped the girl repeatedly, and then shoved a tree limb up her vagina, rupturing her abdominal wall."

"I didn't say the man deserved to live," John told her. "Have I ever accused you or threatened to turn you in?"

Lily had no choice but to lie. "I didn't kill him."

"Hey," he said, "you scratch my back and I'll scratch yours. Isn't that the way the world works these days?"

Lily bit down on the inside of her mouth. Why had he waited all these years to confront her? Knowing John, she had to consider that he might be bluffing. But John and Shana did know things. He knew that the night of the rapes, she hadn't come home until the following morning. And Shana had walked into the garage, catching her mother squatting near the rear of her Honda as she wiped off the black Magic Marker ink she'd used to alter her license plates. In one particular instance, Lily had even blurted out the truth. John had been ranting that he wanted to kill the man who'd violated his daughter. Without thinking, Lily told him it wouldn't be necessary, that she'd already killed him. Since John hadn't taken her seriously, she had recanted and told him her statement was nothing more than fantasy. He knew she was popping Valium to get through the day, so she felt confident that he'd believed her.

"What do you want from me?" Lily asked point-blank.

"You're an attorney," he told her. "I'm going to need someone to represent me. Do you want Shana to find out her father's in jail? She's already devastated that Curazon is back on the streets. That sick bastard . . . he raped my baby. She was just a little girl."

"Calm down," Lily said, hearing him whimpering. "Did the judge set bail?"

"Yeah," he told her. "A hundred grand."

"A hundred thousand!" Lily had expected a lower amount, but vehicular manslaughter carried almost the same weight as second-degree murder. Under those circumstances, bail in this range might be justified. Her original assumption, however, was that the district attorney in Los Angeles had arraigned John on a number of charges. Most defendants were either too frightened to hear half of what was said during their arraignment, or they had difficulty deciphering the legal jargon. In order to charge John with vehicular manslaughter, John had to kill someone with his car during the commission of a felony. "What exactly did you do?"

"You mean what they said I did?"

Now they were going to play this game, Lily thought, having heard the same evasive tactics spewing out of the mouths of hundreds of criminals. She was tempted to bail him out just so she could drive him to a dark alley and smash both his kneecaps with a baseball bat. He didn't mind accusing her of murder on a jailhouse phone, but he wasn't about to admit his own guilt. "Just tell me what crimes the police are alleging you committed."

"The cops claim I left the scene. You know . . . a hit-and-run. When they arrested me, I was sitting on the front porch sipping on a bottle of Jack Daniel's."

"You're on probation, John," Lily said. "You swore you weren't going to drink anymore."

"I know, but it breaks my heart to see Shana scared. She's convinced she saw Curazon last night, poor baby."

"I called the police, remember? You weren't even there. If you didn't want Shana to be frightened, why did you leave her alone last night and go out drinking?"

"I wasn't behind the wheel when they arrested me. Having a drink isn't a crime."

Heaven help me, Lily thought, her thoughts racing. As soon as they concluded their conversation, she would have to call the court and see if they would allow him to post bail with a 10 percent deposit. This was the general rule of thumb unless the judge specified that the defendant fork over the entire amount. Even then, she didn't have ten thousand in cash. She'd have to get a loan from the credit union. Loans took time, but she had to shut John up and the only way was to meet his demands. "Were there any witnesses to this alleged hit-and-run?"

"Not that I know of," he said. "You know the cops never tell you this kind of stuff. They like to get you in an interview room and hammer at you until they get you to confess."

Something was wrong. She knew John was lying, but it was something else she couldn't quite put her finger on. She massaged her forehead, attempting to analyze the situation objectively. When the evidence was weak, most prosecutors allowed the subject to remain at large in the community until they were able to build an airtight case. Once they made an arrest, the clock started ticking and if the defendant was tried and acquitted, double jeopardy came into play and he could never be tried for that particular offense again. "Why did they arrest you if they didn't have a witness or some kind of concrete proof? I don't even know how they identified you since it was a hit-and-run. Was there damage to your car?"

"They found my wallet at the scene of the accident," he told her, not as confident as he'd been before. "The public defender and I decided whoever hit this kid must have been the one who stole my wallet."

Did he really call the victim a kid? Lily started to ask him how old the victim was and then stopped herself. She didn't want to know, not when she was being extorted to bail out the person who had killed him. She already had a nasty taste in her mouth, as if she'd consumed a dozen rotten eggs.

"I need money for an attorney."

"Didn't you just tell me you were being represented by the public defender?"

"I had no choice at the arraignment," John told her. "But even he told me I should hire someone else. I need one of those fancy attorneys who specialize in this kind of thing."

"How can you do this to me?"

"If you'd killed the right guy, I'd have given you a medal and never mentioned it again. But the rapist is back on the street again. Why didn't you shoot him?"

"You're out of your mind, John. Keep talking this way and I won't lift a finger to help you. Let's get something straight right now. No matter what kind of ridiculous accusations you hurl at me, I have no intention of paying for your attorney. They may not be able to charge you with driving under the influence, but both you and I know that the victim would be alive if you'd remained sober."

John's voice took on a sharper edge. "Oh, you'll help me. You can't afford not to help me. I know how much that job means to you, how scared you are of ending up in my position. You know how dirty and cramped it is in prison. Just because you're a woman doesn't mean you'll have an easy ride. You've put your share of women behind bars. Maybe a few of them would like to have a little talk with you."

Lily knew when she was defeated. She picked up a file and threw it across the room, watching as the papers struck the wall and then scattered all over her office floor. Only in the past year had she started to put her life back together. And there was Shana to consider.

"I expect to be out of here by this evening."

Lily swallowed her pride. "I'll do the best I can."

"Just get the job done," John said. "After I begged you to keep it a secret, you told Shana I was broke, made her think her old man was a loser. That's why I fell off the wagon."

"An innocent person is dead, John. I have to walk off my job, scrape together every penny I have, and then drive like a maniac to L.A. to bail out my ex-husband. All these years you've blamed me because Shana was raped. Now you're trying to blame this on me."

"Do you know what it feels like to be humiliated?" John said, his voice laced with venom. "Are you proud of yourself, Lily? Once again you've managed to rip our family apart."

John thought he had disconnected, but Lily heard him talking to someone and bragging about what a good actor he was. She slammed the phone down, knowing he had done more than blackmail her into posting his bail and hiring him an attorney. He wasn't calling from a pay phone inside the jail. She had sensed something was wrong, but she hadn't been able to figure out what it was until now.

John had rolled over on her, parlaying his suspicion that she may have killed Bobby Hernandez into a bargaining chip. He had called her from the district attorney's office in Los Angeles. Every word Lily had spoken had been recorded and was probably right now being analyzed by a team of investigators. She felt herself shaking, wondering how she could have been so foolish. In exchange for his cooperation, the DA would offer John a plea agreement. He'd serve a few weeks in jail while Lily would go to prison. She placed her head down on the desk and cried.

Nurse Peggy pulled Shana's jaw down and deposited several pills in her mouth, and then handed her a paper cup filled with water. Shana tried to spit the pills out, but a pudgy finger pushed them back in and tipped the water into her mouth. "These will help you to sleep."

"I don't want to sleep," Shana told her. "I want to call my boyfriend." She jumped off the bed and ran toward the nearest door, but it was locked and Peggy was moving across the floor behind her. The woman turned sideways, shifted her weight and leaned against Shana, pinning her against the wall.

"George!" she yelled. "Get over here."

The same giant of a man appeared, his muscles straining inside his striped shirt. Together, they lifted the new patient up by her armpits and carried her to a small room containing what appeared to be a hospital bed. "I'm not going in there," Shana protested, her chest heaving. She positioned her legs behind Peggy and George and pushed forward against the backs of both of their knees in an attempt to cause them to lose their balance. Shana's efforts failed, however, as the legs she was pushing against were as stout as tree trunks. "I want a lawyer. What did you give me? You can't keep me here. I'm an adult. My mother has no right to commit me."

George vanished. A few moments later a dark-haired, well-groomed woman in her late thirties appeared wearing a pink sweater and gray pants. With Peggy holding Shana down on the bed, the woman removed her pants and top and began pulling on a pair of green cotton pants, dodging Shana's feet as she kicked out in protest. Peggy and the woman then grabbed her by the shoulders, holding her in place as they placed a matching green shirt over her head. Why were they dressing her in a scrub suit like surgeons wore?

Her vision became blurry and she could no longer focus her eyes. Peggy's image became even more grotesque. As soon as the two women finished dressing her, they left.

The door was open and Shana could see what she assumed was a nursing station and beyond, a large open room where people were milling about. She got up and walked out into the first room, the place where Peggy had pinned her against the wall. She saw a sofa, several chairs, and a television set, but otherwise, the room was empty.

Peggy was sitting at the nursing station with her head down, working on some type of paperwork. A dozen small rooms like the one they had placed Shana in opened off the main area. She went to each room and peered inside. None of the beds were occupied. The drug beginning to kick in, she staggered back to the seating area.

The floor suddenly buckled beneath her. She fell sideways onto the sofa, one arm dangling off the side. She couldn't think or reason. Her mind was mush, an enormous trembling bowl of gelatin. Then the darkness came, crashing down on her like a boulder.

Shana awoke with a start. Her eyes were glued to her eyelids and her chin was jutting out from her face. A piercing scream erupted from her mouth. She tried to swallow and then choked. Saliva dribbled onto her hand. Her body began convulsing. "Help . . . me," she cried pathetically, biting her pulsating tongue as she tried to speak. "God . . . please!"

Shana's head was bent backward. She felt as if her entire body was being pulled toward the ceiling with incredible force. She heard footsteps running on the tiled floor, heard faceless voices speaking in urgent hushed tones. "She's having a reaction to the Thorazine. Hurry, get an injection."

More shuffling feet, then out of the corner of her eye, Shana saw a muscular tan arm encircle her torso. She was thrown facedown on the sofa. Her green cotton pants were jerked down. Cold air swept across her buttocks, followed quickly by the jab of a needle.

"That should do it, George," a woman's voice whispered.

"Dr. Morrow needs to exercise more caution, Peggy," another female voice said. "We don't know anything about this patient. We don't have her medical records. We don't know what, if any, medications she's taking. Did she consent to be treated with Thorazine?"

"Look, Lee," Peggy said, "it's not my responsibility to get consent forms signed. I give whatever medication is prescribed in the chart."

Shana heard the women's footsteps recede, finding herself alone again on the sofa. After an unknown period of time, she managed to pull herself up to a seated position. She sat there stiffly, her eyes still rolled back in her head. She was in Hell. There was no other explanation. Whitehall, they called it.

Hell.

The muscles in Shana's eyes finally relaxed and she could see, even though she still wasn't able to focus. The edges of the sofa across from her bowed out and then caved in, the colors running together like wet paint.

Shana must have fallen asleep again because when she awoke, the room was bathed in light and she could hear noises in the distance. Trying to stand, she crumpled back on the sofa. Thirty minutes or so later, it was as if a great churning engine was pushing her. She felt a compulsion to walk, move, and pace.

The green pajamas were so large they dragged on the ground. Her gait was really more like a stumble than a walk. She was drugged, dazed, and locked inside her body. A woman approached her and touched her arm. Through the fog, Shana thought she saw a face of compassion. "Oh, God, can't someone help me?"

"My name is Lee," the woman said in a soft voice. "I'm going to bathe you."

The next thing Shana remembered was standing in front of a mirror, her hair wet, once again wearing the green pajamas. Lee was slowly pulling a brush through her hair. This is what it must feel like to be a child, she thought. She was completely helpless and careless, swimming in a timeless void. Reality seemed to be drifting away. Lee began blow-drying her hair. Her mother used to dry her hair the same way, gently, unconcerned where it fell, only intent on drying it so she wouldn't get chilled. How could her mother do this to her?

She turned and placed her arms around Lee's shoulders, wanting to embrace her as a child would its mother. For what felt like an eternity, she had been pushed, pulled, jabbed, and terrified. She wanted to be comforted, held, touched.

"Please," Lee said, removing her arms, "we have rules . . ."

The voice, Shana remembered the woman's voice now. She must have been one of the women who had given her the injection. That meant she'd also made the comment about a consent form.

Shana turned and gazed at her image in the mirror, unable to retrieve the exact details of the conversation between the two women. She was so fair, without makeup, her face seemed like a blank canvas.

Lee led her back into the open room and disappeared. On the coffee table was a tray of food: breakfast, lunch, dinner? Shana didn't know and she didn't care. She used her fingers to stuff an unknown substance into her mouth, but when she tried to swallow, her throat constricted. She spat whatever it was out into her hand, and then wrapped it in a paper napkin.

Sometime later, an odd-looking man took a seat on the sofa across from her, studying her like a specimen under a microscope. His eyes looked like black beetles and something about him immediately made Shana bristle—an arrogance, the vague sense that he enjoyed seeing her drugged and disoriented.

"I'm Dr. Morrow," he said. "How are you feeling today, Shana?"

He smiled smugly as he rearranged his slender body to a more comfortable position on the sofa.

"Why am I here?" she asked, appalled that this person might be her psychiatrist. "I know this is some type of mental hospital, but why am I being treated like a prisoner?" Each word required enormous effort. She had to force her mind to retrieve the floating thoughts from her brain and then make her rubbery lips expel them.

"You're here because you're ill," Morrow answered. "You were psychotic."

"I am not psychotic . . . have never been psychotic. You have no right to lock me up in this disgusting place. I'm going to sue you." Shana reached inside herself for the anger and used it to keep herself alert enough to continue. "You release me at once or you'll live to regret it."

Morrow flicked a piece of lint off his black slacks, then leaned over the table and said slowly and distinctly, "Let's get something straight. You may be here a week, a month, or even a year. You might even be here for several years. If you refuse to talk to me now, rest assured, you'll have plenty of time in the future."

Shana was so shocked, she was rendered speechless.

Opening the clipboard he'd placed on the sofa beside him, Morrow crossed his legs and started reading. "Let's see," he said, yawning. "You admitted to extensive use of narcotics, specifically methamphetamine. You had open sores on your arms and legs. Your mother stated that you were delusional, that you had stopped attending law school and had locked yourself up in your apartment." He shut the file with a sense of finality. "I don't think you'll be suing anyone, nor will you be going anywhere for quite some time. Now if you cooperate, the time you spend here at Whitehall can be productive, even pleasant. But if you continue to resist our efforts to treat you, well, you know what to expect. You've been hospitalized before."

"Wait a minute." Shana's pulse was racing. "I didn't admit to using narcotics. Even if I was using drugs, which I'm not, I wouldn't admit it to someone in a place like this. And look," she added, extending her arms, "I don't have any sores. You're confusing me with another patient." Lee's whispered words suddenly appeared in her mind. "You gave me the wrong medication, didn't you? You gave me something that almost killed me."

"We're trying to help you, Shana," Morrow told her. "I understand you haven't been sleeping. Now that you've stopped using stimulants, you'll eventually reestablish a normal sleep pattern. In the interim, I've prescribed some excellent medication for you." He smiled, revealing a row of teeth almost as large as piano keys. "Your situation will be easier to handle once you get a decent night's sleep."

Morrow stood and started to walk off when Shana called him back.

"If I was addicted to meth, I'd be crashing right now. Except for the drugs you people have been giving me, I'm fine."

"You've already detoxed, Shana. It's not a pleasant experience, so it's understandable that you've blocked it out of your mind. The medication you mentioned was a drug we use to prevent seizures when a patient is going through withdrawals. Get some rest. I'll stop by and check on you tomorrow."

Shana remained on the sofa, watching as he deposited her chart in the metal rack at the nursing station, and then waited until they buzzed him through the locked security doors. They were messing with her mind, trying to make her believe things that weren't true. But there was nothing she could do now. She had been in a place like this before, so she knew how they operated. New patients were placed in an isolation ward where their every move could be watched. Once they released her into the general population, she would figure out a way to get out.

Staggering back to her room, she threw herself face-first on the bed. If only her father were alive. He would have never let them lock her up like a criminal. She missed him and yearned to be with him every day. He'd been so much more than her father. He'd been her best friend, something her mother couldn't understand.

People said her grief would eventually become bearable, but it had been nine years and the wound was as deep and painful as the day her father's life had ended. The hatred she carried for the man who had raped her and murdered her father still churned inside of her, poisoning every aspect of her existence.

She had recovered from the rape. It hadn't been easy, but believing her mother had killed the rapist had taken away her constant fear that he would come back. She remembered the terrible day her father had died. She was staying at her mother's place in Santa Barbara when she should have been at home with her father. Knowing he had died alone was one of the things that hurt the most. If she had been at his condo in Los Angeles, she might have been able to do something to save him.

# ELEVEN

SPRING, 2000
LOS ANGELES, CALIFORNIA

En route to his duplex, John Forrester stopped off at a liquor store and bought a fifth of Jack Daniel's, then walked next door to the newsstand to pick up a copy of the *Las Vegas* newspaper, wanting to check out the classifieds section and see what kinds of jobs were listed. He subscribed to the L.A. Times, but he'd been too distraught to read it that morning. Something compelled him to pick the paper up off the stand, sensing there might be something inside regarding the accident. He found what he'd feared— the article about the death of the young man he had run over and left to die, his own name in print for all to see. He staggered backward, dropping his head and ducking back inside the car.

At least the article didn't contain a picture of him. It did state, however, that he had been arraigned on charges of vehicular manslaughter. What choice did he have now but to flee, attempt to establish a new identity? He was no longer John Forrester, loving father and real estate agent. His family name was now publicly vilified. Even if they failed to convict him, he knew his life would never be the same.

While driving to the duplex, John remembered a recent segment on CNN, emphasizing how easy it was for a person to obtain various forms of false identification, even credit cards. On the way out of town, he decided he would drive by one of the places they had mentioned, an area known as MacArthur Park, located at Seventh and Alvarado, hoping he had enough money to pay for what he needed.

The shock of seeing the article caused him to unscrew the bottle of Jack Daniel's and take a swig before he reached his front door, wadding up the paper bag and tossing it into a trash barrel. Swiping his mouth with the back of his hand, once he was in the house, he placed the bottle on the coffee table and headed to the kitchen to check his voice mail, hoping Shana had called. When he heard the nasal voice of a woman inquiring about one of his listings, he smashed his fist into the wall. All he wanted was to say good-bye, tell Shana he was sorry, tell her how much he loved her. How could his life have sunk to such a disgusting level? It was as if Hell had risen up out of the ground and swallowed him.

He had hoped to keep the Buick for at least thirty days, thinking the real estate agent whose identity he had stolen wouldn't find out until the first payment. He had promised the car salesman that he would bring in some type of photo ID the next day. Maybe he could have one of those guys on the street make him a dummy license. With the new seal of the state of California imprinted on each license, it was impossible to simply print one up on a computer. If he couldn't take care of the problem, he would be forced into ditching the car after he reached Vegas. At least his public defender had advised him that his next court appearance wasn't scheduled for another three weeks.

John headed to the front door to retrieve his luggage from the detached garage, grabbing the bottle of Jack Daniel's off the table. The shakes were getting progressively worse. He had to make them stop, and the only solution was to feed his body what it craved. Once he threw some of his clothing and personal items into a suitcase, he would make a pot of coffee to offset the effects of the alcohol before embarking on such a long drive.

As he stood in front of his garage, a car drove past full of young people, loud music blasting through the open window. He imagined families inside the houses on the block, laughing, loving, and enjoying one another. He would never live a normal life again, never see his daughter step onto the stage to receive her college diploma.

He hesitated before hoisting the door to the garage. Inside were the remains of the life he had once lived with Lily: tables, chairs, lamps, items that had been at their home in Camarillo. This time when he tipped the bottle to his mouth, he guzzled it down as if it were water.

John ducked inside when he spotted one of the neighbors out walking her dog, quickly closing the garage door behind him. Beverly Murdock was a white-haired busybody and he was in no mood to deal with her. A small window was situated in the rear of the garage, faintly illuminating the interior. Before he had a chance to turn on the lights, he suddenly froze, hearing a noise in the far left corner of the structure. A neighborhood cat must have managed to sneak inside when he came out a week ago to retrieve his toolbox.

He was feeling along the wall for the light switch when he heard another noise—a strange wheezing sound. Whipping out his pocketknife, he flicked open the blade, fearing the sound had been made by a rabid raccoon or some other type of wild animal. He never locked the garage, almost hoping someone would break in and save him the trouble of hauling the junk inside away. Outside of a few pieces of cheap luggage, there was nothing worth stealing.

He waited and listened, holding his breath. With the alcohol now coursing through his bloodstream, he decided to open the garage door rather than continue groping around in the dark for the light switch.

Just as he reached for the handle to lift the door, John heard something rushing toward him at tremendous speed, like a raging bull. Boxes and furniture tumbled over. The next thing he knew, he was pinned face-first against the wall, held in place by the maniacal force of his attacker.

"Booze, huh?" the man hissed, yanking the bottle out of John's hand and smashing it against the wall.

A dagger of white-hot pain entered John's back as he frantically struggled against his attacker. As he slashed out blindly with his pocketknife, the man seized his arm in an iron grip, a guttural, inhuman sound erupting from his throat.

John screamed in agony as he felt his wrist being bent backward until the bones emitted a sickening crack.

"You thought you were gonna cut me with that pussy knife?" his attacker snarled in his ear, closing the knife and slipping it in his pocket. "You a joke, man. That knife's not good for nothing but cleaning your fingernails."

John felt warm liquid gushing down his back, knowing instantly that it was blood. He had to force each word out of his mouth. "Money . . . I . . . have . . . money."

The man waved the bowie knife in front of his face, a streak of light reflecting off the shiny surface of the blade. "This is what a knife looks like, asshole," he said, his words spoken with a Latin accent. He plucked out the roll of cash and stuffed it into the waistband of his sweatpants.

The man had said something about booze. John thought of Antonio Vasquez, the man he had run over. Had one of his relatives decided to seek revenge? His eyes closed, the weight of his body fell limp in the man's arms. The man's voice and the words he spoke pulled him back.

"You're her daddy, ain't you? Is she in the house? That's who I want, old man. I want that pretty little daughter of yours. You, I don't want. You just a man in the wrong place at the wrong time."

John released an involuntary grunt with each thrust of the knife. He no longer felt the pain, only the pressure of the blade as it passed into his flesh. He had been driving Shana's car the night of the accident. Vasquez's family must believe she had killed their son. He suddenly saw himself inside a sun-filled room. Shana was a little girl again, her eyes filled with love and innocence as she gazed up at him. "Take me to the park," the vision said, her hand tugging on his sleeve.

Shana's image vanished from the light, replaced with the face of the beautiful young boy he had driven over and left to die. He felt himself diving into the same fathomless pool of swirling darkness he had glimpsed the night of the hit-and-run. He mouthed the same exact words Lily had said the night Curazon had dragged her down the hall toward the bedroom where Shana lay sleeping. "Please, God, not my daughter."

A car pulled into the driveway of the duplex on Maplewood Drive at seven-fifteen Saturday evening. When Shana and her friend, Jennifer Abernathy, opened the door and went inside, she was appalled at the filth and clutter. "My father's not only a drunk," she said, angrily kicking an empty beer can across the floor, "he's a pig. He probably doesn't care about leaving the place clean since my mother put up the damn deposit."

"It's okay," Jennifer said, patting her friend on the shoulder. She glanced down at the coffee table and saw a picture of Shana that was singed around the edges. "Look," she said, holding up what was left of the snapshot, "someone ripped your mother out of the picture I took at our high school graduation. Do you think your dad got mad and set fire to it?"

Shana had already started down the hall to her bedroom. When she came to her father's room, the hairs pricked on the back of her neck. Drawers were pulled out, clothes were tossed everywhere, a lamp was toppled. She quickly checked her own room, finding it in the same state of disorder. "Jen," she called out. "Hurry, come here."

"Gee," the girl said, stepping up beside her, "maybe we should call the police."

"That's all I need," Shana said. "The last time my mother called the cops, I was certain they were going to arrest me." She bent down and picked up some of her underwear off the floor, more despondent than ever. "Dad was probably drinking. And

Mom pressured him. She told him he had to be moved out by Monday, or the land-lord would throw everything out in the street."

"Your mom was going to let them throw your stuff out?"

"Of course not," Shana told her. "You don't understand how booze fries a person's brain. My father's desperate for money. He could have taken the clothes from the draw-ers because he was going to try and sell the furniture. I'm so ashamed." She placed her hand over her mouth. "Please, promise me you won't tell anyone. Not just about this, but all the things I told you about my dad and the accident."

"You know I'd never do that. Look, this place gives me the creeps. Since we're not going to call the cops, let's get your stuff together and split."

Shana found a cloth laundry bag in a corner, then began filling it with jeans, T-shirts, blouses, underwear, and several pairs of shoes. After dragging the bag into the living room, she told Jennifer that there might be some empty boxes in the garage. "I want to take as much as I can. I don't want to come back here tomorrow."

Before they went to get the boxes, Shana picked up the phone and dialed the number for her father's voice mail, wanting to see if he had received her messages. She listened to two calls from people inquiring about various real estate properties, then heard a male voice identifying himself as Detective Mark Osborne, asking that her father contact him immediately. According to the recording, the call had come in Friday night.

Quickly checking her own voice mail, Shana discovered that Detective Hope Car-ruthers had left a message on her phone that morning as well. She rushed into the other room, finding Jennifer stacking some of her schoolbooks by the front door. "Th-that guy . . ." she stammered. "The one my father hit with the car . . . Anto-nio Vasquez . . . he was in one of our classes."

"Which class?"

"Philosophy 101."

"I don't remember him, but it's a gigantic class."

Shana wasn't aware that she was holding a tennis shoe in her hand. "The police asked me if he was in any of my classes. They thought I'd been dating him, that we got into a fight and it was me instead of my dad who was driving that night. This is all because I let my dad drive my car."

"From the way it looks," Jennifer said, walking over and hugging her, "the police have already picked up your father. You have to stop freaking out. The world isn't coming to an end, Shana. You've always been tough. I'm the whiner, remember?" She pried the tennis shoe out of her hand, setting it down on the table beside the phone.

"No," Shana said, crying now, "don't you understand? My dad was going to leave me here to take the blame. He's probably left town. I started to feel sorry for him. I tried to call him, see him, tell him I loved him. He doesn't care about me. He doesn't even care if they arrest me."

"Come on now. Get it together so we can get out of here. Where's the door to the garage?"

"Outside," Shana told her, heading toward the front door.

"I can't believe you don't have a garage door opener," Jennifer said, straining as she tried to lift the heavy door.

"This is an old place."

"Something stinks. Can you smell it?"

Shana caught a whiff of something unpleasant. "It's probably fertilizer. The lady that lives next door is out here every day, planting and snipping."

Both girls jumped when Hope Carruthers walked up behind them. By the time the detective had determined that John Forrester wasn't inside the residence, Osborne and the patrol unit had arrived. A Frenchwoman had once told Hope that her highly refined sense of smell could earn her a great deal of money in the perfume industry. But what she smelled inside the garage was far from fragrant. It was the unmistakable odor of death.

"Let's talk over here," she said, anxiously leading Shana and her friend to the street.

"Are you two girls going somewhere?" Osborne asked, the two uniformed officers taking up positions on either side of the two young women.

"I'm just moving some of my clothes out," Shana told them. "I didn't get the message that you wanted to talk to me until I came home about an hour ago. I've been staying with my mother in Santa Barbara. I have no idea where my father went."

Advising the patrol officers to detain the girls on the opposite side of the house, the detectives returned to the garage. Hope flicked on her flashlight, seeing several pools of what appeared to be blood. "Get the crime scene unit and more officers out here." She panned the walls and spotted what appeared to be bloody handprints on the wall near the light switch. "There's a dead body in here somewhere."

Osborne asked, "What about the girls?"

"I didn't see any blood on the girls' clothing. Check them again. If they look clean, get them out of here. We have to find the body."

"I'll have one of the patrol units take the Forrester girl to the station and stash her somewhere. Should we take her friend into custody as well?"

"It's your call," Hope told him. "I think she was just helping Shana move her things."

A short time later, an officer jotted down Jennifer's name, address, and driver's license number and sent her on her way. He waited until the girl drove away to tell Shana that Detective Osborne had instructed him to take her to the station.

Shana was terrified, her back ramrod straight and her arms rigid at her sides as she stared into the open garage. She resisted when the officer tried to get her into the backseat of the patrol car.

"I'm going to have to handcuff you if you keep fighting me," the officer told her, placing his hand on top of her head as he helped her into the car.

Shana stared at the screen separating her from the police officer. She felt like a stray dog en route to the pound, caged and panicked. Peering out the rear window, she saw several more police units and a white van pulling up in front of the duplex. She began gasping for air; certain now that the putrid odor her friend had smelled had not been fertilizer. Unable to accept what her reason was telling her, she fainted, her head striking the back of the seat with a thud.

# TWELVE

Lily was in her chambers waiting for Richard Fowler. She had asked him to approach the bench for a sidebar while they were in session, whispering that she wanted to see him in her chambers during the morning recess. Richard must have assumed it had something to do with the case and was taking his time merely to annoy her.

"Mr. Fowler is here to see you," Jeannie said over the intercom.

"Send him in."

"What did I do wrong, Your Highness?" he said, walking over and flopping down in a chair in front of her desk. "Silverstein's opening statement was seriously over the line and you know it. He practically convicted my client with outrageous accusations and speculations and you sat there and let him get away with it."

"Your client is guilty," Lily told him. "And don't give me a speech about due process. I didn't call you in here to talk about the case. Shana's in a mental hospital."

Fowler looked shocked. "When did this happen?"

"She stopped answering her phone so I flew up there Friday night. She told me she hadn't been sleeping, that a girl was raped in her apartment building, and that she wanted to drop out of school. Oh, she's also decided she doesn't want to be an attorney."

"I agree on the last part," Fowler told her. "I hate this job. If I hadn't lost a bundle in the stock market, I'd try to find another way to earn a living. Defending scumbags is not the way I want to spend my days." He paused and cleared his throat. "Isn't Shana at Stanford?"

"Yes, this is her last year. Or it would have been her last year. I don't know what to do, Rich. She's . . . God, I still don't believe it. She's addicted to meth."

His jaw dropped. "That's one hell of a nasty drug for such a bright woman."

"She has open sores all over her body," Lily told him, forcing back tears. "I couldn't believe it when I saw the picture."

"What picture?"

"She admitted herself, Richard. She looked thin when I saw her, but without her clothes on, she was emaciated. I don't know what to do. Has Greg ever had a problem with drugs?"

"He's a surfer, remember? He starts smoking marijuana as soon as he rolls out of bed every day. He calls it wake and bake. It's never interfered with his work, though. He's a marine biologist now and involved in some enthralling research." Fowler held up a palm. "Let's backtrack. You never answered my question. Who showed you this picture of Shana?"

"The hospital administrator."

"What's the name of this hospital? Is it here in Ventura?"

"No," Lily told him. "It's about twenty miles from Palo Alto, just on the outskirts of San Francisco. I found it on the Internet and it looked like a pretty good place. They told me Shana didn't want to see me or speak to me. She was furious that I brought her there. I tricked her into thinking we were going to a restaurant."

"Wait a minute. Didn't you just tell me she admitted herself?"

"She did, but after I took her to the hospital. She was acting crazy, Richard. Her place was a pigsty and all she was eating was fast food. A girl was raped in her apartment complex and she was terrified she'd be his next victim."

"That's understandable with her history."

"I realize that," Lily told him, her voice rising. "But she wasn't sleeping. She wouldn't even sleep in her bed. She sat on the sofa all night staring at the door. She kept a hammer tucked into the cushions so she could bash the rapist over the head."

Fowler crossed his long legs. "I hate to say this, Lily, but nothing you've told me so far sounds crazy. The meth thing, well, that's serious. I'm surprised she admitted herself. Most addicts would rather die than intentionally put themselves in a place where they didn't have access to drugs."

"I don't think she'd gone that far down," Lily said, praying she was right. "Maybe she wanted help. Her boyfriend broke up with her, which was devastating. She thought the guy was still going to marry her. Shana admitted he hadn't called or seen her for three weeks and she'd deluded herself into believing he was coming back and would proceed with their plans to get married."

"Slow down," he said, a concerned look on his face. "You're talking ninety miles an hour. What caused the breakup?"

"Another girl." She stopped and sucked in oxygen. "I guess he was sleeping with her. You know . . . the new girlfriend. Shana said his infidelity didn't mean anything, that the girl was nothing more than a fuck."

"She was probably right."

Lily's eyes narrowed. "Well, you would know."

"You sure haven't changed."

"I doubt if you have, either."

Fowler stood. "If you brought me in here to fight, I'm leaving."

"I'm sorry, okay? I'm under a lot of stress right now." She placed her hand over her chest. Acid was bubbling back in her throat and the awful taste filled her mouth. "Anyway, now that I know about the drugs, I'm wondering if the boyfriend was her supplier."

"Listen, Lily," he said. "Shana is a terrific girl. She's been through some horrendous experiences. And law school isn't as easy as people think, particularly a high-ranking school such as Stanford. Drugs are readily available in every college in the country. Drug dealers even peddle that shit in elementary schools these days. Shana did the right thing by admitting herself into rehab. People get sick. I doubt if it will show up on her record as long as you provide documentation. Voluntarily entering rehab means she wants to get straight. So what if she messes up a semester? She can make it up next year."

"I'm not sure she wants to," Lily told him, bracing her head with her hand.

"That's just the drugs talking." He repositioned himself in the chair. "In addition to child killers, I also represent drug dealers, so I know. I won't even see them until they get clean. I know you must be upset and disappointed, but everything will work out." He glanced at his watch. "It's time to go back to work, Lily. My adorable client is probably wondering what happened to me." He paused and then added, "I'm curious, why did you come to me with this? Rumor has is that you're involved with Christopher Rendell. I hear he's a fantastic listener. Why didn't you make him your sounding board?"

"Greg and Shana used to be close, remember?" She jotted down the phone number to Whitehall. "Maybe he can call and find out how she's doing. Not today, of course, because she's probably still going through detox. Ask him to call her later on in the week. I have no idea how long it takes to get that stuff out of her system."

"Greg will be happy to call her," Richard said, walking over and picking up the paper off the edge of Lily's desk. Instead of leaving, he just stood there and stared at her, his eyes filled with longing. "I still love you, you know. I always will. And you're still beautiful. You haven't aged a day since I last saw you."

Lily's face flushed with embarrassment. "If you think I called you in here to start something, Richard, you're wrong. I'm in love with Chris. We get along great. Outside of Shana, I'm really happy right now. He asked me to marry him and I accepted."

Fowler ran his hands through his dark hair, now laced with gray. "Jesus, woman, you're getting married again? I thought this time you'd stay single for a while, have a little fun, maybe enjoy your independence."

"You got married," she snapped. "Not that marriage matters to you. I assume your little blond co-counsel is your latest conquest? How old is she? She looks young enough to be your daughter."

"I planned on getting married a few years back, but I realized she wasn't the right woman so I bailed. And Beth Wiseman is my partner's daughter. If I even looked at her the wrong way, Mike would rip my head off. I don't date young women anymore, Lily. I don't have anything in common with them."

"Now I'm late." She stood and threw on her robe. If she wasn't careful, her tardiness would get back to Hennessey.

He stood in front of the door and blocked her. "I didn't get married because I hoped we could get back together someday. Why haven't you called me?"

"It's over, Richard. Move out of my way. I'm supposed to be on the bench right now. You cheated on me, in case you've forgotten. Or I guess it was just a fuck, right?"

"Just once, Lily, and I was drunk. The girl came on to me. You know how I get when I'm drinking. I haven't had a drink in five years. I'm older now, too. I've given up my womanizing ways. Can't we at least have lunch together or maybe go for coffee after work?"

Richard knew everything. If he wanted, he could blackmail her. She knew he would never stoop that low. If he did report what he knew to the authorities, he could be charged with being an accessory to murder. The fact that Lily had placed him in such a position was one of the reasons their relationship had failed.

Even though she tried to deny it, a part of her was still drawn to him. Richard had taught her what it was like to genuinely love someone. And the sex had been great. John had stopped having sex with her as soon as Shana was born. "I can't see you on the side, Richard," she said, gently shoving him away. "I'm with Chris now and even if I wasn't, I would never let myself become involved with you again. Just see what Greg can find out about Shana. Oh, and thanks for listening."

On the third day, they released Shana from isolation and placed her in the general population. The main room was as spacious as the lobby of a first-class hotel. Various seating areas and large round tables were positioned throughout the room. One section reminded her of a reading circle in an elementary school, with plastic chairs arranged in a semicircle facing a television set.

What excited her most were the people. She no longer cared who they were as long as they were alive. Peggy was behind the counter with Lee. Shana scanned the room. Out of the corner of her eye, she saw a flash of green. A man passed her walking fast. Fascinated, she watched as he circled the large room as if he were on a jogging track. Another reason he drew her attention was the fact that he was the only person beside herself dressed in green pajamas. With nothing better to do, she fell in step beside him. Although he failed to make eye contact, he immediately struck up a conversation.

"I find that walking calms me," he said. "It's like I have too much energy and I get aggravated and when I get aggravated people get mad at me. I find that walking calms me, you know. When I'm calm, I . . ."

Live and learn, Shana thought, stopping and letting the man continue on without her. Walking might calm this guy but it certainly didn't calm her. Because he was the only other person decked out in green pajamas, she decided they must be the hallmark of the most seriously deranged. Great, she thought facetiously. Spotting a small group of people at one of the circular tables who appeared fairly sane, she headed in their direction.

Then she saw him.

Unless she was hallucinating, a drop-dead gorgeous guy was standing in the middle of the group of patients. To say he looked as if he'd stepped out of a Calvin Klein commercial was an understatement. His dark hair fell just the right way and his skin was luscious without so much as a hint of a blemish. His dynamite body wasn't overbuilt like so many guys. He was muscular but lean, and his mischievous grin let her know that he knew he had caught her eye and that she liked what she saw.

He was rocking back and forth on his heels. Although it was hard to tell the way he was moving, he had to be an inch or two over six feet, which made a tall girl drool. His white T-shirt was stretched over his toned abdomen and his jeans hung perfectly on his hip bones, low and sexy. His hair was dark and shiny, styled in a conservative cut, which she found refreshing. His nose was nicely slanted and his lips thin but well suited to his face. He looked fit but he didn't possess the type of body she saw on jocks and body-builders. It might mean he was genetically gifted, and would look the same even if he never walked through the door of a gym. She imagined other men and even a few women could be fiercely jealous of him.

Shana took a sharp intake of oxygen, her overall assessment of the man changing as she moved closer. Old movie stars came to mind such as Marlon Brando and Jack Nicholson. Although he looked young, maybe mid to early twenties, he exuded maturity and masculinity.

"That's Milton," he said, tilting his head toward the man who had been circling the room in the green pajamas. "We call him the 'Walking Man.' I guess it wouldn't take a genius to figure out why we decided to call him that."

"Excuse me," Shana said. "Have we met each other?"

"I don't know," he said, giving her a coy smile. "You tell me."

The man seemed so lucid and normal. Shana was almost positive he was flirting with her. She glanced down at her pajamas in renewed humiliation. How could a person make a bad fashion statement in a nuthouse? "I'm sorry," she told him, blinking nervously. "I guess I was mistaken."

At the table behind him, a black woman with luminous eyes and a pretty face was painting her fingernails. They were like claws, at least two inches long, and curled at the end. Each nail was painted a different color. "This is May," he said. "Tell me your name and I'll introduce you to some of my friends."

"Shana," she stated, almost blurting out her last name before she reminded herself where she was. It was her understanding that Whitehall was a rehab hospital, but she didn't see anyone who resembled a drug addict or a stone-cold alcoholic. Except for the few people gathered around the table, the patients appeared to be mental cases.

She couldn't take her eyes off May's fingernails. The woman looked up at her and smiled, blowing on a green nail and waving it in the air to dry.

"May's a psychic," the man said, only a glint of sarcasm in his voice. "She'll give you a reading if she likes you."

Shana wondered if he meant psycho instead of psychic. She was about to ask the man his name when the person seated next to May turned around, and Shana gasped in horror. Every inch of his skin was burned and melded together. In his hand was a portable fan about the size of a flashlight.

"Norman, this is Shana," he said. "In case you're wondering, Norman set himself on fire." He paused and took a deep drag on a cigarette. "The fan eases the pain."

Norman gave her a pathetic look of acknowledgment, his eyes hidden inside the Halloween mask that had become his face. She turned and walked to the far side of the room, her stomach churning.

"I'm Alex," he said, walking up behind her and startling her.

"Why are you here?"

"Why are you here?"

"I asked first," Shana said, managing a weak smile.

"Because my family put me here," Alex told her. "They thought I was going to kill myself."

"Were you?"

"Maybe," he said. "And you?"

"I'm supposed to be a drug addict." Shana was surprised she had rattled off such an embarrassing statement to a complete stranger.

But no matter how desperate she was to escape this hotel hell, her new friend seemed to take the sting out of her situation, making it seem almost comical. She hadn't been standing on a street corner preaching doomsday with a megaphone or eating out of trash cans, but nonetheless, a psychiatrist had looked her straight in the eye and told her she was psychotic. "I don't want to be rude," she continued, "but do you have a clue as to how I can get out of this place?"

Alex shrugged.

Shana glanced back over her shoulder at Norman. Her natural curiosity made her want to ask questions about all the patients, but she knew this wasn't the time or place.

"Are you the one who was singing 'Amazing Grace' in the emergency room?"

"No, why do you ask?"

Alex smiled at her. "I've heard about her but I haven't seen her yet. Maybe she's still in isolation."

"I just got out of there and I didn't see anyone."

Shana suddenly recalled who he reminded her of—a guy she'd fallen in love with her sophomore year in college. Mark Summerfield had the same dark eyes, the same facial structure, the same thick hair, the identical Irish nose. The way Alex held his cigarette, the way he exhaled the smoke, letting it exit one side of his mouth. Mark had been a smoker as well, and during the time she had dated him, she'd picked up the habit. She quit a few months after they had split up, but even to this day, she occasionally yearned for a cigarette. Nicotine had to be the most addictive substance in the world. "It's odd that they let you smoke in here. Smoking is banned almost everywhere today. They won't even let the guys in prison smoke anymore."

"Maybe that's what makes Whitehall so successful."

Shana didn't answer, deciding the most marked resemblance to Mark was the look in Alex's eyes. Wasn't it the eyes that set one person apart from another? Facial features weren't that unique when you thought about it. When she was a kid, her grandmother used to tell her that God only had so many models. Alex's eyes held a sharp, crisp intelligence that shot you down cold, extremely reminiscent of her first love.

Mark majored in English and wanted to be a journalist. He was also an aspiring novelist. It was strange how people who seemed to be so unique sometimes turned out to be so ordinary, which is what eventually occurred with Mark. He was always working on his novel and between that and his work on the college paper, he never had enough time to spend with her.

"Want to play Ping-Pong?" Alex stubbed his cigarette out in an ashtray.

Shana glanced around the room until she spotted the table. She could barely walk, let alone play Ping-Pong. What she wanted to do was beat the shit out of that lying bastard Morrow. That is, when she could remember what he looked like, where she was, her name, little insignificant details. "I can't," she said, staring at the floor. "The medication . . ."

"Sure you can," Alex told her. "Come on, you have to do something."

On the back wall was a black pay phone. Next to it, Shana spotted a blackboard with chalk and erasers resting in the grooved track. Was it really a phone? It wouldn't surprise her if it turned out to be a prop. Everything seemed so surreal. She could imagine Morrow placing a phony phone on the wall to get the patients' hopes up. Then when they picked up the receiver, a message would say, "Got you, sucker."

Not hearing a symphony of cell phones ringing all the time was nice, though. She felt as if she had spun back in time.

She took off in the direction of the phone, her heart pumping against the drugs. She wanted to call Brett but she didn't want him to know she was in a mental hospital. Thinking she'd call her former roommate, Julie, she picked up the phone. It appeared to be real, but she needed money. She turned back to Alex, who'd followed her, thinking she would ask him to loan her a quarter. Not now, she decided. She'd just met the guy. A quarter must be a real prize.

"I'd play," Shana told him, "but my pants are too long. I might trip and fall." She was five-ten so it seemed odd that her pants were so long. Even if they'd given her men's pajamas, they wouldn't drag on the floor. They must have one size of pajamas for both men and women and because she was thin, there was an abundance of extra material. In that respect, she too was genetically gifted, as she'd inherited her height from her mother and could eat a horse and never gain a pound. It was one of the things that made other girls envy her.

Glancing down at her feet, she discovered she was wearing flip-flops, the cheap kind that nail salons gave her when she had a pedicure. For three days, she'd never once looked at her feet. "My shoes . . . I can't play Ping-Pong in these. I'll fall on my ass."

"Here," Alex said, reaching out and unabashedly placing a cool hand under the edge of her pajama bottoms, quickly rolling over the elastic waistband. "That takes care of one problem. As far as the shoes, just play barefoot."

Shana's eyes narrowed. She wanted the quarter. Surely someone could get her out. At the very least, Julie could bring her some clothes. Her thinking was elemental. The drugs had returned her to a state of childlike simplicity.

Everyone else except the "Walking Man" was wearing regular clothing. Several of the women were even wearing makeup. In a way, the hospital resembled a run-of-the-mill health spa. Some of the people were strange, no doubt, such as May with her long multicolored fingernails that curled like talons on a condor, and the tragically disfigured Norman, but others seemed completely normal, almost as if they were on some type of holiday. "Okay, I'll play."

Alex smiled boyishly and set out in the direction of the table. She shuffled along behind him, and they took up positions on opposite sides of the Ping-Pong table. A small crowd of onlookers gathered around. After only an hour or so in the great room, as she'd heard one of the other patients refer to it, she had seemingly been thrust into the role of an entertainer. Here she was playing Ping-Pong in a mental institution with a guy who was a dead ringer for one of her boyfriends, all while she was wearing oversized green pajamas, no shoes, and no underwear.

Through the haze of nameless faces, Shana focused on Norman, knowing her original assessment had to be accurate. She saw herself in Dante's gondola navigating the fiery rivers of the inferno, poor Norman at her side.

"Are we playing?" Alex asked, picking up a paddle off the table. "Or are you going to let the natives gawk at you all morning?"

Shana tossed her hands in the air. "Why me?"

"Why not?" He waved the paddle back and forth over the table. "If you keep asking silly questions, I'll find another partner."

Alex served. Shana managed to return the ball, clear the net, and miss the table. He paused and lit a fresh cigarette, then held it between his teeth as he retrieved the ball and promptly sent it flying over the net again.

"Isn't it time you quit smoking, Alex? The reason they've banned smoking in most prisons is because they don't want the taxpayers to have to pay to treat the inmates when they get cancer."

"Shut up and hit the ball." He slammed one over the net at her. "Prisoners don't pay through the nose to be locked up. Big difference, don't you think?"

They had been playing for approximately ten minutes when Shana felt herself getting caught up in the game. She was actually playing pretty well. Her eyes found the small ball and froze it in her line of vision exactly as if she were peering through a telescope. Once she hit the ball, she easily tracked it across the net and watched it decompress against Alex's paddle before it sprang back at her. In her vision, the ball seemed enormous, a glowing white orb, impossible to miss as it came to her in slow motion.

The drugs had redefined the world.

All at once, Shana became aware that she was having a good time. Her hair was sticking out all over, her skin devoid of makeup, her lips dry and cracked, and her pajama bottoms filthy. Regardless, she was laughing and having fun, far more than she'd been having at Stanford. She was sliding from side to side, returning every shot and either hitting the back of the table or dropping the ball right in front of the net where Alex couldn't retrieve it. She was winning and the group of onlookers was cheering her on.

As they began the third game, several young people entered the room. A young guy of about eighteen came up behind Alex and slapped him on the back, then let forth a frenetic giggle. He was on crutches and Shana couldn't take her eyes off him. Whoever he was, he was absolutely gorgeous. He reminded her of a young Brad Pitt. His hair was a golden blond, his skin smooth and tan. He was wearing shorts and his calves were solid muscle. She immediately thought of Michelangelo's *David*.

What Shana had really wanted to study was the arts. She was a right brain person, not left brain like her mother. For years, she had wanted to tell her mother that she hated the rigidity of the law, but the thought of disappointing her had stopped her. She'd certainly spilled her guts the night her mother brought her to Whitehall. It felt good to finally get it off her chest. Another reason she had stopped being close to her mother was that she'd never really loved Shana's father. He'd made a lot of mistakes in his life, but she'd never once doubted how much he loved her. And he didn't just love her, he had worshipped her.

Alex dropped the paddle on the table and flicked his ashes in a nearby ashtray. "David, my man," he said, turning his attention to the adolescent.

Shana was stunned, wondering if Alex had somehow read her mind. She knew the game was over, just as she'd known the boy's name was David. The unusual experience of *knowing* was over almost the second Alex diverted his attention. Her thoughts turned to the phone again. She had to get the quarter. "Alex, I need—"

"David, this is Shana."

The boy fixed her with lash-fringed blue eyes, a broad grin on his handsome face. Instead of speaking directly to Shana, David turned to Alex and started speaking rapid-fire. "Are you going to marry her? Are you? Are you? Tell me. Tell me. I think you're going to marry her."

Alex laughed and looked at Shana with an arched eyebrow as if to say, Don't forget where you are, looks can be deceiving.

More people joined them on the sofa. Those who couldn't get a seat stood as close as they could to Alex. Seated next to David was a redheaded woman who looked to be in her early to mid thirties. She was neither attractive nor unattractive and it was hard to tell why. Her hair was pretty, Shana thought, even though it was red like her own and she'd always wanted to be a blonde. With what appeared to be a natural curl, it fell just below her ears. Her eyes were green, her skin fair, and her nose and cheeks were sprinkled with freckles. As Shana watched, the woman's head jerked several times to the right and she made a strange noise almost like a bark from a small dog. The other patients acted as if they hadn't noticed, and the woman herself didn't miss a beat in the conversation.

Alex was joking with David, his arm draped around his neck.

"Are we going to play volleyball?" the woman asked. "It starts in five . . ." She turned her head and let forth the same bark. ". . . minutes."

"This is Karen," Alex said. "Karen, this is Shana. Karen has Tourette's syndrome. In case you've never heard of it, there's some information in the hospital library." He gazed at Karen with affection. "Shana hasn't told me why she's here, but I'm sure the truth will come out one of these days."

For some reason, no one seemed disturbed or embarrassed by Alex's recitation of their quirks and illnesses. Some of them appeared relieved that he'd cleared the air and left nothing to speculation. Shana assumed having a disease such as Tourette's placed Karen in a different category from most of the other patients. Suffering from a legitimate disease, even one as rare as Tourette's, was certainly easier than having to admit that you'd set yourself on fire like Norman.

She pondered the last portion of Alex's statement. What would the real truth turn out to be? Had her mother lied about her age so she could have her committed? It didn't make sense given that Lily was so determined that she graduate from law school. Morrow and the woman who dressed like a bank teller had to be at fault. They were the ones who insisted she was a drug addict and had sores all over her body.

Of course, the law allowed for a person to be held in a mental hospital for seventy-two hours if they were deemed to be a danger to themselves or to others. She'd shown her mother her hammer, so maybe she was afraid she'd smash someone's head in and they'd end up suing her.

Her thoughts were heavy with not only the names of the various individuals but their conditions as well. She did a mental exercise: Alex was or had been suicidal; May had landed here for some reason other than her outlandish nails and her psychic ability, so there was at least one mystery to unravel. As for Karen, Whitehall might be a safe haven from the insensitivities of the outside world. When Shana's attention turned to David, she drew a blank. Alex had said nothing about David.

Alex stood and within seconds, the entire group got up and followed him toward the doors located at the back of the room. Halfway across the room, he looked over his shoulder and saw Shana still seated on the sofa. He came back to fetch her. "Volleyball," he said, more of an announcement than an invitation.

"I can't play volleyball."

"Not this again," Alex told her, yanking her to her feet.

Shana glared at him and jerked her hand away. Who did he think he was—the cruise director of this ship of fools? This was a nuthouse, a place for lunatics. For all she knew, the man was dangerous.

The smile disappeared from Alex's face. "Suit yourself," he said. "The day will last forever if you just sit here and wallow in self-pity. Night follows day, in case you've forgotten. Tomorrow we'll have to start the whole process over."

"I'm going to get out," Shana told him, her lower lip extending in a pout. "My boyfriend is a lawyer. I'll just call him collect."

"Long-distance calls are blocked. The only calls you can make from that phone are local."

Brett was probably at Berkeley with his new girlfriend, so she could cross him off the list. She thought of Richard Fowler, her mother's old lover, but she had no idea whether he was still in Ventura.

Alex headed toward the door, where about ten of the patients were gathered, but it was locked and they all stood there as if they were waiting for a department store to open.

Shana glanced at the clock and saw it was only ten o'clock. Time was elongated in this place, she thought, stretched as thin as a rubber band. And there was nothing to snap a person back, to jerk her into some sense of urgency at the ticking clock. She looked around and saw other patients headed for the door. They were going outside. She might be able to escape.

Pushing herself off the sofa, Shana managed to join the group as a muscled man showed up and removed a key from a large ring attached to his belt. The group then trekked across an open courtyard to the gym. Shana's memory kicked in and she finally recognized the attendant. He was the ape from the first day, George, the guy who'd thrown her on the sofa and pulled her pants down when they'd given her the injection.

Shana surveyed Whitehall as they walked, seeing only a series of closed doors bearing the names of various businesses. Whitehall looked like a giant mansion from the front, but inside, it more closely resembled an office building. Falling behind the others, she started reaching out and turning knobs, finding them locked. From what she could tell, there was no way to get to the street other than through one of the offices. Just as she reached for another doorknob, an arm seized her around the waist and lifted her in the air.

"Put me down this instant." Shana tried to wrench away from George but he slung her over his shoulder, carrying her to the front of the line like a sack of cement. "Who do you think you are?" she shouted, beating on his back with her fists. George could obviously carry twice her weight without a problem. "I didn't do anything wrong. Please," Shana pleaded with the other patients. "Can't someone help me?"

Alex tentatively stepped forward. "George." His voice was low and controlled. "Why don't you put the lady down? She's a new kid. She didn't mean anything. Come on, just let her down and get the rest of the patients inside the gym."

As soon as George placed Shana on the sidewalk, she yanked the green pajama top down to cover her exposed abdomen. "Thanks," she told Alex. "What do they feed this guy, steroid sandwiches?"

"I wouldn't try the doors anymore if I were you," he said, his lips compressed into a thin line. "George used to be a boxer. His brain cells are scrambled. I don't think you're much of a match for him. Kind of know what I mean?"

Once they were finally inside the gym, George squatted on the floor to guard the door, massaging one of his muscular calves with a meaty paw. Shana cut a wide path around him but his eyes were trained straight ahead. She wasn't certain about him being a former boxer. She snuck a glance at his forehead, expecting to see a lobotomy scar. The man wasn't human.

Several young people arrived, making boisterous comments as they tried to impress one another. The game began. Shana stayed far in the back court and watched as David hobbled around on his crutches. He suddenly dropped one crutch on the floor and slammed the ball over the net. What was the deal with David and the crutches? For one thing, they were far too short. One foot was encased in a sock, yet she saw David put his full weight on it on several occasions.

Shana became caught up in the game. She moved over the court awkwardly yet she was thrilled to be actually playing a sport. After the rape, she had stopped playing softball and had lost all interest in athletics. She began jostling with her fellow players.

During a break, Shana sat down on the floor beside David. "What did you do to your foot?"

David's amazing eyes lost some of their luster. "I tore a ligament. Man, it hurts. Right now, the pain is a bitch."

"I'm sorry," Shana told him, stroking his hand. "Maybe you shouldn't be playing volleyball. I can adjust your crutches. They're supposed to fit under your armpits. The way they are now, you have to bend over to use them."

Without a word, David got up and hobbled away, waiting at the door alongside George. Alex sauntered over and leaned against the wall next to Shana. "What's up with David?" she asked.

"What's wrong with anyone?" Alex sighed. "Are you referring to his leg? It's called an affectation. David doesn't want to go home so every week he comes up with a new ailment. Last week, I think he tried to convince them he was going blind."

Shana was shocked. "You mean someone really wants to stay here?"

"There are worse places to be," he said, reaching over and tugging on a strand of her hair.

For reasons she couldn't understand, Shana felt a surge of energy, thinking Alex might have a point. Not being under constant pressure was making her feel like a new person. Why had she made such a big deal about Brett ending their relationship? He probably had no intention of marrying her. The whole thing was nothing more than a foolish fantasy.

Her father's murder and her previous stint in a mental hospital had set her back several years. Shana was pushing thirty and the majority of her friends were already married or engaged. Some even had families.

Shana had always wanted what she couldn't have, especially if it belonged to her mother. She remembered raiding her closet on a regular basis when she had more than enough clothes of her own. And the more upset her mother became, the more things she took. Many times she didn't even wear the clothes, and on occasion, she gave them to her friends. When her mother became furious, accusing Shana of stealing, her father countermanded her and told Shana that it wasn't stealing as long as she didn't take things from people outside the family. One of the reasons she'd always worshipped her father was he loved her regardless of what she did, whereas her mother was constantly trying to change her.

Brett had been dating another girl when she'd met him, which was probably why Shana had wanted him so badly. Then later, when he had replaced her with what she perceived as an inferior person, she'd completely lost it. Shana knew she wasn't a good person, but it wasn't that easy to change.

Surfacing from her thoughts, she looked around the room. Except for George, Morrow, and Peggy, most of the people seemed fairly pleasant. The patients might have their various problems, but in many ways, they seemed more tolerable than the people she associated with at Stanford.

A short time later, she realized Whitehall did more than isolate her from the outside world. It was as if it no longer existed.

She walked to the other side of the gym and tried to climb a rope ladder. Halfway up, the ladder began swinging and she became scared she would fall.

Alex was waiting as she climbed back down. When she was on the last rung of the ladder, he placed his hands around her waist and lifted her off. "Don't want to get hurt now, do you?"

Shana felt her sense of well-being evaporate. Twice in one day, this man had touched her. She knew better than to allow a stranger to place his hands on her, particularly in this environment. Had the drugs turned her mind to oatmeal? Here she was climbing ladders and playing games as if she was free to walk out the door anytime she wanted.

"You never answered me before," Shana said, a serious look on her face. "How do I get out of this place?"

"Well," Alex said, reaching for a cigarette and then realizing he couldn't smoke in the gym, "the first step is deciding what you're going to do when that day comes."

He turned and walked off, leaving Shana to mull over his statement.

# THIRTEEN

Mary was back at her desk in Quantico, digging through the stacks of files collected from the Connelly, Thomason, Madison, and Sherman cases. She had already tried to get in touch with Sheriff Mathis but with the three-hour time difference, he had yet to arrive at his office.

Genna Weir stuck her head in the doorway. "I called to see what you were up to this weekend but you never called me back. Was Brooks in town?"

"Not exactly," she said. "We met in Ventura. I wanted him to see my house."

"You mean the one you're going to turn into a nursing home?"

"It isn't going to be that way. Both of our parents are in good health. They just don't see as well as they used to, so we'd rather they not drive."

"I bet they love that."

"They don't drive now, Genna." She didn't know why Weir was always ragging on her about their plan. Both she and Brooks knew it might not work, yet it was worth a try.

"So what did lover boy think?"

"He thought the house was perfect. We ran into a homicide, though. I'm certain it's connected to those suspicious murders the chief asked me to profile. What I need to put it together is the autopsy and ballistics reports from Ventura. Unfortunately, there's no telling how long it will take to get my hands on them."

"Since you're leaving, Adams will probably dump all your cases in my lap. Shit, I'm up to my ears right now. How many other cases are you working?"

"Just these," Mary told her, glancing down at the paperwork spread out on her desk. "Just so you'll know, I'm not giving these cases up."

"How can you not give them up?" Weir argued, placing her hands on her hips. "You took a post in a Podunk town, girlfriend. We're talking about a serial killer who's already snuffed out four lives. Adams won't let you work that big of a case in Ventura, for Christ's sake."

"That's enough, Genna," Mary shot out, tired of her negativity. "I need to get back to work. You're distracting me."

Weir's face fell. "Don't be mad at me. I'm upset that you're leaving. You're the only friend I have around this dismal place."

"I know you wish the best for me. You just have a strange way of showing it." Mary smiled, then opened her drawer and pulled out a pack of gum, offering Weir a piece. "Why don't we go to lunch tomorrow? You know, just the two of us."

"I'd like that," Weir said, popping the gum in her mouth and disappearing down the corridor.

Mary went back to work. Although few were aware of it, she held a degree in biochemistry and had never contemplated becoming a police officer before her father's death. When the LAPD had exhausted all efforts to apprehend the shooter, she had resigned from her high-paying job with AMS Biotech to concentrate on bringing the man who killed her father to justice.

Since the fifth grade, Mary had spent several hours a day on the computer. She had later refined her skills to a professional level, thinking if she bombed out as a scientist, she could establish a career in the computer industry.

Her claim to fame was single-handedly tracking down the man who had murdered her father, achieving something the LAPD had failed to accomplish. And she'd done it without leaving the confines of her apartment. If a person knew how to work the back doors of the Internet, they could find almost anything and anyone.

Mary then decided to enter law enforcement in honor of her father. LAPD had been so impressed with her skills and determination that they had vigorously attempted to recruit her, but Mary had turned them down, preferring to affiliate with a smaller department where she felt there would be more opportunities for advancement and a reduced chance of getting killed. Ventura seemed to be the perfect community. She could indulge her love of the beach as well as her passion for running. She had broken records in the 440 in both high school and college. Ventura was a runner's paradise. It had cool ocean breezes and fresh air. What more could she want?

Once she joined the Ventura PD, she'd moved up through the ranks remarkably fast. After only three years in the field, she received her detective's shield and was assigned to homicide. Some officers went their entire career without making detective. She laughed, thinking about her former supervisor, Hank Sawyer. They were always squabbling about one thing or another. But they had fun, as much as anyone could in homicide. A year or so ago, she'd also befriended a superior court judge, Lily Forrester. Lily's path had crossed with a serial killer and she'd almost lost her life in a shootout.

Lily was an amazing woman. She and her young daughter had been raped at knifepoint by an Oxnard gangster back when she was still a prosecutor. Everyone and their dog knew about it, which Mary thought was sad.

The man who'd raped them had been raised in Oxnard. A sister city to Ventura, Oxnard had recently become a more attractive place to live, after battling a serious problem with violent crime for generations. The majority of the bad actors came from a Hispanic barrio called Colonia. The Oxnard PD had squeezed and squeezed until the area now only amounted to a handful of blocks. But it didn't take a large space to house a lot of gangsters. Since most gangs were formed in prisons today, Oxnard was unique in that respect. She'd talked to kids from Oxnard whose grandfathers were members of the same gang.

Pulling out the stacks of autopsy and ballistics reports on the four unsolved deaths, she began to meticulously examine them, hoping to find something she'd previously overlooked. Almost everything was available online these days, but scanning reports and documents were left to humans, and humans made mistakes. Also, when reviewing autopsy and ballistic reports that contained graphics, it was hard to see the complete picture on a computer screen.

The FSRTC, or, in plain English, the Bureau's $150 million–plus crime lab, had confirmed that the same weapon had been used in all four deaths. One of the programs they used was called Drugfire, a multimedia database imaging system that automated the comparison of images of bullet cartridge cases, shell casings, and bullets. The system was developed by a company called Mnemonic System Inc. (MSI), which allowed examiners from across the country to compare and link evidence obtained in the form of spent cartridges and other ammunition casings.

Drugfire was developed when the Bureau came under pressure to respond to the wave of gun violence gripping American cities during the crack-cocaine epidemic of the 1980s and early 1990s. They subcontracted with MSI to come up with a faster way of comparing and linking evidence from drug-related crimes across the country.

Mary was fascinated with the science of ballistics, and knew almost as much as the Bureau's experts. She knew that low-velocity bullets, such as those from handguns, did virtually all their damage by crushing. Cavitation was significant with projectiles traveling in excess of one thousand fps (feet per second). A permanent cavity is caused by the path of the bullet itself, whereas a temporary cavity is formed by continued forward acceleration of the medium, such as air or tissue in the wake of the bullet, causing the wound cavity to be stretched outward.

Then there were shock waves, which compressed the medium and traveled ahead of the bullet, as well as to the sides. But these waves lasted only a few microseconds and didn't cause profound destruction at low velocities. At high velocities, they generated shock waves that could reach up to two hundred atmospheres of pressure. Bone fracture from cavitation, however, was extremely rare.

The mathematics of wound ballistics worked well for bullets that were in good condition or technically referred to as "not deformed." To demonstrate tissue damage, materials with characteristics similar to the soft tissues and skin in humans was used. Pigskin, for instance, provided an external layer to blocks of compounds such as ordnance gelatin or ballistic soap. After firing bullets into these materials at various ranges, the ballistics technician would then examine them visually, what they referred to as cutting the block, or by use of CT imaging to determine the sizes and appearances of the cavity produced by the bullet.

Wounding was a complex situation involving variables of bullet size, velocity, shape, spin, distance from muzzle to target, and nature of tissue. These factors were interrelated, and the wounding potential was difficult to predict even under controlled test conditions. In an actual forensic case, few of the variables may be known so it's up to the medical examiner to determine what can be known from examination of the evidence.

With information on the wounds in the victim's body and at least one shell casing that wasn't deformed from the crime scene, the murder weapon could be identified. Then *Drugfire*'s enormous database of bullets and shell casings used in various crimes all over the country might even lead to the identification of the shooter himself.

The kink in this perfect scenario was the fact that handguns had an extremely long street life and could change hands a dozen times or more in any given year. The one break that had developed in this particular series of murders was the identification of the murder weapon: a 9mm Walther. For one thing, this particular gun was expensive. Depending on the accessories, a 9mm Walther could cost seven hundred dollars or more. A common criminal might have stolen a gun like this in a residential burglary, but this killer was anything but common.

The murder weapon could tell you a great deal about the shooter. Mary decided her UNSUB possessed both money and class, both of which could ultimately cause his downfall. The best way to get away with murder was to kill someone you didn't know with a gun that would quickly make its way into someone else's hands. This killer liked his gun, though. He liked it enough to kill four, possibly five people with it. Using the same gun showed confidence. His crime scenes were exceptionally tidy: no DNA, no fingerprints, no hairs, basically no evidence whatsoever. He shot his victims in the back of the head, which was the earmark of a coward, but he was not a coward. Mary wondered if he shot the victims in the back because he didn't want them to suffer. They were probably dead before they knew what hit them.

Concern for his victims denoted compassion, something Mary wasn't sure he possessed. Perhaps he'd developed his M.O. to keep the victims from screaming or calling for help, which would draw attention. She estimated he took no longer than five or ten minutes to kill the target, clean up the crime scene, and then flee.

On the other hand, the killings may have gone smoothly because the victims wanted to end their lives. They may have entered into some kind of suicide pact, maybe through a suicide club.

The problem Mary was anticipating was that the sheriff in Ventura might not use the Bureau's crime lab. Some law enforcement agencies relied on their own resources for a variety of reasons. Chain of evidence was of utmost concern, and there was always a possibility that something could go wrong during transit. Contamination was another issue, as was response time. Although the Bureau employed more than seven hundred highly trained forensic scientists and technicians, the demand for their resources was enormous.

As a homicide detective, Mary had been employed by the city of Ventura but the sheriff's office held jurisdiction over the entire county with a population of almost a million people. If things hadn't changed since she'd left Ventura, the sheriff's office relied on their own crime lab under most circumstances. But if the evidence required state of the art equipment, they would turn to the Bureau to process it. Another reason they might use the Bureau's lab was credibility. If the evidence was processed in the FBI's lab, not many defense attorneys would attempt to refute it.

If the SO decided to use their own lab, which she suspected they would, then Mary wouldn't be able to call the FSRTC and gain instant access to the reports and evidence collected in the Washburn homicide. She would have to make a formal request and wait. She didn't have time to wait, not when she was certain the killer would strike again within the next ten days, a pattern he'd established in the four earlier deaths.

She called John Adams and asked if he had time to see her. When he said he could give her a few minutes, she grabbed her files and rushed down the corridor to his office.

He shot her a dark look. "What do you want, traitor?"

Mary assumed he was joking but the look in his eyes said otherwise. She decided the best way to proceed was to ignore his comment. Taking a seat in front of his desk, she immediately began speaking. "Brooks and I went to Ventura this weekend to look for houses. While we were there, the SO discovered a body. The victim was a paraplegic."

"What does this have to do with us? I have a million things to do right now, and this time next week, I'll be short an agent." He held up a picture. "This is Special Agent Labinsky. He's allegedly bright but his eyes look dull, don't you think?"

"I hear he's fantastic."

"I hate it when you lie."

Mary quickly filled him in on the circumstances in Ventura. "This is a perfect fit to the cases I've been investigating. I even found a new will sewn inside the lining of the victim's jacket. I'm certain this wasn't a run-of-the-mill homicide, chief. The victim went up there knowing he was going to die."

Adams let out a long sigh. "I still don't understand what this has to do with this unit. What makes you think this homicide is connected to the others?"

"The victim was a paraplegic," Mary said, her voice louder than she had intended. "I can't believe you don't see the connection. I'm certain there are scores of people who would rather die than live the rest of their lives in a wheelchair hooked up to a catheter. That means we have a possible motive for suicide in a crime that occurred not far from the most recent killings. The victim also had a—"

Adams interrupted her. "You'll be in Ventura in a week. You'll have plenty of time to work on the 'Suicide Killer' case once you get there." He stopped and glanced at the wall of horror, as Mary called it, where crime scene photos of ongoing investigations were tacked up. "Our UNSUB in Chicago killed another child, a six-year-old boy. He grabbed him in a grocery store. The boy wandered over to the candy aisle without his mother noticing. It wasn't her fault. Her other kid, a four-year-old autistic, pitched a major tantrum."

Now she knew why he was in such a foul mood. He'd called her UNSUB the "Suicide Killer." She wanted to ask him if he'd given the case a name without realizing it or if the media had been responsible, but she knew this wasn't the time. "Is Chicago anywhere close to capturing this monster?"

"No."

"I'm sorry, chief, I know you're busy but I need you to make the sheriff see how important it is for him to cooperate with us in this investigation. The most recent crimes occurred in the San Francisco area. My guess is the UNSUB is working his way to Los Angeles. Once he gets there, we may never catch him. L.A. is not only heavily populated, it's spread out all over the place."

"What makes you think the UNSUB is still in the Ventura area?"

"Because he loves what he's doing," Mary said. "He'll kill again in the same general area. He likes to walk among the people, feel their fear and listen to them talking about the murders. This is the kind of killer that we'll end up arresting in a shopping mall or a grocery store. He probably drives a Volvo with a car seat in the back."

Adams's eyes came alive. "Does he steal it, do the murder, and then ditch it?"

"No, he owns it. He buys his cars on Craigslist and probably sells them when he's through with them."

"Interesting," Adams said, one corner of his mouth curling. "Get the sheriff on the phone and I'll talk to him. What's the name of the victim?"

"James Washburn." Mary stood to leave, wanting to get the ball rolling.

"Are you certain you love this guy? You know, Brooks."

"Of course," she said. "Why are you asking?"

"I had to jump through some pretty big hoops to get you assigned to this unit. You were born for this job, Stevens. This homicide in Ventura may turn out to have no connection whatsoever to the other crimes. You're excited now, but it isn't going to last. Someone with your talent doesn't belong in a field office, especially in a town like Ventura."

"We've already gone over this," she told him. "I know what I'm giving up. I love my husband very much. I waited a hell of a long time to marry the wrong man."

"Once I fill your position, you can't come back. You understand that, don't you?"

"Completely," Mary said, sad that she was leaving but eager to push ahead. She'd had a good life in Ventura before she had come to Quantico and she'd have an even better life with Brooks. "The sheriff's name is Earl Mathis."

"Don't leave," Adams said. "I'll see if I can get him on the line right now."

———

"Your daughter is very ill," Dr. Morrow told Lily. "If she refuses to speak to you, there's nothing I can do. That's a problem the two of you will have to resolve when she's released."

Lily was in her office during the afternoon break. She'd stayed awake all night, wondering if she had done the right thing by taking Shana to Whitehall. And Chris had made things worse, insisting that she move Shana to a hospital in the Ventura area where she could visit her and make certain she was receiving the right treatment.

As soon as she'd returned to her office that afternoon, she'd called Whitehall and asked to speak to her daughter, only to be told that Shana refused to take her call. She then demanded to speak to Shana's psychiatrist.

"I don't feel right having her so far away," she said. "I'm sure you take wonderful care of your patients but I'm in the process of checking out some local treatment facilities. As soon as I find something suitable, I intend to transfer my daughter."

"You're making a serious mistake," Morrow said, only a hint of annoyance in his voice. "I'm sorry if what I'm about to tell you seems rude, but you're jeopardizing your daughter's health for selfish reasons. When you should have spent time with Shana was before she developed an addiction to methamphetamine."

His words stung so deep, Lily momentarily stopped breathing. Of course she was at fault. Everything that had gone wrong in Shana's life was her fault. It had all begun that night at the Elephant Bar when she'd gone home with Richard Fowler. After that, it was like a stack of dominos collapsing. John found out and forced her to move out. He'd prepared for that day for years, turning Shana against her so that she would want to live with him instead of Lily. If John got custody, he knew he had a good chance of getting the house, and since Lily's income far surpassed his, she would also have to pay him child support.

When John refused to move out of the house, Lily had tried to rent a nice house, a place where she and Shana could begin a new life together.

"Ms. Forrester . . ."

Lily was holding the phone to her ear but she'd momentarily forgotten that Dr. Morrow was still on the line. "You don't understand. I have a demanding job and Shana doesn't feel safe in Ventura."

"Then why would you want to transfer her, particularly in her present condition?"

She knew she should tell him about the rapes, but something held her back. It wasn't just Morrow's remark about her spending time with Shana, which he'd said intentionally to hurt her and make her feel guilty. His tone of voice was condescending, and she was convinced that he was both manipulative and cunning. Even if he was sincerely concerned about Shana's well-being, she was nonetheless a commodity. Lily had no idea how much the hospital charged, yet she assumed it was a minimum of a thousand dollars per day. She reminded herself to call her insurance company as soon as she got off the phone.

"Your daughter has only been here since Friday, Ms. Forrester," Morrow told her. "She's not even fully detoxed yet. Withdrawal symptoms differ depending on how much and how often the drug was used. Users experience a wide range of problems . . . fatigue, disturbed periods of sleep, mental confusion, irritability, intense hunger, as well as moderate to severe depression."

He had changed his manner of speech, speaking slowly and softly. An intimate quality had seeped into their conversation, as if they had known each other for years. Lily began to relax.

"Psychotic reactions such as Shana experienced happen frequently. Many times users develop symptoms similar to paranoid schizophrenia. May I call you Lily?"

"Okay."

"Don't worry, Lily, these symptoms and behavior will go away once Shana completes our program. At the moment, I'm treating her with an antidepressant called Norpramin which affects serotonin, the neurotransmitter in the brain that deals with both depression and drug cravings, along with a sedative called Dalmane. We're also hydrating her with intravenous fluids. She's responding quite well, but we have a long way to go."

Lily realized it was time to return to the courtroom. "I guess you're right. Shana shouldn't be moved right now. I'd feel a lot better, though, if I could speak to her."

"Just give her some time." He started to conclude the call and then quickly added, "Please feel free to call me whenever you want to talk, or if you have any questions regarding Shana's care. Rest assured, I want your daughter to get well as much as you do. It breaks my heart to see the life of a young, intelligent woman like Shana torn apart by illicit drugs."

Lily eyes moistened with tears. "Thank you, Dr. Morrow."

"Call me Charles," he said. "Shana will be fine, Lily. Once she becomes more rational, I'll do my best to get her to call you."

Once she disconnected, Lily headed back to the courtroom, Morrow's conversation playing over in her mind. He was right. If she had spent more time with Shana, she might not have become involved with drugs. And Morrow sounded like an informed and caring professional. She wasn't certain why Chris had developed such a negative opinion of psychiatric hospitals, but she had to do what was best for Shana. For the time being, leaving her at Whitehall until she became stabilized on the medication seemed to be the most reasonable way to proceed.

# FOURTEEN

Back in the great room, Shana followed Alex and his entourage to the round table designated for smokers. She asked to borrow a quarter, and he pulled several out of his pocket and handed them to her.

"Thanks," she said, rushing over to the pay phone. She deposited her quarter and dialed Brett's number. A female answered and she quickly hung up. Damn him. She'd thought the Berkeley bimbo would be history by now.

Whatever drugs Dr. Morrow was feeding her had eradicated her memory. Desperate to talk to someone, she couldn't recall a single number. All her contacts were stored in her iPhone. No one memorized phone numbers anymore, she thought in an attempt to console herself. She placed her forehead against the wall, trying to bring forth her former roommate's cell number. Feeding another quarter into the phone, she punched in what she thought was her number and a Hispanic woman answered.

Shana returned to where Alex and the others were seated, feeling depressed and isolated. The dryness in her mouth from the drugs, along with the proximity to so many smokers, made her long for a cigarette. Alex didn't sit at the table. His modus operandi was to stand the way she had first seen him. Balancing on the balls of his feet, he would rock back and forth as people came up to him, chatting or asking questions.

"Can I have a puff?" Shana was standing next to Alex. He reeked of cigarette smoke, and instead of repulsing her, it made her long for a cigarette. For some reason, being near Alex gave her a sense of well-being, as if she could do whatever she wanted and nothing bad would come of it.

Alex reached inside his jeans and pulled out a pack of Marlboros, handing it to her. "Go ahead," he said. "I have a whole carton in my room."

"No," Shana said. "I just want a puff. I quit years ago."

"Suit yourself," he said, passing his cigarette to her. "Don't worry. I haven't had a herpes outbreak since last week."

"You're kidding, I hope."

"Yeah, I'm just messing with you."

As she drew in the smoke, she decided if they let people smoke, they should allow her to have her cell phone. She handed Alex the cigarette and headed for the nursing station, shuffling across the floor as fast as she could in her rubber thongs. Peggy was going over some paperwork. Shana waited until she looked up.

"I need my cell phone," she said, her voice shrill. "I can't remember my friends' numbers. I demand you return my property this minute. You had no right to take it from me."

"Well," the woman said, placing her hands on her ample hips, "I'm sure it's been taken care of properly. More than likely, we released your property to your next of kin for safekeeping."

"I don't have any next of kin," Shana said without thinking, covering her mouth in shame when she realized the implications of her statement. Even if she was furious with Lily for committing her, she was still her mother. "I demand to know where my property is, Peggy."

Peggy leaned forward, causing her balloon-sized breasts to squash against the counter. Shana thought any minute she would hear them hiss and pop from the strain. "We don't demand here,

Miss Fancy Pants. And we have plenty to do, so you can go right back where you came from and wait quietly until I have time to check your file." She ran her tongue over her lips and smiled. "It's almost medication time."

"Well, excuse me," Shana said, sucking in a deep breath. "I didn't realize medication time was the big event of the day. Does administering drugs require such a concerted effort that you can't glance at my chart and take maybe three minutes to tell me what happened to my property?"

Peggy let out a loud snort and returned to her task, lining up tiny paper cups across the counter. She then turned around and unlocked the medicine cabinet. Shana wondered how they kept from giving people the wrong drugs as there were no names on the cups. Returning to her position next to Alex, she quizzed him, "How do they keep the pills straight? Someone could pick up the wrong cup. With the type of stuff they give people, the wrongs meds could kill them."

"Follow me," Alex said, walking casually to the counter with Shana trailing behind him. "Peggy darling, I'll take my Prozac now." She smiled and handed him two cups, one with the pill and one with water. Shana had to step aside as the other patients lined up behind Alex, each asking for their medication by name and receiving the same treatment.

Shana grabbed the edge of Alex's jacket and pulled him aside. "My God, are the patients treating themselves? I don't even know what they're giving me. All I know is I don't want any more of it. I'm beginning to feel halfway normal. I mean, not normal . . ." She stopped speaking, placing her palm on her forehead. "If I don't go up there, will they come and force me?"

"Eventually," Alex answered. "First, they'll tell your shrink and he'll punish you by increasing the dose until you can't keep your eyes open. And that's the best-case scenario. The end result could be even worse."

Her eyes widened. "What could possibly be worse?"

"Take a look at poor Wanda over there." Alex tilted his head in the woman's direction. Wanda was sitting in a wheelchair with her head slumped to one side, a trickle of drool running down her chin. "Electric shock," Alex added. "Definitely, unequivocally worse. Get the picture?"

"Say no more." Shana took her place in line. Nice place, she thought facetiously. They probably did frontal lobotomies in the back room. There had to be a way to get out. This was the United States, for God's sake. People weren't confined to institutions without a legitimate cause. Actually, it wasn't easy to get any kind of treatment today. Tons of mentally ill people roamed the streets.

Snorting not once but twice, Peggy placed a pill in a cup and handed Shana another paper cup which she assumed contained water. She glared at Shana until she saw her place the pill in her mouth.

When Shana tried to swallow, she found only a drop of water in the cup. Peggy's mouth puckered in satisfaction. Shana faced her in defiance, tilting her head up and forcing the pill down. She then leaned over and pretended to gag, acting as if the pill had been as large as a golf ball. "Satisfied?" She opened her mouth and stuck her tongue out to show Peggy the pill wasn't still in her mouth. "Am I at least allowed to ask what type of medication I just took, or is that against the rules?"

"Valium."

"Valium?"

"Move aside, please," Peggy told her. "You're not the only patient in this hospital."

The situation was mind-boggling. Shana was incarcerated against her will so she could be treated with a drug as common as Valium. A regular doctor would give her a prescription for Valium in a heartbeat, and she was allegedly going through detox for a meth addiction. One of her friends at school popped Valium like candy, and she wasn't walking around in green pajamas with rubber thongs on her feet. Shit, she could buy Valium on the Internet. She had managed to get a decent night's sleep, though, so she reminded herself to get a prescription for the stuff in case she developed another bout of insomnia.

Her mother used to pop Valium. She even recalled Lily giving her one after they were assaulted. Such a mom, she thought, preparing her daughter for a lifetime of drug addiction. Lily should be in this place, not her.

If they were treating her only with Valium, Shana decided, then they must know that she wasn't going through meth withdrawal. She had assumed her diagnosis had been a mistake, that the hospital had confused her with another patient. Either that or her mother had reached the conclusion that she was on some type of stimulant because she had told her she wasn't sleeping. If the hospital knew the truth that she wasn't on drugs of any kind, other than an occasional hit of pot, then they must have intentionally manufactured her drug addiction in order to have a legitimate reason to commit her.

She pushed Norman aside, failing to notice that she'd touched his charred flesh and caused his little fan to topple onto the floor. He just smiled at her with what was left of his mouth. "I'm sorry," she told him, bending down and retrieving his fan. "I didn't hurt you, did I?"

"Not at all," he said. "Give them hell."

Shana flipped her hair to one side, thrust her chest out, and planted herself directly in front of the nursing station. "I demand to see the hospital administrator. Someone has to be legally responsible for what goes on inside this hospital."

This time Peggy did more than lean over the counter. She stood and the floor moved under her enormous weight. Then she did something unexpected; she stomped her feet like a spoiled child. Shana was sure she was going to summon George and have her carted off to the shock treatment room, but instead Peggy only said one word: "Lunch."

Shana's jaw dropped in surprise. For a moment, she was possessed with a wild interpretation of the woman's words—that

Peggy was going to have her for lunch. She had to get control over herself immediately. Using her tongue, she dislodged the Valium from the corner of her mouth and promptly swallowed it.

Eyeing the pay phone on the back wall, she decided it was time to cry uncle and call her mother. The problem was she couldn't call long distance, even collect. She had to either get her hands on her iPhone, or call Brett again. His parents had gone broke in the stock market crash and she'd been paying his tuition with the extra money she got from her mother. Whether he wanted to be with her or not, the asshole owed her some big favors.

Everyone was walking toward her in the direction of the double doors near the nursing station. Shana felt as if she was part of a school of minnows swimming upstream. It dawned on her that there would be no food trays now that she'd been released into the general population. Once the attendant walked them back from wherever they served lunch, the doors would be locked until dinner.

The people passing her were chatting and smiling. She was now faced with an actual decision for the first time since she'd been admitted. If she stayed and called Brett, she would miss lunch, no doubt one of the highlights of the day, right up there with medication time. She had barely touched food for the past three days and her body was weak from hunger. Besides, she didn't have any recourse. She couldn't handle the stress of calling Brett on an empty stomach.

Shana decided that she would rather remain at Whitehall than beg her mother to get her out. And she refused to call Brett, knowing his new girlfriend would probably answer the phone again.

Actually, the Whitehall thing might work out well for her. She would now have a reason for falling so far behind on her work, and Brett would be hit with a shitload of guilt once he found out he had caused her to have a nervous breakdown.

As she walked through the double doors to the outside courtyard, she saw Alex waiting for her beside a sycamore tree. He fell into step alongside her as they walked toward the cafeteria.

Alex's entourage selected a table, probably the same table they ate at every day. Then they all got in the food line.

"Regular little drones," Shana whispered to him.

He picked up both their trays, balancing them on one hand like a waiter. "Do you want me to get our drinks?" she asked, thinking it was the polite thing to do.

"I'll take some of that red stuff," he said, pointing to the fruit punch.

With two glasses in hand, Shana claimed the empty seat next to Alex. Were they already an item? She felt as if she was married to the man and she had only just met him. Shana stared out over the now familiar faces. What did she generally do in the morning? She went to her nine o'clock class and then came back to the apartment to study. In the same amount of time, she'd discovered an entirely new social scene.

Alex removed her plate from the tray and placed it in front of her. She set their fruit punch down and then returned for napkins. Norman was at the table, as well as Karen and May. The woman's nails were so long she had to hold her fork like a chopstick.

"May," Shana said, "will you do a reading for me sometime?" God, she thought, why did she say that? She didn't put much stock in the supernatural. Her environment was contagious.

"Sure, baby girl," May said. "Let me see your hand."

The woman started laughing, a wonderful sound like silver bells. Once Shana placed her slender hand in May's palm, she experienced a surge of energy, a distinct connection of some kind. Moving a few inches closer, she inhaled May's aroma and wondered if it was cologne. She smelled like apple cider, rich and delicious.

"I see a new man in your life, a dark man." May chuckled again and Shana's hand moved up and down. She quickly trapped it and held it like a tiny bird. "Not a black man . . . a dark-haired man . . . a prince of a man . . . a highly unusual man." May paused and stared out into space, her eyes glassy and fixed.

Shana thought it was a joke. She obviously meant Alex, but no one was laughing. Karen barked a few times but everyone else remained silent. May began rocking, moving her lips without speaking. When she finally said something, she appeared to be in a trance state.

"Woe is me." May spoke in a deep resonant voice. "Woe is me, child. You've gotten yourself into one fine mess. You want Della to make you a grilled cheese sandwich?"

Shana jerked her hand away and stood straight up, almost knocking her chair over. May seemed to snap out of it, gazing pleasantly over the table as if nothing strange had happened. She picked up her fork, loading it down with mashed potatoes.

"How did you know about Della?" Shana asked, her temper flaring. "You must have tricked me somehow." Then she remembered the grilled cheese sandwich. "I'm sorry, May. I'm only trying to assimilate what I just heard."

"I told you May was a psychic," Alex interjected. "What she really does is called channeling. You must have heard about people who channel spirits."

Shana dropped back into her chair, glancing warily at May. "Della was my grandmother's housekeeper. She's been dead for almost twenty years. I know because I went to her funeral. Whenever I went to stay at my grandmother's and got sick, Della always made me a grilled cheese sandwich." Not even her mother knew much about Della. The woman had been so different from Lily, so relaxed and folksy. She remembered asking Della if she could live with her one time when her parents had been fighting. "It was like Della was here, in this very room. You even spoke with her voice, May."

"Everything that ever was still is in the mind of God," May explained, the wisdom of the sages reflected in her eyes. "Don't you know that yet, baby girl? People die but they come back, just like flowers die, only to bloom again in the spring. Right now you may not be able to see this woman who spoke to you through me. She loves you, though, and she knows you're in trouble. One day you'll meet her again."

"Eat," Alex said in a firm voice. "That was the message. Eat your food. If you don't eat fast, it will be time to leave. You're thin enough."

Shana looked at Alex and then grabbed her fork and began shoving food into her mouth. She was traveling in uncharted territory, experiencing things beyond her comprehension. For the time being, the most logical way to proceed was to keep her mouth shut and go along with the program.

On the walk back from lunch, Shana fell in step behind the others, relishing the feel of the warm sun on her body. Inside the hospital, it was freezing. She had no idea what the temperature was, but she felt as if she were inside a meat locker.

May's performance at lunch had unnerved her. Shana had heard about people who could channel spirits, but she'd always assumed they were charlatans. To the best of her knowledge, there was no way on earth May could have known about Della. The fact that someone might have spoken to her from the grave was mind-boggling. Maybe May could channel her father. She felt the hairs prick on the back of her neck and hurried to catch up to the others. No matter how much she loved her father, some things were better left alone.

Inside the great room, she noticed Peggy was no longer at the nursing station. "Lee," she said in excitement. "Can you find out what happened to my stuff? I asked Peggy but she was too busy."

"Sure," Lee said with a kind smile. "Just give me a few minutes to go to the outside office and review your file."

David had returned and was jostling with Alex. "Where's Jimmy?" he asked, glancing around the room. "Did he go home?"

Alex didn't answer. May was engrossed in a novel and Karen was writing in a spiral notebook. Norman had moved to a grouping of people on the opposite side of the room. Milton, the "Walking Man," was asleep on one of the sofas.

Shana dropped down onto the nearest sofa, burying her head in her hands. A short time later, Alex appeared beside her.

"Want to talk about it?"

Shana didn't, but she knew she would. "I have to get out of here, Alex. I have things I have to do."

"Like scoring drugs?" he asked, reaching for a cigarette.

"I told you I don't use drugs. I've smoked pot every now and then, but that's it. I'm in Stanford Law. Before they tossed me in here, I was only a few months away from graduating. How could I possibly handle the work if I was strung out on drugs?" Shana's eyes drifted to the floor, ashamed that he thought she was an addict.

"Interesting," he said, glancing at the television. Some of the patients were watching a rerun of *Charmed*. "Let me ask you something. Do you have decent insurance?"

"Blue Cross."

"Then there's your answer," he told her. "There was a guy named Jimmy here. He called and cancelled his insurance and the hospital discharged him the next day."

Shana gazed out over the room. Alex's explanation seemed too simple. "The hospital can't get away with locking people up just so they can collect on their insurance. For some reason, my mother got it in her mind that I was involved with narcotics. Although I'm pissed she had me committed to this place, I can see how she thought something was wrong with me. I'd just broken up with my boyfriend, so I was going nuts over that, and I hadn't slept in almost a week."

"Now you think you belong here?"

"Maybe I do. I can't even think straight anymore."

Alex gave her a sympathetic look. "I'm not trying to upset you. I've been in this place for four months. How do you think I feel?"

"I'm sorry. I guess I'm being melodramatic. Whitehall isn't a prison."

"Amen to that one," he said, nodding as Karen walked by.

Shana knew Alex was attracted to her. She didn't know why and she didn't care. She was flooded with fuzzy memories of the first few days. "They gave me some type of medication. It caused me to have a severe reaction." She laced her hands through her hair and began pulling. When she let go, strands were wrapped around her fingers. "Now my hair's falling out. I wasn't eating right, either."

"They probably gave you Thorazine. It's a potent antipsychotic drug with some nasty side effects. People who aren't psychotic, which you obviously aren't, are known to have violent reactions. Was it a pill or a shot?"

"A pill, I think," Shana told him, scratching the side of her neck. "They also gave me a shot but I think the purpose was to stop the re-action I was having to the pill."

"The use of antipsychotic medication is highly restricted. Some of the side effects can be permanent. Unless you're under a court commitment, you have to sign a consent form before they can treat you with Thorazine. Did you sign anything?"

"I signed a piece of paper. I don't know what it said, though. I was so desperate to get out of the room where they were holding me, I would have signed my own death certificate."

Alex laughed. "And you're about to graduate from law school."

"Gee," Shana said, glaring at him. "I feel so much better now that you've pointed out what an idiot I am."

"Lighten up. Whatever you did, you did. You may have a case against the hospital. Ask to speak to the patients' rights advocate. Find out if you're here on a mandatory hold from your doctor, or if they conned you into signing yourself in as a voluntary commit-ment. You can demand a hearing. If you signed a voluntary, you can rescind it."

"Thanks, Alex. You're the first person who's told me anything worthwhile."

David walked over and flopped down in a chair, leaning his crutches against the wall. "You two should get married. Are you go-ing to marry her, Alex? You are, aren't you?" He turned to Shana. "Marry him, okay? He's a prince, man. That's what we call him, the Prince of Whitehall. Marry him and I'll come and live with you guys. You can be my parents. How cool would that be, huh?"

"What's wrong with your own parents?"

"They suck," he said. "They don't like my girlfriend. I'm never going back there. I'd rather die."

Alex's eyes narrowed. "Show Shana the picture of your girl-friend, David, the one you had taken at the prom."

David fished in his pocket and came up with a small snapshot. He stared at it for a while before passing it to Shana. In the photograph was an attractive blonde in a frilly pink party dress. She understood why David's parents might not approve of the girl. She looked like an underage prostitute. Although it was a full body pose, taken from some distance away, she could see the girl's face and it was layered with heavy, garish makeup.

"She's very pretty, David," Shana lied. "You make a great couple. You even resemble each other."

David snatched the photo out of her hands and shoved it back into his pocket. Then he seized his crutches, hobbling off toward the back door to return to the adolescent unit.

"Did I say something wrong?" Shana asked. "Why did he storm off like that?"

Alex stood, stretching his arms. "So you think David's girlfriend resembles him? Can you figure out why his parents don't like her?"

"For one thing, she wears too much makeup. And her hair looks strange, almost like a wig. Young girls don't generally wear their hair in such a stiff style."

"Maybe it was a wig."

As Shana thought about the image in the photograph, she real-ized something else that was wrong. Along with the heavy makeup and artificial hair, the girl's knees and thick calves were too mascu-line. "It was David, wasn't it?" she said, her eyes widening. "That was David in the picture dressed up like a girl. Tell me, Alex, am I right?"

"Think you hit the nail on the head."

"How sad," Shana said. "But cross-dressing isn't considered a mental illness. Why is David here?"

A middle-aged man in a brown linen jacket walked up to the

nursing station and Lee handed him a file. "My shrink," Alex said. "I'd like to hear more about you later."

"You should tell me about yourself the next time we talk."

"I doubt if you'd be interested."

"Try me," Shana said playfully.

Alex smiled. "Be careful what you say. You're the best-looking girl in this place. Some of the guys would be more than willing to give you a try, myself included."

Shana swallowed hard, staring at Alex's back as he walked away. Far more dangers lurked inside Whitehall than she had imagined.

# FIFTEEN

"Charles," Dr. Phillip Patterson said, "I need to talk to you."

Morrow was in the isolation section in front of the nursing station. He reached over to retrieve a chart. "Make it quick, Phil. I'm late for an appointment."

"Look, I don't mind covering for you on some of your little schemes," Patterson told him, "but this last referral falls outside the scope of our agreement."

Morrow dropped the file on the counter and faced him, adjusting the frames of his glasses. "In what way?"

"There's something going on that I don't like," the other psychiatrist stated. "I can't quite put my finger on it, but under the circumstances, it's frightening."

Morrow stared at him without speaking. Then he looked over his shoulder and saw Peggy sitting a few feet away. "Don't even think what you're about to say," he whispered tersely. "I explained everything to you. Just go through the motions." He dropped his hand to his side and rubbed two fingers together where Peggy couldn't see. "Not only bucks, buddy, but power. Play the game. That's all I'm asking of you." His mouth opened slightly, exposing his large teeth.

"You've got more than a few shares in this hospital if I'm not mistaken."

"Sure, I've got stock but that's not the issue," Patterson told him. "I do have some ethics left." He looked down at the floor in shame. "Not many, I admit. But I refuse to compromise any more than I already have." Looking up, he waited until Peggy went to attend to a patient before he continued. "In the time I've been working with this particular patient, I've noticed some disturbing things. Is there something you're not telling me?"

Morrow gritted his teeth, the words hissing their way through the cracks. "I don't know shit, okay? And you don't know shit. Sign the orders. Give him whatever he wants. No one asked you to actually treat him. For all I care, you can play tick-tack-toe with the man. Just make sure you see him every day so we'll have it on record."

Patterson shifted his feet around. "I'd feel more comfortable if you handled this one yourself, Charles."

"But why?" Morrow protested, gesturing with his hands. "Is your caseload so heavy that you can't handle this one patient for me? You're getting paid for your time, so what's the problem?"

The other doctor shook his head in dismay. "I wish I knew. Believe me, I wish I knew."

"Forget it," Morrow snapped. He started to walk away and then halted. "Have you forgotten that I'm on the board? Would you like it if I recommend that your privileges at this facility be revoked?"

"You're the biggest prick I've ever met," Patterson exploded, poking his finger into Morrow's chest. "I want it on record that I'm not responsible. I'll play your dirty little game for now, but if your guy steps out of line, I'm going straight to the authorities. You know what you're doing, Charles. You're letting outsiders take control of this hospital, and you're doing it for one reason only, greed."

Morrow tossed his mane of shaggy hair. A longtime astrology buff, he said, "You have a Scorpio moon, right?" He removed his glasses and wiped them with a white handkerchief. "I looked at your chart last night. The next two weeks are going to bring something significant into your life."

"You know," Patterson said, more disgusted now than angry, "sometimes I wonder who the patients are around here."

"The State calls Amber Susan Willis," Clinton Silverstein said, standing behind the counsel table.

Lily watched as a slender young woman approached the witness box. She had jet-black hair and her arms were covered with tattoos. As soon as she was sworn in, Silverstein began to question her.

"Do you know the defendant in this case, Noelle Reynolds?"

"Yes."

"Can you point her out for the court?"

She pointed at Reynolds, who was seated beside Richard Fowler. Reynolds had a blank, detached look on her face. Lily had read in the jail report that she had requested to be placed on antidepressants and the jail physician had complied. Lily didn't believe in medicating a defendant until their crime had been adjudicated. Noelle Reynolds looked as if she was a million miles away. Why didn't they just let the prisoners shoot up with heroin? Lily reminded herself to order the jail to take Reynolds off the medication. A woman who had murdered her child should be alert enough to hear the nails being driven into her coffin.

"And Ms. Reynolds is a friend of yours? Is that correct?"

"I don't know if I'd call it a friendship. She went to some of the same clubs I did. We gave each other rides now and then. That's all there was to it."

Silverstein flipped through some papers, finally finding the one he was looking for. "Were you with the defendant on the morning of May fourth, between the hours of midnight and two in the morning?"

"Yeah, I told you I was."

"And this was one of the nights Noelle Reynolds gave you a ride, correct?"

"Yes."

"Did you have your car that night or did you take Noelle's car?"

"Excuse me," the girl said, her voice laced with sarcasm. "You asked me if she gave me a ride, didn't you? Why would I need a ride if I had my car?"

Silverstein nervously ran his hands through his hair. "On the date in question, did the defendant, Noelle Reynolds, give you a ride in her Ford Taurus?"

"Yes."

"And did you hear anything unusual while you were inside Ms. Reynolds's vehicle?"

"I heard noises coming from somewhere inside the car."

"What kind of noises?"

"Sort of a knocking sound," Willis stated. "I also thought I heard a kid crying, but Noelle told me it was the radio."

"And did Ms. Reynolds stop the car to see where this knocking sound was coming from?"

"No."

"Had Ms. Reynolds been drinking?"

"Sure."

"Do you know if she had used any type of narcotics earlier in the evening?"

"I know she liked coke, but I don't know if she used it that night. She seemed pretty drunk when I got into the car, but when I mentioned the knocking sounds, she sobered up right away."

"Where was Ms. Reynolds taking you?"

"To another club called Swans."

"How far away was Swans located from the club you were at previously?"

"About five miles."

"Did Ms. Reynolds stop during this trip?"

"Yeah, she stopped at Domino's to get a pizza."

"What did she do after she purchased the pizza?"

"She offered me a piece, but I told her I didn't want any. I was trying to watch my weight."

"And what happened after that?"

"Noelle took the pizza and put it in the trunk. I thought it was

odd because she didn't eat any, and I told her it would spoil in the
trunk because it was so hot that night."

Silverstein paused, taking a deep breath before continuing. The
jurors were sitting in rapt attention. "Did Ms. Reynolds take anything else other than the pizza with her when she stepped outside
to open the trunk?"

"Yeah," Amber Willis said. "She took her purse. I resented
Noelle's thinking that I might steal something from her. I don't steal,
you know. I didn't make a big deal about the purse thing because I
wanted to get to Swans. I dance there three nights a week."

"Once Ms. Reynolds went to the trunk and returned, did you
hear any more knocking noises?"

"No," she said, staring at a spot over his head. "The knocking
noises stopped."

"No further questions, Your Honor."


George and Peggy came walking toward Shana as she was flipping
through the pages of a year-old *People* magazine. She glanced behind
her, thinking there was a problem with one of the other patients.
When she turned back around, George and Peggy had taken up a
position on either side of her. George grabbed one arm and Peggy
seized Shana by the other.

Peggy spoke first. "Come with us, Shana. It's time for your medication."

"But I already took my pill," Shana told them. "You gave it to me
yourself, Peggy. You even saw me swallow it." She tried to wrench
away from them. She even tried several self-defense moves she had
learned, such as jerking her arm downward against their open fingers
to release their grip. These people were pros, though. They seized her
underneath her arms and lifted her off her feet.

"Dr. Morrow ordered an injection," Peggy said. "Give us any
trouble and we'll put you in a straitjacket."

Shana felt Peggy's fingernails digging into the soft tissue under
her arm, certain the woman was purposely hurting her. George

made eye contact for the first time. "Just come along now," he said. "You're making things worse by resisting."

"I demand to see the patients' rights advocate!" Shana shouted, trying to recall what Alex had told her. "I rescind my voluntary admission. I'm going to call the police, the district attorney, even the governor. Do you hear me? I demand a hearing! The state will launch an investigation into this entire operation. All of you will be brought up on charges."

Peggy snorted and dug her fingernails even deeper into Shana's armpits. "Demands, that's all we hear from you." She inhaled deeply and then glared at George. "Take care of her, will you? I'm fed up with this one."

As a small group of patients stood around and watched, George tossed Shana over his shoulder and carried her from the great room into the isolation ward. He entered a room and deposited her on her stomach on the bed, holding her down while Peggy yanked her pants down and jabbed a needle into her buttocks.

Once she had removed the needle, Peggy slapped Shana's bare backside with tremendous force, the blow loud enough to be heard in the adjacent room. "Since you've been nothing but a pain in the ass since the day you arrived, I decided it was high time I show you what a pain in the ass feels like." She paused and snickered. "Right, George? We've had plenty of rich girls in here. We know how to handle their demands."

Shana's vision blurred and her arms turned into rubber. George released her but she couldn't move and remained facedown on the bed, her green pajama bottoms around her ankles, the bottom half of her body fully exposed.

"You shouldn't have done that, Peggy," George said in a hushed tone. "You know we're not supposed to strike the patients."

"Oh yeah," Peggy said, shoving her chin out in defiance. "You try working with these people for fifteen years. This girl needed a spanking, so I gave it to her. Now maybe she'll think twice before she causes trouble."

Shana could hear their voices, yet she was once again in a magnified and terrifying nightmare. Every sound seemed as if it was coming out over loudspeakers. George was still arguing with Peggy.

"I'm not supposed to be in the room when you expose a female patient. Why didn't you call Lee or one of the other female attendants? You're going to get us all fired."

All Peggy said was "yeah, yeah, yeah," and then both of them moved out of earshot.

Shana pushed her face up from the bed and groped for the green pajama bottoms in a pathetic attempt to cover herself. Her knees suddenly slid out from under her, and she landed with a thud on the linoleum floor. In seconds, she was unconscious.

Charles Morrow moved out of the lights from the hospital into the dimly lit parking lot. Thinking he heard something behind him, he stopped and listened. Satisfied it was nothing, he continued on to his silver Mercedes.

A man suddenly grabbed him from behind and spun him around, shoving him against the car door. The psychiatrist's breath left his body. A few moments later, the man's face came into focus. "Good lord, it's you. You scared me to death." The man was looming over him. Morrow pushed him away and adjusted his jacket.

"I told you what I wanted," the man said. "You fucked everything up."

"It was a mistake," Morrow said in his high-pitched voice. "Everything's taken care of now."

"There have been too many mistakes. I don't like it, not at all. Do you hear me?"

"Calm down," Morrow told him. "We're accommodating your needs. I can't believe you're complaining about something so trivial."

"Trivial, Morrow? I don't consider anything trivial."

"Fine," the psychiatrist said, deactivating the alarm on his Mercedes. "Enjoy your evening." A strong arm reached in front of him. "What the hell . . ."

"We had an agreement, a mutually beneficial agreement. You're not honoring that agreement. As of today, you're in breach of contract."

"Don't be absurd," Morrow said, his slender body trembling. "Get away from my car. I'm going home."

The man stood there, his feet frozen in one spot. "No," he erupted. "Not again." Darting through an opening in the shrubbery, he made his way down a dirt path leading to another parking lot adjacent to the hospital. When he spotted his car, he reached into his pocket for his keys but they weren't there. He searched his other pocket and still came up empty-handed. Sucking air into his lungs until they were about to burst, he wailed, "No! No! No!"

He began slamming his fist into the window until the heavy glass finally shattered. There was no pain. He didn't feel pain, not physical pain. He wiped his bloody hand on his jeans, then reached inside and opened the car door.

Once inside, he began pulling wires leading to the ignition. Perspiration sprang from every pore. He struggled as he tried to put the two wires together. He didn't have enough light to see what he was doing.

His body stiffened as if he was having a seizure. In an explosion of rage, he kicked the passenger window out as well.

Finally he lay spent, the tempest over.

He imagined himself diving into an azure pool of cool water. On the other side of the water was paradise. Getting out of the car, he headed back up the path. He had to find a way to make it to the other side. At least he was moving closer. This time, nothing was going to stop him.

Chris was driving Lily's white Volvo home from their dinner at a P.F. Chang's, their favorite Chinese restaurant. "How's the trial going?"

"Pretty routine right now," she said, glad he was talking about something other than Shana. Outside of the law, she had never perceived him as highly opinionated. The night before, he'd proved her wrong, arguing with her for hours and insisting that she take

Shana out of Whitehall immediately. He believed all mental hospitals were only interested in making money, and that they'd claim a mule was a drug addict as long as it had adequate insurance.

Whitehall was a fully accredited hospital and after hours researching it on the Internet, she'd failed to come up with even a whiff of impropriety. Even former patients spoke highly about their time at Whitehall.

"Has the medical examiner testified yet?"

"No," Lily told him. "The defense finished their opening statement. Silverstein only just started calling witnesses. The employee of the Oxnard sewage treatment plant who discovered the body testified this afternoon. The killer bagged the boy three times but he was in the water for several months, so there wasn't a lot left of him." She turned to look at him. "He was such an adorable little boy, Chris. How could a mother do such an unspeakable thing to her child? Even the grandfather is at fault. He was a doctor, for God's sake. He knew his daughter was abusing the boy when he took him to the hospital after she fed him Ajax. If he'd contacted the authorities then, the boy might still be alive."

"A lot of kids get into cleaning products and other toxic things people keep in their homes. The grandfather must have assumed it was an accident. How could he have known his daughter did it intentionally?"

"Have you ever tasted Ajax?" Lily asked him. "Kids usually get a taste of it and spit it out. It's extremely caustic and burns like hell. This kid had a substantial amount in his system. The mother must have mixed it with ice cream or something that took the burning sensation away."

"Why didn't the doctor who examined him in the ER report it to the authorities? They're required by law to report any possible case of child abuse."

"The doctor is scheduled to testify so I guess we'll find out."

He steered the Volvo into the driveway and hit the button for the garage door opener. "What are you going to do about Shana?"

Here we go again, Lily thought. "I checked some things out today.

You know I can't take Shana out, Chris. She admitted herself. At the moment, she isn't even taking my calls. If I showed up there, it would be a waste of time. I'm certain she wouldn't see me. I know she's mad at me for tricking her into going to the hospital, but maybe she's also ashamed." She'd tried to speak to Shana again after her last session in court and the receptionist at Whitehall told her the same thing as before. "I did speak to her psychiatrist, Dr. Morrow, and he said it would be a mistake to move her right now."

"The bastard doesn't want to lose his cash cow."

Chris got out of the car and slammed the door. Lily jumped back, startled by the loud noise. She was still trying to accept that Shana had been involved with narcotics and instead of supporting her, Chris was beating her up and making her feel like she was a bad mother. His behavior reminded her of John. She didn't understand what was wrong with him. This was a side of him she had never seen before. He was the optimistic one, the rock, never failing to reassure her. His uplifting personality, easygoing temperament, and genuine compassion for others were the reasons why she had fallen in love with him.

The interior of the car was beginning to cool down. She had expected Chris to come back to get her, but he had walked straight into the house without even a backward glance.

She got out and went inside. Chris was on the sofa staring at the framed pictures of his deceased wife and daughter, Sherry and Emily. His daughter was six at the time she and her mother were killed in a head-on collision with a semi truck approximately four years ago.

When Chris had first received the heartbreaking news, he had blamed the driver of the truck and fantasized about killing him. After the highway patrol examined the skid marks at the scene, they determined that the truck driver had not been responsible. Sherry had drifted into oncoming traffic and must not have seen the semi until it was too late. The officers who had investigated the accident said Sherry's vehicle hadn't left skid marks, which meant she had made no attempt to brake. The driver of the semi had been tired, the roads wet, and the tires on the truck had been low on tread. The investigators believed he'd done his best to avert a collision.

What Chris said had gotten to him the most was that he'd lost his wife and daughter in an "accident." They weren't killed by a murderer, or an act of God such as a hurricane or an earthquake. All it had been was a lousy traffic accident.

Lily tried to sneak down the hall to the bedroom, not wanting to bother him. He saw her, though, and began speaking. "I'm going to take the pictures down, Lily. I can't thank you enough for letting me keep them here so long. This is your house and . . ." He choked up and stopped speaking, then stood and went to the bar, pouring a shot glass full of Jim Beam. "Can I make you a drink?"

Lily took a seat on the sofa. "No thanks," she said, placing a pillow behind her back. Every day the pain got worse. She had put off having surgery, but she knew she couldn't last much longer. Her doctor kept offering her narcotics to help her cope with the pain, but Lily had steadfastly refused. Judges couldn't perform their duties unless they were mentally alert. People's lives were at stake.

"Don't take the pictures down, Chris. Sherry and Emily are your family. Why would you ever think I resented them? I've grown accustomed to the pictures. They're like my own family now. And Emily is such a beautiful girl. I enjoy looking at her smiling face in the morning while I'm having my coffee. Sherry looks like a wonderful person as well, but Emily looks remarkably like you. It gives me an idea of what you must have looked like when you were a child."

He left the shot glass on the bar and rushed over to embrace her. Lily felt a powerful burst of energy rushing through her body. She didn't need pain pills as long as she had Chris. Whenever he touched her, her pain instantly abated. She decided the greatest pain reliever was love.

People at the courthouse said they felt the same way, though. Just being in close proximity to Christopher Rendell lifted a person's spirits and took away their fears. Lily assumed it was because he was such a deeply religious man. When she found out he'd disassociated himself from the Mormon Church, she was confused. But even if he was no longer involved with a specific religion, he still believed wholeheartedly in the existence of God and the basic principles of Christianity. Besides, it was the way a person lived their life that mattered.

Lily asked herself if she was responsible for his present negativity. Maybe Chris didn't belong with a sinner like herself. She had not only killed a man, she had committed adultery. A sin was still a sin regardless of what someone did to you.

"You're a wonderful person, Lily. Forgive me for telling you what to do about Shana. She's your daughter and I have no right to interfere."

"You have a right to express your opinion," Lily told him, tilting her head to one side. "Shana is going to be your stepdaughter. That is, if you still want to marry me."

He pulled her even closer, his large hands entwined in her hair. "Of course I want to marry you. I'm madly in love with you. The mere thought of spending my life without you is intolerable." He paused, thinking. "I can't believe you don't know how beautiful you are, Lily. And you're beautiful both inside and out. I can't think of any man who wouldn't want to be with you. You've got a super body, great breasts, and incredibly long legs. And your eyes . . ." He held her away so he could look at her. "They're such an intense shade of blue, I can get lost in them for hours."

"Ah," she said, trying to lighten up both of their moods, "now I know the truth. You only want me for my body."

"You know that's not true. I was just trying to point out some of your better attributes. You don't see what other people do when you look in the mirror. You don't even think you're attractive."

Lily smiled. "I'm kidding, okay? You're a smooth operator. You're just flattering me so you can get in my pants. It's working. Want to go to the bedroom and have some fun?"

Chris folded his hands in his lap. "I haven't been fair, Lily. I should have told you why I don't trust mental hospitals."

"Most people despise mental hospitals, Chris, but I guess they have a place in society."

"You don't understand," he said, becoming agitated. "Sherry started acting strange about six months before the accident. I know how it sounds, but she believed everyone was a demon, even the man who did our dry cleaning and the nice lady who worked at the post office. We were both heavily involved in the church back then, but Sherry had taken it upon herself to convert every person in Salt Lake City."

"That must have been a short list."

"Not everyone in the state of Utah is Mormon, Lily, contrary to what most people believe. Sherry never thought people were demons before just because they weren't interested in what she had to say about Joseph Smith and the LDS church. I became concerned. Then when she accused Emily's teacher of being a demon, I knew something was seriously wrong with her. Just like you did with Shana, I decided it wasn't physical and took her to a mental hospital. We weren't allowed to make decisions like that without first conferring with the church elders, but I felt it was urgent that Sherry got help. This is probably when my disillusionment with the church began. In reality, they would have told me to take her to a family physician before resorting to a psychiatrist, which is precisely what I should have done."

"You did what you thought was best," Lily said, staring at a spot on the wall across from them. "With Shana, I didn't know what else to do. I couldn't leave her there alone, and I couldn't force her into coming home where I could help her. I still feel awful, though. I'm scared I may have permanently destroyed my relationship with my daughter."

"I understand, Lily," he said, patting her knee. "I'm sure everything will work out between you and Shana. You went through that awful ordeal with her. How can you break a bond like that?"

"It was a complex situation, Chris. In fact, I have to tell you . . ."

He wasn't listening. He had never talked much about his marriage before the accident, so she knew it was important for him.

She was determined to tell him what she had done, though, even if they had to stay up all night.

"As for me," Chris continued, "I didn't agree with the church's position on psychiatry. They believed a psychiatrist would try to steal Sherry away from the church. The church was the last thing on my mind. My wife was demonizing the entire community. I was afraid someone would burn our house down."

Leaving Lily on the sofa, he went over and tossed down the rest of his Jim Beam, then returned and sat down beside her again. "Sorry, but I get upset when I talk about this. That's not true actually because I've never discussed this with anyone before tonight." He glanced at her and then quickly turned away. "Where was I?"

"You were telling me about taking Sherry to a psychiatrist."

"Right, well, it was a private hospital like Whitehall and they committed Sherry on the spot. She remained in the hospital for three months and endured fifty electric shock treatments."

"My God!" Lily exclaimed. "Wouldn't that fry her brain?"

"Not exactly," he told her, the muscles around his mouth tightening. "Sherry was released the day after her mental health benefits ran out. When I picked her up, she looked like a concentration camp victim. She couldn't have weighed more than eighty pounds. She couldn't think straight. She couldn't do anything around the house. She acted as if she didn't even remember Emily. My daughter was shattered. And then Sherry started screaming all the time for no apparent reason. I didn't find out the truth until the medical examiner told me the results of the autopsy." His hands closed into fists. "Sherry had terminal cancer, Lily. It had started in her breast and metastasized to her brain. My doctor felt certain she could have been cured if the cancer had been discovered earlier. Of course, that didn't happen. She would have died even if she'd never had the accident, but Emily might still be alive."

"I'm so sorry," Lily said, clasping his hand. "It wasn't your fault, Chris. You didn't know she was sick. But didn't the hospital try to rule out something physical before they started giving her shock treatments?"

He placed his hands over his ears. "She was screaming in pain. In my nightmares, I can still hear her screaming. The cancer had spread throughout her body. The worst part is that when she left to go to her mother's with Emily, she wasn't going on a vacation. She blamed me for committing her and wanted a divorce. If the accident with the semi hadn't happened, Sherry could have run into a car full of innocent people. In her condition, she wasn't fit to drive."

"The hospital didn't keep tabs on her health?"

"No," he said, outrage shooting from his eyes. "All they did was pump her full of drugs and give her shock treatments." He rubbed his hands over his face. "My wife hated me when she died. And I'll never know how Emily felt about me or what she went through on that road trip. Now you know why I don't trust psychiatric hospitals."

Lily's love for him had instantly intensified. He had opened up and shared a terrible tragedy with her, and it had brought them even closer. She reached over and pulled his head onto her shoulder, cradling him like a child. "You didn't know, honey. Under the circumstances, anyone would have done the same thing. Sherry didn't hate you. She was sick. And Emily was a child. You know God never fails to protect His children. When they die, they're snatched straight up to Heaven. Emily's spirit probably left long before the accident."

Chris began to sob. They weren't tears of sadness but tears of relief. "You're the most amazing woman I've ever known, Lily. You understand things most people can't begin to conceive."

"I don't know about that," Lily said. "But I do know how much I love you."

While he remained on the sofa, Lily tried to get up but the pain in her back was crippling and sharp pains were shooting down her legs, making it hard for her to stand, let alone walk. She staggered to the bathroom, using the walls to keep her upright.

When she reached the medicine cabinet, she popped two Vicodin into her mouth and chewed them. The pills were meant to be swallowed, but she desperately needed the medication. She heard the coffeepot beeping, took several deep breaths, and headed for the kitchen.

Chris was standing on the balcony. He loved looking out over the ocean. The chairs out there weren't that comfortable, so she took a seat on the sofa and waited for him to come back inside.

A few minutes later, he came in and poured them both a cup of coffee. "You're in pain tonight, aren't you?"

"Just a little," Lily told him, sorry that he had noticed. "I'm fine."

"Come to bed and I'll give you a back rub."

"I think I'll stay here awhile longer."

He leaned over and swept her up in his arms, carrying her to the bedroom. "It's stress. You have no idea what stress can do to your body." He put her down on the bed and began undressing her. "I have a perfect cure," he said, "and you don't have to do anything but lay there."

When he buried his head between her legs, Lily sighed in pleasure. "You're right," she said, laughing. "I'm feeling better already."

# SIXTEEN

Shana was in the same position on the floor, her pants wrapped around her ankles. When she opened her eyes, she saw by the clock on the wall that it was almost time for dinner. Since the only thing separating the isolation ward from the great room was the waist-high nursing station, the patients who were beginning to gather for the walk to the cafeteria were able to see her. When she tried to stand, she realized she had injured her leg somehow. The pain was excruciating, but she finally managed to pull up her filthy pajama bottoms.

Limping toward the nursing station, Shana waited with downcast eyes for George to remove his keys and to unlock the door leading to the great room. She possessed an overwhelming urge to take her uninjured leg and kick the burly attendant in the balls. Images of poor Wanda and the shock treatment room flashed in her mind and she decided not to follow through and walked past him.

Dr. Morrow and his band of accomplices had their own private S&M palace, complete with all the necessary tools to torture and drug their victims into submission. The most disturbing element was the fact that they could get away with it by claiming they were administering medical treatment for the well-being of the patient.

Not long after she and her mother were raped, Shana had undergone training in self-defense. Even so, she knew she was no match for George and Peggy. She asked herself what kinds of skills patients like Wanda possessed, or the dozens of elderly men and women she'd observed sitting around in wheelchairs staring blankly into space. These poor people had no way to defend themselves against the blatant abuse that went on inside Whitehall. And she couldn't discount the various alcohol- or drug-addicted patients who appeared either overmedicated or as if they'd also been administered shock treatments.

Even though her mind was clouded by the injection, Shana suddenly saw beyond her own situation. An attorney could sometimes do more than a police officer or a prosecutor. In the O. J. Simpson case, for example, after the courts had failed to convict him, it was the civil case that had finally given the victims' loved ones a smidgen of justice. Granted, it wasn't a death sentence or life in prison without parole, but it was better than nothing.

Shana had fallen into a snake pit but once she crawled out, she would find a way to put Whitehall out of business. Before she could accomplish anything, she first had to graduate from law school and pass the bar.

While the other patients were at dinner, Shana saw a large-boned woman standing at the nursing counter, dressed in an expensive two-piece blue suit with a floral silk scarf tucked in around her neckline. Her hair was dark and loose curls framed her face. Behind her glasses, her shadowed eyes resembled round black buttons with only a small rim of white around them. The pupils were almost totally dilated. Shana shuffled in her direction. "Hi," she said, her words slurred from the drugs. "What's . . . your name?"

"Dr. Ruth Hopkins," the woman answered, tilting her head to one side. "I'm about to see a patient so I don't have time to speak to you right now."

She started to leave when Shana stopped her. "Are you a doctor here?" She studied her face as she attempted to place her. Swaying from side to side, she squeezed the woman's hand to steady herself. "You sure your name is Hopkins? That was dumb. Of course you know your own name. I'm drugged out so just ignore me."

"Let go of my hand, young lady, or I'll have to call an attendant."

In addition to her pupils being dilated, something was strange about this woman. Shana felt it in her gut. She refused to let go of her hand and moved closer to her body. Dropping her eyes to the floor, she then let them rise slowly to the woman's face. A moment later, Shana began laughing. She was laughing so hard, tears streamed down her cheeks. It had to be the drugs. She detested Morrow so much that she saw him everywhere she went. "You remind me of my shrink, Dr. Morrow." Shana placed her hand over her mouth to stifle another burst of laughter. Dr. Hopkins angrily jerked her hand away.

"Hey," Shana told her. "Maybe you can be my doctor. Morrow is a fucking prick. I'd . . . rather a woman doctor treated me. See, I was raped . . ." She realized what she was saying and quickly shut her mouth. The doctor spun on her heels and took off at a rapid pace.

She saw Alex standing in the same location as always and went over to ask him if he knew anything about Dr. Hopkins. She glanced back at the counter and saw Lee, the only Whitehall employee she felt she might be able to trust. Taking Alex's hand, she led him to a corner of the room. "Is Peggy on duty?" she asked, leaning into Alex to keep from collapsing.

Alex looked out over the room and then turned back to Shana. "I don't see her. I think her shift ends at four. What happened to you? Where have you been?"

"They gave me something . . . some type of injection. And that pig hit me. She actually hit me." Shana walked over to the fountain and gulped down water, her mouth dry and her throat parched. Whatever medication they'd administered this time was potent, more so than the others, except for the Thorazine they'd given her the first day she was admitted.

She returned to where Alex was standing. "Is Dr. Hopkins a good doctor?"

"There is no Dr. Hopkins."

"But I just spoke to her. She was standing at the nursing station just a few minutes ago."

Alex laughed. "That woman is a patient, not a doctor. She was admitted around the same time as you but she just surfaced this afternoon. She's the one who was singing 'Amazing Grace' in the emergency room. From what I hear, she's a complete wacko. She walks around wearing a ton of phony jewelry and tells everyone she's a billionaire."

Shana fell back against the wall, massaging her throbbing leg as she waited for the effects of the drug to ease up. When she began to feel more like herself, she turned to Alex. "Peggy hit me today."

Alex steadied Shana with one hand. "Did Peggy really hit you? Is that why you're limping?"

"They fucked me up big time," she told him, placing her hand on her forehead. "I don't know what they gave me but it was serious shit." Her eyelids felt so heavy, they had narrowed to slits.

"Look at me, Shana. Did Peggy really hit you?"

"This is what I remember, okay? Peggy and George came to get me and took me to a room in the isolation section. George held me down while Peggy jabbed me with a needle. Then Peggy just walloped me. She said something to George about me being a troublemaker. No, I remember now. She said I was a pain in the ass. George told her he shouldn't be in the room."

"Why? Peggy gave you a shot in the arm, right?"

"No, she stuck me in the butt like she always does." Shana's eyes closed and her body began swaying as if she were about to collapse.

Alex grabbed her shoulders and shook her. "Don't go to sleep, Shana. Finish telling me what happened."

"I already told you. Peggy pulled my pants down . . . exposed me in front of George." Her eyes blinked as she fought against the drug. "After she hit me, she left me where everyone could see me."

Shana could tell that Alex was furious, but he was controlling himself until she filled in all the details.

"How did your leg get hurt?"

"I fell on the floor after Peggy hit me. I must have landed on my knee or something. All I know is it hurts to walk."

"That's it," Alex said, tossing his hands in the air. "Call an attorney. I'll look one up in the yellow pages. Come on, we'll get in touch with someone right now."

Shana limped behind Alex as he headed to the pay phone, waiting as he flipped through the San Francisco area phone book. The thick book was attached to the phone with a heavy cord so the patients couldn't throw it at each other. He tossed a quarter into the slot and dialed a number. "Here," he said, handing her the phone. "They'll need to hear the facts from you."

"Hello, my name is Shana Forrester," she said, the medication finally leveling off. "I'm being held against my will at Whitehall Psychiatric Hospital. They're abusing me, hitting me and forcing me to take mind-altering medication. I want to sue the hospital and everyone who works here."

"You've never seen Mr. Atwood before?" a female voice asked.

"No, I haven't," Shana told her. "Is he in now? May I speak to him?"

"He's with a client. He doesn't have any appointments available until the end of the month. Would you like to schedule one now?"

No one listened anymore. "If I'm being held against my will, how could I come to Mr. Atwood's office? Don't you have a fucking brain?"

"I don't have to listen to this," the woman said, promptly disconnecting.

Shana turned to Alex. "I shouldn't have smarted off. Now what do I do?"

"Well, you can try calling another attorney or you can call the police. Frankly, I think you have a problem with the police. They get calls from people in mental hospitals all the time. I doubt if your complaints will carry much weight."

Shana walked over and collapsed onto a sofa, exhausted from the effort of holding herself in an upright position.

Alex sat down beside her, a frustrated look on his face. Shana realized it was useless to call the police or more random attorneys from the yellow pages. She was in a nuthouse, for Christ's sake. No one was going to take her seriously. She had no alternative. "I'm going to call my mother," she said, hoping Alex would get the hint and give her some privacy.

"How many times have I told you?" he said sharply. "You can't call long distance on that phone."

Shana was annoyed at the tone of his voice. She felt so agitated and bewildered that she found herself walking in circles around the far corners of the room. After a few minutes, Milton, the "Walking Man," joined her and together they shuffled around the room in their green pajamas.

"Hi, Milton," she said. "How's the walking going?"

"See, the only reason I'm here is I have more brain waves than most people and that makes me excitable. It also causes insomnia and then when I can't sleep, I suffer from sleep deprivation and sometimes act bizarre. How about you?"

"I suffer from sleep deprivation, too. I guess I act bizarre just like you, Milton. Otherwise I wouldn't be here."

"There's this lady in the room next to mine who sings all night. I can't sleep with someone singing all the time."

" 'Amazing Grace,' right?"

"I used to go to church," Milton continued, "but then I get caught up in the Bible. Like I try to analyze it all and decipher it all— the Bible, you know. And then I can't sleep and I suffer from sleep deprivation and exhibit aberrant behavior."

"How aberrant?" Shana asked, seeing Alex out of the corner of her eye grinning at her. Maybe she could get Milton to take out George so she could escape.

"I kill cats, mostly cats."

Shana stopped walking. "Only cats?"

"Once I killed a rabbit," Milton said, "but mostly I kill cats. See,

I don't really like cats. They make too much noise at night and then I can't sleep and I suffer from sleep deprivation. And then . . ."

"You kill more cats, right?" Shana said. "How about people, Milton? Could you kill a person for me if I kept you up all night?"

Milton suddenly halted and looked Shana in the eye with a good deal of lucidity, particularly considering their conversation. "That's not funny, you know. I don't want to kill cats. And I would never kill a person."

The guy was certainly odd, but Shana was beginning to relax. Walking seemed to calm her just as it did Milton. Exercising might counteract the effects of the drugs. "I'm sorry, Milton. Forgive me." She turned and headed off in the opposite direction.

The only hope poor Milton could give her would be to drive George crazy. She wondered if he called the police station and told them he knew who'd killed J.F.K. After she circled the room again, she headed toward the smokers' table, where Norman, Karen, and May were seated. She realized she wasn't limping anymore. Funny thing about Whitehall, it was like living inside someone else's body. In that respect, it wasn't all that bad. But a person could also forget who they were, their loved ones, and even the life they'd had before Whitehall. If they were here long enough, a person could simply disappear.

"What room are you in?" Karen asked once Shana had taken a seat at the smokers' table.

"I don't know." Since she'd been sleeping in the isolation ward, she hadn't given thought to where she would sleep tonight.

"I bet they put you in with Michaela. She says it's the name of an archangel or something. Anyway, she's a plain-looking lady . . . reads the Bible day and night. I think they've been giving her shock treatments. They give them to most of the schizophrenics."

Great, Shana thought facetiously. Just then, Karen's head jerked to the left and she said "Shit, fuck, dick" and then glanced back at her as if nothing had happened.

"You know, Karen, my knowledge of Tourette's syndrome is limited but aren't there drugs you can take?"

Karen looked down at the table and Shana realized her timing had been inappropriate. She should have never questioned her about her illness after an outburst. The spontaneous profanity had to be more humiliating than the barking.

"I was on drugs when I was in school," Karen told her, looking even more disturbed than before. "I have a degree in electrical engineering, but I can't get the medicine anymore. The pharmaceutical companies don't manufacture enough and it costs a fortune. It doesn't matter anyway, I lost my allocation."

"Is that why you came here, because your condition got worse and you couldn't get the medication you needed?"

"Basically," Karen replied, emitting another long string of profanities: "Shit, fuck, asshole, pussy . . ." Then she barked exactly like a fox terrier.

Shana reached over and stroked her hand. "You're a good person, Karen. My mother's a judge and when I get out, she can help me figure out how to lobby against the pharmaceutical companies. No one should be denied the proper medication."

"Thanks," Karen said, a tear running down one side of her face. "You're a good person, too, Shana. We know you don't belong, but we're glad you're here. Maybe you really will be able to help. A lot of people say they want to help, then when they get out, they forget about me. No one could help Jimmy. Now he's dead."

"What happened? Did he die here at Whitehall?"

"No," Karen said, more tears falling. "Someone shot him. I guess they were trying to rob him. It was on the news or we would have never known."

"What was wrong with him?"

"Paranoid schizophrenia," she said, brushing a finger underneath her nose. "He developed it when he was in high school. You know the profile, smart guy, perfect grades, everyone liked him. Then all of a sudden the floor dropped out from under him. Jimmy hated the side effects of the medicine so he refused to take it. That's how he ended up here at Whitehall."

"What a terrible illness. Isn't there a cure of any kind?"

"The only good thing I know about schizophrenia is the symptoms sometimes go away or lessen when the person gets older."

"That's not so bad then. How old was Jimmy?"

"Thirty-seven," Karen said, massaging her neck. "The symptoms don't diminish until a person is in their seventies or eighties. By then, they could be dead so it wouldn't matter. I don't know why the hospital released Jimmy unless his insurance was tapped out. He was psychotic the day he walked out of here. He had a wife and kids and I was afraid he might hurt them. He'd hurt them before. That's why the court committed him. It was either Whitehall or jail."

"Heavy," Shana said.

"He talked about killing himself a lot, so I guess he got what he wanted. Jimmy had a tough life. I'm happy he's in a better place now."

Shana didn't see how being dead was a better place, even when stacked up against a lifetime inside a mental institution. She occasionally got depressed and overwhelmed, but she would never kill herself. Although she'd stopped going to mass, she was still a Catholic and knew she would rot in Hell if she took her own life.

The church had changed its position on suicide in recent years, finally taking into account people with special circumstances such as a lifetime of excruciating pain, acute mental illness, or those facing a prolonged and agonizing death.

That didn't mean God had changed his mind, however. The church liked to think they had a direct link to God, but Shana wasn't sure that was the case. The Vatican reminded her of a private club for stuffy old men who'd lost touch with reality. And what was the deal with the costumes? Didn't they know what century it was? Maybe if they dressed like normal men, people might take them more seriously.

The big dogs at the Vatican liked to boast that God lived there. My ass, she thought. The church had sheltered sex offenders, which left her believing that God had moved out of the Vatican a long time ago. Criminals were criminals. A priest's collar wasn't a get-out-of-jail-free pass.

But she still believed enough that she wasn't willing to go against the church's teachings. Hell was supposed to be repetition and she couldn't stand repetition.

She turned to Karen and clasped her hand tightly. "I promise I won't forget you when I get out. I'm only a few months shy of graduating from law school. I'm certain I can find a way to help you. It may take time, though, so don't give up hope."

"Don't worry," Karen said. "I have another person who's going to help me."

# SEVENTEEN

Visiting hours at Whitehall were from seven to nine every evening. Shortly after seven, people started appearing at the doors. Patients were allowed to leave and follow their visitors to the outside court-yard, the area they passed on the way to the cafeteria. Various chairs were placed in small groups throughout the area.

Shana watched, wondering if her mother would show up. Damn it, Lily had put her in this place. The least she could do was come to visit her, see how she was doing. Of course, it was Monday and her mother was in trial, which was obviously more important than seeing her supposedly drug-addicted daughter. Had Lily committed her to Whitehall to punish her for wanting to drop out of law school, or was it so Morrow could knock some sense into her? The hatred she felt for her mother intensified. While she was locked up in this awful place, Lily was back in Ventura with her new fuck buddy, waiting for Dr. Morrow to call and tell her when she could pick up her pathetic offspring.

What her mother didn't know, and Shana wouldn't stoop to tell her, was Morrow was not going to release her until her insurance ran dry. Even then, he could always persuade Lily to pay out of her own pocket. Shana had already established that her mother was vulnerable and would try to buy her way out of just about anything. How many parents would dish out the kind of money Shana had been getting without asking so much as a single question? Besides, Morrow was a doctor and Lily would never question a doctor.

She recalled breaking her leg while on a ski trip when she was seventeen. The doctor at the tiny hospital in Mammoth, where the ski resort was located, hadn't felt the need to call in an orthopedic surgeon, even though Shana was certain her leg needed more than the average cast. Her mother believed the doctor and Shana was sent home in a cast. After three months of agony, Lily finally gave in and took her to a specialist who ended up inserting a metal plate and five screws. Lily had told the surgeon, "The man was a doctor. I didn't know anything about broken bones. Why wouldn't I trust him to give my daughter the right treatment?"

When it came to money, Lily was one of those people who cried poverty when they had a fortune tucked away somewhere in a bank account. She might have taken a modest hit when the stock market crashed, but she knew her mother hadn't lost that much because she was too conservative when it came to her finances.

Shana sank to the bottom of her chair, consumed with self-pity. She fantasized that Brett would come bursting through the doors and the patients and staff would snap to attention. He would bring her clothes to wear and makeup. He might even bring a hairdresser with him, or send one over before he arrived so he wouldn't have to see her looking like a bag lady. Brett loved to spend money.

She imagined the look on her mother's face when she found out that she'd not only been paying for her education but for Brett's, someone she had never even met.

But it wasn't as if Shana had intentionally taken advantage of Lily. Brett came from a wealthy family and would pay her back as soon as his parents sold their three-million-dollar home in San Francisco. Unlike Lily, Brett's family had lost almost everything they owned in the stock market. He was a good student and wanted desperately to get his law degree. One of the reasons they'd broken up was her constantly nagging him to pay her back.

Shana knew it was wrong to make her mother pay for Brett's tuition, so in that respect, her punishment was well deserved. She also knew that asking for extra money all the time had given Lily good reason to believe she was abusing drugs. Nothing, however, could justify her mother having her committed to a place like Whitehall. Shana had been convicted before she'd been found guilty, treatment she wouldn't expect from a superior court judge.

As she watched, a whole gang of people appeared for Alex. Instead of walking out with them, he returned and took Shana's hand.

"Since your family isn't here, why don't you share mine? Come on, I'll introduce you."

"No," Shana told him, embarrassed by the hideous green pajamas and her disheveled appearance. She felt the back of her head. Her hair was so matted, it felt like a bird's nest. "I'll be fine, but thanks for the offer."

"I insist," he said, giving her the stern look he'd used in the cafeteria.

He gave a forceful pull to Shana's hand and yanked her to her feet. Before she had a chance to protest, she found herself following Alex out the double doors to the courtyard. It was twilight and the air was crisp and chilly. She wrapped her arms around herself to stay warm.

Alex's family was assembled in a circle of lawn chairs. "This is my father, William; my sister, Gwen; my brother, Raymond; and of course, my mother, Nadine. Everyone, this is Shana."

Something was very strange here. Shana picked up on it instantly. It might be due to her drug-induced hypersensitivity, but regardless, it concerned her. She felt as if she were surrounded by a cast of actors. Everyone exchanged pleasantries and smiled, yet there was an undercurrent of tension and subterfuge.

Alex's father was a distinguished-looking man with dark hair and a spattering of gray at the temples. He was dressed in an expensive pin-striped suit and a white shirt and tie. Raymond had lighter hair, more in the brown tones. He was attractive and neatly attired. Gwen resembled Raymond with slightly more elongated features. Nadine also appeared as if she'd just left work. Her clothes were stylishly tailored and she was wearing nylons and heels.

Alex's father, brother, and sister easily broke into a fast-paced banter and the atmosphere was relaxed and friendly. Not so with Alex's mother. Nadine blatantly stared at her, to the point that Shana felt as if she was being examined under a microscope. Nadine was trying to make her uncomfortable so that she would leave. Leaving would be awkward, though, and she wanted to find out more about Alex.

Alex held court in the center of the group, tilting his chair back on its hind legs. Shana couldn't imagine sitting around and chatting with her mother, nor could she fathom why Alex was still speaking to his parents if they were responsible for his hospitalization. Then she reminded herself that Alex had been suicidal. There had to be more than that, she told herself. He must have tried to kill himself and something went wrong.

Shana tried to follow the conversations, several going on simultaneously, but Alex's snooty mother kept asking her questions.

"So, are you from California?"

Shana overheard a few words exchanged between Alex and his father, something about their recent acquisition of a printing company. "I don't know if we're going to make a profit on this one, Alex."

"Are you kidding?" his son told him. "The Komori five-color Lithrone SX29 printers are worth more than we paid for the entire company. They remind me of the press I built five years ago. We blew it when we didn't get a patent on it."

Shana turned back to Nadine. "I live on the outskirts of Los Angeles, Ventura to be precise."

"Then how did you end up here?"

"I'm in my last year at Stanford Law." Shana knew Nadine was fishing for a diagnosis but she didn't know what to tell her. Helping a serious student finish his education wasn't an illness.

"That's a long way from your family. Couldn't you have found a school closer to home?"

"Stanford is an excellent law school."

Nadine's eyes drifted over to her son. "Alex lived with us until he was twenty-six. Or was it twenty-five, darling? Sometimes my memory fails me. We've been overwhelmed with business matters lately. You know, it's difficult when Alex isn't with us. He's our mastermind. Last year, he invented a new medical laser. We're having trouble keeping up with the demand for it."

Alex and Gwen were discussing a spreadsheet on another company they'd recently acquired. She handed him some papers to sign.

"Alex is an entrepreneur as well as an inventor," Nadine told her. "He didn't have time to move into his own place. He wanted to become a physicist when he was younger, but he couldn't stop inventing new machines. He's also a brilliant businessman."

"Impressive," Shana said, adjusting her position in the chair. "Your son is an industrious man, Nadine. I'm sure you're very proud of him."

Alex smiled smugly, appearing pleased that his mother had boasted about his accomplishments. "Tell my mother what you need, Shana. She'll pick it up for you tomorrow."

"I-I . . . I don't need anything," Shana stammered, desperate for something to wear so she could rid herself of the stigma of the green pajamas. Nadine was glaring at Alex, though, and she didn't feel comfortable asking favors from strangers. "Your offer is very gracious, but I'm doing fine with what I have."

"Wrong," Alex said, pulling out a cigarette. "You need some clothes, makeup, some toilet articles. Those are the primary items I've heard you mention. You might want an iPod and some music to listen to when you're in your room. Tell Nadine what type of music you like and she'll take care of it."

Shana opened her mouth to protest, but Alex spoke directly to his mother in a flat, authoritative voice. "When you come tomorrow, bring Shana a few pairs of jeans and some sweaters. She gets chilled from the air conditioner. Also, buy the kind of things women need. You know, a brush, shampoo, lipstick, cologne, maybe some makeup. Size four on the clothes. The sweaters should be white."

Nadine didn't answer. She shifted nervously in her seat, never taking her eyes off her son. Shana felt her face flushing as the air filled with tension.

Alex suddenly stood and within seconds, they were all standing. "I want that other matter dealt with by this time tomorrow. I expected it to be taken care of by now." He moved until he was only a few inches from his father's face. "Do I make myself perfectly clear?"

His father merely nodded and then let his gaze drop to the ground. Alex made a gesture with his hand as if he were dismissing a board meeting. Everyone but his sister walked off. Gwen turned to Shana. "It was nice to meet you. I guess we'll see you tomorrow."

"Thanks," Shana said, hoping Whitehall would be history by then.

Alex took her hand and led her back to the great room. Life in the funny farm, she thought, was not always fun. Had Alex really been a boy genius, or were his family members merely giving in to his delusions? He was lucid and he was here—more than she could say for her mother or Brett. Another reason Alex was looming pretty large on the horizon was that he had arranged for her to get some clothes. If she had to spend one more day in the green pajamas, she might be tempted to tie them around her neck and hang herself.

She chastised herself for not asking Alex's sister if she could borrow her cell phone. Admitting her circumstances would have been too embarrassing, though. How could she tell someone that her own mother had dumped her at Whitehall as if she was an out-of-control child that she could no longer deal with?

Something came to mind and she turned to Alex. "Karen told me about what happened to Jimmy. What was he like?"

"Hopelessly insane," Alex told her, his brows furrowed. "What else did she tell you?"

"That someone killed him a few days after he was released. If he was so ill, why did the hospital release him?"

"He cancelled his insurance."

Okay, Shana thought, wishing she could do the same. But her mother took care of her health insurance. She doubted if the insurance company would allow her to cancel without her mother's consent, which would never happen.

In this environment, it was easy to grow close to people. She could tell by the expression on Alex's face that he would prefer not to discuss Jimmy's death. Had Alex taken Jimmy under his wing the way he had her, or was there something deeper?

She was over six feet tall and looked as if she could play football for the Dallas Cowboys. Although her size was intimidating, her face appeared pliable and kind. Shana rushed to the counter, seizing a possible opportunity. The woman was wearing a pink knit sweater and the name tag pinned on her chest read Betsy Campbell.

"Excuse me," Shana said in an intentionally nonchalant tone. "I need to speak with the patients' rights advocate. Could you please put in a call to this person?" She looked at Betsy and smiled pleasantly. "I love pink, don't you?"

"That would be Linda Allen," Betsy said, reading the name off a list in front of her. "I'll put a call in to her, but I can't promise when she'll call you back. And your name?"

"Shana Forrester. Will you call her now, please? I'll wait."

Betsy looked around the room and then turned back to Shana. "I just started here yesterday. I'm not sure what the procedure is regarding the patients' rights advocate. I should probably leave a note for the day shift. They might not take too kindly to me calling folks at home at night."

The woman's self-confidence fell short of her size. "Please," Shana pleaded. "I'm sure you'll only reach her answering machine. This person isn't a doctor so the number you have is more than likely her office. The day shift is always so busy. If you don't handle this for me, they may think you're lazy."

Betsy's hand reached for the phone. Shana hoped against reason that the number was Linda Allen's home and she would answer.

Leaning over the counter, she was ready to snatch the phone and plead her case.

"It's a recording," Betsy said, holding the phone away from her ear.

"Leave a message . . . quick . . . tell her to contact me as soon as possible." When Betsy just stared, frightened by Shana's intensity, Shana grabbed the phone out of the woman's hand and began speaking. "This is Shana Forrester at Whitehall. I need to speak to you right away. I'm formally rescinding my voluntary commitment. If you're listening to this message, you're legally obligated to contact me or you'll be named in a lawsuit."

Betsy straightened to her full six feet, easily retrieving the phone from Shana's hand. "I should have known not to listen to you. You'll get me fired. Now you get along, you hear me?" The phone back in the cradle, Betsy started waving her hands as if she were shooing Shana away.

Shana realized she still didn't know her room number. "I don't know where I'm supposed to be sleeping. You'll have to find out for me."

Betsy gave her a wary look and then rummaged through some papers. "Room sixteen."

Shana headed off in the direction of the room, only two doors away from Alex's and directly across from the smokers' table. The room was dark so she assumed her roommate was asleep. When she stepped inside, she saw a large, shadowy image rocking back and forth on the bed, and heard a wheezy sound that she assumed was the woman breathing. A pungent odor assaulted her nostrils. She assumed it was body odor but it smelled like rotting flesh. Shana began back-stepping to the door.

God, she thought, who was this creature and how could she possibly sleep in the same room with her? According to Karen, Michaela believed she was an angel. For all Shana knew, the woman was a homicidal maniac. Nonetheless, her name did refer to the archangel Michael, one of the few named angels in the Bible. Catholics prayed to Saint Michael in conjunction with the rosary. She remembered her grandmother teaching her the prayer as a child and how frightened she had been. She hadn't said the prayer for a long time, but she would never forget it. "Saint Michael, Archangel, defend us in battle. Be our protection against the wickedness and snares of the Devil. May God rebuke him, we humbly pray. And do thou, O Prince of the Heavenly Host, by the power of God, thrust into Hell Satan and all the other evil spirits who prowl about the world seeking the ruin of souls."

No wonder Catholic kids were so tough, Shana thought. They went to bed with visions of Satan and evil spirits trying to destroy them. Thinking the Devil was out to get you was a Hell of a lot worse than imagining a nondescript monster was hiding under your bed. The name Michaela must be the female version of Michael, although the Vatican would never give power to a woman, even an archangel.

May was filing her nails at the round table. Karen was watching TV on the sofa with Norman. He was holding his small fan to his charred face. Alex was chatting with a remarkably normal-looking man in his late forties or early fifties. When Alex saw Shana, he ran to catch up to her as she began circling the room at a fast pace.

"That guy is a priest." Alex matched her stride and fell into step beside her. "Can you believe it?"

Shana felt agitated and overwhelmed. "I can believe anything . . . absolutely anything. You should see who they selected for my roommate. I'll probably be dissected during my sleep."

"Michaela is practically catatonic. She won't hurt you. You'll be fine."

"Sure," Shana said, cutting her eyes to him. "That's easy for you to say. You don't have to share a room with her. I'll never be able to sleep." She thought of Milton, the "Walking Man," and wondered if she'd suffer from sleep deprivation, exhibit bizarre behavior, and start killing cats. "What's the priest in here for? The usual, molesting kids, or does he believe he's the Virgin Mary? All we need is Jesus and we'll have a nativity scene."

"Nick makes a good Jesus," Alex told her, pointing at a tall, skinny man with a scraggly beard and what looked like a cane carved from a baseball bat. "They're getting ready to open the kitchen. It's open from eight to nine every evening. They even have bagels. Everyone else is glued to the boob tube. Some kind of big disaster just happened."

Shana tried to see the television but there were too many patients blocking the screen. News, she thought. What news? What world? Everything seemed so remote, so out of context. War, killings, disasters, all served up with a smile. Whitehall was similar to being in your mother's womb, hearing her heartbeat and knowing she was somewhere but not knowing where.

"You don't want to watch that," Alex told her, clasping her hand. "We'll be alone in the kitchen. We can talk in private for a change."

The kitchen opened up off the great room. Inside was a refrigerator, a microwave, a toaster, and a small table. Alex hoisted himself onto the counter and Shana did the same. "Do you know what happened?"

"Another plane crash or something."

They gazed at each other in silence. Shana finally pulled her eyes away. "You know what one of the patients said to me this morning? 'Tomorrow is the last day. Prepare yourself.' Don't you ever get freaked out by some of these people? Who knows? Maybe they're right and the world really is coming to an end."

Alex scowled. "We're in a mental hospital. When the mind begins to splinter, certain individuals convince themselves that the world is coming to an end. It's the sense of impending doom they experience that causes them to develop this line of thinking. A person having a heart attack generally has a similar sensation. It's the brain's way of warning you something serious is happening to your body. Most of the patients here at Whitehall are schizophrenic. So it's their brain that's taking off in a different direction or a portion of their psyche."

"Why are there so many schizophrenics?"

"Because most of the other mental illnesses no longer require hospitalization. They're easily treated with medication and the people are seldom dangerous." He tilted his head. "You're not going to start preaching, I hope."

Shana ran her hands through her hair. "Dr. Morrow might have been right when he said I was psychotic. If I wasn't, I would have never let my mother trick me into coming here."

"You're here because you can pay," Alex said flatly. "Greed is a more rational explanation for your predicament than Armageddon."

Shana found herself standing between his legs, swimming in his dark, expressive eyes. Part of her wanted to flirt with him, while another part wanted to run away. She didn't know if what he had just told her was true or if he had merely made it up to impress her, but it made him sound like a shrink instead of a patient. "How do you know I'm not insane, Alex? I mean, this is an insane asylum."

"Whitehall isn't an insane asylum. It's a highly lucrative business." He smiled mischievously. "People are here for a variety of reasons, most of them having nothing to do with mental illness. Now your new roommate, Michaela, or whatever her real name is, certainly isn't playing with a full deck. Anyway, move over. I'm ready for a snack."

Alex slid off the counter and he grabbed a bagel from a large basket. After slicing it with a plastic knife, he put the two pieces into the toaster. They were standing so close now that Shana could feel the heat emanating from his body. The dreadful cold had penetrated her bones.

"I don't know," she said, still pensive. "A shrink would say I have unresolved conflicts from my childhood. I also have some pretty weird thoughts when I don't get enough sleep."

"You are not mentally ill," Alex said emphatically. "Everyone has strange thoughts from time to time. If you're crazy, then I'm a certifiable lunatic."

"Why? You seem perfectly normal to me."

"Because of the way I get when I'm working. The psychiatric term is mania. More creative people call it inspiration. When I get an idea for an invention, I can work for days at a time without sleeping or eating. The energy just keeps flowing. Michelangelo, Einstein, Da Vinci, and a lot of other famous people would be classified as mentally ill by today's standards. Good thing these geniuses lived before psychiatry. In Michelangelo's time, working for days without sleep or food meant he was receiving inspiration directly from God. Granted, Michelangelo had his problems but no one locked him up in a loony bin and drugged him into normalcy." He stopped speaking and stared off into space. Turning back to her, he said, "Let's talk about something more uplifting, like how amazing your eyes are. Green eyes are rare, you know."

"I've heard that but I don't know why." Shana resisted the urge to press her body against his long enough to get warm and feel the touch of another human being. Alex spread cream cheese on their bagel and handed her half. His kind words and nurturing manner were becoming addictive.

"The reason why green eyes are so rare is that the genes that produce green eyes are themselves rare. One set of genes has a brown and blue version, one set has a green and a blue version, and one set controls shading in brown eyes. The best explanatory theory right now actually suggests that brown is dominant to all other colors, which means a person with a mix of genes is probably brown-eyed. Green is dominant to blue," Alex continued, pausing to take a bite out of his bagel, "so a green-eyed parent and a blue-eyed one will have some green-eyed kids and blue becomes completely recessive. The reason blue is more common than green as an eye color is that there are just so few green-eyed genes in the population. Cool, huh?"

"It's good to know something about me is unique." Shana thought of her mother and how much they looked alike except for their eye color. She wrapped her arms around her chest, shivering. "Why is it so cold in here? They don't even have blankets on the beds, only sheets. I guess I'm not accustomed to air-conditioning."

Alex tossed what was left of his bagel into the trash can and then jumped back onto the counter. "They keep it cold because of the psychos. Cold temperatures keep them calm." He rolled his eyes around. "These are my psycho eyes."

"Funny." A few moments later, she blurted out, "Were you really going to kill yourself?"

"The IRS decided I was making too much money," Alex explained, taking the napkin out of her hands and disposing of it. "I'm practicing in case they send me to prison."

Shana took a step back in shock. "You're hiding, then?"

"More or less."

What a brilliant idea, she thought, chewing on a ragged fingernail. Who would ever think of looking for someone in a place like Whitehall? "Can't the IRS track you by your Social Security number?"

"Whitehall doesn't report Social Security numbers. Why would they? It doesn't matter anyway. I gave them a fictitious one."

"Couldn't you hide out somewhere other than a place like this?"

"Let me explain," he said, becoming animated. "The economic downturn along with the stock market crash created unprecedented opportunities for individuals with liquidity. I took advantage of those opportunities and increased my wealth substantially. The only problem was I failed to set aside enough money to pay my taxes." He leaned over and ran a tapered finger down the center of her nose. "You're beautiful, you know. I don't know why you're worried about makeup. Your skin is perfect, and your hair, the color is fantastic. You can't get something like that out of a bottle."

For the first time, Shana wasn't chilled. She even felt flushed. He was so close, she was certain he was going to kiss her. With his face next to hers, she could feel his breath on her cheek and it was warm and sweet.

"As soon as Morrow raises your level," Alex told her, "you'll be able to go outside to the courtyard from nine to nine-thirty every evening."

"Alone?"

"I can come along if you want. We can take a walk in the moonlight. We won't even have to contend with your buddy, George. He gets off at nine."

Shana fantasized about them necking in the night air. They weren't that far apart in age and since Brett had left her, she was free to do whatever she wanted. Alex poured her a glass of punch from the refrigerator. "Thanks," she said, taking a long sip. "When are you leaving?"

He mistakenly thought she was referring to the courtyard. "There's nothing for me to do out there by myself, so I usually stay inside. Tomorrow, ask Morrow to raise your level. I can go anywhere I want."

"Really? Why do you get special treatment? Do you pay an extra ten grand a week?"

Alex hesitated before answering. "I was scheduled for discharge the day you were removed from isolation. Once I saw you, I decided to stay."

Shana was flattered but somewhat taken back. "You're not serious, I hope."

"Dead serious," he told her, getting down off the counter and taking both of her hands in his own. "Why don't we leave together? You know, when you're released."

Shana became caught up in his fantasy, imagining the two of them whiling away the days on a sun-drenched beach in some exotic location. No more papers to write or books to study. And she wouldn't have to stay up all night worrying that she'd flunk the bar exam and humiliate her mother. She could simply vanish, walk away and never look back.

"Will you come with me?" Alex whispered. "I have money. I can take care of you. We can go to France, Spain, Greece, anywhere you want. We could spend the rest of our lives together."

Shana stared at a spot above his head. Brett had made similar promises and she'd been stupid enough to fall for them. How could Alex ask her to run away with him? They hardly knew each other.

"Don't answer," he snapped, storming out of the room.

Shana started to call after him and then decided to let it go. Whitehall had intensified her vulnerability. Regardless of the confidence Alex projected, she sensed an aura of desperation around him. Why had he run off and left her in the kitchen? What had she said or done to piss him off?

From this point on, Shana would have to exercise more caution. As attractive and appealing as Alex seemed to be, there was something underneath the surface that frightened her.

# EIGHTEEN

Shortly after Alex left her in the kitchen, Shana headed to her room, removed the pathetic green pajamas, and crawled into her bed. She had wandered around and found the laundry room, seeing a clean stack of pajamas, so at least she didn't have to wear the same pair every day.

The clock read nine-forty and she was already sleepy. Her eyelids had started getting heavy even before Alex had stormed off. At least her stay at Whitehall had accomplished something. Her bout of insomnia seemed to be broken.

A swatch of light streaked across the room. The hospital required that the doors to patients' rooms be left partially open at all times. Shana preferred it to be completely dark when she slept, but she doubted if anything could keep her awake tonight. She pulled the sheet tightly around her body. The temperature seemed lower in the room than it was in the rest of the hospital and she was shivering.

Although she'd never heard the woman who called herself Michaela speak, she could see the outline of her body and hear the bedsprings straining under her weight.

Shana couldn't understand why her mother hadn't called to

check on her. She wasn't too busy to fly up here and ruin her life, but she couldn't find the time to make a single phone call. No wonder she'd fantasized about being with Alex. The only person who loved her had abandoned her.

She knew her relationship with Brett was history. More than likely, he had dumped her so he wouldn't have to pay back all the money he owed her. For all she knew, the money could have gone for something other than his tuition. Maybe he was the one who was using drugs.

Her life reminded her of two separate movies. The first one was filled with toys, friends, parties, and laughter. Then that life abruptly ended. Even her memories of that first life were vague, so much so that she didn't know what was real and what she had imagined. Her second life began as a horror movie, then later became a tragedy, and finally became as close to normal as it would ever get. Whitehall fit perfectly into her second life. She had somehow recovered from the rape when the man who had raped her and her mother came back and took the life of her beloved father. She was destined to end up in a mental institution. In a way, she was relieved that it had happened. When she got out, she could move forward with her life, knowing the worst was behind her.

She felt guilty for the lies she had told her mother. One of Lily's best traits was her generosity. She had given her the money without questioning her. Abusing her trust wasn't right. As a county employee, her mother was far from rich, which made taking advantage of her even worse.

With her father, nothing she ever did was wrong. A good parent would teach their child the right thing to do and punish them when they did wrong. Her father didn't care if she stole things or lied. The only person who'd ever punished her was her mother, and she'd only done so to make certain Shana would become a responsible law-abiding adult.

Her eyes closed and she fell into a deep sleep.

She saw Brett's face floating in front of her. He was kissing her breasts, her stomach, stroking her between her legs. Her mouth fell open in pleasure.

"Oh, Brett," she panted. She reached out to bring him to her body, to feel him inside her, to smell him, taste him. She suddenly found herself sitting upright in the bed. Michaela was wheezing now and the sound was so irritating, she got out of bed, got dressed, and staggered out into the great room.

Betsy was performing her nightly duties, checking to make certain the patients were in their rooms and accounted for. No one was at the nursing station. Shana ducked back into her room, peeking around the corner of her doorway until she saw Betsy enter one of the patients' rooms. She then rushed to the nursing station, entering through the side door, and snatched the phone out of the cradle.

Squatting down so Betsy couldn't see her, she dialed her mother's number in California. Instead, she was connected to the hospital switchboard. Even the employees were not allowed to call long distance. Depressing the button to end the call, she dialed nine and finally reached an outside line.

"Brett," she said in a hushed tone.

"Shana," he exclaimed. "God, what time is it?" He yawned and then continued, "Everyone's been looking for you. Julie called me when you didn't show up for class today. I guess that would be yesterday now. She went by your apartment but no one was there. Where the hell are you?"

Shana clasped the receiver with both hands. "I had a dream that we were making love. It was so real. I was certain you were here with me."

"I'm sorry I hurt you. I felt like you were suffocating me, dragging me down. It's not what you think about Trudy. We're just friends. My parents couldn't pay the rent on my apartment and she offered to let me live with her for free."

"You really expect me to believe that you're not sleeping with her? Give me a break, Brett. I paid your tuition. Don't you think I'd let you stay with me?" As she spoke, the suppressed anger replaced the longing. "You're a damn leech, that's what. When I told you I wasn't going to ask my mother for more money, you decided to find someone else to support you. I'm sorry your father lost all his money in the stock market, but my mother is a county employee and can't afford to pay your damn tuition. I demand you pay back every dime or—"

Betsy appeared at Shana's side, wrestling the phone out of her hands. "Get back to your room this minute."

"No!" Shana shouted. "You can't keep me here without contact with the outside world. All I want is five minutes."

Betsy seized her from behind, placing her arm around her chest.

Without thinking, Shana spun around and slugged her.

Betsy took several steps backward, rubbing her chin. Then she shook her finger. "You're going to pay for this, young lady."

"I didn't mean to hit you. I was talking to my fiancé and he said something that upset me."

Alex and some of the other patients had heard the commotion and came out of their rooms. "Go on," Betsy said, waving them away. "There's nothing to see here. Everything is under control. Go back to sleep."

Alex motioned for Shana. As soon as Shana left the nursing station, Betsy picked up the phone to make a call.

"Sit down," Alex said, patting a place beside him on the sofa. "Fold your hands in your lap and act like nothing happened."

A short time later, two male guards came walking out. One was carrying something large and white.

Alex stuck two cigarettes in his mouth and lit them both at the same time, handing one to Shana. He leaned back on the sofa and crossed his legs. "What's the job market like in Los Angeles?"

Shana inhaled the smoke, wondering if Alex was trying to prepare her or protect her. "Great," she said. "Everything's wonderful." She'd never been that much of an actress, particularly under duress. Her hand was shaking so badly, the cigarette almost fell out.

"I see," Alex replied. "Unemployment is high around here,

especially if a person isn't educated. There's a shortage of registered nurses, but most of the employees here at Whitehall aren't
accredited. They're lucky to have a job, if you know what I mean."

Shana tried not to look at the two attendants or the dreaded
straitjacket, but her feet were tapping involuntarily against the
floor. Alex squeezed her hand even tighter, locking eyes with the
two attendants. "I know people who have lost their jobs over a
simple error in judgment. All they need to do is to stop and think
about what they're doing."

One attendant nudged the other one, ignoring Alex's attempts
to intimidate them. "Let's go," he said, striding toward Shana. When
he got to the sofa, he planted his feet and placed his hands on his
hips. "No one, and I mean no one, strikes a staff member. You're
either going to spend time in the jacket or in the Quiet Room. It's
your choice."

"The room," Shana said quickly, knowing she couldn't stand
being restrained in the jacket. She assumed she would be placed
back in the isolation section of the hospital for the night. Slipping
her hand out of Alex's, she stood and walked off with the attendants.

In the corridor leading from the great room to the isolation
unit, the taller guard took a key off the ring attached to his belt and
unlocked a door. Once he had shoved Shana inside, she heard the
key turning in the lock.

The Quiet Room was a padded cell!

Nothing she had experienced could compare to the fear she
now felt as she stood in the center of the small room and turned
slowly around, looking at the white padded walls. She began hyperventilating, certain she was going to suffocate. Her eyes searched for
the air-conditioning vent. She saw a small opening on the ceiling
with rusted metal slats. There was air, not much, not moving, but
nonetheless air.

She sat down on the floor and inched her way into the corner,
thinking that in the corner, the walls would seem farther away.

The whiteness was marred in various places, in what appeared to be rips in the vinyl padding. These became like her wall decorations, her paintings. She stared at a silver patch, trying to see her reflection.

Shana had finally hit bottom. Only a week ago, the whole world had been accessible. Now it had shrunk to an eight-by-six padded box, an oversized coffin without so much as a mattress. What kind of country would allow this to happen? People could commit heinous crimes and be released on bail. There were no bail hearings at Whitehall. No one cared because they never thought they'd end up inside a mental hospital.

Punching Betsy in the face might go down as the dumbest thing Shana had ever done. By hitting a staff member, she'd given substance to the premise that she was mentally ill. Even if she managed to get a court hearing, the court could determine that she was not only disturbed but dangerous, and her life as she had known it would cease to exist.

They could lock her away for years, and she would sink deeper into the quicksand. With every pill-filled cup, every injection, another piece of reality would fall away.

Her mind turned to Alex. He was now interwoven into her new abbreviated existence, whereas Brett and her mother seemed far removed—a voice, a face, a few memories. Among the comforting sights and sounds of what had once been her life, with freedom to come and go as she pleased, Lily had become an outsider with no possible comprehension of the degradation her daughter was being forced to endure.

Shana had read stories about prisoners of war, and how they were subjected to brainwashing and behavior modification. Now she was experiencing it firsthand. Once she walked out of the Quiet Room, she would never break the rules again.

# NINETEEN

Whiteness, everywhere she looked. Her eyes strained against the glaring white walls of the so-called Quiet Room. She tried to swallow, choking and coughing until she managed to push the saliva down her constricted throat. She beat the cushioned walls with her fists and then kicked them with her feet. "Let me out!" she screamed. "Please . . . I'll do anything, sign anything, say anything. I can't take it anymore."

Shana knew she had to stop sucking up oxygen. Her cries for help were futile. The room was soundproof. She curled up in a fetal position. If she let her mind roam, she would crack. She had to focus on something.

Recalling the erotic dream, tears streaked down her cheeks. She had believed Brett when he'd told her she was too uptight when they had sex. She should have never told him she'd been raped. From that point on, he had pushed her to do things he must have known would upset her. He wanted to pin her arms over her head, but it made her panic. And there were other things, things too offensive to remember. She knew now that he'd become aroused by the thought of her being raped. They had talked about it for hours,

Brett insisting on knowing every sick detail. Everything had happened so fast; there wasn't much to tell. Shana started making things up just to satisfy him.

The one thing she had never told anyone, the unspeakable truth she had lived with all these years, was that her mother had killed the man she believed was the rapist. Lily had risked her life driving to the most dangerous area of Oxnard to end the reign of a violent criminal. Instead of being a judge today, her mother could be sitting in a prison cell. She knew Lily hadn't wanted to kill the rapist simply for revenge. Even though she'd killed the wrong man, she had done it to protect her child, and for that alone, she would always be Shana's hero.

Her thoughts turned to Norman and his awful injuries. Then there was May and her ability to channel dead spirits. Karen suffered from a tragic disease, yet in some ways, she appeared more normal than some of the others. Her roommate, Michaela, was like a rotting, wheezing corpse. For all practical purposes, Alex was her only anchor on reality.

Her muscles began cramping from sitting. Shana stood and began peeling off the silver duct tape. She then proceeded to pluck out the stuffing. She wasn't certain what it was, but it was white and fluffy and drifted on pockets of air to the floor. She tried to block everything out but the task—to peel off the masking tape from the rips in the vinyl and see how much stuffing she could get out.

The floor was soon covered in downy whiteness. If she could just get enough of it out, it could serve as her mattress. She made the holes bigger by holding the torn edge and pulling until the rips were enormous. The more she thought of her predicament, the more she dug her fingernails into the padded walls.

Shana felt a pressing urge to urinate. "I have to go to the bathroom!" she shouted. "You can't lock me up without a toilet, you barbaric monsters."

She was now standing midcalf in fluff. Betsy and the others may have forgotten to tell anyone they'd placed a patient in the padded cell. Without a clock or a watch, she had no idea how much time had elapsed.

The fullness in her bladder was unbearable. Shana was repulsed by the fact that she had no choice but to pee on the floor like a dog. Finally she gave in, squatting on the floor and relieving herself. Then she went to the wall and furiously plucked out more padding to cover the spot on the floor.

Keys were rattling outside the door. Shana was crouched in the corner, her arms wrapped around her chest. The door flung open and the space was instantly filled with Peggy's enormous body. Stuffing rose off the floor and floated on air from the open door.

"You insufferable little brat," Peggy said, turning and yelling. "Lee, come here. You've got to see this to believe it."

Shana's hair and clothing were covered in white fluff. Peggy shook her head as she stepped through the doorway. "I told you about this one," she told Lee. "No one ever listens to me."

Shana was so thrilled to see a human being, she grabbed Peggy and kissed her on the cheek. The woman briefly smiled in surprise, then pushed her away. "Get out of here now, you hear?"

When Shana entered the great room and saw the clock, she was shocked. It was a few minutes past eleven and since it was daylight, she knew it had to be morning. She'd been in the room almost twelve hours without food, water, or a toilet. Even the most heinous criminals would not be forced to endure such treatment.

Alex saw her and rushed over, hugging her tight to his body. "Thank God, you're okay. What did you do to yourself? You look like you've been tarred and feathered."

"I guess you could say I had a run-in with the Quiet Room," Shana told him. "In case you don't know, the Quiet Room is a padded cell. At least it used to be padded."

She looked around the now familiar room. She waved at Karen and May at the smoking table, then she walked right up to Norman and kissed him on his scarred cheek. "That didn't hurt, did it?"

"Nah," he said. "You can kiss me anytime you want."

White fluff was falling from her body and drifting across the floor. "Milton," she called out as he circled the room. "Come here, I want to kiss you." Milton gave her a perplexed look and picked up his pace. As he reached the Ping-Pong table, Shana caught up with him and planted one on his forehead. "Let's run off together, Milty. We can go to the animal shelter and have a blast. I hear they have a surplus of cats."

Shana was laughing so hard, tears were running down her face. She started picking the white stuffing from her hair and tossing it at May and Karen. Soon, everyone in the room was laughing.

She was free. She was out. Nothing else mattered.

"I think you need to shower and change your clothes before lunch," Alex told her. He raised his eyebrows and gave her that look with his psycho eyes.

Shana made a face and tried to outdo him, then hurried off to her room. Michaela wasn't there, but she saw a stack of packages wrapped in red paper. Each package had a sticker that read, "To Shana, from Alex." Nadine must have gone shopping the night before, or hit the stores as soon as they opened that morning. She began ripping open the packages and then walked to the door and yelled, "I love it, Alex. I love you. I love all of you. It's Christmas."

Inside the boxes were jeans and cashmere sweaters, makeup and cologne. One box contained a black pantsuit with a white silk shirt trimmed in delicate lace. Shana was beside herself with joy. She tossed the green pajamas on the floor, then kicked them out the door. A round of applause resounded.

Inside the steaming shower, Shana soaped her body and washed her hair. "Thank you, God," she said, looking up at the ceiling. "Thank you, Alex. Thank Heaven for small favors."

After Lee came in and dried her hair, she started playing with the cosmetics. All the colors were wrong, but she didn't care. She had complained about Brett's insistence that she wear makeup and dress in provocative clothing, but once a person began wearing makeup they felt naked without it. The lipstick was a bright red, a color she would never wear. She eagerly smeared it over her chapped lips, then stood back to look at herself in the mirror. Shana had full lips and extremely fair skin. With the red lipstick, her mouth looked like a juicy red apple. The only other makeup was black eyeliner and mascara. She quickly applied it and her eyes became the focal point in her face. Since Lee had blow-dried her hair, it was wavy instead of curly and frizzy.

The only thing missing was underwear. She pulled on one of the white cashmere sweaters. There, for all to see, were two protruding nipples. What difference did it make, she decided. She hadn't worn underwear since her admittance. The jeans fit her waist and hips perfectly. Then she slid her feet into the soft suede shoes, marveling that they, too, were exactly her size. How did Alex know so much about her? She finished with the earrings and sprayed herself with cologne, a fresh innocent scent. Returning to the mirror, she saw a woman she'd never seen before.

"This is me," Shana said to her mirror image. "This is the real me." She turned her head upside down and brushed her hair until it was smooth and shiny, then walked out of the room, a new woman.

Everyone turned and stared. One by one, they stood, and Karen started clapping. Shana modeled for them, glide-walking across the floor and spinning around in circles. She walked up to Alex. "I feel so good," she said. "I don't know how I can ever repay you."

"We'll think of something," Alex said, a broad grin on his face. "We have time for a quick game of Ping-Pong before lunch. How about it, gorgeous?"

"You're on," Shana said, tossing her hair to one side. "But don't think for a minute I'm going to let you win."

# TWENTY

Mary Stevens was on her way to John Adams's office when she ran into him in the hallway. "The Ventura PD found another body last night. They haven't had a chance to compare the wounds to the Washburn homicide, but the MO is identical. The victim was killed with a single shot to the back of the head."

"Tell me more," he said.

"This is the first time the UNSUB has killed a female. At this point, there are no immediate signs that the victim was suicidal. Of course, we'll know more once the autopsy is completed." Adams headed back to his office and Mary followed. He waited for her to enter and then closed the door before taking a seat behind his desk.

"There's a pattern developing," Mary continued, placing her hands on the back of the chair rather than sitting. "The most recent homicides in San Francisco occurred within a seven-day period. The two bodies surfaced in the Ventura area only a few days apart, and my bet is they were killed in the same time period. The tension must build up inside of him to such an extreme level that one killing no longer satisfies him. The homicides that occurred prior to the San Francisco crimes were approximately a month apart. His bloodlust is intensifying."

"And you need to be in Ventura right now. Isn't that what you're trying to tell me?"

"Yes." She stared at the wall where photos of ongoing cases were pinned up, hoping Adams would comprehend the implications of her next statement. "And I need the full force of the Bureau behind me, sir. Regardless of my suspicion that some or all of the victims may have hired the UNSUB to kill them, we have a serial killer who has now taken six lives. If he keeps killing at the rate he is now, that number could double in a matter of months."

Adams leaned back in his chair. "We don't know that as a fact."

"No," Mary said, pacing. "But I believe we have enough circumstantial evidence to establish that the crimes are connected. Every one of the victims was shot in the back of the head. I pulled up computer statistics on every homicide that occurred in the country last month, and other than the cases I've already identified, only three victims were killed by a single gunshot to the back of the head. We have stabbings, multiple gunshot wounds, strangulations, poisonings, and a variety of other means of death, but only four individuals were killed by a single perfectly placed shot to the back of the head."

"Pack your bags," Adams said, standing. "And get every piece of evidence you have on these cases to me by four o'clock so the team can work on perfecting your profile. You've done good work here, Stevens."

"Thank you, sir."

"Now get out of here and continue working. I should have listened to you sooner. Take my word. You'll have the full resources of the Bureau at your service until we capture this maniac." He paused, patting his shirt pocket as if he'd forgotten something. "You're in charge, Stevens. I'll call your husband's SAC in Dallas and get his transfer date moved up. I want both of you in Ventura by tomorrow evening. Do you think the UNSUB is still in the Ventura area?"

"Doubtful," Mary told him. "I think he's hiding out somewhere between San Francisco and Ventura. I'm not even certain the murders occurred in the same area where the bodies were found. Washburn's last known residence was in Stockton. We need to consider the possibility that the UNSUB came to Ventura strictly for the purpose of dumping bodies."

"Smart," Adams said, looking somewhat bewildered. "Now I remember. I'm late for another damn meeting. Don't let them seduce you into taking a supervisory position, Stevens. You'll spend the majority of your time kissing ass and wading through paperwork." He rifled through his drawers, finally coming up with his car keys. "You can share the rest of your thoughts with the team at our four o'clock meeting. If I'm not back in time, you can stand in for me."

Mary walked out of Adams's office beaming.

Dr. Phillip Patterson's face was flushed in anger. He spotted Morrow heading down the hall. "Charles!" he yelled, but the other man kept walking. He picked up his pace and caught him in front of his office. "Stop right there," he said, grabbing his arm. "I have to talk to you."

"Take your hands off me, Phillip," Morrow snapped. "What's wrong now?"

"I've had it, you hear me? No one is going to tell me what to do, certainly not a patient in my own hospital."

Morrow place a hand over his mouth and yawned.

"You're a weasel, Charles, a disgusting weasel," Patterson ranted. "You know what he said to me . . . your guy . . . your guy? He had the unmitigated gall to waltz into my office and order me . . . you got that? Not even ask me, but order me to discharge my patient, Michaela Henderson. You know why? You know why?"

Morrow removed his glasses and calmly wiped them with his handkerchief before replacing them on his nose. "You're repeating yourself, Phil. Maybe you should write yourself a prescription."

Patterson ignored him. "He thinks Michaela may hurt your prize, the redheaded bombshell. Michaela Henderson has never exhibited an act of aggression in her life. She's a self-mutilator. I refuse to discharge her. If I do, she may kill herself. All your man wants is a piece of ass and a room to do it in."

"What's the big deal, Phil?" Morrow said, his eyes narrowing. "The Henderson woman's insurance ran out yesterday. Her husband is a truck driver. In case you've forgotten, Whitehall doesn't take charity cases. We're losing money as we speak. I don't know what kind of meds you've got her on, but the last time I saw her, she looked like a walking corpse. A little fresh air might do her good."

Patterson was a large man, a former college linebacker. He seized the skinny psychiatrist by the shoulders and lifted him several inches off the ground, then dropped him. "I'm not discharging a suicidal patient, Morrow. And don't threaten to have my privileges revoked because two can play the same game. You want this person inside this institution, you play shrink to him. Count me out or I'll take my story to the press." He glared back at Morrow before he turned and took off down the corridor.

Inside his office, Patterson fingered an open case file. Instead of dictating as he usually did, he scribbled some notes in longhand. Then he swiveled his chair toward the wall where his diplomas were mounted. He was leaving on a three-week vacation beginning tomorrow, traveling to Los Angeles to visit his ailing father.

Why had he let himself become involved in the underhanded dealings that went on at Whitehall? For forty-five years, his father had been a respected practitioner. While he was in L.A., he'd make some inquiries. He might be able to buy an established practice. Along with his father, his adult children also resided in the L.A. area.

Patterson picked up the file and ripped it apart. Why leave any evidence that he'd treated this individual? He massaged his temples. The man couldn't be classified as actively psychotic. There was no evidence of paranoia, no loss of reality, and no sign of mania, nothing that would fit a specific diagnosis. But there was something there, something menacing. He saw it in his eyes, a steely control; a concocted disguise of normalcy practiced to the point of perfection.

Morrow could go down with this spook house and his income-producing schemes, but he was getting out. If he didn't disentangle himself fast, he might end up as a patient.

"God forbid," he said, tossing the remnants of the file in the trash can.

QUANTICO, VIRGINIA

At precisely four o'clock that afternoon, six special agents, including Mary Stevens and SAC John Adams, were assembled around the long table in the conference room. Mary had arranged to have folders prepared for each agent. Inside were the police and forensic reports from the five unsolved homicides. The folders contained so much material, she had been forced to use spiral binders.

Copies of the crime-scene photos were pinned up on the large board similar to the wall in Adams's office. A projector was mounted on the opposite wall and a drop-down screen was located in the ceiling above the poster board. Most agents preferred to use the projector for their presentations. Mary had all the crime-scene and autopsy photos on computer and could have done the same, but it was her belief that an actual photograph made a more lasting impression than a slide flashed on a screen.

As soon as she tacked up the last image, she took her seat and waited while the agents took turns examining the images. The name of each victim was scrawled in Magic Marker above their photographs, along with the place and date of the crime.

Outside of papers crackling and feet shuffling, there was no talking or gossiping or cell phones ringing. This was serious business and the agents needed time to focus all their energy on assimilating the materials.

"I'm going to hand this over to Special Agent Stevens now." Adams didn't need to elaborate. By his introductory statement, the agents knew it was Mary who had discovered the similarities in the homicides and Mary who was now in charge of an investigation that could require the expertise of hundreds, even thousands of FBI and other law enforcement personnel over an unknown period of time. This wasn't television, where killers were captured in a few days. Mary, along with several other fellow agents, could end up investigating this case for the remainder of her career.

Today she was wearing a green wool blazer over a navy blue blouse and matching slacks. From the day she had signed on with the Bureau, she had ferociously fought the dress code, seeing no reason to dress like an undertaker in order to profile serial criminals. Adams had ordered her to tone down her clothing on more occasions than he could recall. She would follow Bureau standards for a while and then rebel again as she had today.

Mary had taken a seat squarely in the middle on the left side of the table, which enabled her to make eye contact with the other agents. "The first victim that we know of is Joseph Connelly, a fifty-one-year-old white male. He was married with two children but estranged from his wife at the time of his death. Connelly's body was found in a remote area on the outskirts of Dallas. As you can see from the photographs taken at autopsy, Joseph Connelly was killed by a single shot to the back of the head. A gunshot wound to the back of the head, as we all know, can damage the higher centers but as long as the brain stem remains intact, the victim will survive.

"The UNSUB who I believe killed each of the five individuals we will be discussing today made certain that didn't happen. The medical examiner in the Connelly case as well as the medical examiners in the subsequent homicides of Ralph Thomason, Gerald Madison, Richard Sherman, and James Washburn all came to the same conclusion." She paused and scanned the faces around the table. The female victim the Ventura PD had discovered had yet to be identified and had not yet been autopsied, so Mary had decided not to include her until she received more information. Since the other victims were male, it was possible that the female was not related, even though she had been killed by a gunshot wound to the back of the head.

"The various medical examiners' conclusions were that the UN-SUB either shoved the victims' heads forward onto their chests or ordered the victims to do it themselves and then proceeded to fire a single shot into the inion of the victim's skull, assuring that the path of the bullet would strike perfectly in the midline. The bullet ripped up the center of the inferior portion of the cerebellum and continued forward through the floor of the fourth ventricle, plowing through the medulla, the pons, and the midbrain, destroying the centers that made the victim function."

Mary looked up from the autopsy report. "In layman's language, the UNSUB killed the brain stem and therefore the victims."

"How did he get the victims' heads down to expose the brain stem?" Genna Weir asked. "The victims were alive at that point, right, so there should have been some type of struggle? Did any of the autopsy reports indicate the victims were knocked unconscious prior to death?"

"No," Mary answered. "There was no sign of assault or injury other than the single shot to the back of the head. If you will turn to page thirty in the materials I've prepared for you, you will see an image that superimposes the injuries in all five victims." She waited while the agents flipped through the packets to the page. "As you can see, there's no more than a few millimeters difference in each wound."

George "Bulldog" McIntyre, a huge man who roared to work on a Harley, spoke up. "The UNSUB is obviously a sharpshooter. Maybe he's a disgruntled cop out to use his skills in a different way. Want me to put out a bulletin to law enforcement agencies in the areas where the killings occurred?"

Mary glanced over at Adams, expecting him to answer and then realized he was actually placing her in charge of the entire investigation. "Good idea, Bulldog." She wondered if Adams was simply trying another avenue to keep her in the unit. It wouldn't work, even though she was flattered he trusted her to run an investigation of this magnitude. The recent homicides had been in the southern California area, and she and Brooks would have a better chance of tracking and possibly even apprehending the killer if she went forward with the transfer.

"Okay," she said, placing her hands on the table. "You can study the crimes in more detail on your own. The most important thing is to establish a credible profile. There's another aspect of these crimes that I haven't mentioned. All of the victims had either a past incident of attempted suicide, served time in a mental hospital, or suffered from a debilitating illness. One of the most recent victims was a paraplegic."

"Interesting," Pete Cook, the unit's psychologist, said. "So there's a possibility they all wanted to die. Is that what you're saying?"

"Precisely."

Mark Conrad was in his late fifties and was a quiet, somewhat withdrawn individual, but his knowledge base and insight were second only to John Adams. "If I may render my opinion?" he said in his slow articulated fashion. "The victims all had families or loved ones to support, but they no longer found life worth living and they purchased life insurance policies. I presume this was less than two years before their deaths, so a suicide would not be covered." He paused for a long time, the team knowing he was gathering his thoughts before continuing. "Somehow they managed to hire a professional assassin to fulfill their desires." He looked at Mary, who was astonished that he had put things together so fast.

"But how did they hire the same assassin and where did they come up with the money to pay him?" Weir interjected. "They couldn't be well-off or they wouldn't care about the life insurance money."

Bulldog laughed. "Nobody has any money today, so that could apply to just about anyone."

"I agree with Weir," Adams said, turning toward Mary. "What have you found out about the victims' finances, Stevens?"

"We don't know a great deal about the most recent victim's finances, but the earlier ones were either living in poverty or only slightly above it, which makes it highly suspicious that they would expend money on life insurance. Before we go too far with this, I'd like to tell you the premise I've developed. The victims had someone kill them, but I don't believe they paid him. I think they found this person in a suicide club."

"Shit," Mark Conrad said. "Sorry, chief, but this is one hell of a scary situation. Are you saying there could be a serial killer prowling the Internet looking for willing victims?"

"Yes," Mary answered, "and he's finding them in suicide clubs. If you look in the right places, suicide clubs aren't that hard to find. Killing yourself has become trendy."

"We need a profile of this UNSUB," Adams told them, glancing at his watch. "He's moving fast so we need to move faster. Mary, who are we dealing with?"

"I believe he's a white male, mid to late twenties. I disagree that the UNSUB is a former marksman or sharpshooter for a law enforcement agency, nor does he have military training. When you think about it, anyone could make a perfect shot with a stationary, compliant subject. He's an elitist. He's also confident and knows he's superior but he possesses no need to brag. We're not going to get a letter or any type of communication from him like the BTK or the Son of Sam, regardless of how long this goes on or how many people he kills." Mary paused and took a sip of her water. "He could be big and strong or he could be small, depending on whether or not he disposes of the body or kills them on-site and leaves. Oh, we've confirmed that he uses a 9mm Walther. He's either wealthy or someone wealthy supports him. A Walther isn't a street gun, so we have to assume he has access to money."

"He's killing all over the map," Bulldog said. "Is there any pattern?"

"The first kill that we know about was in Dallas, the next in Houston. Then sometime during the summer, I think he decided he didn't like Texas and moved to California. Maybe he didn't like the heat or he wanted to be near the beach. That's another reason I believe this is a fairly young man. Another possibility is he somehow exposed himself in Texas."

"Explain how the suicide clubs work," Adams told her, sitting sideways in his chair to make room for his long legs.

"Some of the sites are free, and others charge a modest fee, generally in the range of ten to fifteen dollars. Which sites are legitimate and which are merely making money off these pathetic individuals is difficult to discern."

"They're probably all scams," Mark Conrad said, the unit's skeptic. "Besides if you were depressed enough to want to kill yourself, would you really try to find help over the Internet? Stuff you put on the Net never goes away. When you're eighty, your grandkid could find out you once joined a suicide club."

"You're already dead, remember?" Weir said. "And who cares what people are going to think about them thirty years down the line? Have you looked at the crap people put on YouTube? There's no such thing as pride anymore."

The unit's psychologist spoke up again. "I think all of you are taking this far too lightly. The statistics on suicide are staggering. I've seen some of these sites. Type the word 'suicide' on Google and see what comes up. People want to know recipes for poisons, different medications that can kill them, how long it takes to starve to death. It's gruesome stuff. Have you forgotten how popular Dr. Kevorkian was?"

"Hey," Bulldog said, chuckling. "Why do we have to bust our balls to track down a guy who's giving people what they want? He wants to kill. They want to die. Everybody's happy."

"I'm going to pretend I didn't hear that," Adams said, scowling. "Please continue, Stevens. Explain about the list."

"Okay, when a person joins one of the clubs, they're placed at the bottom of a list. They then have to assist the person's suicide at the top of the list. No one reveals why they want to die. Nothing like that is required." Mary rolled her neck around to relieve the tension. "Since none of this is legal, there's no way to know which person is serious or if they just stumbled onto the site and decided to hang around and bullshit someone into thinking they're suicidal. Most sites have chat rooms and members instant message each other, so I'm sure this kind of thing eventually comes out. Anyway, after you provide proof of the person's death, you move up a notch on the list. How soon it takes for you to die depends on how many people are on the list."

Pete Cook was beginning to get excited. "And because most of this is transpiring over the Internet, members of a suicide club could live anywhere in the country. What's the price of an airline ticket if you want to die and you're too chicken to do it? You don't have to pay the person who's going to help you. All you have to do is transport them to your location."

"You can't carry a gun on a plane," Genna Weir said. "I bet you a thousand bucks that one of these wannabe suicides slipped through the noose and may know what our UNSUB looks like, even his real name and other identifying factors. I'll put some ads on Craigslist and see if anyone bites."

"Has anyone considered that the UNSUB may actually be suicidal?" Cook asked. "Maybe everyone in the group decided to use the same method, even share the same gun. They could ship the Walther to each other."

"It's obvious you aren't a shrink anymore, Pete." Weir smirked, folding her arms across her chest. "I doubt if you could get a bunch of depressed people to agree on anything, let alone the exact means and method of their deaths."

"I agree that's a stretch, Pete," Mary said, having already considered something along those lines and discarded it. "We have to get a fix on where this man is or we'll never be able to stop him." Her face muscles twisted and her eyes narrowed. "He loves what he's doing, understand? I mean he absolutely loves killing people and walking away without any guilt whatsoever. This is paradise to him. All those terrible desires he's held inside over the years are worth something now. He's a fucking humanitarian. That's what makes me so furious."

"We understand, Mary," Adams said, rocking back and forth in his chair.

"You're right," Weir said, walking over to fill up her coffee cup. "This one's a bastard straight out of Hell. He doesn't even have to work for it. All he has to do is find these pathetic people."

Bulldog slammed his fists together. "We'll get him, Stevens."

Mary placed her head in her hands for a moment, then looked up. "Excuse me for getting carried away."

Mark Conrad was sitting next to Mary and patted her on the shoulder. "We've all been there."

"Okay," she continued, composed now. "I believe he has a hiding place, more or less a base of operation where he can come and go at will without anyone noticing. But this isn't a house or an apartment. I don't even think it's a hotel. It could be a motor home, but it doesn't fit my image of him. I know this sounds silly, but I see this place along the lines of a cave, somewhere unique, somewhere we'd never think to look."

"So he's driving," Bulldog said. "You don't think he's the type to travel by bus or motor home, so he has to be driving some kind of car. All that does is take care of the gun. He could be driving an Aston Martin from the way you've described him, Stevens."

"It's about a four-hour drive from Houston to Dallas," Mary told them. "And it's six between San Francisco and Ventura, where the most recent murder took place. What if he organizes his kills and takes only suicidal individuals who live in the same general area? That way, he can knock off one and then kill the other before moving to another hideout."

She stopped speaking, momentarily losing her train of thought. She had only had a few hours' sleep during the past two days. In addition to preparing the materials for the meeting, she'd had to line up a moving company and call her mother to tell her they were leaving. Luckily the Bureau would pay for it because she wasn't going to have time to pack and that made it costly.

People were beginning to fidget so she picked up an eight-by-ten paper that she had pasted onto cardboard and held it up for the agents to see. "I picked this up off the Net at three-fifteen today."

The mood in the room instantly changed. Seeing what appeared to be a handwritten note was sobering. "Saturnalia refers to the Roman dedication of the temple of the god Saturn which was held on December seventeenth," Mary explained. "Now we have a date, and perhaps this computer placard or whatever it is gets you into a specific suicide club. If you continue to follow these types of leads, you may eventually find the actual URL for the suicide club. For all I know, it's a physical address, but I have no idea how to find it. This club may be located in the San Francisco area or the person who posted it uses a server out of San Fran. Tracking down random postings on the Internet is time consuming."

With a smug look on her face, Weir said, "What you have is nothing."

"Exactly," Mary said. "But since it's January and it alludes to December, I don't think we should spend a lot of time on this one."

Putting the paper down, she continued. "Three teenagers killed themselves in Palo Alto just the other day by stepping in front of a Caltrans train. Our UNSUB hasn't killed a teenager yet, but if you ask me, it's only a matter of time."

"Good work, Stevens." Adams stood and pushed his chair back to the table, his way of signifying that the meeting was over.

———

After lunch, Shana curled up on the sofa next to Norman, exchanging playful glances with Alex from across the room. Dr. Morrow burst through the double doors, stopped off at the nursing station to pick up her file, then gestured for Shana. She had her head resting on the arm of the sofa, her feet in Norman's lap. When she didn't budge, Morrow walked over. "I'll see you now," he said, looking down at her. He turned his head and looked at Alex, then turned back to Shana.

"I'm busy right now," she told him, furious over her night in the padded cell. Norman snickered, but Alex shook his head. Smoothing down her sweater, she stood and followed Morrow. When they passed the window, she stopped and stared at the sunny courtyard. "Let's talk outside. You're a big shot here. It's not like I'm going to escape or anything. I already tried that the first day."

Morrow reached into the pocket of his baggy black slacks and came up with a large key ring. A short time later, they were standing in the afternoon sun. The weather was perfect and Shana walked ahead of him at a brisk pace, wishing she was free to enjoy the day. The weather in the San Francisco area was strange, with the hottest months being September and October. Today, it had to be in the low seventies, which was unseasonably warm.

"The staff says you're hanging out with Alex. They say you're with him all the time. They even observed you embracing him on several occasions."

"What's it to you?" Shana tossed over her shoulder. She suddenly halted and Morrow almost collided with her. "I'm formally rescinding my voluntary commitment. Take me to court. No matter what you write in your report, I'm going to get out of here. When I do, you can kiss your medical license goodbye. You've held me against my will, administered drugs you had no right to give me without my consent, and one of your staff members exposed me in front of a male attendant. She also struck me."

Shana gave thought to reminding him that her mother was a superior court judge, but it was hard to know where Lily stood since she was responsible for her being at Whitehall. To be fair, though, she doubted if her mother had any idea what went on inside the hospital. Even she had been deceived by the hospital's appearance. "There's still a chance, though."

"Let's talk, okay?" Morrow said, brushing his hair off his forehead. "If I raise your level and give you access to the courtyard, will you sign a consent for treatment?"

Now he was bribing her, which gave credence to the fact that he couldn't treat her with Thorazine without her consent. Shana kicked a snail off the sidewalk, looking down at her new suede shoes. "I'd be an idiot to sign anything at this place. You tricked me the first time. Keep playing games with me, and you'll lose more than your medical license. This entire hospital will be history. Do you think I don't know what Whitehall is all about? You're raking in a ton of money off defenseless people."

"Okay, okay," Morrow said, holding up a palm. "Sign the papers and I'll stop the injections as well as agree to release you this Saturday. That's only four days. Force me to take you to court and you could be here far longer. I can present a good case for commitment. Once a judge officially commits you, you might never go home again. Are you prepared to take that great of a risk?"

It had to be more than the Thorazine. Her suspicions about the hospital's unscrupulous practices must be accurate. The events of the night before passed through her mind, and she was fearful of pushing the psychiatrist any further than she already had. "Why do I have to sign a consent?"

"It's just a formality. I'll have the staff prepare it this afternoon." He glanced at his watch. "I have another patient waiting. We have to go back now."

"It's the Thorazine, isn't it?" Shana said. "You failed to get me to sign a consent for treatment with Thorazine. You knew I wasn't psychotic. I had a severe reaction. Shit, the drugs are more dangerous in here than they are on the street. Of course, you know I don't have a drug problem."

Morrow spun around. "You struck a staff member. You're a

violent person, Ms. Forrester. Perhaps you should spend about ten years in the state hospital instead of Whitehall."

Shana wasn't a poker player, but she knew this was a hand she had to play. "I'll sign, but I want my release date in writing."

Morrow smiled, exposing his large teeth. "I did your astrology chart, by the way. Tell me what time you were born, and I'll research it more thoroughly. It's highly unusual. Your coordinates form a circle with a star inside."

"What does that mean?" The heavy jeans and sweater had felt wonderful inside the frigid hospital, but perspiration had started dripping between her breasts. She took the edge of her sweater and held it away from her body, hoping a breeze would come along.

Morrow's eyes were focused on her chest. The dampness had made the white sweater even more transparent. "I'm not really certain what it means," he told her. "You're either someone extraordinary or something extraordinary is about to happen to you."

"And this isn't extraordinary?" Shana said, shocked that he'd shifted from locking her away forever to a discussion about astrology. "Trust me, I don't need any more extraordinary events in my life."

Morrow took off again and Shana tagged along behind him. She saw the keys come out of his pocket and was tempted to snatch them. Even with the keys, she doubted if she would be able to make it to freedom. Only four more days, she told herself. Now wasn't the time to take chances.

"You know," he told her, inserting the key in the lock, "I've become accustomed to skeptics. Astrology and physics are the keys to the universe. I never intended to go into psychiatry. Whether you believe me or not, I do know what I'm doing."

"As a psychiatrist?" she asked. "Or do you mean as an astrologist? I haven't been through Hell to be treated by a fucking astrologist, have I?"

"You'd rather be out here than in the hospital, so I'm going to explain something to you," Morrow told her. "The human body contains somewhere between seventy to eighty percent water, and the Earth itself is covered by three hundred and twenty-six million trillion gallons of water." He paused to give her time to absorb what he was telling her. "Yes, I said three hundred twenty-six million trillion. Lots of water, right? Well, an ocean tide is the cyclic rise and fall of seawater. Tides are caused by slight variations in gravitational fields between the Earth and the moon. The Earth and the moon have a geometric relationship with locations on the Earth's surface. Tides are periodic primarily because of the cyclical influence of the Earth's rotation. The moon is the primary factor controlling the temporal rhythm and height of tides. The moon produces two tidal bulges somewhere on the Earth through the effects of gravitational attraction. The height of these tidal bulges is controlled by the moon's gravitational force and the Earth's gravity pulling the water back toward the Earth. At the location on the Earth closest to the moon, seawater is drawn toward the moon because of the greater strength of gravitational attraction. On the opposite side of the Earth, another tidal bulge is produced away from the moon. However, this bulge is due to the fact that at this point on the Earth the force of the moon's gravity is at its weakest."

Shana stopped him. "I know the argument you're presenting. Since our bodies are made up of so much water, we're subject to the same forces that act on the Earth's water. You're trying to convince me that astrology is science. Your analysis is anecdotal and therefore flawed. Science is not based on assumptions. You must have proof and you don't have it." She stopped, feeling like lashing out at him but knowing it would only make matters worse. "Let me tell you something. You could do a million charts and you'll never know me. Now if you don't mind, I'd like to go inside."

Once he pulled open the door, they were hit by a blast of frigid air. "If you refuse to listen to anything," Morrow said, "at least listen to what I'm about to tell you. You're in over your head with Alex."

The psychiatrist started to walk off when Shana tugged on his sleeve. "Two o'clock," she said. "I was born at two o'clock."

"Morning or evening?"

"Are you going to tell me about Alex?"

"I've told you all you need to know." Morrow glanced at her

chest again. "Whoever brought you the clothes should have brought you some underwear. You're titillating the male patients. Some of these men haven't been with a woman for years. I suggest you take my suggestion seriously. If you don't correct your clothing, we'll have to put you back in the clothes we provide for you."

The green pajamas, Shana thought, disgusted at the thought of having to wear them again. "I'll take care of it."

Everyone lined up for medication before dinner and Shana stepped to the back of the line behind Alex. Under her white sweater, she now had two Band-Aids covering her nipples. She hoped her solution would satisfy Morrow, as she refused to let him put her back in the green pajamas.

"Maybe I don't have to take the Valium since I'm going to be released in a few days," she whispered to Alex. "Should I get out of line and see what happens?"

"Suit yourself," he said, shrugging.

"Why cause problems?" Shana said, answering her own question. "I've been taking the pills all along."

Peggy handed her two cups, one with a pill and the other filled with water. Shana removed the pill and examined it. This pill was round and white, whereas the Valium was oval and pink. "I'm sorry," she said, "but you've made a mistake. This isn't my medicine."

Peggy slapped her meaty paws on the counter. "That most certainly is your medication. Dr. Morrow ordered it for you a few hours ago."

"But I don't even know what this is," Shana told her. "You can't expect me to take something if I don't know what it is you're giving me. I've had bad reactions to some of the medication."

Peggy stood and the counter shook like a small earthquake. "You take that pill this instant or I'll have you placed back in the Quiet Room. Are we clear?"

The mere mention of the Quiet Room was sufficient. Shana tossed the pill in her mouth and swallowed it dry. She started to take to the sides of the room for a brisk walk. Milton was already circling, though, and she wasn't up for discussions about sleep deprivation and aberrant behavior. She opted for Norman and the sofa.

"Alex says you're leaving Saturday," he said. "Everyone will miss you. Alex is leaving, too. This place won't be the same without you guys."

"What about you, Norman? When are you going home?" Shana stared at his face without cringing. His entire scalp was burned, leaving only a few strands of hair. He had no eyelashes or eyebrows, and his nose consisted of a flat surface with two holes. The tiny fan was held between the stubs of his right hand. Two of the fingers on his left hand were melded together. Shana thought of gloves with the slots for five fingers, then thought of mittens and wondered if the person who had invented them had been a person like Norman.

"Can you talk about what happened?" she asked, reaching over and gently touching his free hand.

He looked at her and sighed, moving the small fan in front of his face. "It just happened, you know? Not many people really understand." He leaned forward in his seat, shifting his body closer to Shana. He kept his voice low, looking around to make certain no one was listening. "All my life I felt like there was this hideous thing inside me. I knew it was there even though no one could see it. Now it can't hurt me anymore."

Shana asked herself how anyone could set themselves on fire. What had possibly driven Norman to such a desperate act?

"I lost my job," he continued. "Last December . . . you know, only a few days before Christmas. I was a department head at Macy's. Seven years I worked for that store and they fired me for absolutely no reason. They said they were cutting back due to the economy. That was a lie. I wasn't a strong enough manager. The employees in my department took advantage of me."

"With your experience," Shana offered, "surely you could have found another position."

"They said I could stay with the store, but I had to go back to the sales floor. My salary would have been a fraction of what it had been before, and it wouldn't have been enough to support my family. I'd already promised my son a new bike for Christmas. We were two months behind on our mortgage and my wife was pregnant again. How could I tell my family I'd lost my job? This horrible thing inside me kept tormenting me, pushing me."

Norman stared out over the great room. "I went to the bicycle shop and smashed the window. I took the most expensive bike on the floor. I wanted my son to have the best." His words were generally slow and measured. Now they were coming out rapid-fire. "I hid the bike in the garage. That's when I saw it . . . the can of gasoline for the lawn mower. The voices kept screaming at me, 'Take it . . . take it.' I put the can in the backseat of my car and told my wife I was going out to finish the rest of my Christmas shopping."

They were sitting so close, their bodies were touching. Shana was staring out over the room as well, her mind chained to Norman's in those agonizing hours.

"While I was driving around, I thought of my insurance policy. With that money, Gladys and the kids would be okay. I didn't want them to lose the house. Gladys loved that house. It meant the world to her. I'd failed her, failed everyone. More importantly, I'd failed myself. If I set myself on fire inside the car on the highway, the police would think the engine exploded and it would be classified as an accident." The fan fell unnoticed from his fingers as he glanced furtively at Shana. "I drove on the freeway, parked, and grabbed the can from the backseat. I threw the key to the car out the window into the bushes. Then I locked all the car doors, afraid I'd panic and try to get out. The windows were automatic and wouldn't work without the key in the ignition. Then I soaked my clothes with the gasoline. All I had to do was light a match and drop it in my lap."

Shana saw the burning car with the image of Norman inside, consumed in the flames. She could imagine his terrified screams, and how he must have placed his palms against the cool glass of the windows. "I'm so sorry, Norman," she said. "Thank God you survived."

"I didn't want to survive," Norman shot out, a muscle in his face twitching. "How did I know the fire department had a station only a block away? My wife lost our home and had to file for bankruptcy because of my medical bills. I even failed at killing myself."

"Well," Shana said, wishing she'd never brought up the subject, "I'm glad you survived, and I know Alex and the others feel the same. Life is precious, even though we sometimes forget it. I know about depression, the feeling that everything is collapsing around you and there's nothing you can do to stop it. Then someone smiles at you, calls you, holds you, and you realize how lucky you are to be alive." She stopped and inhaled. "Regardless of how you look, Norman, you're still the same man. Everyone loves you."

"You don't know anything about the others," Norman told her, his tone even more agitated. "You're just a tourist here. Saturday you'll go back to your life, and we'll be nothing more than a colorful story to tell your college friends."

"I'm sorry you feel that way, Norman." Shana pushed herself to her feet, completely drained. Someone should have told her not to talk to Norman about his injuries. He'd seemed so relaxed and open. Her vision suddenly blurred and she felt drugged and disoriented. What had they given her now? Saturday, she told herself. All she had to do was hold on for four more days. But four days at Whitehall was like a month, a year, a lifetime. Peggy marched over and handed her a clipboard.

"Sign on the red X," she said. "Dr. Morrow ordered it."

Taking the clipboard, Shana walked to a small table and sat down in the chair. She certainly wasn't going to sign whatever Peggy had given her without reading it, but the drug had affected her vision and she had to strain to make out the words on the piece of paper. She'd already made a mistake in the emergency room. Her excitement at catching Morrow at his dirty tricks helped to sharpen her state of alertness.

Shana held the document close to her face. There it was. Not on the first page, but the second. It was a consent form to treat her with psychotropic medication, specifically Thorazine. A sentence was typed at the bottom stating that she was to be released that Saturday, so at least Morrow had held true on one promise. She signed her name and dated it with the current date, then handed the paper back to Peggy.

She watched as Peggy walked away, her hips swaying underneath her blue shirtwaist dress. She glanced over her shoulder at Norman. Of course he was bitter. What was he going to do with the rest of his life? Where could he get a job with such severe deformities? He certainly couldn't work in retail sales.

Her own predicament came to mind. What was she going to do when she got out on Saturday? She had told the others that she was going to Ventura, but it would be difficult to live with her mother after what she had done. Witnessing the greed and corruption at Whitehall had changed her mind about becoming an attorney. Even if she didn't want to practice, she could use her credentials to tackle a plethora of problems. She was too far behind to catch up, though, so she would have to make up the semester in the fall. She doubted if her mother would continue to pay rent on her apartment, particularly when she came clean about paying for Brett's tuition, which she fully intended to do. Although she hated to admit it, being removed from all of her problems had been good for her. She felt more mature and confident. Of course, no longer having to carry the burden of Brett's problems and the demands he placed on her was partially responsible. How could she let anyone take advantage of her, let alone a man? And Brett's sexuality simply wasn't compatible with someone who'd been raped. It wasn't that she didn't enjoy sex because she did. She had normal desires and needs. What she couldn't tolerate was a man telling her what to do in the bedroom.

Shana placed her head in her hands. Her new cashmere sweater already reeked of cigarette smoke. Except for Norman and herself, most of the people who hung out with Alex were smokers. All she could think of was charred flesh. Did Norman still smell it? Would the scent of burning flesh ever go away?

A nasal voice she immediately recognized as Peggy's jolted her out of her thoughts. "Sign this again," Peggy said. "The first one was torn up in the copy machine."

Shana took the clipboard and signed her name. She checked to be certain the sentence about her release date was still present. It was, but something was missing. Then she saw it. There was no date. The section next to her name where she had written in the date had been deleted.

Peggy reached for the clipboard, but Shana refused to let her have it. She slapped the document on the table and printed the word "date" next to her signature, then entered the current date.

Shana understood the game.

"Here you go, Peggy," she said. "And don't tell me this one got torn in the copy machine. You'll be wasting your time. I won't sign it."

Peggy snatched the clipboard and stomped off. The hospital was trying to protect itself from a lawsuit. She had Morrow and his cohorts on the run. They wanted the date to match up with the date she was admitted. Before she checked out on Saturday, Shana would demand to see the form again to make certain it hadn't been altered.

# TWENTY-ONE

When Chris and Lily ate at home, they cooked as a team. Tonight they were making fish, one of Lily's specialties. Chris was chopping up vegetables for their salad while Lily prepared the sea bass, baked potatoes, and fresh asparagus. A bottle of Sauvignon Blanc was open on the counter.

"I want you to call tonight and see if you can get through to Shana," Lily told him, covering the sea bass with a light lemon butter sauce she had prepared earlier.

"That doesn't make sense. Why would she talk to me? We've never even met." Chris removed a bottle of honey mustard dressing from the refrigerator, shaking it and then dribbling it over the salad.

"You're going to pretend to be Brett." Lily placed the fish in the oven and then walked over to the sink to wash her hands. "She won't refuse a call from him."

"That's cruel, Lily." The muscles in his face tightened. "I thought you wanted me to develop a good relationship with Shana. If I do what you want, you'll be sabotaging any chance of that happening. You can't start a relationship with a lie."

"What else am I supposed to do?" She dried her hands with a

dish towel. Taking a sip of her wine, she added, "Maybe there's something physically wrong with her. I haven't spoken to her since she was admitted."

"I know you're concerned, but you put her in that place. If it was me, I wouldn't talk to you, either." Seeing Lily turn away, he walked over and captured her face in his hands. "Look at me, honey. I'm not criticizing you. If anyone should understand, it's me. I did the same thing with Sherry. The chances of something being seriously wrong with Shana are remote. From what you've told me, she's a healthy young woman. Now let's sit down and enjoy our meal. The fish smells delicious."

"I'm not hungry," Lily said, sniffling.

"Come on," he said. "You were too busy to have lunch today. You have to be famished. You'll get sick if you don't eat. Besides, I like my women with some meat on their bones." He tossed the salad and then carried it to the table, returning for the bottle of wine.

Lily was quiet throughout their meal. Chris's statement about not starting a relationship with a lie had hit too close to home. Once she had cleaned up the kitchen, she asked him to come outside on the balcony. The evening air was chilly with a brisk ocean breeze. A storm was working its way north and heavy clouds were forming on the horizon. She went to her bedroom for a sweater and brought along one for him.

Her conversation with Dr. Morrow had left her feeling confident that Shana was in the right hands and would soon be herself again, but oddly, she became tense when she was alone with Chris. His story about his wife had been unsettling to say the least, but it was far more than that. She had to tell him the truth. The same uncomfortable feeling was surfacing again. Hiding the truth from Bryce had made her miserable. Even a louse deserved to know the person he was sharing his life with.

"Remember when I told you I did something wrong?" Lily asked, the wind whipping her hair back from her face.

"Yes, but Lily . . ."

"You have to know, Chris. I didn't shoplift something from a department store. I killed someone."

His expression remained the same, almost as if he needed time to digest what she had told him. Some time passed and then he blurted out, "Who did you kill, for God's sake?"

Her voice cracked with emotion. "I caught sight of the rapist in the light from the bathroom when he was fleeing. A siren scared him off. Unfortunately, no one had called the police, even though Shana and I had screamed for help. But something about the rapist was familiar. I was certain I'd seen him before but I couldn't remember where. After John took Shana home, I figured out where I had seen him. I convinced myself he was the suspect Clinton Silverstein was prosecuting on a rape case. When the victim failed to appear at the preliminary hearing, we had no choice but to drop the charges and release him."

Lily stopped speaking and massaged her back. It had started throbbing as soon as she'd brought forth the memories of that night. Chris was sitting in rapt attention, so she knew she must continue. "The suspect was released the same day we were assaulted. I built this whole picture in my mind, how he'd watched me getting in and out of my car from the windows of the jail, then followed me home when he was released. I had the report with his mug shot in my briefcase. When I took it out and looked at it, I was certain it was him. He was wearing the same red sweatshirt and an identical gold crucifix around his neck. I was so full of rage I couldn't think straight. I took my father's shotgun out of the garage and drove to the address on his booking sheet. I even altered my license plate with a Magic Marker." She stopped and placed her hands over her face. "Then I waited for him. I sat there all night watching for him to come out of his house so I could kill him. And when he came out early the next morning, that's exactly what I did. I blew him apart."

"You killed the wrong man? Is that what you're trying to tell me?" Chris clasped Lily's hand, but there was something artificial about his gesture, almost as if he did it without thinking.

Lily turned and linked eyes with him. "I killed Bobby Hernandez.

Have you heard about the Lopez/McDonald murders? It was one of the most atrocious crimes ever committed in Ventura. I doubt you know about it because it happened before you moved to Ventura." When he shook his head, she continued. "The victims were teenagers, lovers. The boy was beaten and bludgeoned. The girl was raped and mutilated. The killers were five Hispanic gang members. They played target practice on the girl's breasts. They shoved a tree limb up her vagina. Bobby Hernandez was the ringleader, Chris. That's the man I killed."

"I need a drink," Chris said, getting up and going inside.

Lily remained outside, wondering if he would return. The sea seemed to mimic her emotions, as an enormous wave barreled its way to the shore beneath her. He would leave her now. Her back pain had disappeared. The horrible secret she had carried inside for so long was finally out. There was no statute of limitations on murder. The minutes ticked off inside her head. What would Chris do?

He finally joined her again on the balcony. "I don't know what to say, Lily. I don't condone vigilantism and from what you've told me, what happened is a perfect example of why people shouldn't take the law into their own hands. I'm not going to turn you in, if that's what you're worried about. No one can say how they would react under the same circumstances. At least you didn't kill an innocent man. I guess you could say you brought a killer to justice. Are you certain Bobby Hernandez was involved in the deaths of the teenagers?"

"The police had eyewitness identification," Lily told him. "One of the other gang members also rolled over on Hernandez, targeting him as the ringleader. Unfortunately, DNA wasn't available back then. After Hernandez was murdered, though, the police were able to search his house. They found the girl's necklace as well as other evidence that linked him to the crime."

"This man was a monster," he exclaimed. "I just don't understand this kind of brutality. Where does it come from? How could they violate a young woman like that? It's sickening, evil."

"You haven't heard the whole story." Chris looked at her in astonishment. "The attempted rape case we dismissed turned out to be a homicide. The victim didn't show up for the preliminary hearing because Hernandez had killed her."

"Listen to me," he said, the wind howling now. "What you killed wasn't human. You'll probably think I'm a religious freak, but evil entities exist. They roam the earth looking for empty vessels like Bobby Hernandez and his gang buddies and then they use them to commit unbelievable acts against mankind. You and Shana were forced to make an enormous sacrifice for the benefit of the greater good. But God choose you, Lily. He chose you to go to battle for him. This was a great honor, don't you see? No one else other than God himself could have organized this, brought all the details together."

"But Shana . . ."

"It may be hard to believe now," Chris told her, having to shout over the wind, "but both you and Shana will be rewarded for the pain and degradation you suffered. It may not happen today or tomorrow, or even during your life here on earth, but God knows what you did and he won't forget." He stopped and smiled at her. "I wouldn't kill anyone else, though. I believe it's highly unlikely that God would ask you to do something like this again."

A sense of overwhelming relief washed over Lily. Someone finally knew the truth and understood. When Chris stood and pulled Lily into his arms, tears of joy streamed down her face. She visualized a lifetime of unsuccessful and many times psychologically damaging relationships floating out to sea with the ebbing tide. At last, she had found her soul mate. The sky opened and it began pouring but neither of them made a move to go inside. Side by side, they turned and faced the churning ocean, letting the rain wash over them.

WEDNESDAY, JANUARY 20
SAN FRANCISCO, CA

"Are you going to the dance tonight?" Alex asked Shana on the walk across the courtyard to lunch. "They hold it in the gym. Mostly it's for the juveniles, but sometimes we all go."

"A dance?" she asked, incredulous. "They're really having a dance in this place?"

Alex arched one eyebrow and then the other, making funny faces to get her to laugh. Shana had been moping around all day, refusing to talk to anyone. She'd spent the afternoon watching television or nodding off.

"Get your ball gown out," Alex quipped. "This is a big affair. I hear they bill your insurance ten grand."

"I wouldn't doubt it." Shana finally managed to smile, but it barely lifted one corner of her mouth. "Are you going?"

"Certainly," he said. "Wouldn't miss it for the world."

At lunch, Alex carried their trays to the table while Shana brought their two glasses of fruit punch, the napkins, and the silverware. She took her regular seat beside him. The chair where Norman generally sat was empty. Shana turned around and checked the food line to see if he was there, but she didn't see him. "Where's Norman?"

"He's in a session with his shrink," Alex told her. "Norman's been talking about going home. He's voluntary, so he can leave anytime he wants."

"I'm not sure if he's ready," Shana said, her face etched with concern. "He seemed really depressed yesterday, almost hostile. I shouldn't have asked him about the fire."

"He was fine," Karen jumped in. "Norman's more than ready to leave. I've talked to him about the fire before and it didn't bother him. He was probably in pain today. I think he's going in for another operation."

With the talk of the dance and the news that Shana and Norman would soon be discharged, May announced that she was scheduled for release the following week. No one said anything about Alex leaving, so Shana kept her mouth shut. "Do you have family here, May?"

"They all dead now." She looked sad and then a few moments later, she perked up and smiled. "I've got me a job lined up in L.A. The company is called Dial-A-Psychic. They pay good money, too. Movie stars call in all the time. They say I can make up to fifty dollars an hour just chatting with lonely souls on the phone."

Everyone chuckled at the thought of May as an L.A. Dial-A-Psychic. "Sounds like you're going into the entertainment business," Shana told her. She forced herself to swallow a spoonful of rice. Lately, she'd almost completely lost her appetite. She assumed it had something to do with the medication.

"I'm not gonna cheat people. I'm gonna give them a real reading. I can do it over the phone. I've done it before."

"Hey," Shana said, "I'm not mocking you, May, not after what I've seen and heard. I'm probably going home to Ventura when I get out. It's not that far from Los Angeles. We'll have to keep in touch, maybe have lunch one day."

A loud ting rang out as Alex dropped both his knife and fork on the table at the same time. "Excuse me," he said, standing. "I need some fresh air."

Shana attempted to ignore him and finish her lunch. She picked at her chicken until it was broken up into tiny pieces.

"Alex doesn't want you to leave," Karen told her, turning her head to one side and muttering, "Shit, damn, suck." She composed herself and then continued, "But he doesn't think you should stay in this area because of your boyfriend. He hurt you, didn't he? There are so many abusive men out there. It makes me glad I'm single."

"Brett didn't hit me," Shana said, wondering what Alex was telling them.

Karen and May stopped eating and stared at her with a look that said they didn't believe her. Shana went to find Alex. He was sitting in a chair in the courtyard smoking a cigarette. She pulled up a chair and sat down beside him.

"Want a cigarette?"

"No, thanks," she said. "The last thing I need is to get hooked on cigarettes again."

Alex stuffed the pack back in his pocket, exhaling a thin stream of smoke out of the corner of his mouth. "What would it take for you to stay here?"

"You mean in the San Francisco area?"

"No," Alex said, "I mean here at the hospital. What would it take for you to be happy here?"

Shana was shocked. "You mean permanently?" Something was seriously wrong. Why in God's name was he asking her such an insane question? She was counting the hours until her release, and Alex was asking if she could stay at Whitehall indefinitely.

Leaning back in the plastic lawn chair until the front legs came off the ground, he flicked his cigarette ashes into the grass. "When you think about it, Whitehall isn't that bad. You get three meals a day and a roof over your head. They clean your room, wash your clothes, and keep people you don't want to see from hounding you. When you get right down to it, what does a person really need in life? Do we really *need* all these cars, houses, clothes, and other possessions? You want a computer, we can get you one. You want books. Write down the names and the staff will get them for free from the library. Do you really need to own so many things, store so many things, maintain so many things? The economy is a disaster. We've destroyed the planet. We're running out of oil, and more importantly, water." He paused, taking another puff of his cigarette and then extinguishing it. "Now that Morrow has raised your level, we can take walks in the courtyard every evening." He laughed. "And don't forget, no one can bust you for using drugs."

"Funny," Shana said, wondering if he was serious or merely seeking an interesting conversation. "There's no freedom to come and go here, to make your own decisions, to develop a lasting relationship, or simply do something other than sit around all day. Life isn't just three meals a day and someone to hang out with. Sure, the world isn't always a pleasant place. That's what makes life challenging, though, the struggle to overcome all the various obstacles. And you're forgetting responsibility. What if everyone decided to abandon their jobs and disappear? Who would deliver the newspapers, stock the shelves with groceries, grow our food, and educate our children? What about doctors? What if all the doctors decided to drop out of society?"

"I didn't ask for a speech," Alex said, "just an answer to a hypothetical question."

Listening to herself, Shana realized how much she had grown in the short time she'd been at Whitehall. What had she been thinking? She'd never been a quitter. Brett's grades were lower than hers, so it was understandable why he was so anxious about getting his degree and passing the law exam. The situation was directly opposite to what Brett had told her. He had dragged her down, caused her to panic. When you were intimate with someone, you took on their problems and concerns.

Shana believed she'd held up her end of the conversation, but Alex was evidently seeking a more precise answer. "There're too many rules and regulations here. The staff has too much power over the patients."

"And there aren't rules in the outside world?" Alex argued. "What about the law?"

"I'll give you that point. The rules at Whitehall are similar to laws. The problem is there are no courts or judges. Whitehall isn't a democracy. It's a dictatorship, a fancy prison."

Alex was persistent. "There's no pressure, no need to compete and excel. Here there's no failure, no rejection, no deadlines to meet. Three months at Whitehall would be comparable to three years on the outside. Stay here and ten years from today, you'll look about the same as you do today."

They stopped speaking as the doors to the cafeteria opened and patients started coming out. "I know this is only a philosophical conversation, Alex," Shana remarked, "but I could never remain here at Whitehall. I've decided to finish school and get my law degree."

"You think you'll ever be important in the overall scheme of things? Trust me, you're nothing. The only value you possess rests in what good you can contribute to humanity. What can a lawyer do?" Alex stood and slipped in with the group headed for the main building.

Shana remained there until everyone had gone inside. He was wrong. If she got her law degree, she might be able to close down unscrupulous hospitals like Whitehall, or help people like Karen who suffered from a rare illness and couldn't get medicine because there wasn't enough profit in it for greedy drug manufacturers. Another alternative was to get a government job, perhaps even work her way into politics. She realized she had to bring in some kind of income, but material possessions had never mattered to her. Maybe she could become an advocate for the mentally ill. The possibilities were endless.

Now that everyone had returned to the main wing of the hospital, Shana saw George walking toward her. "False alarm," she said, pushing herself to her feet. "I'm not going over the wall today, George. You can call off the dogs."

Inside the great room, Milton was walking and Karen and May were the only members of their group at their customary table. "Look," Karen said, holding her hands in front of her. "Aren't they great? May painted my nails gold with green tips. For the dance, you know."

Every time Shana looked at Karen, she tried to imagine what she would look like with a different hairstyle and makeup. People always wanted what they couldn't have. She'd never liked her own red hair but Karen's was a more brilliant shade. A vision of Karen appeared in her mind—a different Karen. "Have you got any makeup, May? Alex gave me a few things, but . . ."

"May has everything, baby doll," she said, opening up a large metal case where she kept all her nail polish. "You name it, I got it. I got a bunch of stuff the lady who was in my room before me left behind." She chuckled. "Some of it's a little light for me, if you know what I mean, but it would probably look real nice on you or Karen."

Mimicking Arnold Schwarzenegger, Shana said, "I'll be back." She went to her room to collect some of the makeup Alex had given her. Michaela was in the same position she'd been in the last time Shana had seen her, turned on her side with her face toward the wall. Sometimes the woman was in the room, and at other times, the bed was empty. Shana never saw her in the cafeteria, and never saw a tray or any traces of food in the room. As she opened the drawer in her nightstand where she'd placed the makeup and the other toiletries Alex had given her, the bed creaked and Michaela got up and walked to the bathroom, pulling the door closed behind her.

Shana grabbed the bottle of cologne Alex had given her from the top of the nightstand. Before she had time to spray the room with it, she heard the toilet flush and darted out of the room.

"It walks," she told Karen and May, tilting her head in the direction of her room. "Heaven help us if it starts talking."

"Poor Michaela," May said, her lyrical voice dropping to a masculine level. "This life isn't for her, you see. Next life will be better."

"I shouldn't have made such an insensitive remark."

"It's all right," Karen told her, clapping her hands. "What are we going to do?"

Shana dumped all the cosmetics onto the table, along with the hairbrush. "We're going to play dress up," she said. "My first victim will be . . . let's see . . . Karen. My second sense tells me it must be Karen. Are you game?"

"Sure."

Shana pulled out a chair and gestured for Karen to take a seat. She started with foundation, covering almost all of Karen's freckles. She then added blush, eye shadow, lipstick, eyeliner, and mascara. The difference was dramatic. Shana then told Karen to bend over, and brushed all of her hair to the top of her head. "Rubber band, please," she said to May, extending her hand like a surgeon in an operating room. May rummaged around in her metal case and handed her an elastic hair tie. Once she had secured Karen's hair on top of her head, she pulled a few strands down around her face.

"Voilà!" Shana exclaimed, stepping back. Karen jumped up and headed to her room. Shana followed. May was heavy and didn't move around all that much, so she stayed behind at the table.

Shana stood in the doorway while Karen looked at her face in the mirror. "I can't believe it. I look so different. I look . . ." she grimaced and an aborted bark came out, "almost pretty. I never tried to fix up because I didn't think it mattered."

"Only pretty," Shana said, grinning in delight. "You look gorgeous. Guys are going to chase you like wild. Tomorrow, I'll show you how to do it by yourself. I'm sure May won't mind letting you have most of the stuff since she said she couldn't use it."

When they went back to the great room, Norman was seated at the table beside Alex. Shana stood at one end of the smoking table and analyzed his face. Then she picked through the various tubes, jars, and brushes in May's case until she found the items she needed. "Come on, Norman," she said. "Step into my office. I think we have something for the men in here, too."

Norman glanced behind him, thinking Shana was speaking to someone else. When he saw Karen, he put it together and reluctantly sat down in the chair. Shana leaned near what had once been his ear but was now only a small hole. "Will it hurt if I touch your face?" she whispered. "I promise I'll be gentle."

"I'll be fine."

Shana seized a jar of makeup in a warm healthy shade that must belong to May, plunging her fingers into the jar until she had a glob of it. She gingerly began applying the foundation to Norman's scarred face. After using a cover-up, she applied a second layer and dusted his face with powder. Next, she painted on eyebrows, and faintly outlined the scar tissue around his eyes with eyeliner. She used a dark pink to make Norman a mouth and finally finished with a flesh-colored lipstick belonging to May. The makeup gave Norman the appearance of having lips. He didn't look normal, of course. Sadly, he would never look normal again. Nonetheless, it was a substantial improvement.

Shana stepped back and dropped her hands to her side. Filled with compassion for this tragic soul, she bent down and pressed her lips to the ones she had just created for him. "You look so hand-some, Norman, I couldn't resist." Shana handed him a small plastic mirror from May's case.

He shoved the mirror away. "I try to avoid looking in mirrors. You would too if you looked like me."

"Oh, come on," May said, encouraging him. "Go ahead and look, honey. You look mighty fine to me. I feel like giving you a smooch myself."

"You're just placating me," Norman said, rising to his feet. "Anyway, men don't wear makeup."

Alex walked over and took a seat in the chair. "You're wrong, buddy," he said. Then he spoke directly to Shana. "See that scar over by my eyebrow? I hate that damn thing. Can you cover that up?"

"No problem." She reached for the foundation and dabbed it over the scar. Out of the corner of her eye, she saw Norman watch-ing. "Doesn't he look better? What do you think, Alex?"

Norman walked off and Alex reached for Shana's hand, pulling it to his chest. "I think you're one of the most beautiful human be-ings I've ever met, both inside and out. I don't want to lose you."

Even though his voice was low, May overheard and smiled. "You've done made the grade, sugar. Alex is our prince. Now we got ourselves a princess." She flicked her wrist. "Oh I know what you're thinking but you're wrong. We might not be the cream of the crop in some folks' eyes, but I know one thing for sure . . . the man upstairs loves us."

The rest of the day passed in a blur of anticipation. The patients played volleyball in the afternoon, and Shana asked David if he was going to attend the dance. When he said he was coming, Shana wondered if she'd recognize him. The crutches were gone, but his arm was now in a sling. He told her he had fallen out of bed that morning. He was such a beautiful young man, so handsome and fit. Why would he feel compelled to manufacture injuries?

Karen's new look had caught everyone's attention. Patients came up and complimented her, asking her what she'd done to herself.

Even several members of the staff asked Shana if she would give them a makeover.

Karen didn't exhibit one symptom of her illness during dinner or volleyball. Perhaps the strange outbursts associated with Tourette's were triggered by nerves, and Karen's newfound confidence gave her the strength to control them.

After spending the rest of the afternoon giving makeup lessons, Shana headed to her room to shower and change for the dance. She breathed a sigh of relief seeing the empty bed. Either Michaela had been discharged or they'd moved her to another room. Tossed across Shana's bed was a garment bag and what looked like a shoe box. She unzipped the bag and found a white lace dress with a high neckline, a dropped waist, and a full skirt. Holding it in her hands, Shana thought of a wedding dress and then changed her mind, deciding it was more like a high school prom dress. Inside the box was a pair of white satin pumps with small heels.

After her shower, Shana found a perfect white rose on her bed, along with a rhinestone hair clip. She was certain the rose and the clip hadn't been there before she'd entered the bathroom. Next to it was a white slip with a built-in bra and a pair of white silk panties. Alex must have placed the items in her room while she was in the shower. She dressed and sat down on the edge of the bed, trying to decide how she should handle the situation. It wasn't right for Alex to come into her room without her consent, but his gifts were sweet. She worried, though, as surely none of the other patients had evening clothes. Deciding what the hell, she patted down the puffy skirt, and walked out of her room.

When Shana stepped into the great room, her mouth fell open in shock. All the patients were dressed in formal wear. In less than an hour, the hospital population had been transformed. Alex was wearing a white tuxedo, while all the other men were wearing black. Karen had on a green taffeta dress with a short skirt. May was wearing red chiffon with a plunging neckline that exposed her ample breasts. There was such a mixture of men's and women's cologne that Shana felt as if she were in a flower shop. Alex must have purchased all the clothes, the shoes, and given each patient their own bottle of cologne.

"Can I offer you a cocktail?" Alex said, bowing at the waist.

Alex was an attractive man, even in his T-shirts and jeans. He had that rare combination of rugged masculinity and elegance, reminiscent of the James Bond character. Tonight he looked as regal as a prince, and it was clear why the patients had given him such a title.

She asked herself what else Alex had done for them. Many of the hospital patients had no one. When visiting hours came every day, only a few people showed up. And how could they afford an expensive private hospital like Whitehall? Sure, some of them had insurance, but insurance seldom covered everything. Did Alex pick up their tabs, rather than let them be forced into a state facility, which were notoriously overcrowded and understaffed. Compared to a state institution, Whitehall must seem like a palace. She had finally met a man with real empathy, who cared not just for her but for others. The word *magnanimous* passed through her mind.

"We're all having a cocktail before dinner," Alex told her. "You might as well join us."

"You're pulling my leg," Shana said, smiling coyly. "They won't let us have alcohol in here."

"It's all a matter of perspective," Alex told her, arching an eyebrow. "A cocktail is a tool of relaxation, isn't it?" He turned to the people assembled in the room. "Ladies and gentlemen, the bar is officially open."

One by one, the patients lined up behind Alex at the nurses' station. "I'm feeling a little tense tonight, Betsy," he said, placing his elbow on the counter. "I'd like two of my Ativans, please."

Betsy checked Alex's chart, and then put the two pills he'd asked for in a cup. Soon everyone was asking for two doses of their medication instead of one, and tossing the pills in their mouths like candy. Shana tugged on Alex's sleeve, then whispered in his ear, "How can they double their medication? Doesn't Betsy know better? Someone might overdose."

"The majority of medications, particularly tranquilizers, are written to take 'one or two as needed' every so many hours," Alex explained. "Almost everyone here has a prescription for some type of antianxiety drug in their chart. It's pretty common in this type of place. And as long as Betsy has it on file, there's nothing she can do." He smiled, full of himself.

"I'll pass," Shana said, giving him a stern look. Buying the patients fancy clothes was one thing. Enticing them to mess around with their medication was dangerous.

"You don't want to ruin our party, do you?" Alex tilted his head, giving her a puppy dog look. "It's not like we do this all the time." He glanced at Norman, Karen, May, and Milton, lined up next to each other on the sofa. "Think about what this night means to some of these people. Don't you think they deserve a few hours of happiness?"

Shana understood. Norman's disfigurement made him terribly shy. The extra medication probably helped him just as it did Karen. The same applied to Milton and his constant state of agitation. When her turn came, Shana told Betsy she'd been suffering from a bout of insomnia and was handed two pink pills.

Alex could have been right in some of his earlier assessments. Where would she ever find friends as unique as the people she'd met at Whitehall? More importantly, where would she ever find a man like Alex? She wanted to drag him to her room and make passionate love to him. He had to be a wonderful lover because he possessed such an overwhelming desire to please. Most of the men she'd had sex with were selfish pricks. She fantasized about them getting married and having a houseful of kids. A vision of Alex tenderly rocking their baby in his arms flashed in her mind. He would make the perfect husband and father. She chuckled under her breath, imagining the day she introduced her mother to her new fiancé. Lily would freak, terrified her daughter had fallen in love with a lunatic. The more she thought about it, the better it sounded.

———

Dozens of balloons floated near the ceiling. Music was playing from two large speakers. In various corners of the gym people were congregating in groups. In one corner, George stared into space as he leaned against the back wall. When Shana walked in with Alex, everyone stopped what they were doing and stared.

"Shall we dance?" Alex said, swinging her away from his body.

They were the only couple on the dance floor. Brett and the other guys Shana had danced with over the years had only shuffled their feet from side to side. She was amazed at how well Alex could dance, deciding he must have taken lessons. He held her tight as they twirled around the slick surface of the gym. Other couples began slowly making their way onto the floor.

Karen was dancing with Norman; May had her arms wrapped around Milton's waist, a strange couple to say the least. David was dressed neatly in a sweater and a pair of dark slacks. On his arm was a pretty brunette from the adolescent unit. He was no longer wearing his sling, nor had he come decked out in women's apparel. Wanda, the woman Shana had seen drooling in the wheelchair after shock treatment, was wearing a bright blue dress and dancing with the man Alex had told her was a priest. They were smiling and snuggling close.

Shana asked herself if it was the drugs or if everything she'd experienced at Whitehall was a delusion. The patients no longer seemed to be aware of their various illnesses or limitations. She envisioned the collective group along the lines of actors on a stage.

Alex's voice jolted Shana out of her thoughts. "I could spend my life right here with you. There's nothing more I'd ever need or want."

Shana didn't know how to respond. After the song ended, they sat side by side in folding chairs along the wall. "Alex, it's none of my business, but have you ever been married?"

"No," he said, gazing out over the dance floor.

"Really? You must have dated a lot of girls. You're a good-looking man, Alex. Surely you fell in love at least once or twice."

"Once."

The music changed and rock and roll began blasting out of the speakers. "What happened?" Shana yelled over the noise.

"The teenagers must have complained."

"Not the music . . ." Shana said. "What happened to the girl you were in love with?"

"We were too young," Alex told her, staring at the floor. "Things didn't work out."

Shana moved her chair closer. "Did your parents cause the breakup?" She thought of his mother, Nadine, believing she could chase away anyone.

"No," he said. "She left me."

"I'm sorry."

Shana saw Norman walking toward her. "Hey, Norm," she called out, "you look like a million bucks in that tuxedo. How about a dance?" Just as she stood, she felt fingers digging into her forearm. Instinctively she jerked away. "That hurt, Alex! I have the right to dance with anyone I want."

Once they reached the dance floor, Shana snuggled up against Norman, thrilled that he appeared to be having such a good time. "When you leave the hospital," she said, "promise me you'll take your wife out dancing."

Her eyes scanned the room but Alex had vanished. She had no idea what was wrong with him, and her arm still smarted from where he'd grabbed her. He hadn't hurt her by accident. She was almost certain he'd done it intentionally.

After she finished dancing with Norman, Shana saw Milton and pulled him onto the dance floor. Milton danced like a crazy teenager, so in this respect, his boundless energy served him well. Next she danced with David and even the priest. Her feet were killing her but she couldn't stop dancing. As soon as one dance was finished, someone else would approach her and she felt obligated to go back onto the floor.

Seeing Alex again, she returned and took a seat beside him. "Whew," she said, feeling perspiration soaking through her dress. "That's it for me."

"You mean your dance card is full."

"No, my toes are crushed. I appreciate these nice shoes you gave me. I'm not certain they're my size, though." She removed one of the white satin pumps and massaged her aching foot. "Everyone's having a wonderful time, thanks to you, Alex. You're a generous man." She looked down and saw the inflamed area on her arm. "You almost twisted my arm off earlier. What was that about?"

Ignoring her question, Alex handed her a cold glass of punch. "I got you a fresh drink. You looked like you needed it."

"You're always so considerate, Alex. That's why I—"

"We can go now. Because Morrow raised your level, you can leave anytime you want."

Shana stifled a yawn. The extra dose of Valium, coupled with the physical activity, had made her feel woozy. "Shouldn't we wait for the others?"

An awkward silence ensued. "I didn't mean to hurt you, Shana. I just wanted to get out of here. The music is giving me a headache."

Shana forgot about her arm as he obviously hadn't meant to harm her. He was a big man, and men were always doing things like that to her. She'd gone out with a football player once, and he'd almost broken her back when he had hugged her. Men didn't realize how strong they were. She was ready to leave the dance anyway. She wanted to find a way to get Alex alone.

George unlocked the doors and they both waved good-bye to the other patients, still dancing and mingling about in the gym. She swung her shoes back and forth in her hand as she walked barefoot on the sidewalk.

Suddenly Alex stepped in front of her. "I'm in love with you," he told her. "I can make all your dreams come true if you'll only give me a chance. We don't have to stay here in San Francisco. We can live in Bora-Bora if you want."

Shana grabbed him by his lapels and pulled him into the shadows. "I'm falling in love with you, too, Alex."

He led her to an alcove where no one could see them. Without speaking, he kissed her forehead and then grabbed her cheeks in his hands and kissed her passionately on the mouth. "I want you so bad, Shana. I've wanted you since the day I saw you."

Before she could stop him, he dropped to his knees on the concrete and buried his head between her legs, moving her panties aside with his tongue. She wanted to resist but she couldn't. Her state of arousal was so intense, the probing of his tongue so delicious and exciting, she experienced a powerful orgasm. "Oh, Alex," she said, panting, trying to unzip him, wanting him more than she'd ever wanted a man before. Just as she reached into his pants and pulled out his erect penis, she heard laughter and talking.

Alex moaned and then said, "The others must be coming back from the dance, damn it."

Shana was completely obsessed with him now. She wanted to make love to him until the sun came up. "They can't see us, can they? I mean, it looks like we're pretty well hidden."

He quickly repaired his clothing. "If we don't go back, George will come looking for us. I don't want the memory of the first time we're together to involve George, do you?"

She laughed and then grabbed his hand and placed it between her legs. How could she be aroused again? She'd just had an orgasm. "George can watch for all I care. I don't want to stop. I can't believe I want you so much. You're a fantastic lover."

He was speaking fast now as the footsteps became louder. "I think they discharged your roommate. After bed check, I'll come to your room."

The moment was shattered; Shana patted her puffy skirt down. "What makes you think they discharged Michaela? If anyone needs to be here, she does. I'm terrified she's going to suffocate me with a pillow."

"We both have the same doctor and I'm sure he mentioned discharging her."

"But all her things are still in the room."

"Did she have anything of value?"

"Not really, just a stinky gown and a pair of slippers."

"Just come to my room, then. I don't have a roommate."

As soon as the group of patients walked past them, Alex pulled Shana from their hiding spot and they slipped in with the others. May saw them and smiled. Alex had lipstick smeared all over his face and one side of his shirt was sticking out of his pants.

"We don't have to go in yet," he whispered. "All we have to do is let George see us."

"But I'd like to take a shower so I'll be perfect for you."

"You're already perfect." The others went inside and Alex picked a flower for her, a gardenia. "This is what you smell like." He nuzzled her neck. "And you taste like honey."

They were standing next to the gardenia bush and the delightful fragrance filled the air. "Can I see your scar?" he blurted out. "The one on your leg."

Her leg had been broken in a ski accident. The doctors had implanted a plate and five screws. She wondered how he knew about it and then decided he must have felt it when they were fooling around. "Why do you want to see my scar? I've had plenty of guys who wanted to see my tits, but no one has ever asked to see my scar."

"When I was twenty-four, they found a malignant tumor on my leg. They removed it, but I was certain it would come back and they'd have to amputate my leg." He stepped to one side of the door where he couldn't be seen, unfastening his belt and unzipping his pants, then slipping them down to his thighs. He took Shana's hand and placed it on his left leg, wanting her to feel the abraded scar tissue. As soon as she did, he quickly repaired his clothing.

Shana was flabbergasted. Alex's scar felt exactly like hers. It was on the same leg, about eight inches above his knee, and appeared to be the same width. "My ski accident happened when I was seventeen." She thought Alex was the same age as she was, if not several years younger, but she had never asked him. "How old are you?"

"Thirty-five."

"Really?" Shana said, shocked. "But you look so young. When I first saw you, I thought you were in your early twenties. I thought my accident might have happened around the same year you were diagnosed with cancer. That can't be true because I'm only twenty-eight."

"But it did happen the same year, exactly eleven years ago."

She did the math and realized he was right. When she had been seventeen, Alex had been twenty-four. "Amazing."

"What month?" he asked, excited.

"December."

"They removed my tumor in December."

"What are the chances of something like this happening?"

"Astronomical," he said. "Don't you understand, Shana?"

"Not really," she said, brushing her hair behind one ear. What point was he attempting to drive home? It was nothing more than a coincidence, although she had to admit it was a strange one. Were their matching scars supposed to be proof that they were soul mates? "Just because we both have scars doesn't mean anything. A lot of people have scars."

Alex kissed her on the mouth. "We're destined to be together. What are the chances of two people such as us ending up in a place like this at the same time in history? Maybe these things happened to us because God was trying to move us in another direction. He wanted us to be together, don't you see? That's why we both had to come to Whitehall."

Shana's face glowed. He believed in God. Most people laughed at her, especially when she told them she was a Catholic. She could count on her fingers the number of people she had met at Stanford who believed in God and weren't embarrassed to admit it. It was one of the reasons she didn't fit in.

She had to admit that some of what Alex said made sense. When she was close to him, she felt intoxicated, almost mesmerized. This must be what it felt like to fall in love. Maybe they were meant to step off the edge of the world together. She visualized them falling, their hands linked together like skydivers, their matching scars touching in the air. They were twins, cosmic twins. Shana felt her finger on the buzzer and saw Betsy crossing the floor to the door. "Destiny, right?"

"Destiny," Alex proclaimed, smiling.

She had fallen so hard for Alex it was difficult to leave him, even though she knew it was only for a short time. "I'll meet you in your room. How long should I wait after bed check?"

"Come as soon as you can, just be careful. Sex between patients is one of the worst offenses you can commit here."

"Are we talking Quiet Room?"

"You better believe it."

Shana tensed and then smiled. She was flying so high, nothing could bring her down tonight. "That makes it even more exciting. Besides, they only have one padded cell and I pretty much destroyed it, so they'd have to put us in there together."

Alex arched an eyebrow. "There's always the straitjacket."

"Thanks for reminding me." She placed her palm in the center of his chest. "I love you, Alex."

"I love you more, much more."

"Why?"

"Because I loved you from the moment I saw you," Alex told her. "You didn't know what to think or do about me until tonight."

"Whatever," Shana said, pecking him on the cheek before she depressed the buzzer again to go inside.

# TWENTY-THREE

George handled bed check that night because of the dance, checking the patients off as they left the gym since there was no way to get out of the courtyard. Most of the lights in the hospital were either off or dimmed. Betsy was on duty and had her back turned, probably busy filling out reports. Shana decided it was as safe as it would ever be and headed to Alex's room.

She crept along the walls. When she got there, she knew she couldn't knock so she merely opened the door and stepped inside. The room was so dark she couldn't tell if he was even there. She flipped on the lights and then quickly turned them back off. Alex was sitting up naked in his bed. "Hi, baby," she whispered. "This is so exciting. Are you ready for me?"

"More than ready."

Making love in a twin bed was awkward because they were both so tall. He stroked her breasts and took one of her nipples into his mouth, then scooted down her body to her navel, titillating her with his tongue.

He finally got out of the small bed and positioned her on the edge with her legs up in the air. Then he lifted her lower body up until he could reach it with his mouth. She was thrashing and moaning, overwhelmed with pleasure. He stopped just as she was about to have her second orgasm of the night and placed a finger over his lips, reminding her that she had to be quiet, a difficult proposition for someone that intensely aroused. When her body began violently trembling, he thrust himself inside. He exploded a few moments later, tossing his head back and letting out a long whoosh of air.

They lay side by side in the tiny bed, their foreheads touching and their legs entwined. Their bodies were hot and slick with perspiration. "You better go back to your room," Alex whispered. "I'm afraid we'll go to sleep and Betsy will come in and catch us."

Shana pouted. "But I don't want to leave you."

"We only have until Saturday. After that, we'll be together for the rest of our lives."

"I want to ask you so many questions. I mean, we know each other but then again, we don't know each other. Where do you live?"

"I live here for the time being."

"Don't you have a house or an apartment?"

"I gave it up."

"That might pose a problem. My mother may not pay the rent on my apartment if I don't go back to school, and going back to school is another problem because I'm too far behind in my work."

His eyelids were heavy. "I have money, Shana. I told you I'd take care of you. Pick a place and we'll live there. As long as you're with me, I'll be happy. We can buy a house and start making babies if that's what you want." He captured her face in his hands. "You don't get it yet, do you? You can have anything you want, anything. I'm really, truly rich."

"What about the IRS problem?"

"I don't have a problem with the IRS."

Shana was confused. "But isn't that why you're here?"

"No," he said. "I'm here because I amassed a fortune but I somehow lost my will to live. All I wanted was someone who loved me for myself instead of the money. You've met my mother so you know. She drives me crazy. Here, she can't get to me unless I let her."

"What will we do about her when we get out?"

"I won't tell her where I'm living. That's why I dumped my house in the city." He gave her a nudge in the side. "We can talk about all this tomorrow. You need to get back to your room now."

Shana got out of bed and then tripped into what appeared to be a table or a desk. "What is this?" she said, feeling something with her fingers. When she touched what she recognized as a keyboard, she blurted out, "You have a computer! Why didn't you tell me? I could have e-mailed some of my friends. They would have come and helped me get out. All this time and you had a damn computer. I can't believe it. I just can't believe it."

"Calm down. I don't have an Internet connection. I use the computer to type things up regarding my businesses. Please, Shana, go back to your room now. Someone may have heard you just now. You don't want to go back to the Quiet Room, do you?"

"You should have told me you had a computer," Shana argued. "We could have hooked up to someone's wireless."

"Please . . ."

"I'm going, okay, but you should have told me."

Before she opened the door to leave, Alex was snoring.

VENTURA, CALIFORNIA

At eight o'clock Thursday morning, Lily had a meeting in her chambers with Clinton Silverstein and Richard Fowler. Noelle Reynolds had suddenly opened her eyes and realized she might get the death penalty. As her attorney, Fowler had to present her offer to plead guilty to the district attorney. And since this could conceivably terminate the trial, it was mandatory that a judge be present.

"My client is willing to plead guilty to first-degree murder in exchange for a sentence of life in prison."

"Oh, really," Silverstein said, his shoulders squared off for a fight. "Tell her to stick her finger in a light socket. I refuse to let this cold-blooded murderer get away with life in prison. She deserves to die just like her little boy."

"Remember," Lily told the prosecutor, "you've given the jury only two choices and one of those is acquittal."

Silverstein gave Lily a dirty look. "The only reason Reynolds wants to plead out is she knows the coroner is about to testify that she fed her child pizza laced with Ajax."

Fowler jumped in. "Just because Ajax was found in the boy's system doesn't prove Noelle fed it to him. Children are famous for eating toxic chemicals. You have to do better than that, Silverstein."

"For Christ's sake, Fowler," Silverstein shouted. "She locked the kid in the trunk of the car while she went out partying. You used to be a first-rate prosecutor. How can you even defend this monster?"

"We're trying to settle this," Lily said, turning to Richard. "What do you have that would mitigate this crime?"

"As you both should know, looks can be deceiving. Dr. Reynolds spent a fortune on psychologists and tutors." Fowler opened a brown leather litigation case, pulling out a stack of stapled papers and handing copies to both Lily and Silverstein. "What you're looking at is an IQ test that was administered to my client a week ago at the jail. I just got the report yesterday. If you'll look at the last page, you'll see that her score was seventy. Seventy or below is considered retarded, or to be politically correct, developmentally disabled."

Silverstein hadn't taken the time to condition his permed hair and the dryness in the air made it stick straight up all over his head. He looked either ridiculous or terrifying, like a villain out of a slasher movie. "How could she be retarded? Give me a break, Fowler. She graduated from high school. She even got accepted at UCLA."

"Which she could not have done without help, as you yourself pointed out in your opening statement. I have other psychological and intelligence tests that were administered to Ms. Reynolds as early as age five. Her father desperately wanted her to fit in with normal children and spent an enormous amount of time and money to make certain this happened. He hired a long chain of tutors. He sent Noelle to special summer camps for learning disabled children. When she entered puberty, Noelle even went to modeling school so she could learn table manners and how to walk and carry herself."

Both Silverstein and Lily were hanging on his every word. There were no indications the defendant was developmentally disabled in the police reports or the subsequent investigations conducted by the homicide detectives and the DA's office. Lily and Silverstein were completely astounded.

"Now," Fowler continued, "considering that my client is borderline retarded, the stress of trying to support herself as well as care for the demands of a toddler was more than she could handle. So she cracked, lost touch with reality. For all we know, she could have become psychotic. Her mother is dead. Her father abandoned her. She had no one to teach her parenting skills. We know she's been self-medicating with various illegal substances for years. Perhaps she even believed that the boy was safer in the trunk than he would be somewhere else. The only babysitter Noelle could afford was a fourteen-year-old girl named Rhonda Westin. She's on my witness list, so she was going to testify on Noelle's behalf." He paused and cleared his throat. "Noelle claims Ms. Westin was the one who was watching Brandon when he got into the Ajax. She used Rhonda because she only charged a dollar per hour, whereas the older sitters charged far more. We also have to consider that Brandon may have suffered from some of the same disabilities as his mother, which could explain why he consumed toxic substances."

Silverstein seemed to shrink in his chair. It wasn't a perfect defense, but it was enough to place doubt in the minds of the jurors. The criteria for a guilty verdict was that the jurors must find the defendant guilty beyond a reasonable doubt. The most damning point of all was that the Supreme Court had ruled against capital punishment for the mentally disabled. If Fowler could prove that Noelle Reynolds was retarded, the death penalty would be lost, which meant the only sentence left would be life without the possibility of parole. Silverstein picked up his briefcase and held it tight against his chest. "I-I won't agree to life. If I did, she'd be eligible for parole in approximately fourteen years, which would be a miscarriage of justice. The child also had trace elements of arsenic in his body. Is the babysitter going to admit she fed him arsenic as well?"

"We have an expert witness who will testify regarding the arsenic."

Silverstein knew he was defeated and had to push for the longest sentence possible. "The only thing I'll consider is life without the possibility of parole."

Fowler stood and picked up his papers and briefcase. "I'll have to discuss this with my client and her mental health advocate."

"Now she has a fucking mental health advocate! You're a bastard, Fowler. When did murderers stop deserving punishment? When they started padding your bank account?" Silverstein sprang to his feet, dropping his briefcase on the floor and lunging at Fowler. "If you dummied this up, I'll . . . I'll rip your fucking throat out."

"Take your seat, counselor," Lily said through clenched teeth. "You're accusing a respected member of the legal community of manufacturing evidence. Are you certain you want to do that?"

Silverstein was red-faced and panting. A trickle of drool ran out one corner of his mouth. He wiped it away with the back of his hand. "Any deal will be based on the People conducting their own intelligence tests."

"No problem." Fowler quickly slipped out the door, evidently fearing Silverstein would come after him again.

Lily turned to Silverstein. "You should have had Reynolds tested months ago. If you had, Fowler might not have been able to sandbag you like he just did."

"But we did psychological testing. I didn't test her intellect because she seemed to be perfectly normal. The only thing that was at issue was her sanity and her ability to cooperate with her defense. Dr. Williams said she was immature but otherwise perfectly normal."

"You didn't look deep enough, Clinton. Get two independent psychologists over to the jail to test Reynolds immediately. If you get the results after hours, call me at home. I doubt if Fowler would stoop low enough to manufacture evidence in a case this serious, but let's do our best to keep him honest."

Lily was already exhausted and the day had just begun. It wouldn't be a bad resolution to the case if Reynolds agreed to life without the possibility of parole. Then the trial would be over and she would have time to focus all her attention on Shana. She had already purchased a ticket to fly up there Friday night. Maybe she could bring Shana back with her. At the noon break, she would look for a local addiction specialist who worked with patients on an outpatient basis.

She called Richard on his cell phone. "Was Greg able to get in touch with Shana?"

"No," he said. "He called but the hospital told him she was refusing all calls. I don't know what to tell you, Lily. Oh, thanks for backing me up in there. Clinton's always been a little wacko, but . . ."

"I didn't back you up, Richard. I was doing my job."

"See you in court."

"Yeah," she said, disconnecting.

Life was funny. The man had once been the love of her life. Now he was nothing more than another annoying, egotistical attorney.

# TWENTY-FOUR

On the walk to lunch, the sky was overcast and the air heavy with moisture. Shana suspected a storm was moving in. Although her days were spent inside an air-conditioned hospital, Shana knew it had been far too warm for this time of the year. It had to be global warming. At least the rain would give the area a respite from the unseasonable heat they had been experiencing.

The patients seemed to be experiencing a letdown. The magic of the night before had been vanquished in the light of reality. "Are you still going back to Ventura?" Karen asked, as if she knew what had happened the night before in Alex's room. "Why don't you stay here with Alex?"

"Oh, Karen," Shana said, sighing. "You know I'm not going to stay here at Whitehall."

"Alex loves you," Karen told her. "You're the perfect couple. He's an important person. He even told me I could work for one of his companies when I get out."

"I'm happy for you." Shana draped an arm around her shoulder. "I'm sure you'll make a wonderful employee."

In the cafeteria, Shana carried her own tray to the table. Alex

hadn't been around when they'd left for lunch, so she assumed his
session with his shrink had run late. She took a few bites out of
her turkey sandwich, and then dropped it back on the plate,
wondering what had happened to Norman. May and Karen were
discussing hairstyles and makeup, so she waited until they stopped
talking. "Where's Norman?"

"I don't know," Karen said. "I haven't seen him around all day.
Maybe he's in bed or something. We stayed up pretty late last night."

Shana didn't feel well herself and decided to skip lunch and go
back. When she stood, though, the room began spinning and she
sat back down.

Alex appeared and placed a glass of orange juice in front of her.
"Drink this," he said. "It will stabilize your blood sugar."

"Are you sick, sugar?" May asked, seeing a line of perspiration
on Shana's forehead.

"I don't know," Shana told her. Karen looked as lovely as she had
the night before, only now she had four eyes, two mouths, and two
noses. Shana began giggling. David had joined them and started
throwing paper napkins and chunks of his dinner roll at her.

Alex slapped his palm down on the table. "Stop it, David. You're
acting like a child. If you want to eat with adults, you have to act
like one."

"It was my fault," Shana said. "Don't blame David. He thought
I was joking around because I was laughing."

David shoved his chair back from the table, shot Alex a black
look, and then stormed out of the cafeteria.

"I'll go talk to David," Shana said, placing her napkin on the table.

Alex's dark eyes were flashing with anger. He reached for the
back of her chair, pushing it closer to the table. "Eat your lunch."
One side of his lip curled. "Don't baby him. He was acting stupid."

"Maybe that's why he's here." Shana tried to stand again, but
her arms floated in the air like wings. Karen jerked her head to one
side and barked. Shana responded with a high-pitched giggle. She
placed her hand over her mouth, fearful she had hurt Karen's feelings. "I'm not laughing at you, Karen. I promise."

Karen fingered a strand of hair. "It doesn't matter. I'm used to people making fun of me." Then she blurted out, "Shit, damn, asshole."

"Please don't take offense." Shana felt guilty that she'd caused an outburst. "Dr. Morrow gave me some kind of new drug that must be causing me to laugh. Besides, everyone says bad words when they're angry or frustrated. We all have those words inside of us. Maybe if some of us could release all the anger trapped inside, we'd be better off."

Karen had returned to her lunch when Shana was struck by another fit of uncontrollable laughter. Karen leaned over and hugged her. "It's the medication. Here," she said, picking up a forkful of mashed potatoes. "You have to eat, Shana. Food will help absorb whatever chemicals they've given you."

"I can't . . . eat," Shana told her between giggles. "I . . . I'll choke."

A few of the other people at the table began snickering. "Stop it!" Karen shouted. "She didn't say anything funny. She's having a reaction to the medication. None of you have any idea how terrible it is not to be able to control yourself. Let's get out of here, Shana." She stood and took her hand, leading her away from the table.

The two women made their way to the courtyard. Shana was laughing so hard that she wet her pants. Karen's concern intensified. Inside the great room, she headed straight to the nursing station. Peggy was thumbing through a copy of the *National Enquirer*.

"You have to give Shana something to counteract the other medicine," Karen demanded. "She can't stop laughing. She can't even eat."

Shana giggled again.

"She's not having a drug reaction," Peggy said. "None of the drugs we administer cause a person to laugh. We don't dispense laughing gas or LSD."

"You and that stupid Morrow make me sick!" Karen yelled, flinging her arms around. "Call someone now or I'm going to come over this counter and strangle you."

Just then, Shana stopped laughing. She'd never seen Karen mad before. She waited a few moments to make sure, and then said, "I think it's over, Karen."

"Are you certain? Because if you're not, I'll keep at them until they do something."

Shana slipped her hand out of Karen's. "I'm going to my room. I appreciate what you did. It takes guts to butt heads with Peggy."

Karen looked down at her shoes, her face flushed in embarrassment. "It was nothing. You've been wonderful to all of us. This place was the pits before you showed up." She held up a palm. "Don't worry. I'm not going to ask you to stay. We all know you don't belong here."

"Thanks," Shana said, walking off toward her room.

# TWENTY-FIVE

A loud clap of thunder rang out. A flash of lightning followed, visible through the plate-glass window. The sky opened up and rain poured down in transparent sheets. Shana watched as the others darted through the rain as they returned from the cafeteria.

Karen had wandered off somewhere, but Shana remained in the great room at the smokers' table, waiting for Alex to show up. Besides lunch, she hadn't seen or spoken to him since the night before, and a queasy sensation had developed in the pit of her stomach. Had he said things he didn't mean just to get her to have sex with him? She chastised herself for overreacting to the fact that he had a computer in his room. For all she knew, the hospital rules didn't preclude a patient from having a computer as long as it wasn't connected to the Internet. Her heart began to sink as the minutes clicked off on the big clock on the wall.

Another loud crack of thunder rang out, and a second later, the lights went out. Some of the patients panicked and began screaming. At least a third of the great room was plunged into near-total darkness. Shana stood up, put her hands out in front of her, and kept walking in the same direction until she felt what she thought was her doorway. "Thank you, God," she said, relieved that she had made it to her room. Not everyone at Whitehall was harmless. Being in a mental institution during a blackout was dangerous.

Trying to stay close to the wall, Shana felt her leg brush up against what she thought was a mattress. She tripped and fell forward. Her chest and elbows struck a soft surface. A noxious odor rose to her nostrils, far worse than Michaela's usual body odor. She pushed herself off whatever it was she had touched, and then slipped and fell in what she assumed was a puddle of water.

"Michaela," Shana called out, scrambling back to her feet. "Is that you, Michaela? I'm sorry, but we're having a storm and the power went out. The roof must be leaking. There's water all over the floor."

Was she in the wrong room? She heard people milling about outside, but inside the room, there was no sound whatsoever. She listened for Michaela's heavy breathing, holding her breath so she could hear. As her eyes adjusted to the darkness, she could see a form on the bed. There was no rocking, no squeaking bedsprings, no wheezing. She started to return to the great room to get away from the awful smell when an eerie feeling came over her and she returned to the edge of the bed.

"Michaela!" she said again, this time louder. "Answer me." She reached out and nudged the body on the bed, hoping that what she feared wasn't true and Michaela was only sleeping. Leaning over the top of the bed, she turned her face sideways to where she thought Michaela's mouth was, waiting to feel the woman's breath on her cheek.

"Please help me!" Shana cried out. "Michaela's not breathing!" She wanted to run from the room and keep running, out the doors and as far away as she could get, but she was frozen in that one spot by Michaela's bed. How could she stand by and do nothing? Since she had taken a course in CPR, she might be able to save the woman's life. She placed her finger on Michaela's neck, searching for a pulse.

She was probably in cardiac arrest.

With her fingers, Shana pried open Michaela's mouth to begin ventilating. At the same time, she touched the soft flesh of her abdomen, and then ran her fingers straight up to what she hoped was her sternum. Placing one hand on top of the other, she began the compressions.

A commotion broke out in the great room, followed by the sound of pounding feet. "Here!" Shana screamed. "I'm here. Follow the sound of my voice. Here! Here!"

Outside, Betsy was running with a flashlight. The patients were huddled together in small groups. "George!" Betsy shouted. "Call an ambulance. And bring another flashlight. Something has happened to Michaela Henderson."

Betsy shoved aside several people in her path as she rushed into Shana's room. Shining the flashlight toward the bed, she saw it was empty. She quickly checked the other bed and found it empty as well. A second later, she heard Shana yelling again from what appeared to be a nearby room.

"Oh, my Jesus!" Betsy exclaimed as the beam of the flashlight struck Shana. She was covered in blood—her face, her hands, and her white cashmere sweater. Sitting astride Norman, Shana was pressing down on his chest. With the light from the flashlight, Shana saw Norman's charred face. Something silver protruded from his throat. On impulse, she reached to grab it, and then realized he would bleed to death if she pulled it out. Whatever the object was, it was in the same area as Norman's carotid artery.

"Norman's been stabbed in the throat," Shana said rapidly. "I thought I was in my room. That's why I said it was Michaela." She bent down to ventilate again. "Not sure . . . suicide or murder. Call the . . . paramedics." She sucked in another deep breath. "Quick or he'll die."

"Lord God Almighty, you've killed him!" With an enormous swing of her body, Betsy rammed the left side of Shana's rib cage, smashing her into the wall. The last thing Shana saw was Betsy bending down over Norman, his eyes open and empty.

———————

"Ms. Forrester, can you hear me?"

A beam of light filled Shana's right eye. She saw an unknown male face peering down at her. The beam of light retreated and Shana saw a dark-haired doctor she'd never seen before standing next to Betsy. She watched as he placed the small penlight back in the pocket of his starched white coat.

"How do you feel?" he asked. "You appear to have suffered a mild concussion."

Shana tried to raise her arm when she met resistance. "That doesn't explain why I'm tied to the bed."

"I'm not on staff here," the doctor said. "I'm Dr. Rolheiser. I was called in to take a look at you. Do you know where you are?"

"What happened to Norman? I was trying to resuscitate him. Instead of helping me, the woman standing next to you shoved me against the wall and knocked me unconscious." Shana's head and left shoulder were throbbing.

Rolheiser remained expressionless. "You didn't answer my question."

"I'm at Whitehall Hospital. I don't know the exact address but it's somewhere near San Francisco."

"Correct," he said, making a notation in his clipboard.

"Do you want me to recite the Pledge of Allegiance?" she said, thrashing against the restraints. "There's nothing wrong with my mind. If you aren't affiliated with Whitehall, for God's sake, get me out of here. They've been holding me against my will. They kidnap people to collect on their insurance."

"Norman's dead," Betsy said, stepping in front of the doctor. "You stabbed him. I saw the knife in your hands. Dr. Morrow warned us to keep an eye on you."

Rolheiser's curiosity got the best of him. "Did you really kill someone?"

"What do you think?" Shana said, outraged that Betsy would make such an accusation. "Not many murderers try to resuscitate their victims."

The doctor placed his hand on Betsy's back, steering her to a corner of the room. "Neither of us should be asking Ms. Forrester questions about the crime," he whispered. "Advise the police officers they can interrogate her now. She's alert and cognizant. I'll stop by later to check on her. I think she suffered a mild concussion."

Betsy and Rolheiser left. A short time later, two men entered. One was a fresh-faced young officer in uniform, with short cropped hair and a squared-off jaw. The other man was in his late forties, had disheveled brown hair, and the ruddy complexion of a drinker. He had to be a detective, Shana told herself, as he was wearing a gray suit and looked the part. The younger officer was smacking a wad of chewing gum.

"San Francisco Sheriff's Office," the plainclothes officer said. "I'm Detective Lindstrom. Officer Prescott and I need to ask you some questions about Norman Richardson." He reached inside his pocket, removed a small card, and began reading Shana her rights. He ended by saying, "Do you understand?"

"Yes, damn it," Shana shot out. She pulled hard against the restraints and then let her hands fall back to the bed. She felt as if someone had hit the rewind button, but this time the nightmare was worse. "I'm a law student at Stanford. My mother is a superior court judge in Ventura. These people tricked me into signing a voluntary commitment order. They gave me drugs . . ."

"I see." Lindstrom's tone was flat and disinterested. "We'll verify your history once we complete our preliminary investigation." He pulled out a microcassette player and pushed a button. "I need it on record that you are officially waiving your right to have an attorney present during questioning."

"Ask me anything you want." Shana was certain that once she told them the truth, they would no longer consider her a suspect. "I'll talk to you without legal representation as long as you promise to listen to my side of the story."

Officer Prescott pulled out a small notebook and pen to take notes. Lindstrom placed the tape recorder on the end table beside the bed. "Tell us everything that happened from the time you went to the cafeteria until you were discovered standing over Mr. Richardson's body."

"Take off the restraints," Shana demanded. "Otherwise I'll wait for an attorney."

The two officers exchanged glances. Lindstrom nodded, watching as Prescott reached down and unfastened the arm restraints. "You can sit up," the detective told her. "I'm not going to remove the leg restraints."

Shana rubbed her wrists, first one and then the other. "Can I have a drink of water, please? My throat is parched."

The younger officer left, returning with a pitcher of water and several plastic cups. After he handed her the water, Shana gulped it down and then held out her cup so he could refill it. She stared off into space as she tried to recall the events of the last few days. "Norman seemed depressed, but at the dance, he acted as if everything was okay. He didn't show up at lunch today. When I asked where he was, one of the other patients said he was either sleeping or his session with his psychiatrist had run over."

"Let's backtrack to the dance last night," Lindstrom said. "What time did you get back to your room?"

"I can't tell you the exact time. My guess is it was around midnight. The hospital generally requires that we be in our rooms by ten. Because of the dance, curfew was lifted, and patients were still in the gym when Alex and I left."

"Who is Alex?"

"One of the patients."

"What's his last name?"

Shana placed her palm on her forehead. "I don't remember. Maybe it's because of the concussion. I believe he gave me a telephone calling card. That should have his last name on it. Can't you get information on Alex from the hospital? He's been a patient here for several months. He practically runs the place."

"Are you sure this man is a patient?" Lindstrom asked, placing his hands on his hips. "Could you be confusing him with a member of the staff?"

"Not at all," Shana told him. "The staff is made up of idiots. Alex is a smart man. I even met his family. His mother is overbearing and rude, but that doesn't have any bearing on what happened to Norman." She wondered if she should tell them that Alex had originally told her he was hiding from the IRS. Right now, she didn't know what to think about anything. She decided to keep her mouth shut. If she admitted that she was in Alex's room, Morrow might refuse to release her.

Officer Prescott flipped through his notebook. "We don't have anyone on the patient roster with the first name of Alex. Are you certain that was his name?"

"That's what everyone called him," Shana said, reclining on the pillow. "Norman bled to death, didn't he? How long had he been dead?"

Lindstrom shuffled his feet around. "We'll know more after they complete the autopsy."

"I woke up sometime during the night," Shana said, interrupting him. "Dr. Morrow's been giving me enough dope to put me in a coma. What I'm trying to tell you is something must have caused me to wake up. I wish I'd looked at a clock so I could help you establish a time line. All I know is it was between two and seven this morning."

Both Lindstrom and his partner were listening intently now. The average mental patient wouldn't consider things such as timelines. "I had a strange dream," she said, clasping the railing with both hands. "I wouldn't mention this if I didn't feel it might be related to the crime. I was certain I'd stopped breathing. I saw someone standing in front of what I perceived as my father's car. Maybe that person was really there, and my mind just filled in the blanks."

"Are you trying to suggest that you saw the killer? Were you sleeping in Norman Richardson's room last night?"

"No, no," Shana said, shaking her head. "But the killer could have come into my room by mistake. That's how I ended up in Norman's room when the lights went out. Maybe the killer was shopping for a victim." She gave more thought to her next statement.

"What I was originally going to say is that the killer may have held a pillow over my face. You know, that may have been why I felt like I was suffocating. For all I know, I was the intended victim."

"Nice try," Lindstrom said. "Since the assailant was successful, reason says you'd be dead if you were the intended victim. Did you actually see or hear anyone in your room last night?"

"Nothing more than what I've told you." Shana winced in pain, touching a swollen knot on the side of her head. It was useless to complain about Betsy. She could see how a person might jump to conclusions. "Something else happened that might be important. Morrow changed my medication for no reason. I asked Peggy, one of the nurses here, what the medication was and she told me the bottle wasn't labeled. Not long after I took it, I began to have a reaction. I feel foolish saying this, but I couldn't stop laughing. Maybe Morrow is your killer. To say he's strange is an understatement."

"How's that?" Lindstrom asked.

"He's more interested in astrology than psychiatry. He wanted to know what time I was born so he could do my chart."

"Are you sure this was a prescription drug reaction?" Prescott wanted to know. "You didn't sneak in some weed or Ecstasy now, did you?"

"Shut up, Prescott," the detective said. "This is a murder investigation, not a traffic stop."

"The killer got a knife in here. How do you know they don't smuggle in illegal drugs? They find drugs all the time at the jail."

"The victim was stabbed with a kitchen knife," Lindstrom told the younger officer. "We're almost certain it came from the dining room. This isn't a jail, Prescott. They let the patients use knives and forks as long as they don't take them back to the main portion of the hospital."

"But that's what the killer did, right?"

"They had to assign me a rookie," Lindstrom said, linking eyes with Shana.

Shana relaxed somewhat, believing she'd finally broken ground with the gruff detective. "It was a prescription drug reaction, all right. There's not a lot to laugh about in this place. I was borderline hysterical. Talk to the people at my table. I was laughing so hard I couldn't eat."

"Is that why you left the cafeteria early?"

"Yes," Shana said. "I left with Karen. I don't know her last name. This isn't the kind of place for last names. The patient I'm referring to is a redhead with Tourette's syndrome. When we walked into the great room—"

"What's the great room?"

"The recreation room where the TV is located," Shana said, trying to remember as many details as possible. She tried not to think of Norman, but it was difficult. She wondered if he had killed himself. The police must have considered suicide, so she didn't want to waste their time with her own speculations. She kept returning to the conversation she'd had with him about the night he set himself on fire and how agitated he had become. Had she caused him to take his own life by forcing him to revisit that awful night? She hoped that wasn't the case.

"Okay," she continued. "Peggy was at the nursing station. Karen told her I was having a drug reaction. By then, whatever it was had passed, thank God."

"And this was before the blackout?"

"Yes," she answered. "The rest of the patients got caught in the rain. Most of them went straight to their rooms to change out of their wet clothes. Then the power went out. You know the rest."

"Where were you when the electricity went off?"

"On the way to my room," Shana said, clearing her throat. "There was some light coming in from the windows, but as I got closer to the patients' rooms, there was no light at all. Norman's room is two doors down from my own. I thought I was headed in the right direction, but obviously I wasn't."

"What happened when you entered the room?"

Shana took another drink of water. She still had a cottony taste in her mouth from the drugs. "I tripped and fell against the bed.

There was a person there. I assumed it was my roommate, Michaela. The smell was terrible. She always stinks, but it's usually from body odor. I knew something was wrong. That's when I slipped in what I thought was a pool of water. I kept calling out to Michaela to see if she was okay. When no one answered, I checked to see if she was breathing. I yelled for someone to call an ambulance, and then I began CPR."

"Why didn't you wait for help?"

Shana crushed the paper cup in her fist. "I can't believe you would ask such a stupid question, detective. I'm certified in CPR. It would have been irresponsible of me to stand around and do nothing. I didn't know Norman was already dead. The patients were freaking out. Some of them are like little children and they panicked when the lights went out." She paused and adjusted her position in the bed. "Anyway, look what happened when the so-called help arrived. Betsy is supposed to be a nurse, although I have no idea what kind of credentials she holds. What kind of nurse would tackle someone while they were administering CPR?"

Lindstrom picked up the only chair in the room, turned it around, and then straddled it. "Betsy claims she saw you with the knife in your hand. Is that true?"

"No," Shana said, a degree of fear setting in. "The first time I saw the knife was when Betsy came in with the flashlight. To be fair, I can understand how she might have thought she saw me with the knife in my hand. I was working near Norman's face and sternum."

"Outside of you and this Karen person, did any other patients return from lunch at the same time?"

"I can't say for certain. I didn't pay that much attention." Shana remembered waiting for Alex, and was shocked the hospital had no record of him being a patient. He must have another name, but she wondered why he hadn't told her. They had been talking about running off together and starting a life. Now poor Norman was dead and Alex had disappeared. Her head began pounding. Why would Alex kill Norman? It didn't make sense.

"Did you touch the knife, try to pull it out?"

"You mean are my fingerprints on it?" God, Shana thought, was she a suspect? What else could happen to her? She expected a plane to crash through the window at any moment. "I didn't try to pull the knife out, detective. I could have easily touched it, though, either while I was giving Norman CPR or when I was feeling around in the dark trying to see what was wrong with him."

Things were starting to add up in Shana's head and the prognosis was grim. An eyewitness had seen her standing over the body. Her fingerprints were most likely on the murder weapon. Betsy had probably told the police that Shana hit her, establishing that she had a propensity for violence. The one thing they didn't have was a motive. In that respect, a mentally ill person might not need a motive. "What about suicide? Norman set himself on fire. That's how he became so horribly disfigured. Maybe he didn't want to go through life like that anymore, so he decided to kill himself again and this time he succeeded."

Lindstrom stood, glancing over at Prescott. "I might tend to agree with you under the circumstances, but we have to rule out homicide first. We have an eyewitness who claims she saw you stabbing the victim in the neck."

"I know you aren't going to believe me," Shana said, rubbing her eye with her finger, "but this hospital is blatantly kidnapping people for money. I'm not crazy or suicidal, nor do I have a drinking or drug problem. I agreed to speak to you without an attorney present on the condition that you'd report what's going on here and help me get out. They've restricted me from making any outside phone calls. If nothing else, please let me call my mother."

"We'll put in a call to the attorney general's office," Lindstrom told her. "The hospital isn't your problem right now, Ms. Forrester. You may need to hire a good defense lawyer."

"Dear God, you're going to file criminal charges against me?" Shana's stomach was rolling over like a beach ball. After everything she'd been through, they were going to arrest her for murder! The situation was mind-boggling.

"Not at the moment," the detective said, walking around in a circle. "We're going to write a report and submit it to the district attorney. If you were on the street, we'd probably have to arrest and arraign you. But since you're in a somewhat secure environment, there doesn't appear to be any reason to take you into custody."

"Listen to me," Shana said, adrenaline flooding her veins. "Talk to the shrinks, find out if any of the patients has a history of violent behavior. Let me go to my room and find the phone card with Alex's last name on it. He's not a figment of my imagination, if that's what you're thinking. I have no idea why he isn't on the patient roster. The hospital staff knows him. Everyone knows him. Alex is a good source of information. He can help you sort through this thing."

"I can't let you go to your room, Ms. Forrester. The only way I can justify not booking you is under the hospital's guarantee that you'll be detained."

"Please," she pleaded, digging her fingernails into the mattress, "don't make them put me back in the padded cell. I'd rather be in jail."

"Calm down," Lindstrom said. "I'm not going to insist the hospital keep you in a padded cell. Until the DA makes their decision as to how they want to proceed, Dr. Morrow has agreed to hold you in this room. That's not so bad now, is it?"

"Without the restraints?"

"I'm sorry. The hospital believes you're dangerous. They say you struck one of the attendants and had to be restrained on a previous occasion." He paused and then added, "Could one of the other patients have set you up?"

A cloak of silence fell over the room. Shana could hear the TV and people talking in the great room, but all she could think about was Alex and the night they had spent together. Strings of questions danced in her mind. He had said once that he was at Whitehall on a voluntary commitment and could leave anytime he wanted, but surely he would have told her good-bye. Why wasn't he on the patient roster? Could he have killed Norman? What possible reason would Alex have to kill Norman? Everyone loved Norman. And

Alex's feelings for her had seemed so sincere. How could he swear undying love for her one day and abandon her the next? She hadn't pegged him as a player. He had made love to her so tenderly, so unselfishly. It had been one of the best sexual experiences of her life. What did she do to push men away? Tears welled up in her eyes. She needed her mother. Why wouldn't the cops at least let her call her mother? They had said she needed an attorney, so they had to give her access to a phone.

"Ah, Ms. Forrester," Lindstrom said. "I asked you . . ."

Shana blinked back the tears and then a moment later exploded in anger. "I remember what you asked me. You wanted to know if someone had set me up. How could anyone do that? Don't you know how moronic it is for you to even ask me something like that? Maybe one of the patients has the power to bring on a rainstorm. And the power failure, isn't it possible it was caused by the lightning strikes? If the lights hadn't gone out, I wouldn't have gone into Norman's room instead of my own. Now can I please make a phone call?"

"We can't go against the rules of the hospital," Lindstrom said, as disinterested as he was before, as if he was merely going through the motions. "Your chart says you were admitted because of an addiction to methamphetamine. Drug abusers tend to call either their dealers or other users. The hospital wants to break those connections so you won't return to drugs when you're released."

"Bullshit." The restraints were worse than the Quiet Room. How much could a person take before they became a raving lunatic? "I've never used meth in my life," Shana said. "For God's sake, look at my arms. My chart probably says I had track marks. Everything in that chart is a bold-faced lie, except for the massive amount of psychotropic drugs they administered to keep me under control. They're holding me here for no reason except to collect on my insurance."

Lindstrom picked up the tape recorder and slipped it back into his pocket. "The only advice I can give you is to ride it out. We're not in the business of arresting innocent people. Once the crime lab works up all the evidence, you may be ruled out as a suspect."

"I won't get to go home on Saturday, will I?"

"I'm afraid not."

Shana erupted again. "What the fuck am I supposed to do? Stay strapped to this bed until you get off your ass and decide if you're going to arrest me or not? I demand that you arrest me right now. Otherwise, you have no authority to hold me."

Lindstrom abruptly walked out of the room. Prescott shrugged, and then turned and followed him. Shana had opened up her mouth at the wrong time. She was forcing their hand. They would probably be back tomorrow with an arrest warrant. At least if they took her to the jail, she might be able to make a phone call.

Shana fought against the restraints, even though she knew she could never break through them. Why was God so pissed off at her? Anyone who ended up in a nightmare like this had to be on God's shit list. She hadn't gone to mass in years. Catholics were supposed to go to Mass and partake of the blessed sacraments on a regular basis. She hadn't confessed her sins, although she didn't know very many Catholics today who did. But it didn't matter what everyone else did. Each person was responsible for their own soul. Right now, her soul was stained by sin. She needed to ask for forgiveness for taking money from her mother to pay for Brett's tuition. She had lied to and cheated her own mother. She was a worthless excuse for a daughter. And it wasn't the first time she'd taken advantage of Lily. She would have to remember that if she ever got a chance to go to confession.

Had she imagined what had transpired between her and Alex last night? She must be crazy just like everyone thought. If she could just get out of Whitehall without going to prison, she would never complain about law school again, never let some idiot guy exploit her, and she would appreciate all the sacrifices her mother had made to pay for her education and give her a good life. How could she not respect a person who had killed to protect her?

Something flickered in the back of her mind, something she had done everything in her power to suppress. And it was big, a far more serious sin than taking money from her mother. She was a demanding, selfish bitch, used to getting everything she wanted from her parents. Although her mother had made every attempt to discipline her and teach her the right thing to do, up until his death, her father had spoiled her to the point that she treated him like a slave. Didn't he know the monster he had created?

Memories from a day shortly before her father's death flooded her mind. Because of her, an innocent young man was dead. She tried to push the memories back, but being strapped to a bed with nothing to do but think made her powerless to stop them.

"Dad," Shana called out from her bedroom. "Where's my ice cream?"

John Forrester was asleep in a brown leather recliner in the two-bedroom duplex he shared with his eighteen-year-old daughter. Located on a tree-lined street, the exterior was constructed out of stucco, the pale pink paint cracked and faded. The yard consisted of a small patch of grass. Even though the living room was sparsely furnished, it appeared cramped and cluttered. A green velvet sofa was backed up to a large picture window over-looking the street. Shana had insisted that her father rent a place with a fireplace, which limited their wall space. If they hadn't placed the sofa in front of the window, they wouldn't be able to see the television. The only other furniture was an oak coffee table, the top littered with glasses, newspapers, and stacks of unopened mail.

Dressed in jeans and a black tank top, Shana left her desk to see why her father hadn't answered. "Wake up," she said, shaking his shoulder. "You promised you'd go out for ice cream. The chicken you made tonight tasted like an armadillo."

"What time is it?" he asked, looking at his watch. "Why didn't you wake me up before now?"

"Because I was busy writing a paper. Can't you get rid of all this trash? You know I can't concentrate when the house is a mess. A cluttered house is symbolic of a cluttered mind."

John stared up at her, his eyes groggy from sleep. Up until her first day in college,

Shana's room had been a pigsty. Now the pendulum had swung the opposite direction. The duplex had to be kept in perfect order. He stood, tucked his shirt in, and stepped into his loafers. At five-nine, he wasn't a large man. His daughter stood five-nine, only an inch shorter than her mother. If Shana hadn't possessed Lily's intelligence and drive, she would have had no difficulty earning her living as a model. Her red hair fell to the center of her back, but tonight she had it tied up in a ponytail on the top of her head.

"Baskin-Robbins might be closed," he told her, brushing his hand over the top of his head. The only hair he had left was a fringe around the base of his skull. To make matters worse, his hair had turned gray during the past year and he now had to have it colored twice a month. "Don't worry," he said, picking his car keys up off the coffee table. "Ralph's is open all night. Peanut butter and chocolate, right?"

"I don't want ice cream from the grocery store," Shana protested. "I missed so many classes last week, I had to stay up until three o'clock this morning studying. Please, Dad, don't go back on your word." She grabbed one of the glasses off the coffee table and brought it to her nose. "Were you drinking this afternoon? Is that why you burned our dinner?"

"Of course not," he said, snatching the empty glass out of her hand. "One of my deals fell through. I was trying to see if I could salvage it. That's why I burned your dinner."

"Maybe you should get a regular job." Shana picked up the remote to lower the volume. Her father watched TV incessantly, and she was starting to suspect he was losing his hearing. He kept the volume at such deafening levels, it made it almost impossible for her to study, one of the reasons she stayed up so late. "Mom says you're not cut out for real estate. She thinks you'd be better off getting a job that paid you an hourly wage. You know, something you could count on every month."

John bristled. "When did you talk to your mother?"

"Yesterday." Shana scooped up the old newspapers and dumped them in the trash can in the kitchen, and then walked the short distance back to the living room. "Mom's already paying my tuition. It isn't right for her to pay for everything, especially with all the money I've been giving you. If she finds out you're driving my car without insurance, she'll be furious. It's not like she's rich or anything. She's a district attorney, Dad. She works for the county."

"She's makes more money than I do," he said bitterly. "Why didn't she go into private practice? I'll never understand why she wanted to be a DA."

Shana hated being trapped between two individuals who were constantly arguing. People thought divorce affected only young children but they were wrong. As much as she loved her parents, the situation was sometimes maddening. She felt like a lawyer forced to defend both the criminal as well as the victim. "Mom's worked hard all her life. I'm proud that she's a district attorney again. She didn't belong in that boring job at the appellate court. All day she was locked in a little room trying to find out if a judge screwed up. She's too good in the courtroom. Because of her, tons of violent criminals are in prison."

"Lily could have done the same thing in Los Angeles." John's jaw protruded like a petulant child's. "You could have seen her more often. Then I wouldn't have to listen to her complain that I monopolize all your time."

"Can't you please stop it?" Shana shouted. "After the years she spent in L.A., Mom wanted to be near the beach. She had to take whatever position was available, anyway. You're talking stupid, Dad. I'm too tired tonight to listen to this crap." She turned to head back to her room and then stopped. "Hurry and make it to Baskin-Robbins before they close. I bought all those groceries yesterday. I lied and told Mom I needed the extra money for schoolbooks."

"Why didn't you buy ice cream?"

Shana flashed her dynamite smile, displaying a perfect row of white teeth. "Come on, Dad. You don't like ice cream from the grocery store any more than I do. Most of the time it's burned from the freezer." She licked her lips. "I know what you want . . . a great big sundae with nuts and whipped cream. Doesn't that sound yummy?"

John lumbered out the front door, climbed into his daughter's Mustang, and backed out of the driveway. Making Shana happy was the focal point of his life, even if she did have a tendency to treat him like an errand boy. He had given up on women years ago. Now that he was in his fifties, certain things weren't as important. After college Shana would be entering law school. He had no doubt that she would become a successful attorney. And she certainly wasn't going to follow in her mother's footsteps if he had anything to do with it, working for peanuts as a county prosecutor. He envisioned her in one of those skyscrapers down on Wilshire, where all the high-powered lawyers had their offices. Those were the people who raked in the big bucks. If Shana played her cards right, she might even get her own TV show someday.

Pulling up at a stop sign, John glanced over at one of his listings, a three-bedroom fixer-upper with a swimming pool. When he'd decided to get his real estate license, he had anticipated earning a large income with a minimal amount of effort. Instead, he spent every day jabbering on the phone or chauffeuring people around. Resigning from his job with the government might have been a mistake, but there was nothing else he could have done. He ran into some financial trouble a few years back and cashing out his retirement had been his only option.

Outside of his relationship with Shana, his future didn't hold a great deal of promise. He had to get his career as a real estate agent off the ground or he would end up living the remainder of his life on Social Security. The day before, he had suffered the embarrassment of having to call Lily and tell her the truth: that he couldn't afford to continue paying the rent on the duplex. The fact that she had immediately told Shana made him furious. No man wanted to look like a failure in the eyes of his daughter.

A black Mercedes came from out of nowhere, causing him to swerve to avoid a collision. "Idiot!" he yelled out the window. Behind the wheel of the Mercedes, a pretty blonde had a cell phone to her ear. "Try driving instead of talking."

Before the divorce, John and Lily had owned their own home. Maybe it wasn't a palace but it was certainly better than where he was living now. He missed his old yard, the backyard barbecues, chatting with his neighbors. While Lily devoted herself to prosecuting criminals, he had coached Shana's softball team, prepared their meals, and dropped whatever he was doing to rush to her school when she got sick. Lily was responsible for what had happened to his daughter. She had refused to listen to him. If she had quit the county and opened her own law practice, she wouldn't have lured a criminal home and thrown all their lives into chaos.

Shana's face flashed in his mind, the disgusted way she looked at him. So what if he had suffered a financial setback or needed a little help making ends meet? Why hadn't Lily kept her mouth shut? He had begged her not to tell Shana. But no, she had jumped on the opportunity to degrade him. And his ex-wife was far from perfect. He knew things about her that could send her to prison. Unlike Lily, though, he didn't run around telling people. "Bitch," he mumbled, wishing he had the money to stop for a stiff drink.

When he reached the corner of Melrose and Santa Monica Boulevard, he spotted the pink-and-white neon sign for Baskin-Robbins. The clock on his dashboard read 8:55. He punched the accelerator and careened into the parking lot, missing the driveway and running up over the curb. He couldn't continue to drive forward as there was a large metal container in front of him, a receptacle for people to place items in that they wanted to donate to Goodwill. Throwing the car into reverse, he revved the engine, wanting to make certain the Mustang cleared the curb.

"Shit," he said, hearing a loud thud.

Slamming on the brakes he looked in the rearview mirror, certain he must have struck a tree. The area was so dark, all he could see were the lights in the office building across the street. He rubbed his neck, wondering if he could put in a claim for whiplash, then reminded himself that he was no longer insured. After his DWI arrest, his premiums had skyrocketed and he had been forced to sell his car.

He got out to survey the damage and saw a body on the ground, the legs twisted at an unnatural angle. A faint voice pleaded, "Help . . . me."

John stood frozen. He couldn't breathe, think, or move. He watched in horror as the young man's eyes closed and his head flopped to one side. "No!" he shouted, falling to his knees. "Please, God, don't let him be dead."

There was no blood, at least none he could see. Positioning his face over the man's mouth, he felt a whisper of breath on his cheek. He reached toward his legs, certain they were broken, and then yanked his hands back as if he were reaching into a flame. What if he regained consciousness? He couldn't let the man see his face. "Are you satisfied now?" he said, blaming Lily. "This would have never happened if you hadn't upset me."

He had to remain calm, figure out a game plan.

John decided the man must be a pedestrian, as there were no other cars in the parking lot. Dressed in beige khaki pants and a white T-shirt, the victim appeared to be in his late teens or early twenties. His dark hair was long and unkempt, but there was an incredible softness to his features, causing John to question if the person might be female. To make certain, he bent down again and lifted his T-shirt. When he failed to detect breasts, he decided his first assumption was accurate. Regardless, the young man was astonishingly beautiful. A light seemed to emanate from his face.

John rocked back and forth on his knees, overwrought with emotion. How could he call the police? He had been driving too fast. He hadn't been paying attention. The worst was that Shana had been right when she had accused him of drinking. After losing the only real estate contract he had written in months, he had consoled himself with alcohol. "What have I done? Dear Lord, what have I done?"

THURSDAY, JANUARY 21
SAN FRANCISCO, CALIFORNIA

Fifteen minutes after the police officers left, Lee came in to place the restraints back on Shana's wrists. "You know these aren't necessary, Lee. Betsy was wrong to accuse me. I was trying to save Norman's life."

"I'm only following orders, honey," Lee said, her hands trembling as she fastened the straps.

"Look at me, Lee. Do you believe I killed Norman?"

Lee let her hands fall limp at her sides. "No," she said weakly. "Someone made a terrible mistake. They made it a long time ago."

"Who made a mistake?" Shana said. "For the love of God, tell me, the police are going to charge me with murder. Do you want that on your conscience?"

A slender woman in her early forties, Lee had never married. She'd been severely abused as a child, and still bore the scars on her body. "I need this job. I took in two foster children five years ago. Because I wanted Kate and Jacob to know how much I loved them, I legally adopted them last year. I now have to support them without any help from the state."

"You're a good woman," Shana said, managing to touch Lee's hand as she tucked in the sheet. "I understand your position. You have to tell me what you know, though. I swear I won't mention your name."

"I can't," Lee said, moving away from the bed. "People make promises they can't keep."

Shana felt helpless. She couldn't let the woman leave, not when she might have information that could clear her. Then she thought of Alex. "You know Alex, don't you? The police claim there's no one by that name on the patient roster."

Lee's anxiety intensified. She rubbed her hands on her black skirt. "I wouldn't talk about that man, Shana. Not that man."

"Did he leave the hospital already? Is that why he wasn't listed as a patient?"

Lee stared through the open doorway. "He's right across the hall."

The way the bed was positioned, Shana couldn't see beyond the nursing station. "Close the door, Lee. No one will be able to hear you."

Lee's chest rose and fell as she contemplated her decision. Finally she walked over and closed the door, then returned to stand beside Shana's bed. "His name isn't Alex. Don't ask me his real name because I don't know it. All I know is he can do whatever he wants. When he wants to leave, he leaves. Sometimes he comes back in the middle of the night. One of the other nurses told me he keeps a car in the side parking lot." She stopped and sucked in air. "He even has a set of keys!"

Shana couldn't believe her ears. "Are you certain? Alex has keys to the doors in the hospital?"

Lee nodded, her lips compressed. "I have to leave."

"No, please, you have to tell me. Is it money? Is Alex paying Morrow or some other staff member to stay here? He told me he was hiding from the IRS."

Lee leaned over the edge of the bed again. "Someone told me he owns part of this hospital."

"Who ordered the restraints?" Shana was outraged. She felt as if she had been raped again. "Was it Morrow? Call him and tell him I want to see him. Please, Lee. No one will know you told me. You have my word. Something terrible is going on here in the hospital. I'm not saying Alex is involved or that he killed Norman, but if he can come and go as he pleases, he can also give other people access to the hospital. Do you understand?"

"I shouldn't have told you. I have to go now."

"If it turns out Norman didn't commit suicide, whoever killed him is diabolical." Shana's eyes flashed with intensity. "What possible reason could anyone have to kill a person like Norman? This was murder for the sake of murder. The killer enjoyed it. His next victim may not be a patient. How would you like to run into this maniac in a dark corridor? Think about me. How can I defend myself if I'm strapped to the bed? You have to release me, don't you see?"

Beads of sweat were glistening on Lee's forehead. She left and returned a few minutes later, pulling a pair of surgical scissors out of her pocket. "I'm cutting the restraints where they're attached to the bed. That way, if someone comes in, all you have to do is keep still and it will look like they're still on." Once she finished the arms, she moved to the legs. "If someone asks me if I did this, I'll deny it. Dr. Morrow is out of town until tomorrow, and Peggy has already left for the day." She pulled the sheet back over Shana and returned the scissors to her pocket. "We may all be out of a job anyway. Norman's family has already hired an attorney."

"Who told you about Alex?"

"You ask too many questions," Lee said, leaving the room and closing the door behind her.

The police had seized the clothing she had been wearing, so Shana was back in the disgusting green pajamas. She paced inside the small room, the hours clicking off in her head. The police could burst through the door with a warrant any minute, but knowing how bureaucracies worked, she assumed the paperwork wouldn't be processed until the following day.

Every sound caused her to jump. Alex as part owner of this contemptible hospital was enough to make her blood boil, but Alex as a homicidal maniac who might kill just to keep her within his grasp was truly terrifying.

She had to get in touch with her mother somehow. Had Lily been calling and the staff had prevented her from receiving her calls? It wasn't like her not to call. She should have put it together by now. She thought of sneaking out and trying to use the phone, but it was ten at night and Betsy was on duty. If they found out someone had cut the restraints, the blame could fall on Lee and she didn't want anything to happen to her.

Her mind raced as she tried to put together the pieces of the puzzle. The hospital, as she saw it, was Alex's playground. He couldn't have simply purchased a few shares of stock in the hospital or they would never allow him to do the things she suspected he'd done. After achieving success in the business world, he must have decided to purchase his own mental hospital for reasons she couldn't fathom. A prince, the patients had called him. What better place to set yourself up as a prince and play the ultimate game? The majority of the patients were weak and pliable. Because Whitehall was privately owned, the risk of discovery was minimal.

Something Morrow had said came to mind. He said a person had reported them for their unscrupulous practices, but that person lacked credibility as he was a former patient. Maybe that person was Alex, and he knew enough to not only close the hospital's doors but to have criminal charges brought against Morrow and the other psychiatrists.

What Lee had told her was hearsay. It might be nothing more than rumor and insinuation. Betsy had accused her of murdering Norman, so it wasn't far-fetched that the staff had conjured up Alex as some type of villain. The man was assertive and smart, and had won the support of most of the hospital population. This alone placed him on the opposite side of the fence in regards to the nurses and attendants.

If Alex had paid a large sum of money to disappear inside Whitehall, it only made sense that being able to come and go as he wished would be part of the bargain.

Another scenario came to mind. Alex could have slipped underground to avoid a financial disaster, but once inside, he'd gone mad. He seemed so lucid, so normal. She went to the bathroom and stared at her image in the mirror, seeing a woman with ghostly pale skin and hollow eyes. Wondering how much weight she had lost, she glanced down at her body and saw her ribs and her pelvic bones protruding. Whitehall had done the trick. After less than a week, she now looked like an addict.

Like a person trying on shoes, Shana kept coming up with different scenarios to see if they might fit. If Alex was one of the primary owners of Whitehall, this might provide him with enough clout to manipulate the psychiatrists and force them to administer whatever medication he selected to specific patients. Her bet was the hospital was a hotbed of corruption before Alex ever appeared on the scene. Being an astute businessman, he may have figured out they were kidnapping patients and used it as additional leverage.

At a few minutes past three in the morning, Shana dropped down on the edge of the bed, exhausted and wired at the same time. Maybe Alex handpicked some of the patients. Now that she thought about it, it was hard to imagine that a psychic like May would have the kind of insurance Whitehall required. Norman and Karen probably had insurance coverage as they had been previously employed and they both had legitimate medical and psychological problems. Most insurance plans had a cap, though, and from what she gathered, Norman and May had been at Whitehall for quite some time.

Shana got up and started to pace again, and then stopped herself, afraid she was going to end up like poor Milton. Milton! She'd forgotten all about Milton and the cat killings. Could his self-proclaimed aberrant behavior have escalated into murder? Through posthypnotic suggestion, or by utilizing the arsenal of drugs the hospital had at its disposal, Alex could have turned Milton into a killer.

Her energy was finally depleted. She removed the green pajamas, climbed under the sheet, and instantly fell into a deep slumber.

The cat and mouse game was over. A horrendous crime, which Lily had been certain would end up in the hands of a jury, had now been resolved. All the months of preparation, the dozens of motions, the time spent selecting the jury, along with the hours of court time were wasted. The jurors were stunned when they were dismissed. Just like that, it was over.

Noelle Reynolds was either beginning to suffer guilt over killing her child, or Richard Fowler had convinced her that life in prison with no chance of parole was a far better outcome than a death sentence. Silverstein was devastated, of course, but Lily was relieved. Since her calendar had been blocked off for the next two weeks to cover the trial, she would now have time to devote to Shana. She went to Judge Hennessey's office and requested vacation leave. Amazingly, the old buzzard agreed.

"We settled the Reynolds case," she said, sticking her head into Chris's chambers. "Life without parole."

"Are you happy with that?"

"I'm thrilled." Seeing he wasn't busy, she came in and took a seat in front of his desk. She was somewhat jealous because he had such a large, well-appointed office, while her office was crap. Although she'd been a prosecutor for most of her career, Chris had received his judgeship long before her. She was the last judge appointed to the Ventura bench, so she had the worst chambers. He had mahogany bookcases and a gorgeous desk, plus a ton of open space. Her office wasn't much bigger than a walk-in closet.

"I told Silverstein from the outset that the death penalty would never fly," Lily told him. "Fowler pulled a fast one on us. He managed to get a psychologist to give the Reynolds girl an IQ test. She scored seventy, which means she's borderline retarded."

"You're kidding me. She seemed far too manipulative to be developmentally disabled. And why didn't Silverstein know about this before now? It should have been revealed during discovery. Fowler can't drop a bomb like that and get away with it."

Lily smiled because he was politically correct to an extreme. She would never use the word "retarded" in public, but she was talking to her lover in the confines of his office, where she should be able to say anything she wanted. The phrase "developmentally disabled" covered too broad a spectrum of physical and mental disabilities.

Chris was giving her a curious look so she quickly became serious again. "Richard Fowler was formerly one of the best prosecutors the DA's office ever had. If he stumbled onto something during the course of the trial which he thought would better his client's case, he was obligated to bring it to the court's attention, particularly something of this nature. I'm certain you're aware that the Supreme Court recently ruled that a mentally disabled defendant can't be put to death. Fowler must have had this brainstorm after we went to trial. He had her tested a week ago, and just got the results back the other day."

"Do you think it's true?"

"Yes," Lily told him, having had time to think about it. "Something had to be wrong with her, don't you see? No one could be that cruel, nor could they be that stupid. According to Fowler, her father, Dr. Reynolds, spent a fortune hiring tutors and other professionals to work with her. It's sad, really. He desperately wanted her to be normal. He knew she had problems, which might be the reason he wanted nothing to do with her when she got pregnant. She told the psychiatrist that she'd been on birth control since she was fourteen. When she gave birth to the child, her father should have stepped in and made certain both she and the boy were taken care of properly. He's partly responsible for the child's death."

"The press will have a field day. First she's the devil and now she's pathetic."

"No one will care." Lily shrugged her shoulders. "The reality is less interesting than what everyone believed. Evil is exciting. What happened here is frightening. People know it could happen to them. Unfortunately, we can't pick our children."

"What about the arsenic and the Ajax?"

"The kid must have eaten the Ajax, even if it did taste like shit. Maybe the mother forgot to feed him. As to the arsenic, they found only a trace of it in his system. Everyone has daily exposure to arsenic because it's a naturally occurring chemical element that's normally found in water, soil, indoor house dust, air, and food. Of course, you know that."

"So you're going to have some time on your hands."

"I just got out of Hennessey's office," she said. "He agreed to let me take two weeks' vacation. I'm going to try to figure out what to do about Shana. Something's not right, Chris. I can feel it. I had a terrible dream about her last night. We've had arguments over the years, but she's never gone this long without speaking to me."

"Are you going to fly up there?"

"Yes," she said, standing to leave.

Chris walked over and embraced her. "You're doing the right thing. Unfortunately, I have to be on the bench. We'll talk more at lunch, okay?"

Lily sighed. "I'm going home. I'll pick up some food for dinner. Then I'm going to pack. If I have to, I can stay in Shana's apartment.

I've got to get her out of Whitehall. You were right all along, Chris. She doesn't belong in a place like that."

He nodded. "I'll do whatever I can to help you."

"We have to get you dressed," Lee said, finding Shana sprawled out on her bed naked. "Your mother's on the phone."

Shana rolled over and squinted. Light was streaming in through the window. She tried to wake up but something was pulling her back under. She closed her eyes and fell back to sleep.

Lee was working frantically. She placed the leather restraints she had cut into a plastic garbage bag, and then attached the new ones she had brought from the supply room to the bed. "Wake up," she said, shaking Shana by the shoulder. "Your mother can get you a lawyer. Peggy has a doctor's appointment and everyone else is at lunch. Otherwise, they wouldn't let you speak to her."

Shana sat up, her eyes roaming around the room. "My mother? She finally called me?"

"Yes." Lee held a clean pair of pajamas in her hand. "Your mother has called dozens of times, Shana. Dr. Morrow left strict orders that you weren't allowed to speak to her or anyone else. He said it was part of your treatment."

As soon as Shana was dressed, she followed Lee across the isolation ward, where her new room was located. The clock on the wall read twelve-fifteen. She had slept all morning. Lee handed her the phone from the other side of the nursing station.

"Mom," she said, tears gushing from her eyes. "Please come and get me out of this place. The hospital made everything up. I was never addicted to drugs. Please, you have to believe me. They wouldn't allow me to call you or receive calls. You don't know what I've been through. They've been giving me all these horrible drugs. They even locked me in a padded cell."

"My God, Shana, are these things you're telling me the truth?"

"I swear, Mom. Please help me. You have to get me out of here. Something terrible has happened. One of the patients was murdered and the police think I did it." Shana's shoulders shook as she sobbed. "I'm sorry I said those ugly things to you. I love you. I was just depressed and stressed out. Please, come fast."

"I'll catch the next flight out. If this hospital has done the things you say, I'll mop the floor with them. Try to be strong until I get there, Shana. I'm so sorry, honey. This is my fault. I should have never taken you to that place. Will you be safe until I get there?"

"What about your trial?"

"The DA cut a deal this morning. Don't worry about my work, Shana. You're the only thing that matters right now. I don't know what I'd do if anything happened to you. A murder? Dear God, did you really say you were a suspect in a murder?"

"Yes," Shana said. "What if they won't let me leave?"

Lily's shock had turned to anger. "They'll have me to answer to, and I guarantee you they'll let you leave. If Whitehall gives me any trouble, I'll slap a cease and desist order on them and close their doors. I am a judge, remember?" She paused and took a breath. "Listen to me, Shana. I'm coming to get you out and take you home. Just stay safe until I get there? Can you do that?"

"I'll try."

"If you feel you're in any immediate danger, I'll have the local police dispatch an officer over there to protect you until I get there."

"No!" Shana shouted. "Didn't you hear what I said? The police think I killed someone. They won't protect me, Mother. They'll arrest me."

"Everything's going to be all right," Lily said, her voice cracking with emotion. "I promise I'll never betray your trust again."

Shana handed the phone back to Lee and headed back to the room. The floor suddenly rose up to meet her and then tilted on its side. She slapped open the door to the room and headed to the bathroom to take a shower and try to look presentable for her mother. When she got out, she rubbed a spot on the mirror and stared at her face. Her head still felt groggy and her eyes were swollen from crying. She brushed her teeth twice, squeezing a glob of toothpaste onto the brush and moving the toothbrush back and forth until her gums began to bleed, trying to get the cottony feeling out of her mouth. Why did she feel so drugged? The last medication she remembered taking was yesterday morning when she couldn't stop laughing. Was someone other than Morrow drugging her?

Every day at lunch, she sat next to Alex. They always drank the same fruit punch, but some days he picked it up in the cafeteria line and other times she did. Maybe Alex had given her Ecstasy or some other type of hallucinogenic. That could explain the laughing fit as well as the intense pleasure she had experienced the night they had sex.

Shana tried to block the door to the bathroom with her body, a scream trapped inside her throat. It would take at least four or five hours for her mother to get here. A lot could happen in that amount of time. A person could get themselves killed.

# TWENTY-SEVEN

Alex's mother, Nadine, appeared at the door to the great room wearing dark sunglasses and a green raincoat. Even though the sky was clear and the sun was out, another storm front was supposed to be moving through. Nadine's hair was covered with a paisley scarf and she was carrying a briefcase.

Alex gestured to George and he lumbered over and unlocked the door. Mother and son then made their way to an isolated section of the courtyard. There was only one lawn chair, so Alex had to find another one and carry it over to where Nadine was sitting.

"I brought the last of the papers," she told him.

Alex stared at her, tipping his chair back on its back legs. His eyelids looked heavy and his normally relaxed face was tight with tension.

"Everything's been taken care of . . . everything's in order."

Alex's full weight fell forward as he leaned over his knees. "What's the rush? There's time."

"No, Adam, there isn't." She opened her purse and pulled out a tissue, dabbing at her eyes.

He sat upright in the chair, his mouth rigid, and his teeth gritting the end of the cigarette. "What did you call me?"

"You're my son," Nadine said, tears welling up in her eyes. "That's the name I gave you. It was your grandfather's name." She looked down at her hands. She was nervously rubbing the thumb and forefinger on each hand together. It was a lifelong habit. When he was a child, he used to tell her it reminded him of a fly. "I was so proud of you. You were the smartest boy in your elementary school, the smartest in your junior high. You won all those awards for your inventions in the science fair. You won a scholarship to MIT."

"Well, I didn't win any awards for popularity, did I? I didn't have time for friends or school activities."

"You were a gifted child, Adam."

"I wasn't a child, Nadine. You never allowed me to be a child."

She slipped the scarf off her head. Her hair was slicked back in a tight knot at the base of her neck. "You can't stay here because of that woman. We can't put everything on hold, not after what's happened. This is serious, Adam. We have to move now. The police are going through the records at the hospital and checking all the patients."

"There's nothing in my file. Morrow assured me he took care of it."

"Don't you think that alone is suspicious?" Nadine argued. "What kind of hospital doesn't keep records on their patients? My God, Adam, that's a red flag to the authorities. What if they start taking fingerprints? You can't just stay here. You're risking everything."

"I can do anything I want."

"Yes, you can," she told him. "You can do anything you set out to do. You've proven that, proven it to everyone. You've always said I pushed you to excel. But you did succeed, didn't you? You accomplished more than you ever dreamed you could. You built a fabulous empire, all created and fueled by your brilliance and vision. And no one is going to stop us. No one stopped us before and no one is going to stop us now. We bought controlling shares in this hospital. We did everything exactly the way you wanted. The hospital will always be here for you if you have problems in the future. You just can't stay here after what's happened." She picked up her purse, opening it and removing a piece of paper which she handed to him. "Do you remember, Adam? Other people remember, people who loved her."

He held the paper in his hands, transfixed, immobile. It was the picture of a young girl, the edges of the paper frayed and yellow with age. His chest started to rise and fall as if he were having difficulty breathing.

Nadine spoke, her voice a controlled monotone, any traces of the earlier display of emotion gone. She was using his distress, feeding on it, growing stronger. Her mouth compressed into a thin, straight line. "I should have known you were in trouble when you demanded that I bring all those things to the hospital for that girl." She paused, wanting her words to sink in. "It's over, Adam. I'll call you later this evening and tell you what to do. Your father's made all the necessary arrangements."

Nadine stood and waited. He was staring into space, lost in his memories. The paper fluttered out of his hands and Nadine stooped down to pick it up so she could return it to him. When he made no move to accept it, she stuck it inside his shirt pocket. Then she opened the briefcase and placed it on the chair, removing two documents. She placed the papers in his lap and handed him a pen. "Sign these, Adam. These are the last."

His eyes locked with hers and lingered. After some time had passed, he bent down and signed his name. Nadine removed the papers from his hand and placed them back in the briefcase. Without saying good-bye, she turned and headed back into the hospital. Once she was safely inside, the sky opened up and it began pouring. A few staff members from the adolescent unit were running across the courtyard, holding newspapers over their heads to protect them from the downpour. No one saw Alex sitting there long after the others had gone inside, a soggy cigarette dangling from his mouth, his eyes fixed and blank, rain washing over his face and soaking his clothing. He remained there, perfectly motionless, oblivious to the rain, racing back in time to the day he'd been released from the Camarillo State Mental Hospital, two days before his eighteenth birthday.

Nadine was screaming at him, her face a mask of twisted fury. They were in her long bronze Cadillac and had just driven past the gates of the hospital. "You got that girl pregnant? How could you do that, Adam, after everything we've been through? You went in her room and had sex with her. If I hadn't gone to the head of the hospital and pleaded with him on my hands and knees, they would have never released you."

"Where is she, Mother?" he asked, his voice eerily calm.

"Look, honey," she said in a calmer tone. "Forget about that girl and I'll buy you that contraption you want. Some very important people from Switzerland have expressed interest in the paper you wrote for Young Scientist magazine. One of the gentlemen is with a place called CERN. I still don't understand why you need such an expensive toy."

"That contraption is a computer," he said, his eyes coming alive. "I need a fast computer with a large memory to do the math. CERN is the European Organization for Nuclear Research. I can't believe they called me."

"Nuclear?" his mother said, alarmed. "You'll blow yourself up. You can't be involved with those people if they make nuclear bombs. I thought they were just a bunch of math professors. Besides, why would they call themselves CERN? That's not an acronym for what you just told me."

"They study the atom. I think they use the word nuclear because it refers to the nucleus. The original name was in French. That's why the letters aren't right. In certain parts of Switzerland, the people speak French."

"Don't talk down to me," she told him, cutting her eyes to him. "I know what a nucleus is. Just because I studied English doesn't mean I'm stupid. Science and math don't interest me like they do you and your father."

"Forget the computer," Adam said, intense again. "I have to find Jennifer. Where is she? Where did they take her? I promised her I wouldn't leave her. We're in love, Mother."

"You're too young to be in love. It's natural for boys your age to want sex. Sex is not love, Adam."

"Take me to her house."

"Forget you ever knew that girl. You're going to college. You have a tremendous future ahead of you. She's mentally ill, that girl. She's never going to be normal."

"And what am I, Mother?"

Nadine pulled into a gasoline station and parked. "I have to get gas." She told the attendant to fill it up and then turned back to her son. "Don't compare yourself to the people in that awful place. You're nothing like those people. You're brilliant, Adam. Ordinary people can't comprehend genius." She opened her purse and took out her wallet.

"You went to Jennifer's parents and told them to take her away, didn't you?"

"Stop it," Nadine snapped. "You're being ridiculous. Once the hospital discovered the girl was pregnant, of course they released her. They didn't want to be responsible for a mentally ill pregnant girl, especially one who'd have sex with anyone." She stopped and took a deep breath. "What difference does it make if I contacted her parents? They've probably had her abort it by now and we can forget about this whole sordid mess. Whatever they did, it's over now. Just be thankful her parents didn't press charges against you or you'd still be in that filthy hospital."

"I love her, Mother. No one's going to kill our baby." He reached over and snatched Nadine's wallet out of her hands, then leaned over and opened the driver's door, shoving her out onto the pavement.

"Adam, stop! My God, what are you doing?" The attendant rushed over to Nadine but it was too late. The Cadillac was speeding out of the gas station. It fishtailed onto the interstate, then headed north into the afternoon sun.

"Gosh, lady," the attendant said, bending down and extending his hand to Nadine. "You want me to call the police? Did that guy rob you?"

"Get your greasy hands off of me," Nadine snapped, staring down the road as she dusted off her clothing. "No, I don't want you to call the police. That was my son."

Adam arrived at the address Jennifer had given him at five o'clock in the morning. He parked a few houses down and got out, prowling around the house and peering into the windows as he tried to find her bedroom. Seeing a window ajar, he entered and crept through the house.

In the den was a large, glass-enclosed gun case. He tried to open it but it was locked. Finding a towel in the laundry room, he wrapped it around his hand and broke the glass, reaching in and removing a pistol. In the bottom of the gun cabinet, he found the ammo clip and shoved it into place. No one was going to take Jennifer away from him. He would not allow anyone to murder their baby.

Moving like a cat through the dark room, he opened doors and looked inside. He found a room with a white bedspread and several stuffed animals on top of it and knew it had to be Jennifer's because she was an only child. The bed was made, though, and Jennifer was nowhere to be found.

He sat down on the edge of her bed and brought her pillow to his face. They were so much alike. Before he'd met her, he had felt totally alone, separated from the world because of his differences. In her arms in the small twin bed at the hospital, he had finally tasted happiness and a sense of belonging. In a black nightmare of pain, he had somehow found paradise. Now it was gone. They had taken it away from him, robbed him of the only good thing he had ever had. Consumed with anger, his fingers locked on the gun.

Dropping the pillow on the floor, he walked toward the bedroom where her parents were sleeping, his rage unchecked and his body rigid. He stood over their bed and wailed like a wounded animal, the sound coming from somewhere deep inside his body. "Jennifer . . ."

"Oh my God, Fred!" the woman shouted in total terror, bolting upright in the bed. "It's him! It's that boy from the hospital. He's got a gun. He's going to kill us."

Adam leapt onto the bed on top of the man, shoving the barrel of the gun into his gaping mouth. "Where is she? What have you done with her?"

"Don't hurt him," the woman begged. "Please don't hurt him. Jennifer isn't here. She ran away. She said she was going to Oakland. That's where we used to live. Please leave my husband alone. He has a heart condition. Help us!" she shrieked, her eyes darting around the room. "Someone call the police. He's going to kill us."

Adam fled the house and escaped into the night before the neighbors heard Jennifer's parents' terrified screams. Back in his mother's car, he found the freeway and headed toward Oakland.

Once he arrived in the city, he drove all day without stopping, searching the streets, the cheap hotels, the shelters, stopping at phone booths to call the local hospitals to see if Jennifer had been admitted. If her parents hadn't forced her to abort their baby, it would be almost time for her to give birth.

When night fell and he became too exhausted to drive, he parked in a shopping center and slept in the car. The next morning he awoke at dawn and started his search again. His stomach rumbled with hunger, but he refused to stop to eat or drink.

Then he saw her.

She was walking down the street, alone, carrying a small suitcase, her blond hair stringy and limp, her eyes dazed and her face ashen. He stomped on the brakes and put the car in park, jumping out and grabbing her. Sweeping her up in his arms, he carried her to the passenger side of the car and fastened her seat belt. Through her clothes, he could feel her rib cage and her skin was cold and clammy. "What happened to our baby, Jennifer?"

"It came out," she told him. "Then I killed it. It was a little girl. I wrapped my sweater around its face and held it tight until it stopped crying. I left it in the trash can."

He seized her thin shoulders and shook her. "How could you? I could have taken care of you and the baby. The hospital released me yesterday. I can get a job and make money. We could have had a life. Why? Why? Why did you kill our baby?"

Jennifer dropped her head and then slowly raised her eyes. "It wouldn't stop crying. I couldn't stand it. The noise made my head hurt."

Adam drove to a nearby motel and rented a room using Nadine's credit card. He placed his arm around Jennifer's waist as they climbed the stairs to the room. Once inside, she sat on the edge of the bed and he fell to his knees in front of her, placing his head in her lap. They sat there in silence for a long time, neither attempting to move.

Thoughts were racing inside his head. There was no place for people like them in the outside world. They were defective, mistakes of the universe. He thought of the freaks in the circus, people with two heads or a third leg. Even they were better off than he and Jennifer. People would pay to see them, laugh at them, point at their deformities, but even the freaks had a place of their own and freedom to come and go whenever they wanted, something he and Jennifer would never have. All they had was a cold, indifferent institution that refused to allow them to be together. No matter what they were, they deserved to experience love.

Jennifer's soul was locked inside her tortured mind. The court would commit her again once they found out what she had done. And he would have to go back as well because he'd broken into her parents' home and pointed a gun at them. He lifted his head and captured her face in his hands, forcing her to look at him.

"Listen to me," he said, his voice high-pitched and agitated. "We have to start over, die. It's the only way. If we die together at exactly the same time, we'll be together forever in paradise. We'll force the universe to give us another chance. Can't you see? It's all meant to be this way. We'll be together with our baby girl."

"We'll all be together." A glimmer of hope appeared in her dull eyes. "I'll never have to go back to the hospital?"

"No, you'll never have to go back." Tears were streaming down Adam's face. She was so beautiful, so perfect. She was eighteen, but her body was as fragile as a twelve-year-old's.

White was her favorite color. She was wearing a white dress today, but it was dirty and stained with blood. She had killed their child. How could they go on?

He pushed himself to his feet and removed the pistol from his back pocket. On the drive to Oakland, he had inserted the clip into the gun, afraid that Nadine or the police might track him down and try to stop him.

"You promise, Adam?" Jennifer said. "We'll all be together?"

"I promise, Jennifer. We'll all be together on the other side. There has to be another world, another lifetime. The doctors are always giving us drugs that make us sleep. Death is just like going to sleep except you wake up in another world, a better world than this one. Everyone is happy and people who love each other are together forever."

She folded her small hands in her lap, and then tilted her head slightly as if she was posing for a photograph. She even tried to smile, but the edges of her lips were trembling. "I'm ready. Do it now."

He bent down and embraced her, then released her and stepped back. His body was shaking so hard the gun was jumping up and down in his hands. She looked into his eyes and sat up straight, raising her chin with pride.

"Do it, Adam."

He was sobbing, choking, mucus dripping from his nose. "I love you, Jennifer. When you get to the other side, just count to ten and I'll be there."

He fired.

The explosion was deafening. The bullet struck almost squarely between her eyes, propelling her frail body backward with tremendous force. Fresh blood stained her white dress and spilled out on the bedspread. He held the gun to his head as he stared down at her lifeless body. "I'm coming."

When the police broke down the door, Adam was rocking her body in his arms and sobbing hysterically. "I couldn't do it," he told the officers. "Oh God, I promised her. Shoot me, please, I'm begging you. I want to die. I want to die."

Adam saw the gun on the bed and lunged for it, hoping the officers would open fire. But one of the officers grabbed him from behind just as his fingertips touched the gun and wrestled him to the floor.

One year later, Adam Pounder, wearing an expensive suit his mother had bought him, was standing in the courtroom with the best defense attorney money could buy at his side. Except for the tortured look in his eyes, Adam resembled a clean-cut college student.

Adam stood, glancing over at Nadine and then back to the jury foreman. "On the charge of murder in the first degree, we find the defendant not guilty by reason of insanity."

Nadine jumped up and embraced him. "I told you, darling," she whispered in his ear. "They can't send you to prison. You were sick when that awful girl made you shoot her."

The judge shot a stern look at Nadine and she sat back down in her chair. "Mr. Pounder, you are hereby committed to the California state hospital for the criminally insane at Vacaville where you will be held until you are no longer a threat to society." The gavel came down and Adam was removed from the courtroom.

Two years later, he was released.

"Mr. Pounder is an extremely intelligent and industrious young man," the report from Vacaville stated. "During the time he has been at this institution, he has exhibited no abnormal or violent behavior, has participated willingly in therapy, and has been working actively toward obtaining his college diploma. Mr. Pounder has a supportive family structure, an excellent chance for employment and continued education, and no longer appears to pose a threat to the community."

The case was closed, and the court was relieved of the responsibility of releasing a potentially dangerous individual back into the community. Vacaville, like most of the California prisons, was enormously overcrowded. A young man like Adam Pounder, with a family to support him and the possibility of contributing to society, was a calculated risk but one both the institution and the court had no choice but to take.

Adam walked out of the courtroom a free man exactly twenty-four months and three days after he shot and killed Jennifer Rondini. It was the second occasion where he had been convicted and released after committing an act of violence.

# TWENTY-EIGHT

Lee knocked on the door at two o'clock that afternoon. "Open the door, Shana. I have to know that you're okay."

Shana's muscles were strained from staying in bed so it was a relief to move. She removed the chair she had used to block the door. "I'm fine. I just don't want anyone to sneak in here and kill me."

"Relax. No one is going to hurt you. Everyone went to the gym to play basketball. You can walk around now if you want, stretch your legs."

Shana was hesitant but decided to take her up on her offer. Depending on which flight Lily had managed to get on, she might not arrive until late that night. Staying in the room so long was making her paranoid, the last thing she needed right now. "Is Alex still at the hospital or did he leave?"

"I haven't seen him," Lee told her. "That doesn't mean he won't be back. One time he left for a week."

She walked to the door and cracked it, peering out into the great room to make sure it was empty. Lee walked to the door separating the isolation section from the great room and unlocked it. Placing the keys back in the pocket of her sweater, she slowly raised her eyes to Shana. "Thanks for not telling them I cut the restraints."

Shana hugged her. "No one else would have helped me, Lee. You're an angel."

In the great room, Shana saw the police had posted a notice on the door to Norman's room that identified it as a crime scene. She went two doors down and snuck into Alex's room. Closing the door, she flipped on the light switch. The bed was neatly made and she didn't see any personal items on top of the end table or chest. Even the computer was gone, so it could be Alex was gone for good this time. When she looked into the closet, though, it was crammed full of Alex's clothes. She couldn't believe he had so many things here, and then remembered that Lee was convinced Alex could come and go whenever he wished. If she was right, he used Whitehall like a hotel room with great drugs and excellent security.

She was about to close the closet door when she saw what appeared to be a loose tile on the floor. Dropping to her knees, she used her fingernails to try to dislodge it. She was about to give up when she saw a ballpoint pen on the end table. She poked around the edges of the loose tile with the pen until it finally popped out. Underneath the tile, someone had chipped a hole in the concrete. Seeing a glint of something metallic, she reached in and pulled it out.

"Hot damn!" she exclaimed, holding a microcassette player in her hands. She depressed the play button and was startled by what she heard. Wheezing, combined with the sounds of a bed squeaking, then followed by a period of heavy breathing. These were the only noises she had ever heard Michaela Henderson make and they were all contained on this one recording. Had she been sleeping next to a corpse?

The hairs on the back of her neck pricked. What kind of devious charade had been going on? No, she told herself, Michaela had been alive. A corpse didn't get up and walk to the bathroom. She recalled the day she had seen Michaela get out of bed. All she had really seen was a large shadowy image swaddled in a thick bathrobe. There was only one explanation for the tape. Alex must have hidden in her room disguised as her roommate. If she wasn't mistaken, the night she had seen Michaela get out of bed had been the night she had dreamed she was making love to Brett.

Had her sexually explicit dreams been real?

Shana was horrified. Stuffing the tape recorder into the back pocket of her jeans, she started to leave and then decided to look inside his drawers. Inside the top drawer of the chest, she found Alex's wallet hidden underneath a stack of jockey shorts. She flipped it open and scanned the credit cards in the plastic slots. There were other papers inside the side compartments in the wallet. She pulled them out and started reading them. Most of the papers were credit card receipts and business cards. One of the receipts caught her eye and she slipped it into her pocket.

The next thing she found was a torn and yellowed newspaper clipping that had been folded into a small square. Shana put everything back except the receipt and the clipping, and quickly returned the wallet to the drawer where she'd found it. She was about to leave when she saw him.

Alex was standing there watching her.

Shana gasped. A moment later, she collected herself and managed to smile. "I'm sorry, Alex," she said. "You must think I'm terrible to be going through your things. I wanted to call my mother and I remembered you had a calling card, so I thought you wouldn't mind if I borrowed it."

Alex had closed the door while she was speaking and now placed his hands behind his back and leaned against it. "Did you find what you were looking for?"

Shana heard him but she couldn't speak. His eyes were burning through her and she felt as if she were naked. "No, I-I wasn't . . ." she stammered. "I didn't . . ."

"No?" he said, tilting his head. "That's strange."

Shana swallowed hard. Never had Alex looked at her this way. What she saw was sheer insanity. His face had transformed into rigid lines and a strange light emanated from his eyes. She started walking toward the door, and then stopped inches away as if he had thrown up an invisible force field. "Why is that strange?"

"It was right there in my wallet."

Alex's eyes said it all. He must have been standing there the entire time. Then she played it over in her mind. She remembered glancing at the door while she was going through his wallet and no one was there. He was bluffing. "No, I didn't find your wallet. I thought it might be on top of your chest, but I didn't see it. I was about to leave when you walked in."

He continued to glare at her for several moments and then pushed himself off the door. Going to his dresser, he removed his wallet and handed her the calling card. "They're not going to let you leave, you know," he said. "You're deluding yourself if you think otherwise. Homicide investigations take time, and from what I understand, you're the prime suspect."

"We'll see," Shana said, her blood boiling. He knew how much she wanted to get out of the hospital. If he had set out to push her buttons, he had succeeded. What riled her most was that if Alex was one of the owners of the hospital, he could have arranged her release. How could he have stood by and watched when they tossed her in a padded cell and pumped her system full of dangerous drugs? And he had to be aware of the patient snatching. Even if he wasn't a killer, he had turned out to be a fake. The way it looked now, he was also a rapist. "I have to call my mother," she said, pushing past him.

Walking in the direction of the pay phone, Shana darted inside her old room and found Michaela's bed empty. Had she been murdered as well? If so, why didn't the police mention it? Since she was her roommate, if something had happened to her, Shana would be the most likely suspect. Of course, Michaela could have been released, although she seriously doubted it. The woman was almost catatonic. She closed the door and started walking rapidly toward the isolation ward.

"Your mother hired a guard to watch over you," Lee told her, unlocking the door to the isolation wing when Shana appeared. A fresh-faced young man in a brown security uniform was seated in a chair in front of her room. He stood when he saw Shana. "Are you the lady I'm supposed to protect?"

"Shana Forrester," she said, extending her free hand.

"Will Andrews," he responded. "I've never worked in a place like this before. Is there anyone in particular you want me to look out for?"

"Everyone," Shana said, rushing inside her room. She went to the bathroom and shut the door, sitting down on the commode and pulling out the two pieces of paper she had taken from Alex's wallet. She placed the credit card receipt and the calling card on the counter by the sink and unfolded the newspaper article.

The girl in the picture was a young blonde, more than likely in her late teens. It was funny but she faintly resembled Shana. Her hair was a different color, but it was the same length and appeared to be naturally curly. The girl had fair skin like Shana and green eyes. The photo looked as if it had been taken from a driver's license or identification card. She read the caption above the article.

MURDER VICTIM DEAD BABY'S MOTHER.

Newspapers and their headlines, she thought. They'd sure captured her attention. They had everything working in this story, not only a dead woman but a dead baby as well. "Death sells," she said, turning her eyes to the article and eagerly reading the text.

"Police authorities advise Jennifer Rondini, the eighteen-year-old female shot and killed yesterday in what apparently started out as a suicide pact, was the woman described by several passengers in the Greyhound bus terminal where the body of a newborn infant was found dead in the women's restroom . . ."

The rest of the article was missing. The newspaper was the *San Francisco Chronicle* and the date was January 15, 1992. Alex had told her he was thirty-five, so that would make him eighteen at the time.

She stared at the receipt and tried to recall why she had taken it. It was just an old credit card receipt for gas. She started to wad it up and toss it into the trash can when she noticed the date was only two days ago and Alex had signed it. Lee's statements had been true. Alex not only had carte blanche inside the hospital, he could come and go whenever he wanted.

Thank God her mother was coming. As soon as she got home, she would insist that Lily cancel the mental health benefits that were part of her policy. She had to make certain something like this didn't happen again.

Halfway to the door, Shana suddenly halted. If she was right and she hadn't lost track of time, today was January 15th, the same date the article on Jennifer Rondini was written. It was just a coincidence, she told herself, and she'd never put much stock in coincidences. On the other hand, the young girl in the article had been murdered and Alex had carried that piece of paper in his wallet for almost twenty years. Right this minute, Shana didn't care what crimes Alex had committed. All she wanted was to get out of Whitehall alive.

When she got the nerve to go to the great room, she glanced around at the patients. The stories they told could all be lies. "Consider the source," her father used to tell her. She saw the man Alex had said was a priest and wondered if he had killed Norman. He might not even be a priest. What caused her to believe Alex was sane when he lived in a mental hospital? The drugs Morrow had given her had robbed her of her common sense.

Everything about Whitehall was not what it seemed. Looking back at the nursing station, she saw Lee wearing the exact same dress she had been wearing since Shana was admitted. No one wore the same dress every day of the week unless it was a uniform and the dress didn't look at all like a uniform. The only explanation had to be a contrived plan. Since they snatched people off the street and shot them full of drugs, seeing the staff in the same clothes could cause the patients to lose track of time and reality. The way she saw it, the goal at Whitehall was to drive the patients crazy. The hospital didn't profit from restoring their sanity.

She started counting heads and came up with forty-three patients milling around inside the great room. As far as she could tell, Lee was the only attendant on duty today. She wasn't up on the licensing standards for psychiatric institutions, but anyone with half a brain would know Whitehall was dangerously understaffed. Norman's family would win a lawsuit for negligence and wrongful death hands down. With this in mind, her eyes found Alex, seated at the smoking table as he chatted and laughed with Karen and May. If he was, in fact, one of the principal owners of the hospital, he certainly didn't appear concerned. But of course, Alex had moved on to larger stakes. He was playing with human lives now instead of a portfolio of investments. She headed to the pay phone to call her mother with Alex's calling card, wanting to make certain she was on the way.

"Mom," she said, "what time does your plane leave? I thought you'd be in the air by now."

"I'm at the airport. My plane is about to take off. It's not easy to book a flight on the spur of the moment. I got one, though, and the flight gets in at six-thirty." Her voice was momentarily drowned out by interference. "Did something else happen? I hired a private security guard to look after you until I get there. Has he shown up yet?"

"Yes, thank you. So if your plane gets in at six-thirty, you should be here by seven-thirty at the latest. Is that right?"

"Are you really that frightened, Shana?"

"Yes, I am, Mother. I don't want to spend the rest of my life in prison. The man who died had burns on ninety percent of his body. I really liked him. I would never do anything to hurt him. When the nurse saw me straddling him, I was trying to give him CPR. Remember, I took that class and got my certification the summer I worked as a lifeguard."

"Just stay in your room and let the guard do his job. I bet you're not in your room right now."

"How did you figure that out?"

"Listen to me, Shana. I know you're anxious and stir crazy, but the guard can't protect you if you don't stay in your room. I instructed the security company to tell the guard to call the police if anything even slightly suspicious happens. I love you. I promise I'll make everything right when I get there. Try to stay calm, and for

God's sake, don't go out of your room until I get there. What if there's another murder? I'm trying to make sure you have an alibi. Do you understand?"

"Yes, Mother, I understand. I'm going back to my room as soon as I finish talking to you."

"Go now," Lily told her. "They're calling my flight."

Shana hung up and started walking back to her room. She wanted to call the police and report what she'd found out about Alex, but she knew she couldn't. Detective Lindstrom thought Alex was a figment of her imagination. Besides, the patients and the staff, outside of Lee perhaps, believed she was enamored of Alex. Even her suspicions about him and the mysterious newspaper article wouldn't carry any weight with the authorities. The police would think she was trying to implicate Alex to clear herself. How could she recount the complexities of her relationship with Alex to a courtroom of strangers?

Only one thing remained. She still had to get out of Whitehall. Shana had learned an important lesson, though. Money was important, something she'd never thought about until now. And Alex must have plenty if he had purchased his own hospital.

Nodding at the guard, she entered her room and flopped down on the bed. No matter how much money Alex had, he could never go up against her mother. She wasn't rich but she had power, and power might be the only thing that could clear her. She also reminded herself that her mother was an esteemed superior court judge. When Marco Curazon had raped her, Lily had put her life and her future on the line to make certain he would never hurt her again. It didn't matter that she'd killed the wrong man. What mattered was that she did it to protect her.

Shana didn't expect her mother to kill Alex or anyone else, but she knew she would fight for her with every ounce of strength she possessed. The cavalry was on the way. All she had to do was wait.

# TWENTY-NINE

"Shana, your mother is here."

No better words had ever been spoken. "Thanks, Lee," Shana yelled through the closed door. "Tell her I'll be right out."

She started to change into one of the other cashmere sweaters Alex had bought her and then threw it aside like a snake. Dropping to her knees, she reached under the bed for the green pajamas. Once they were on, she ran out of the room. In her excitement, she forgot to put on her shoes. Lily was standing at the counter waiting for her.

"Mom!" Shana yelled across the room. Before Lily was able to take two steps toward her, Shana sprinted across the room and engulfed her. A moment later, her shoulders shook and tears gushed from her eyes. It was strange how a person didn't appreciate someone until they lost them.

Lily pulled her daughter's wet face to her chest. "Don't cry, honey. Everything's going to be all right. I'm here now and we're together. That's all that matters."

Shana relished the warmth of her mother's body and the unique smell of her skin. She had worn the same cologne, Chanel No. 5, for as long as she could remember. Several pleasant moments

passed before her frustrations erupted. "Why didn't you come before now? Why did you leave me here, in this place, with these
horrible people?"

"You have to believe me, I called every day," Lily told her. "They
kept telling me you wouldn't speak to me."

Lee came over and directed them to an empty room, not wanting
the patients to bother them. Lily took a seat on the side of the bed
and Shana remained standing. "I assumed you were mad at me.
Then when Dr. Morrow told me you were doing so well in your
treatment, I thought I was doing the right thing by staying away. He
called me yesterday, and I was shocked at what he told me."

"Morrow," Shana said, spitting his name out like piece of rotten
food. "That lying piece of shit. I never refused your calls. Lee, the
nurse who let us use this room, told me Morrow left a standing order with the receptionist not to put any of my calls through. He
was afraid you'd wise up if you talked to me. What did Morrow tell
you that you were shocked about?"

"That you'd fallen in love with a male patient."

"You're shocked about me hooking up with one of the patients,
but you're not concerned that I'm the prime suspect in a murder?"

Lily's face drained of color. "I didn't mean it like that."

"Yes, you did," her daughter argued. "If I told you I'd met a nice
guy at Stanford, you'd be ecstatic. You're prejudiced, Mother. I guess
you look down on me, too. I've spent time in a mental hospital
thanks to you, and not once, but twice."

"I'm sorry," Lily said. "You're right, I guess."

Shana would one day tell her mother what had transpired between her and Alex, but she couldn't discuss it right now. The
wound was too raw. "Morrow was lying, Mother. Every word that
comes out of his mouth is a lie. Did he tell you I was violent, that
I had to be locked in a padded cell? This is an awful place. It's also
a dangerous place." She waved her arms around. "My God, the police are ready to charge me with murder. Doesn't that give you a
pretty good picture of what goes on here?"

Lee stuck her head in the door and whispered, "She's here, so be careful. I wouldn't want anything to happen to your mother."

Lily's back was turned and she didn't see Lee wink. She must have overheard their conversation and decided to give Shana a little help.

"What is she talking about?" Lily said, standing and walking over. "I'm a judge, in case you don't know. I don't think they'd have the gall to lock up a judge."

"We've had a number of patients who were judges," Lee told her, her eyes drifting downward. "You need to get your daughter an attorney and get her out. This isn't the first person who has died here. They always say it's suicide, but I'm not certain. I've already turned in my resignation. This is my last day."

Shana looked over her shoulder and saw Peggy had just come on duty. She was putting her purse under the counter at the nursing station. Shana lunged forward as if she wanted to rush out and attack her, her chest rising and falling with emotion.

Gently taking her arm, Lily pulled her back from the door. "Now isn't the time to make a scene. Be smart, Shana. Once we get you out of here, we'll put this hellhole out of business. Right now, you have to go along with the program."

"See that woman at the counter, the heavyset woman? She's the one who put me in the padded cell. I was in there for almost twelve hours. I didn't have any food or water. I had to pee on the floor like a dog." She became emotional and started crying. "You have to get me out of here, Mother. You have to get me out of here today."

"I'll do everything I can, Shana. I'll hire an attorney first thing in the morning, but I can't promise anything. I don't know what's involved yet."

Shana started to lose it, grabbing the lapels of her mother's jacket. "Not another night here. You don't understand. I'm in danger. Pay someone, bribe them, anything. All they want anyway is money. You can't leave me here. Please, please . . . for the love of God, get me out of here!"

Lily pried her daughter's hands off her jacket and clasped them in her own. "Calm down, Shana. You have to calm down. If you don't stop acting this way, I'll never get you out. Acting like this is how you got here."

Shana saw that it was more than her behavior that was bothering her mother. With the baggy green pajamas, no shoes, and her unkempt hair, she must look completely mad.

"Are you sick or something?" Lily asked, one hand moving to her chest. "My God, Shana, you're emaciated. You look like you've lost ten pounds."

Shana slipped her hands out of her mother's and let them fall by her sides. "It's the pajamas, but you're right. If I keep shaking things up, Peggy will have them put me in a straitjacket."

"You've lost far too much weight. Haven't you been eating?"

"Losing weight is the least of my problems," Shana said. "Please, Mom, can't you even try to get me out today? It's only a few minutes past eight. You might still have time to find an attorney. Go to the jail. Lots of attorneys put their cards there. The police haven't charged me, so they have no right to hold me. Am I right?"

"Okay . . . okay," Lily said, her nerves jangled. "I'll leave now. As soon as I get the wheels in motion, I'll be back." She kissed Shana on the cheek. "It's almost over, honey. You've made it this far so just stay safe until I get back."

Shana felt bad for her mother. Desperate for someone to help her, she'd completely overwhelmed her. Lily was a judge and her daughter was now a suspect in a homicide. That alone was enough to drive a person over the edge. None of her problems had easy solutions, and she was demanding that her mother fix them instantly. The last thing she wanted was to leave Lily with the impression that she belonged in a hospital like Whitehall. She forced herself to calm down and spoke in a calm, moderated tone. "Can you please bring me some clothes? I can't leave in these pajamas."

"Just relax. I'll take care of everything."

After Lily left, Shana rushed back to her room. She was upset when she saw the guard had gone, but she doubted if he could have protected her anyway. The battle had begun and it wasn't between her and the police. Morrow couldn't afford to let her walk out of the hospital, not with the information she had uncovered. It was more than the hospital losing their license, which she felt confident her mother would make happen. Kidnapping was a serious crime and she was only one of what might be hundreds of victims. If Morrow was convicted on numerous counts of kidnapping, the psychiatrist could spend the rest of his life in prison. He would do his best to keep her here and he had more than enough tools to do so. He could drug her and have his minions transfer her in their fake ambulance to a state mental institution where she might be lost forever. No matter who came or what they said, short of a fire, Shana wasn't leaving her room until her mother came back to get her.

After an hour or so had passed, she heard a knock on her door and jumped up, thinking it was her mother. Instead she heard May's lyrical voice. "I'm leaving, Shana. I wanted to tell you good-bye."

Shana was tempted to open the door and let her in, but thoughts of Alex standing behind her stopped her. "I'm sick. I just threw up, May. I'll come out as soon as I stop barfing."

"You promise, sugar?"

"I promise."

No one else came to the door. At least Alex had the sense to stay away. She remembered the newspaper article and rushed to her closet, digging in the pocket of the jeans she'd been wearing. It was gone. She searched the entire closet, tossing everything out into the center of the room, but the frayed piece of newsprint was nowhere to be found.

Alex must have snuck into her room while she was outside talking to Lily. Had he bribed the guard to leave? What other reason could there be? Of course, Lily may have only hired the guard until she arrived, but it seemed foolish to leave her alone now that she'd left.

She peeked outside, hoping she would catch Alex walking away with May. Peggy wasn't at the counter but she could see a portion of her enormous frame inside the isolation wing. Alex had surprised her when she had searched his room. The newspaper article must be important to him. She remembered the dates and names, though, so she could find the article in the newspaper's archives when she was released.

Maybe there was something else in Alex's room that would shed light on some of the things that had occurred. She knew she was placing herself at risk, but her desire to figure out a man she'd felt so passionately about overcame her fear. This would be her final excursion.

Keeping her back pressed to the wall so she could keep track of what was going on in the great room, she sidestepped to Alex's room and quickly ducked inside. The bed was made and the room looked unoccupied. She'd already decided that Alex was a neat freak.

Shana flung open the closet door and stared in astonishment. Empty! Where were all his clothes, his wardrobe for every occasion? She heard a voice somewhere and ran to the back of the room, fearing that if Alex was still at the hospital he might be at dinner. Dinner was served at six, but Alex liked to linger outside in the courtyard afterwards.

For the first time she realized Alex had a window. Most of the rooms didn't have windows, but she should have known that he would have the best room in the hospital. Now that she looked at it in the light, she saw his room was considerably larger than the others. She whipped back the curtains and found a brick wall outside, probably the back of one of the offices she'd seen in the courtyard.

There were handprints all over the glass. She saw a dried substance, almost like dirt or mud. Using her fingernail, she chipped it off into her hand and then brought it to her nose. Blood! She had once cut her hand trying to cut up a chicken and had bled all over the kitchen in her apartment. She had tried to get it all up, but evidently some of the blood had seeped underneath the refrigerator. A few weeks later, her small apartment had started stinking and Brett had moved the refrigerator, finding what they later determined was dried blood. She couldn't be certain without a lab analysis, but once a person smelled old blood, they never forgot it.

A short distance away, there was laughter in the courtyard and the shuffle of feet. She managed to sneak back to her room without anyone seeing her. Just as she was about to get back in bed, she heard another tentative knock at the door.

Lily drove to the sheriff's office and asked to speak to the detective assigned to the Norman Richardson homicide. A short time later, a man who appeared to be in his late forties, with messy brown hair and bloodshot eyes, came out to speak to her. "What can I do for you?"

Lily shook his hand and then told him, "My name is Lily Forrester. I'm a superior court judge in Ventura County. I believe you spoke to my daughter, Shana, regarding the Richardson homicide."

"You're really a judge, huh? Holy shit, I thought she . . ."

"Lied," Lily said with a stern gaze. "No, she didn't lie and I resent the fact that you didn't take her seriously." She reached into her purse and pulled out her ID, practically shoving it into his face. "Before the people at Whitehall kidnapped her, my daughter was only months away from receiving her law degree from Stanford. Shana intends to become a prosecutor. She would never jeopardize her reputation by falsifying statements to the police. Unless you possess sufficient evidence to charge her in the death of Norman Richardson, tell me why my daughter has been strapped to a bed and denied her free will. Can you do that, detective?"

Lily felt certain the detective was an alcoholic. He began breathing heavily and she could smell bourbon on his breath. Either that or the alcohol in his bloodstream had reached such a toxic level that it was seeping through his pores. His cheeks were ruddy and the veins in his face were indicative of a person who consistently abused alcohol. She also noticed that he was jaundiced, which meant his liver was already damaged or on its way to complete failure.

"Listen," he said, dark stains dampening his armpits. "We're not the ones who ordered the restraints. The hospital did. We considered your daughter a person of interest in the Richardson case because one of the nurses at Whitehall found her standing over the victim's body. When you showed up, I was about to call the hospital and tell them to release her. The medical examiner ruled Norman Richardson's death a suicide today. He made a previous attempt to kill himself by setting himself on fire. According to his shrink, Richardson's suicidal tendencies were the primary reason he was at Whitehall." He paused and coughed. "I saw him at the scene and trust me, I wouldn't want to live either if I looked like this guy. He had burns over ninety percent of his body."

"So my daughter is free to leave?"

Lindstrom ran his fingers through his hair. "She's free to leave anytime she wants, okay? I assume she'll be returning to Ventura with you, so I'd appreciate you giving me her contact information in case we need any additional information from her. I don't think we will, but that's standard policy in cases of this nature. I mean, a man did die."

Lily was relieved but she maintained the same stoic demeanor. She should just walk out the door and forget it, but alcoholics destroyed an untold number of lives. "It's my professional opinion that you're incompetent to operate a motor vehicle, detective. I don't see how you can continue your duties as a police officer if you can't drive. I would also suggest that you see a liver specialist as soon as possible."

The detective looked down at the floor. "I already have," he told her. "I need a liver transplant, but as you probably know, I'm not likely to get one. People like me go to the bottom of the list. I'll more than likely die before I get a new liver. And as to your comment about me performing my duties as an officer, I put in my resignation last week. Thirty days, and I'm a civilian."

"That's too bad," Lily said, sorry to see another man's life destroyed by his drinking habits. She'd heard her ex-husband, Bryce, was finally on the wagon and attending AA on a regular basis, but you could never count on a drunk. An alcoholic usually had to hit bottom more than once before they either died or decided to maintain their sobriety.

"Good luck," Lily told him. "You still might be able to turn your life around. If you keep drinking, though, and your doctor finds out, you definitely won't get a new liver. For whatever it's worth, I'll keep you in my prayers."

"Open the door, Shana," Lily said, knocking louder. "It's me, your mother."

Shana opened the door and pulled her inside, then quickly closed it again. "Was there anyone out there?"

"A lot of people."

"Was there a good-looking man out there with dark hair?"

"What's this about, honey?"

"It's a simple question, Mother. Was he out there or not?"

"I saw that heavyset lady and a man in green pajamas who was walking fast. He had a frenetic look in his eyes. Is that the man?"

"No, that was Milton."

"Oh," Lily said, setting her suitcase down by her bed. "I didn't book a hotel room. I was going to stay at your apartment but that won't be necessary now."

Shana dusted the dried particles of blood she'd scraped from Alex's window into a department store bag where the makeup Alex had given her had been. "You pay the rent, Mother. You can stay at my apartment anytime you want." Having completed her task, she turned and faced Lily. "Were you able to hire an attorney?"

"I started to call you several times, but I wanted to wait until I had some news." A broad smile spread across Lily's face. "Pack your things. You're going home."

Shana felt an infusion of energy and almost choked Lily when she grabbed her around the neck and squeezed her with joy. "How did you manage it? Did the attorney make them release me? What did he find out about the investigation? I have to get in touch with the police as soon as I get out of here. I think I know who killed Norman. If I told you everything now, you wouldn't understand."

"Well," Lily said, taking a seat on Shana's bed, "start getting your things together and I'll tell you what happened. You don't need to play detective, Shana."

"Didn't you hear what I just said? I think I know who killed that man. Whether you realize it or not, that's not playing detective. A person was murdered."

"I called an attorney and he suggested I approach the police on my own before bringing him into the picture," Lily told her, recounting what had transpired at the police station with Lindstrom. "The coroner ruled Norman Richardson's death a suicide. I guess this man set himself on fire in the past, so he has a history of that type of behavior."

"It was a ruthless, senseless murder," Shana told her. "The killer knew Norman had tried to kill himself before. It was titillating to him."

Lily looked lost. "What was titillating?"

"Norman was the perfect victim, don't you see? The killer couldn't resist because he knew he could get away with it, that the medical examiner would call it a suicide. When you die in a mental hospital, it's always suicide."

"Right now I don't care what it was, Shana. You want to stay here and solve murders, fine. I'm going home." Lily got up and headed for the door.

"I'm sorry," Shana said, chasing after her. "You're right. I'll do whatever has to be done when I get home. I'm clear, then? I'm not going to walk out of here and find the police waiting to arrest me?"

"You're clear."

"Fabulous," Shana said, smiling. "You did great, Mom. I'm ready to go. The few things I have here are worthless. Did you bring me something to wear?"

"We're about the same size so I thought you could wear something of mine. That's why I brought my suitcase."

Shana unzipped her mother's bag and pulled out a pair of jeans and a blue sweater, dropping the pajamas on the floor and quickly changing.

"I thought we'd relax tonight at the apartment," Lily told her, "then we'll catch the first flight out in the morning. That way, you can pick up some of your things to take back to Ventura with you.

I took some vacation time, so we can figure out what to do with the apartment later."

To Shana's relief, Alex was not in the great room. She made the rounds quickly, saying her good-byes. May came over and hugged her. She'd already written her phone number down on scraps of paper and handed one to both May and Karen. She started to give one to Milton and then decided it wasn't a good idea.

"I'm not leaving, you know," he said. "They won't let me out. I haven't been sleeping since Norman died and I'm suffering from sleep deprivation. They think I'll exhibit aberrant behavior. They're wrong, you know. They're wrong."

Shana tried to reach for him, to at least shake his hand, but he took to the walls and began circling.

Peggy stepped from behind the counter and stood there as if she expected Shana to hug her like she had the others. Instead Shana walked up to one side of her bulky frame and gave her a swift and unexpected kick in the ass. Peggy jumped, but with all the padding back there, it was doubtful if she felt any pain. Her face twisted in indignation and then Shana reached over and hugged her. "You're not such a bad egg, Peggy. But if I were you, I wouldn't spank any more patients or you'll be out of a job."

Peggy just snorted and repositioned herself behind the counter. She placed a piece of paper on the counter and reminded Shana that she couldn't be released until she signed it.

"Look, Mom," Shana said, handing her the document. "What you're reading is a consent form to treat me with Thorazine. I signed it so Morrow would agree to let me out, but I put the current date at the bottom. Peggy brought a new form back to me, claiming it was destroyed in the copy machine. We danced around with this three or four times, but each time they erased the date I'd inserted. They want to backdate it to the day of my admission." She stopped speaking and laughed, looking over at Peggy. "My mother is a judge, so I've asked her to represent me. Mother, should I sign this? If I don't, does that mean they can hold me like Peggy over here is implying?"

"Absolutely not," Lily said, glaring at the heavyset woman. "I wouldn't sign a fucking thing these people give you. Come on, Shana, let's get out of here. I've had about as much as I can stand of this place. See you in court."

When George lumbered over and unlocked the door, Shana finally stepped through to freedom.

At the curb was a white stretch limo. The driver jumped out and took Lily's small suitcase, placing it in the trunk and then rushing back to hold the door open for her. Shana got inside and leaned back against the plush leather seat. "I can't believe you hired a limo, Mother. You never spend money on things like this."

"Well," Lily told her, "today is special. Besides, I was too anxious to drive. I asked for an executive car but they were all taken, so I got this for the same price. I thought you might enjoy a nice ride after everything you've been through."

"I do," she said. "It's great."

Shana vowed to appreciate the woman beside her and the life that stretched ahead of her. Turning in the seat, she watched as the hospital got smaller until it finally disappeared.

# THIRTY

Shana had been home a week and things were going well when Lily got a call from Mary Stevens, inviting her to lunch. The former Ventura PD detective was now an FBI agent and was assigned to the Ventura field office. Lily was excited to see her, and had no qualms about leaving Shana home alone.

They had lunch at an Italian restaurant called Giovanni's. Mary looked stunning in a fuchsia silk dress with a scarf tucked in around her neckline so it looked like a blouse. When she leaned over, her cleavage was exposed but not to the point of being distasteful. Once they were seated, she told Lily, "One of the nice things about my new job is I can dress any way I want and there's no one around to report me. Our work is depressing enough as it is. Dressing like an undertaker makes it worse."

Lily laughed. Not only was Mary smart, she had an upbeat personality. "At least you don't have to battle the PD like the agents before you did. I never understood why the local authorities resent the FBI so much. Can't you get along? You're all working toward the same results."

"It's territorial, Lily, like one dog pissing in another dog's yard.

The PD knows we have more resources, better training, and a world-class crime lab, so maybe they're afraid we're going to one-up them."

"Are you and Hank Sawyer still close?"

"Of course," Mary told her, flagging the waitress over. "The food is great here, but the service sucks." She ordered linguini with clam sauce and Lily settled for a chicken Caesar salad, along with a bottle of chardonnay.

"Hank and I have a love/hate relationship," Mary said, placing her napkin in her lap. "The good news is there's a lot more love than hate. He's just mad because I left the PD to become an FBI agent."

"Was he in love with you?"

"If he was," she said, "he never did anything about it. I'm glad he didn't, to be honest. Hank's a super guy but he's quite a bit older and he's short. You and I are about the same height, so you should understand. I don't like staring down at a man's head, especially one who's losing their hair like Hank. The picture keeps changing, you know? You go, wait a minute, wasn't there a hair there yesterday?" They both howled with laughter and then Mary picked up where she'd left off. "Hank and I knew too much about each other. Brooks lived in another state until we moved to Ventura. Talk about love at first sight. Whew, this guy blew me right off my feet. Less than eight hours after I met him, I was in bed with him." She leaned over and whispered, "I had six orgasms the first time we made love. Now that's chemistry."

Lily laughed again, wondering if Mary would believe her if she told her about the day she and Chris had made love in her office at the courthouse. She was finally beginning to heal from the ordeal with Shana, and being able to laugh again felt wonderful. "I'm glad you're happy, Mary. Finding the right man isn't easy."

Their orders arrived and they both began eating. Mary stopped twirling her linguini. "Congratulations, Lily, I hear you're engaged to Judge Rendell. Good for you. From what I've heard, Rendell is quite a catch."

Lily set her fork down on the table. "I'd like to run some things by you if you don't mind."

"Shoot."

"My daughter, Shana, was in her last year at Stanford Law when she had some kind of meltdown. She broke up with her boyfriend. She was exhausted from the workload, and to make matters worse, a girl in her apartment complex was raped. You can imagine how traumatic that was with her background."

Mary stopped eating, her plate already clean. "I'm sorry, Lily. That was a long time ago, though."

"Sixteen years," Lily told her. "About a month ago, Shana stopped calling me or taking my calls, so I flew up there to see what was going on. I'm not going to bore you with all the details, but I felt she needed some kind of medication, maybe an antidepressant or a tranquilizer. The poor girl couldn't sleep. She claimed she hadn't slept in weeks and I believed she was exhibiting symptoms of sleep deprivation." She paused and rubbed her forehead. "I did a stupid thing, Mary. I took her to a mental hospital."

"What's stupid about that? She needed help. Sleep deprivation can be serious."

"She was in a hospital named Whitehall that I found on the Internet. I didn't check this place out, which was irresponsible, but I had no intention of having her admitted. I just knew she couldn't get the kind of medicine she needed in an emergency room."

"You're right about the ER," Mary said. "An internist might have been able to sedate her. I suffered a terrible bout of insomnia when my father was killed. I turn into a righteous space cadet. I even had hallucinations. The good thing is once you catch up on your sleep, you're fine."

"I mistakenly thought she could be treated at Whitehall as an outpatient," Lily continued. "When we got there, they told me they would evaluate her and asked me to wait outside. When I came back, they said Shana was addicted to meth and showed me a naked snapshot of her with oozing sores all over her arms and legs. I was devastated."

"I can imagine. That stuff is poison. Between meth and crack, people are dying like crazy. But they can't kick a drug like that without help. You did the right thing."

"Shana had always taken a strong stance against drugs. She may have taken a puff or two of marijuana, but that's nothing. Even I tried it once when I was in high school. Shana's not a kid, Mary. She's twenty-eight."

"You don't look like you're old enough to have a daughter that age. I'd have pegged you for thirty-five. Anyway, go ahead. I shouldn't interrupt you. I can tell by your face that talking about this is upsetting you."

"I need your help," Lily said. "Shana was about to graduate from Stanford so it was hard to believe that she was a drug addict. But photographs don't lie." She paused, thinking. "Oh, there's another component to this story. For about six months, Shana had gone over her budget. I was always busy when she called, so I just gave her the money."

"How much money are we talking about?"

"Over a thousand a month. Of course, after seeing the picture, I knew where the extra money went. Then they told me that Shana had signed a voluntary commitment order, and that really blew my mind."

"I'm so sorry you had to go through this, Lily. How is she now?"

"She's fine, Mary. In fact, she was fine when I took her to Whitehall. The hospital looks like an old Southern mansion. According to Shana, the exterior was a façade. In addition to the hospital, they rented out individual office spaces." Lily's shoulders rolled forward. "I'm telling you this for a reason. More than the exterior of Whitehall is a façade. They basically kidnapped Shana. I don't know how they created the picture of her with the sores, but I guess you can do anything with a computer."

"Are you saying she didn't have sores?"

"Not one," Lily said, her mouth compressing into a thin line. "Her skin is fair like mine and if she'd had so much as a pimple, it would have left a mark. Shana's skin is absolutely perfect and she swore she'd never used meth, nor did she commit herself. They locked her up in a room, then they sent someone in with papers for her to sign, telling her that was the only way they could release her." She paused and sighed. "Of course, she signed. Anyone would under the circumstances. It only gets worse from here."

"This is terrible, Lily."

"You're telling me. They gave her psychotropic drugs and locked her in a padded cell. What they did was torture her." Lily's face became flushed with anger. "My daughter, Mary, they tortured my daughter! I'd like to wipe that place off the face of the earth, and charge every person who worked there with a dozen felonies."

"Calm down, Lily," Mary said, checking the wine bottle and finding it empty. "You can take them down if what you say is true. It's going to take time, though."

"I'm just so enraged that they could get away with this kind of shit. Listen to this, while Shana was there, one of the patients died and they tried to blame my daughter. The police have ruled the death a suicide, thank God, but I need all the help you can give me. Shana also told me that they were dangerously understaffed and she suspects some of the nurses didn't have credentials."

"That's happening in all the hospitals today," Mary said. "It's one of the reasons Brooks and I don't want our parents in a nursing home. They need at least one RN to dispense medication, though, particularly the type of drugs they give in mental hospitals."

Lily hated to burden Mary with her problems, but she had to go back to work soon, and so far, she hadn't accomplished anything. "While she was there, a person who called himself Dr. Morrow laid a line of bullshit on me that you wouldn't believe. He claimed Shana was refusing my calls when he was intentionally keeping her from having any contact with the outside world."

"You know," Mary said, setting down the bread she'd been nibbling on. "I've heard of this kind of thing before. They had a huge problem with private psychiatric hospitals in Texas. The attorney general's office went to town and shut most of the worst ones

down. I'm surprised you didn't hear about it. The story was in all
the papers."

"Whitehall is as corrupt as they come," Lily told her. "All they're
interested in is money. Shana said they release people the second
their insurance runs out, even if they still need treatment." She
stopped and took a long drink of water, her voice hoarse. "Oh, and
Morrow called and told me Shana was in love with one of the patients, which really upset me. She said it wasn't true, that the man
was just a friend. Then one of the nurses told her that this man
owned part of the hospital and they let him come and go whenever he wanted."

Everything slammed together in Mary's mind like a train wreck.
She'd suspected their UNSUB might have money. She grabbed her
purse to find her phone and knocked over her water glass. The
waitress rushed over to clean it up. "Where is this hospital located?"

"I don't know the exact address," Lily told her, "but it is between Palo Alto and San Francisco. All you have to do is Google the
name on the Internet and it'll pop up. Remember, that's how I
found it. I called the attorney general's office but I haven't heard
back. Can you help me? We simply have to put this hospital out of
business before what happened to Shana happens to someone else.
And then there's the man who died. Even if it was a suicide, the
hospital should be held accountable. A mental hospital is where
you send someone with suicidal tendencies."

Mary was like a racehorse waiting for the gates to open. Whitehall
was a perfect hiding place for her serial killer, especially if this patient could come and go whenever he wanted. The fact that there
was a recent suicide added flame to the fire. Their UNSUB could
leave, kill someone, and then disappear back into the hospital. Someone on the team mentioned a Batman cave, and she believed she'd
just found it. Maybe the killer even picked up potential victims at the
hospital. "Listen," she said. "I'm going to get some people over to
Whitehall right away. I can't guarantee how the cards will play out,
but I promise I'll do everything I can." She glanced across the room

and saw the waitress taking an older couple's order. "All I need is one favor."

"What?" Lily said, leaning forward over the table. "I'll do anything."

"Take care of the check. I need to get on this right away. I'll treat next time. Oh, and make sure you give her a nice tip." Mary got up and dashed out of the restaurant, leaving Lily sitting alone at the table.

Her mother had finally picked a good man. Chris was great. His positive outlook and easygoing manner made Shana feel comfortable and relaxed. The beach house was also a winner, and she loved taking long walks on the sand. Her mother had gone out to have lunch with a friend, and Chris was on the golf course. Shana had to fend for herself, so she made a ham and cheese sandwich and took it out on the balcony. After a few bites, she heard the phone ringing inside the house and assumed it was her mother. She left her food on the small table and rushed inside to answer it.

"Shana," a female voice said. "Do you know who this is?"

Actually she didn't, but the voice had a familiar ring to it. "No, I'm sorry."

"Karen . . . you know . . . from the hospital."

"Karen, my God, how are you? It's so sweet of you to call and check on me."

"I thought you'd want to know. Alex is dead."

"Alex is dead?" Shana sat down at the kitchen table, reeling in disbelief. "That can't be true, Karen. Are you sure you're not mistaken? He seemed to be in perfect health. When was this supposed to have happened? Was he still at Whitehall?"

"No," the woman told her. "Right after you left, he checked himself out. He had a brain aneurysm. They found him dead in his car. The aneurysm burst and he died instantly. At least he didn't suffer." She stopped speaking and coughed. "Did you know he owned a controlling share of the hospital? I was shocked when I heard. I thought he was just another patient, but he did buy us a lot of extravagant gifts."

Shana stared at the mirror on the wall across from her. Instead of herself, she saw Alex's face. She tried not to look but her eyes were drawn to the mirror like a magnet. His image was still there, but this time his eyebrows arched in that "I told you so" expression and then he vanished. "I'm sorry, Karen. This is a shock to me, too. When did he die?"

"I don't recall the exact date, but they said it was the day after I was discharged, so I guess he died almost a week ago. He might have died before then and they didn't discover his body right away. Anyway, I wanted to call and let you know as soon as I heard, but I misplaced your phone number."

"Did you go to the funeral?"

"Yes," Karen told her. "I spoke with his family. His mother said Alex had known he had the aneurysm for a long time. He didn't know when it would happen, but he knew it would eventually burst and kill him. She said Alex checked into Whitehall because it was a stress-free environment and he thought it might buy him more time." She paused and then added, "It's sad but I thought you'd want to know."

"Thanks, I did."

"Well, I have to go. I'm training for a new job. I got hired at Raytheon. Before he left, Alex paid for a year's worth of my medication. I still bark on occasion, but the profanity has almost stopped. The profanity was what made working impossible. No one wants to listen to that when they're trying to focus on their work. Alex was one of the nicest men I ever knew. I can't believe he's really dead."

"Take care of yourself, Karen."

Shana held the receiver in her hand long after the call had ended. Her eyes were glued to the mirror, but all she saw now was her own image. She went to the guest room, where she was staying, and climbed into the bed, rolling over onto her back and staring at the ceiling. She hadn't told Lily about the gift the airline stewardess had handed her while her mother was in the lavatory. She'd been certain Alex had sent it because it was a single white rose, identical to the one he'd left on her bed the night of the dance. She'd asked the stewardess who'd sent the rose and she'd told her that an unknown individual had left it at the gate under the name of Forrester. At the time, she'd been so mad at Alex that she'd told the stewardess to trash it.

Her mother came home at two, wanting Shana to go shopping with her. She knew she wanted to buy her clothes, but she didn't really need anything. Besides, she'd taken enough of her mother's money. But mothers always thought a girl needed party dresses, heels, and at least one pricey black purse with shoes to match. College kids didn't dress up, but arguing with her mother was pointless. As a prosecutor, Lily had been relentless.

The best news so far was that Lily had managed to get her back into Stanford, but she'd done it by telling the dean about her ordeal at Whitehall. When her mother told her what she'd done, Shana was furious. She didn't want anyone to know she'd been in a mental hospital. The stigma associated with mental illness was awful. Once a person found out you'd spent time in a psychiatric hospital, you could never convince anyone that you weren't crazy. It was similar to being a suspect in a crime. It stuck with you forever, even if you were innocent.

Regardless of how her mother had made it happen, she was thrilled that she could go back to school. Lily had decided to keep her apartment and Shana was looking forward to taking summer classes, hoping to be caught up by fall.

In the Volvo on the way to the mall, Lily turned to her. "You look upset, Shana. Did something happen while I was gone?"

"Someone died."

Her mother slammed on the brakes. "Who died? Why didn't you tell me? Good lord, it's Marie. I knew she was going to have a heart attack. Did you see her last time?"

"Stop, Mom. Marie didn't die. It was someone from the hospital."

Lily was relieved. "If your Aunt Marie doesn't lose some of that weight she's carrying, she's going to drop dead. The last time I saw her, she had to weigh over two hundred pounds." She thought a few minutes and then asked, "Was it that man?"

"What man?"

"Don't be coy, Shana," Lily said, turning to look at her. "The man Dr. Morrow said you were in love with."

"Mom, I've told you ten times, I never told Morrow I was in love with this person. But yes, he was the man who died. His name was Alex and we were friends."

"How old was this man?"

"In his thirties," Shana said, gazing out the passenger window. The man in the car beside them glanced over at her and for a minute, she thought it was Alex. All their strange discussions about death made sense now. While she was blaming him for everything, even poor Norman's death, the man was living his last few days on earth. She hadn't even told him good-bye.

When they returned home that evening, Chris gave both of them a hug, then went to the bedroom to watch the news. The house wasn't that large and the way it was designed, there wasn't room for a television in the living room. The bedroom was huge, though, so they had purchased two recliners and mounted a plasma TV on the wall. It worked well for Chris and Lily, but Shana didn't feel right watching television in their bedroom only a few feet from where they had sex. Besides, there were only two chairs, so Chris had to bring one of the chairs from the kitchen. The chairs were contemporary and uncomfortable. Lily offered to buy a television for the guest room, but Shana told her she'd rather catch up on her work than waste time watching television.

The doorbell rang and Lily sent Shana to answer it. A florist's van was parked at the curb and a young delivery man was holding a vase full of white roses. "Give me a minute," the boy said, handing her the vase. "I have more in the van."

"Mom!" she shouted. "Come and help me. Someone sent you flowers."

Once they had carried in all the vases, Lily went to the bedroom and climbed on Chris's lap. "Oh you . . . you're such a hopeless romantic. You must have spent a fortune on those flowers. There're so many." She kissed him on the mouth. "Thank you, darling. You're the best."

Chris was as rigid as a sheet of steel, but Lily failed to notice. She rushed back to the kitchen to decide where to put all the arrangements. There were a total of five vases, all full of white flowers. There were white lilies, white carnations, white tulips, and of course, the two dozen white roses.

As Shana inhaled their delightful fragrance, she remembered the single white rose she'd received on the plane. Maybe Chris had sent it to her mother and the stewardess had accidentally given it to her. It was understandable since they had the same name. It was too bad if Chris had sent it because she was so mad at Alex then, she'd handed it back to the stewardess and told her to toss it.

Chris walked in and stared at Lily. "I didn't send them."

"What?"

"I didn't send you these flowers, Lily."

Lily and Shana searched all the vases but there were no cards other than the one from the florist shop. "You're kidding," Lily said. "Who else would have sent them?"

"I'm not kidding," Chris said, scowling. "I had nothing whatsoever to do with these flowers. How many times do I have to tell you?"

Shana's heart was doing a tap dance inside her chest. She didn't want to get caught in the middle of an argument. In addition, the flowers were something she could see Alex doing if he was still alive. She grabbed the card with the name of the florist on it and dialed the number. The shop had already closed for the day, so she quietly disconnected.

"Maybe your boyfriend sent them," Chris said with an angry, jealous tone.

"Look, honey, don't get upset," Lily told him, holding up a palm. "The florist must have delivered them to the wrong house." She glanced over at Shana. "Is that who you just called?"

"They're closed for the day." Shana turned to Chris. "I didn't want to say anything, but I think the flowers were meant for me. There was this guy I met at the hospital. He more or less fixated on me. He sent me a white rose on two occasions, so it makes sense he might have sent me these. I'll call tomorrow morning as soon as the florist opens. Until then, why don't we enjoy them?"

"Is this the man Dr. Morrow mentioned?" Lily asked.

"Yeah," Shana told her. "I felt abandoned and alone at the hospital so I flirted with him. He was great looking and seemed perfectly normal. Later, I realized there was something wrong with him and ended it."

"Did you give this man our address?"

"I don't know what I did, Mother," she said, becoming annoyed. "They pumped me full of drugs, okay? There's no telling what I told him. He won't come knocking on our door, so don't make a big deal out of it."

Chris jumped in. "How do we know that, Shana? What was wrong with this man? Was he violent?"

Shana was becoming frustrated. "He wasn't violent. He told me his family insisted he go to a mental hospital because he wanted to kill himself. I know he won't come here because he's dead. Now can we stop talking about him?"

Both her mother and Chris looked perplexed. "What you're telling us doesn't make sense," Lily said. "How do you know this man is dead?"

"A friend of mine from the hospital went to his funeral."

Chris said, "Dead men don't send flowers."

"Apparently this dead guy does. Maybe he ordered them last week before he died. Once a year on her birthday an unknown person sends flowers to Marilyn Monroe's grave." She shook her head as if to clear it. "I'm going to my room to study. I'm not hungry, so forget dinner. We'll probably find out tomorrow that the flowers belong to the next-door neighbor. Damn it, they're only flowers. Someone didn't send us a dead chicken. Why are you making such a big deal about it?"

In her room, Shana tried to study but she couldn't stop thinking about Alex and the night they'd made love. When she turned off the lights and tried to sleep, she felt a strange presence all around her and became convinced it was Alex's spirit. "Where are you?" she whispered, peering into the shadows.

He had said they were destined to be together, that they could step off the edge of the universe and find paradise. Was he alone when he died? Death left behind so many unanswered questions.

As the clock ticked and she still couldn't sleep, Shana whispered again, "I'm sorry, Alex." Almost as soon as the words left her mouth, her eyelids closed and sleep finally found her.

# THIRTY-ONE

Only a few feet away, on a bus bench, sat Alex!

Shana had taken Lily's car to go to the drugstore and pick up some shampoo and mascara. She slammed on the brakes with both feet. Cars honked behind her. She craned her neck around, but Alex was gone. Only one person was sitting on the bench now, a disheveled man who appeared to be in his mid to late fifties. From the looks of the sacks and blankets he carried, he was homeless, more than likely dumped on the street by a state mental facility. "Did you see a man?" she yelled out the car window. "He was sitting next to you just a second ago?"

The man hugged his dirty blankets to his chest as he mumbled something under his breath. Shana grabbed her purse and jumped out, opening her wallet and handing him whatever cash she had. He stared at the bills in his hand as she got back in the car and drove off.

Tears of self-pity and confusion spilled from her eyes. It might be her one day sitting on a bus bench with nowhere to go and no one who cared about her. Alex was dead. She had just seen a dead man. Only lunatics saw dead people.

At dinner that night, Shana was quiet, speaking only a few words. She spent the rest of the evening on the balcony, staring out at the ocean. Lily came out with a sweater, but otherwise left her alone.

At midnight, when Chris and Lily had gone to their room for the night, Shana finally headed to bed. She had just managed to fall asleep when her cell phone started ringing. The illuminated dial on the nightstand read 3:15. She seized the phone, not wanting to wake up her mother and Chris.

"Hello?" All she heard was heavy breathing. "Is anyone there?"

Through the silence, Shana felt a presence reaching out for her. She sat up on the edge of the bed and groped for the light switch. "Alex," she said, "is that you?" There was no answer even though the line remained open. "If it's you, Alex, please talk to me." She heard a click and knew he had hung up.

Shana stayed in bed until two o'clock the following day, ignoring the phone when it rang and burying her head under the covers. If she told anyone what was happening, she might end up back where she started, maybe not at Whitehall but somewhere similar. Was she hallucinating or had she really seen Alex?

She got up and put her clothes on, not wanting Lily to come in and find her still in bed. Before they'd left San Francisco, they had gone to her apartment and picked up some of her things. She removed her laptop from the carrying case and set it up on the small desk that also served as a vanity. She went to the homepage for the San Francisco Chronicle and searched through the archives. As soon as the article popped up, she stared at the girl's picture, the image far better than what she'd seen on the crinkled piece of paper she'd found in Alex's wallet. The girl looked so young and fragile. She started to read through the text when she saw another photo at the bottom of the page, the picture of a young man with thick dark hair standing beside what appeared to be a detective. The younger man's head was down and he was obscuring his face with his hand. She zoomed in, but it was impossible to make out the man's facial features. Was it Alex? She couldn't tell.

The first part of the article she had already read. She jumped down several paragraphs and began reading.

> Eighteen-year-old Adam Pounder was arrested at a local hotel af-
> ter police responded to a call of shots fired. Pounder was found
> holding Ms. Rondini's body with the murder weapon a few feet
> away. "I couldn't do it," he allegedly told officers. "I promised
> her, but I couldn't do it."

Shana leaned back in her chair. "Adam," she said, noting how similar it was to Alex. She'd seen a police show once where they had said that people who assume fictitious names frequently incorporate elements of their real names. Both names began with the letter "A" and consisted of four letters. She continued to read.

> Pounder and Rondini met while institutionalized at Camarillo
> State Mental Hospital, and from what Pounder told authorities,
> they entered into a suicide pact after Rondini gave birth and left
> the newborn child to die in the restroom of the Greyhound bus
> terminal. Pounder allegedly failed to follow through on his end
> of the pact after he shot and killed Rondini.
>
> Police advise the suspect had been placed at Camarillo State on
> an order of the court following an incident where he threw acid in
> a female student's face while in a high school chemistry lab.
> Pounder was found not guilty by reason of insanity on these earlier
> charges and committed to the state facility. Three months later,
> Pounder was released. The injured girl, a minor, has asked to re-
> main anonymous; however, when contacted, her parents stated
> they were shocked and outraged that Pounder had been released so
> quickly after the horrendous damage that was inflicted on their
> daughter. "It's a sorry state of affairs," the girl's father stated, "when
> a person as dangerous as Adam Pounder is released back to the
> community after only a brief period of hospitalization. My pre-
> cious daughter is scarred for life. You call that justice? I don't, but at
> least my daughter is alive. Now he's gone and killed someone."

When asked if he placed the blame on the legal system for releasing Pounder to commit another violent act, the victim's father
stated, "Damn right I do. They should lock him up and throw
away the key. How many people does he have to maim and kill before they stop him?"

Shana felt trapped inside the house and took off in her mother's
Volvo. She glanced at the faces of people in the cars that passed her.
Any one of them could be dangerous. Criminals generally looked
like criminals. Not so with the mentally ill, and Alex was the perfect
example. He had seemed so normal, so sane. She would have never
suspected he might be dangerous. People like Alex had jobs and families, but they were ticking time bombs, ready to explode and point
a shotgun out the window and kill an innocent person, slaughter
their entire family, or hack the head off their neighbor with an axe.

Could Adam Pounder and Alex Purcell, the name she had seen
on the telephone calling card, be one and the same? Pounder had
met Jennifer Rondini in a mental hospital, exactly how Alex had
met Shana. It was a chilling thought to say the least, but Alex was
dead, so he couldn't hurt anyone now. Was it the pressure of the
world we lived in that caused things like this to happen, people to
just crack? Were they too flawed and fragile to cope with the fractured economy, the corrupt politicians, or the skyrocketing unemployment? Things were coming apart at the seams, the very seams
that were necessary to maintain society.

Was it the chemicals in the food they ate, the toxic dumping, or
the polluted environment? The light changed, but Shana was lost in
her thoughts. The car behind her started honking and she stepped on
the gas, her eyes darting to the rearview mirror. She expected the man
behind her to stick a gun out the window or ram her with his car.

Was Alex really dead?

Shana had seen him on the bus bench and then there were the
white flowers as well as the phone call. She began hyperventilating.
Was he still out there? Had Karen made a mistake?

When she turned onto her street, she saw Chris's Volkswagen

parked in front of the house with one wheel up over the curb. Then she saw Lily pacing back and forth on the sidewalk. As soon as she saw the Volvo turning the corner, her mother started running toward her.

Shana pulled into the driveway and parked, wondering what had happened. Lily flung the car door open. "Where have you been? My God, I've been calling all the hospitals. I thought you'd had an accident. I was out of my mind with worry."

"I'm fine, Mother," she snapped, resenting being treated like she was incapable of driving two blocks down the street. Climbing out of the car and closing the door, she glared at her mother. "In case you've forgotten, I've been driving since I was sixteen. You know what happened at Whitehall. Why are you acting like I'm crazy and have to be watched every second of the day?"

"Shana, please," Lily said, "no one thinks you're crazy. You should have asked to take the car, told me where you were going. The hospital gave you a lot of drugs. How do we know they're out of your system? Chris and I are just concerned for your safety."

"I tried to find you to ask you if I could take the car. When I couldn't, I decided you must have taken a walk on the beach, so I left and drove around. I just needed to get out of the house."

"I did take a walk," Lily said, somewhat embarrassed. "In the future, just let me know where you're going so I won't worry. I contacted the flower shop and they don't know who sent the flowers, but it wasn't a mistake. Whoever it was gave them our address. They said an attractive, dark-haired man walked into their store in Santa Barbara two days ago and paid cash. I'm afraid of this man Alex. Maybe he's not dead, Shana. You told me he was obsessed with you. Could you have misunderstood this girl who told you he was dead? She was a patient, so perhaps she's delusional. Or maybe Alex made her call you and tell you he was dead to gain your sympathy, or to make you feel bad that you didn't care for him. I'm just speculating. You knew the man."

Shana couldn't believe it. They were taking her life away. They might as well dig a hole and bury her. "Karen has Tourette's syndrome. There's nothing whatsoever wrong with her mind. She even has a degree in electrical engineering. The only reason she was at Whitehall was she lost her allotment of medication and it's hard for her to hold down a job or be around people who don't understand her condition. The man you're so scared of wasn't someone off the street. He was a successful businessman and inventor. Karen said he paid for a year's worth of her medicine. Because of Alex, she was able to leave the hospital and get a job at Raytheon."

Lily reached over and hugged her. "Forgive me, honey. I was wrong to get so upset. Have you been able to get in touch with any of your friends here?"

"What friends?" Shana said, looking down at her feet. "I've been at Stanford forever. And since I stayed there twelve months a year, whatever people I knew in Ventura have either moved or gotten married. I'm trying to connect with some of my high school friends on Facebook and MySpace, but I haven't had any luck."

Chris stepped in. "Let's go inside and relax. I left work early so we can go to a movie if you ladies are interested."

"That sounds great," Lily said, smiling. "I'll go see what's showing, shower, and be ready in thirty minutes." She paused and then added, "Maybe you should pick the movie, Shana."

"No problem," Shana said, willing to do anything to get out of the house, especially to someplace where her mother couldn't talk. She remembered the substance she had scraped off Alex's window and decided to call Detective Lindstrom tomorrow and see if they had checked the fingerprints in Alex's room. She would also offer to send him what she was certain was dried blood, as well as tell him how he could retrieve the newspaper article.

They went to see a movie called My One and Only starring Renée Zellweger. It was good, but it didn't hold Shana's attention. She stared out into the dark theater, angry and confused. She couldn't accept that she was hallucinating, not after all she had been through.

If Alex Purcell was Adam Pounder and he was alive, why in God's name was he back on the street? Could a person really throw acid in

a young girl's face, shoot and kill a second girl, and then, after managing to become a successful businessman, possibly stab another
helpless individual in the throat and still manage to remain free? It
was mind-boggling.

Shana sighed, her eyes glued to the screen but still trapped inside
her thoughts. Law school and having a judge for a mother had taught
her a lot. A person might have gotten off with an insanity defense in
the past, but not today. She thought of John Hinckley, the man who'd
attempted to assassinate Reagan. He would never get out of his mental institution. Alex even reminded her of Hinckley, the strong family
background, the wealth. But Hinckley hadn't been a successful person in his own right like Alex claimed to be. Only in the United
States, she thought, the land of opportunity, opportunity to kill and
kill again.

Under the new laws, a person could be found sane under absolutely any circumstance, even if they were as crazy as a loon. The
new criteria made it impossible for a person to plead not guilty by
reason of insanity and avoid imprisonment. All they had to prove
was the person was aware their actions constituted a criminal act. A
person would have to be brain dead to think sticking a knife in
someone's throat or shooting them wasn't illegal and wrong, so that
eliminated almost everyone. And if a person was actively psychotic
at the time of the court proceedings, they were simply sent away until they were competent to stand trial. The pendulum had swung in
the opposite direction.

It was sad, really. In trying to correct the problem, the court had
bypassed the obvious: even though they might know their actions
were wrong, these tortured souls couldn't stop themselves. How
would she feel if someone she loved was seriously mentally ill? Was
a person like that really the same? An individual who committed
a crime in the throes of madness versus a sociopath committing an
intentional act of violence? Should they stand side by side in a state or
federal prison, no distinction between them? Was there any resolution to this horrendous problem?

But that didn't matter at this point, Shana told herself. Only one thing mattered right now and it filled her with abstract terror. And she knew it was true. What she had seen had convinced her.

Alex was alive and in Ventura.

# THIRTY-TWO

Alex was certainly busy for a dead man. Karen had gone to his funeral, and people just didn't make those kinds of mistakes.

In her bedroom with the door shut, Shana dialed the number she had for Karen. "Thank God, I got you," she said when the woman answered. "I need to ask you something."

"Sure."

"You told me you went to Alex's funeral, right?"

"Right."

"Was it an open or closed casket?"

"Closed. Shana, what's this about?"

"And Alex's family was there? You saw them and talked to them?"

"I spoke to his mother, Nadine," Karen told her. "She's the one who told me about the aneurysm. I didn't speak to his father because I'd never met him."

Shana let her mind run free. Alex had told her he was in trouble with the IRS, then said it was a lie. He had access to money, which could buy almost anything, even a coffin loaded with rocks. Alex also knew doctors such as Morrow who were outright whores and might produce a phony death certificate for the right amount of money. What else did he need? It was perfect. Alex made the police look like a bunch of baboons. It was all part of his enormous ego, a more dangerous and exciting way to play the game.

"I'm certain I've seen Alex here in Ventura, Karen, just yesterday to be precise. You should see the newspaper article I have on him. Please trust me on this. I think his real name is Adam Pounder, not Alex Purcell. Who knows how many people he's killed over the years?"

"I don't agree with you," Karen said. "Alex was a good man. He would never physically hurt anyone. I think your mind is playing tricks on you, Shana. Everyone knew you guys were in love. That's why you can't accept that he's dead."

"I was in love with Alex for about three hours, and I'm certain he put Ecstasy or acid in my drink. I would be perfectly fine accepting his death if he didn't keep popping up all over town."

"Be rational, Shana. A lot of men resemble Alex. In most cases you wouldn't notice these look-alikes, but right now you're in a hyper state of awareness. You're seeing Alex because you long to see him. You're in denial, plain and simple."

Shana liked Karen but she refused to listen to her psychobabble. "I better go. I'll let you know if anything else happens."

"Please do."

The next person Shana called was Detective Lindstrom. She told him what she had found out about Alex, and asked him to check if Whitehall had ever admitted a patient named Adam Pounder. She hesitated telling him everything. Her story was implausible and too complex, especially since the detective had only a few minutes to give her.

"I'm not saying I'm not going to help you," he told her. "But you've hit me with a shitload of speculation. To prove this man faked his death, you'll have to get a court order to exhume the body. I assume he's buried here in California, but I need the address of the cemetery. I can make an attempt to get the authorities in that area interested, but you have to give me something solid. Do you have any fingerprints or DNA on this Pounder person?"

"I don't carry ink pads in my purse," Shana tossed back. "Why would I have his fingerprints?" She thought of something and added, "Wait. I may actually have his prints. He gave me this plastic case for my makeup." She'd left the clothes Alex had given her at Whitehall, but she still had the plastic makeup case and the telephone calling card. Her mind began clocking at lightning speeds. "I'm going to put what I have together and mail it to you. Give me your address and I'll send it FedEx so it won't get lost."

Shana then told him about the substance she'd scraped off the window in Alex's room, and Lindstrom appeared to be genuinely interested, asking her to send it along with the other things she had collected. The only problem was once she handed off what she perceived as valuable evidence, it could end up buried on top of someone's desk or in the trash can. She was beginning to think like a lawyer, which was cool. At least one thing positive had come out of her experience at Whitehall.

Ending her call with the detective, Shana decided to make copies of the newspaper article and the calling card. As to the substance she thought was dried blood, she would divide it equally and send Lindstrom his share.

She began digging through all her things. The telephone calling card showed up in one of her bathroom drawers. Seizing a pair of tweezers, she picked it up and carried it to the bed.

She yelled for Lily but she didn't answer. She found her in the bedroom, stretched out on the recliner, an open law book in her lap. "I'm going to FedEx. I thought you'd want to go with me. That way, if I see Alex, you'll see him. Then you'll know I'm not hallucinating. I assume you have a plastic baggie in the kitchen."

"I keep them in the drawer next to the dishwasher," Lily told her, placing the book on the nightstand and getting up. "I don't think you're hallucinating, Shana. Is what you're sending some type of evidence?"

"I'll tell you in the car." When Lily gave her another questioning glance, Shana ignored her and rushed to her room with the baggie. Her mother followed her and watched as she placed the makeup case and calling card inside one baggie, then separated the contents of a plastic makeup case and put them in another baggie.

"These are some things Alex touched. I'm sending them to Detective Lindstrom to see if he can get his fingerprints."

"I have a friend who's an FBI agent," Lily said. "I had lunch with her the other day and told her about Alex and Whitehall. She's in the process of checking them out. I also notified the attorney general's office, but I haven't heard back from them yet. Why don't you send whatever you have to my friend, Special Agent Mary Stevens? I spoke to Lindstrom, remember? He told me he was resigning next month, that he had a less stressful job lined up or something along those lines. Listen to me, Shana, Lindstrom doesn't care. They never do if they're leaving. Mary will work twenty-four/seven for you. She's the one who saved my life last year. If you send this stuff to Lindstrom, you might as well throw it away."

"Alex isn't dead," Shana said. "I tried to tell you guys that last night. But I agree with you about Lindstrom. I could tell he didn't give a shit when he interviewed me. Do you have Agent Stevens's address with you?"

"Yes, it's in my iPhone." Lily cleared her throat. "I realize what happened to you was horrible. It was enough to make anyone paranoid. But you—"

"Listen to me carefully, because I'm only going to tell you this one time," Shana said firmly. "If I am right and the Alex that I knew at Whitehall is Adam Pounder, then this man threw acid in a young girl's face. He shot and killed another girl and he may have stabbed the man at Whitehall. He knows where we live. He knows what kind of cars we drive. He has a blueprint for our entire lives. You think about it, okay? I'm trying to do something to stop him."

He was dozing in a rented blue Chrysler parked behind the guard shack when the white Volvo sped past him.

An older man in a navy blue blazer and khaki pants walked up to the car window. "You can start tomorrow night," the man said, handing Alex an identical blazer. "Shift starts at midnight. Don't be late. And bring those employment forms with you."

"Thanks, buddy. See you tomorrow."

As soon as the man walked away, Alex slipped back down in the seat and closed his eyes. Inside his head was a whirring, jarring noise that never went away. Sometimes the sound became low, similar to the brush of a broom across a floor, but since Shana had left, it had turned into the roar of a jet screaming inside the skies of his mind, crashing from one side to another and scattering wreckage and debris in fireballs throughout his brain.

His mother always said he was gifted. This became the stock answer to every question he had about his life or his bizarre behavior. He recalled stabbing his goldfish with a fork and lining them up on his desk while he was studying. Nadine would flush them down the toilet and the next day, the tank would be filled with more goldfish from the pet store on the corner. He'd never been in the pet store, never saw a movie, never went to a sporting event, and never had a friend. "You're not like the other children," Nadine would tell him. "Other children play because they have nothing better to do. They're not smart enough to study physics or read Nietzsche."

Nadine was far from a genius or child prodigy, something she told him on a daily basis, emphasizing how grateful he should be for his "gift." Both of her parents were university professors and renowned scholars, completely submerged in the egomaniacal waters of academia. They believed a child was a product to display, a combination of their superior gene pools. But as many hours as Nadine spent studying, she remained a borderline student, hanging on with a steely, desperate grip. Then she gave birth to a baby boy and her parents reveled in his brilliance. They analyzed and computed his potential until his mother realized her son could take her where she had never been able to go, and win her the respect she craved.

That's when Alex began imagining his mother in the little red wagon he pulled behind him wherever he went, loaded down with puzzles and books. Even as a young child, he knew he must pull more than just his own wagon. He had to pull Nadine as well. As time went on, he realized that Nadine not only wanted him to pull her in his now symbolic red wagon, she expected him to pull the entire family.

When he was eight, he began suffering from migraine headaches, headaches so severe he felt as if someone had lopped off the top of his head and filled it with piranhas that furiously fed on the gray matter of his brain. The headaches, according to Nadine, were the result of his "gift." When he had to remain in a dark room for days at a time, she refused to allow him to be medicated. Medication, Nadine believed, would dull his mind.

Normal children were repelled by him, while the teachers in the exclusive private school he attended found him brilliant, although obnoxious and undisciplined. Report after report recommended that Nadine's son be sent for a psychological evaluation for his aggressive and antisocial tendencies.

All he recalled about his first major act of violence was that the girl who had been assigned to be his lab partner was slow and clumsy. The court understood about the frustrations of genius. What they didn't understand, the former judge Nadine had hired to represent him was more than willing to explain. The court offered a stint in a mental hospital in lieu of a jail sentence and a felony conviction. Nadine told her son it would be like a vacation.

He was committed to a state hospital, a filthy, inhuman hole where the defectives of the earth were herded and watched like animals. He was drugged, poked, and probed, as well as forced to endure a seemingly endless battery of tests. He was also sodomized on two separate occasions and stabbed in the leg by another patient. He stopped speaking and spun out of control in the hurricane of his mind. For one three-month period, he wore disposable diapers.

Then he met Jennifer and experienced his first taste of happiness. They met at the weekly dance during one of his lucid periods. Jennifer was wearing a beautiful white dress, identical to the one he had purchased for Shana.

His mind was still awash with memories of Jennifer when a hand reached through the window of the car and shook his shoulder. His dark eyes sprang open and he grabbed the hand in an iron grip.

"Let go of my hand," the guard said, yanking his arm back and rubbing it. "You've got to move your car. You can't sleep here on the grounds."

The noise was screaming inside his head, piercing his eardrums. He brought forth the imagery of the pond, the only constructive thing he'd learned from a lifetime of therapy, and tried to find the stillness. Under water, there was no noise. "Sorry, Ralph," he told the guard. "I've been traveling. I haven't been able to find a place yet. I'll move my car right now."

After driving around in the area for thirty minutes, he finally found a phone booth and stopped to call Nadine. He never carried a cell phone as he knew cell phones could be traced. Pay phones were disappearing, though, so he knew he would have to find another way to communicate. He had given thought to developing a system that would allow a person the option of blocking their whereabouts while still being able to use the various functions of their cell phone. People deserved privacy.

"Where are you?" Nadine said. "My god, what's happened? God help us. God help us."

The hot sun had turned the phone booth into a sauna and he was perspiring. He leaned his forehead against the cool glass. "Nadine, I'm surprised at you. You told me there was no God when I was five. I think He was insulted, so I doubt if He'll help you now."

"You have to come home," Nadine told him, ignoring his sarcasm. "We're all here. The movers delivered the furniture yesterday and the house is unpacked. I even found a local doctor. He'll prescribe some of those new pills you like so much. Your brother is checking into a hospital here in case you ever need one. We'll set it up just like before. Everything will be foolproof just like you like it. Please, darling, come home."

"Home?"

"We're your family, darling. We had to leave San Francisco because of the police investigation at Whitehall, but that doesn't mean we don't love you and support you like we always have."

"It's over," he told her. "You said so yourself."

"No, no," Nadine protested. "We can rebuild. With your genius, we can do anything. I meant that woman in the hospital, the redhead you fixated on. I didn't want you to get involved with her for your own good. You know what happened in the past, but because of our precautions, no one else knows. Now that we've all moved again, no one will ever know. We're safe, son. You died, remember? We buried you. It was a brilliant plan and it worked perfectly."

He opened the doors to the phone booth and stretched the phone cord so he could talk in the open air. "It's so beautiful here, Mother. It's so clean, so peaceful. It's almost like paradise. I wish you could see it."

Her voice was urgent, compressed into tight hard sentences. "Listen to me. We may need you, but you need us as well. Don't think for a minute you don't. They'll catch you and put you in prison. They could execute you. Come home this minute."

"I'm already dead." He dropped the phone and the cord snapped it back, striking the glass in the booth.

# THIRTY-THREE

Once they had dropped the plastic makeup case, the calling card, and the sample of dried blood off at the FBI office, Lily gunned the Volvo and headed in the direction of their house. "I forgot to ask. Do you want to head home, or is there somewhere else you'd like to go?"

"Let's go for a walk on the beach. I prefer McGrath. The sand is nicer there."

They parked and walked down the steep steps to the sand. The sun had gone behind a cloud and it was overcast and gray. Surfers waited for waves on their boards, and here and there, people were spread out on towels waiting for the sun to reappear. When the Santa Ana winds blew in, they could have ninety-degree weather in January, but today was chilly, so Lily suspected the sunbathers were out-of-towners who believed Southern California had warm weather all year long.

Shana walked near the water's edge and Lily trailed along behind her. "I know who you can call," Lily said. "Greg Fowler. Do you remember him?"

"Of course, but I'm not interested in talking to him. I mean, he's a nice guy but he's a stone-cold pothead. He starts smoking as soon as he wakes up and stays high all day. He also tries to force you to surf with him. I don't like to be pounded by waves. My balance isn't good enough to stand up on a moving board in the ocean."

The damp air had caused their hair to fall limp around their faces and necks. Shana walked a few feet into the surf, oblivious to the fact that she was soaking her shoes and the bottom of her pants. Lily followed her and together they stood side by side in the shallow water. "You have to do something, Shana. My vacation is going to be over soon. I don't want you to be sitting around all day at the house."

"Why can't I go back to Palo Alto and get a job until the summer sessions starts? Maybe I could even pay the rent on the apartment."

"That's not necessary. I'll take care of your rent like I always have. I started saving for your education the day you were born."

"No, Mother, it is necessary," Shana told her. "I took your money and paid Brett's tuition with it. That's why I needed so much cash all the time."

Lily's jaw dropped. "Why couldn't he pay for his own tuition? Weren't his parents wealthy?"

"They were until they lost everything in the stock market. Brett was a good student, Mother. I felt sorry for him and didn't want him to have to drop out of school. But I was wrong. Brett's a user. The only reason he moved in with that Berkeley girl is his parents told him he'd have to give up his room in the dorm and come home."

"Why didn't he move in with you?"

"I had a roommate, remember? She didn't want to share her bathroom with a guy. Julie was a perfectionist and Brett was a pig. You saw how the place was trashed when you came. That was left over from Brett." She stopped speaking and linked eyes with her mother. "I feel so bad for lying to you and taking your money. I know you're not rich. I can work as a waitress and tutor undergraduates." She reached over and pulled her mother into her arms, both of their eyes moist with tears. "You're a wonderful mother. You didn't deserve the things I did to you. I want to make it up to you."

"If that's what you want, I'm all for it. All I've ever wanted is to make you happy." Lily tenderly brushed Shana's hair off her forehead. "You've gone through too much, honey. You've always hidden your problems from me. Promise me you won't do that anymore. I'm the best friend you'll ever have. Next time you become overwhelmed or down, give me a chance to help you. I know I made a terrible mistake this time, but I promise I won't make that mistake again. Will you promise to stay in touch and let me know when you need help?"

"I promise," Shana said, smiling. Her expression suddenly changed and she grabbed Lily's hand. "There's an enormous wave coming in. Don't look back, Mom, just run as fast as you can."

They jogged through the water and kept on until they reached high ground. A moment later, they fell to the sand, both of them laughing.

"I needed a good laugh," Lily said, trying to sit up and then collapsing back on the sand. "Is that little thing your humongous wave?"

"Okay," Shana said, giggling even harder. "It looked scary from a distance. I guess it petered out on the way in. I told you I don't like to be pummeled by waves. Now you know."

They got up and dusted themselves off, then walked hand in hand in the direction of the car. An older lady approached them. "You're such beautiful twins. I love the color of your hair."

Lily waited for Shana to explode as she had in the past, but she just smiled at the woman and thanked her for the compliment. "You didn't mind that the woman thought we were twins?"

"Of course not," she said. "You look great for your age. I hope I look that good when I get older. We need to get our pictures taken together like we used to. We haven't done that in a long time."

For Lily, it was a perfect ending to a perfect day.

Chris and Lily were in bed and the house was quiet. Shana tried to sleep but found it impossible. When she was at school and she couldn't sleep, she would go out in her car and drive around. She suspected it was the movement of the car that relaxed her.

She crept into the living room and started looking for her mother's car keys, then decided she must have left them in her purse. When she couldn't find Lily's purse, she decided she had taken it to her bedroom. She gave thought to taking Chris's Volkswagen but she couldn't find his keys, either. Then she remembered that she was at the beach, and decided a walk would be even more relaxing than a drive. She needed to exercise more, but school had left her with no time to do anything but study. Next year would be different. She would set aside time to exercise every day and stick to it.

Stopping on the way to the door, she thought of Alex and knew she should probably forget about going out. But even though she felt certain she'd seen Alex in the area, Karen was insistent that he was dead. Even if she was somehow mistaken and Alex had faked his own death, she doubted if he would consider roaming around at night on foot. For all she knew, Alex could have already moved on, or gone back into hiding with his crazy mother and the rest of the clan. If he had wanted to hurt her, he'd had every opportunity at Whitehall. She'd even slept with the guy.

"Fuck you, Alex," Shana said under her breath. She refused to let another man ruin her life and turn her into a recluse.

Disengaging the alarm system, she slipped out of the house. She couldn't get to the beach from the balcony because it was elevated and if she jumped, she might break her leg. She went out the front of the house and decided it was fun walking around at night. She traveled down the sidewalks lined with blooming flowers and glanced in windows, thinking she might see someone having sex or walking around naked. But it was a quiet community with big houses built close together. Most of the homes were dark except for the outside lights.

She was plodding down the dirt ravine heading to the sand when she heard something behind her, a noise like someone stepping on an acorn. She turned around but no one was there. She decided it must be some kind of animal like a dog or a squirrel.

Off in the distance, she could see the water and hear the sound of the surf. The ocean was beautiful in the light from the moon, shimmering, expansive, and mysterious. She liked that type of thing. She was a romantic and a loner. No one ever saw that side of her. For years, she thought it was because she was an only child and her mother was gone all the time. Later she realized it was just her nature. People were disappointments. They lied to you, let you down, and said bad things behind your back. It was better to be alone sometimes than to get hurt. She had broken that rule with Brett, and look what had come of it.

Shana started down the long flight of stone steps that led to the sand, her eyes focused on the water as she breathed in the fresh, salty scent of the ocean. She relished the wind whipping across her face.

Her stomach started rumbling. Chris had treated them to Mexican food and it sometimes upset her stomach. She looked back up the stairs and saw the public restroom. There was a small light under the overhang and flies and mosquitoes were buzzing around it. The interior of the building was dark. She hesitated, but the rumbling was getting worse.

"Probably no toilet paper," she said, taking the stairs two at a time, the urge overwhelming now. "Dark and spooky or not," she said, wanting to hear the sound of her voice, "when you gotta go, you gotta go." She looked around at the bushes and thought of squatting but then remembered the coyotes that roamed the beaches and decided the restroom was more appealing than having a coyote bite her ass. She stood at the door to the restroom, peering into the darkness. Hesitant but desperate, she finally took a giant step and was inside.

She made it to the toilet in the nick of time. Dropping her jeans she sat down in a stall, easily finding it by the stench. She had seen these places during the day and they weren't even real toilets, even though they had a seat. They were just holes in the ground with sewage tanks underneath.

Shana kept hearing things, little things, but nonetheless unsettling. She strained, trying to go faster so she could get the hell out of there. She didn't even care if she walked on the beach now. She just wanted to get home safe. Something terrible could come crawling up from the hole in the ground.

"I've been looking for you, Shana," a voice said from somewhere inside the room.

The voice sounded so loud. In the stillness, it sounded supernatural. It was magnified by the human electricity of fear, her fear, which was now raging. "What the fuck?" Shana bolted to her feet, grabbing at her pants, then tripping and falling against the door to the stall. She scrambled back to her feet and tried to open the door. It wouldn't budge. How could it be locked from the outside?

"Who's there?" she screamed. "Is that you, Chris? Stop it. Let me out, damn it. I'm not a kid you can punish for leaving the house without your permission."

Shana charged the door with her shoulder. It moved half an inch but that was it. Then she heard someone breathing, a raspy sound. The person was leaning against the door, trapping her inside. She would fight to her death before she would let some man rape her again.

"Just relax, Shana," a man's voice said, air whooshing in and out of his nostrils. "I'm going to open the door but you have to promise you won't scream. You must be perfectly silent. Those are the rules."

Shana froze, unable to breathe, terrified beyond all reason. She knew Chris's voice and it wasn't him. It had to be Alex. She tried to scream but her vocal cords were paralyzed. Her heart was leaping, pounding. In seconds, she was drenched in sweat.

Slowly, the door opened. The figure standing there was illuminated from behind by the exterior light but his face was bathed in shadows. Shana backed up until she collided with the commode and stopped.

"Don't be afraid, Shana. It's me. You know me."

"Alex?" Shana said, coughing up the word. "Alex?" Jesus, Alex had found her! Was it his ghost or was it really him? There was a fetid odor in the air, something terrible and sick. She started to move forward when an arm seized her and smashed her into the stall partition.

The building seemed to shake in an eruption of tremendous power and movement so fast it couldn't be detected. Doors rattled, walls popped and cracked as if they were being blown apart by an explosion. The man's fury almost leaped from his body and became an entity of its own.

"Help me!" Shana cried in a high, shrill voice. The shadowy figure suddenly froze and then began kicking out with his feet, smashing into the commodes and sinks. There was the sound of gushing water. One of the fixtures had broken.

Shana lunged for the door when the man placed a hand over her mouth and his other arm around her neck in a choke hold. How could it be Alex? It could be a maniac rapist or killer. Her eyes fluttered. She gasped for breath. The pressure on her throat increased. All she could hear was the sound of her own heartbeat and the low eerie monotone of his voice. For just that instant, Shana thought there were two attackers, two men in the room with her. She couldn't fathom one human being with such raw strength.

"I'm not going to hurt you. This is just a process we have to go through. It's called transformation. You want to see your mother, don't you, your real mother?"

Kicking the door out of his way, the man started dragging Shana from the building up the hill to the road. The waves were breaking and crashing onto the shore. Cars zipped by on Harbor Boulevard only a few feet away.

"As soon as we get your mother, we'll all leave. We'll leave together like a family, the way we should have left years ago."

Alex opened the trunk of the blue Chrysler, glancing around to see if anyone was nearby, then gently lifting Shana and placing her in the trunk on top of a stack of blankets. "I'm going to close the lid, but don't panic. You can breathe. There's more than enough air in there. We'll take a short ride and then I'll take you out. We can talk about our journey, make plans, and get something to eat. Before you know it, your mother will be here with us."

Shana was unconscious and close to death. The choke hold had deprived her brain of oxygen. A trickle of saliva ran from her mouth. Her eyes were open but unseeing.

Alex closed the trunk and climbed into the driver's seat. He was perspiring and used the sleeve of his shirt to wipe his face. Shana wasn't heavy, but she was unconscious and therefore a dead weight. The whirring noise inside his head was deafening and painful, like a malignant cancer expanding his skull. He thought of his brain more like a human heart, a lifeless, bloodless heart. He stared at the ocean and brought forth the imagery of the pond.

"The pond." Alex whispered the words as if they were something delicious on his tongue, something reverent and holy. "We're almost there, Jennifer."

# THIRTY-FOUR

Lily's eyes sprang open in darkness.

She felt her gown and discovered she was drenched in sweat. In her dream, she had been trapped in the midst of a brackish red funnel cloud spinning through space. All the things from her house, things she recognized—chairs, tables, beds—were twirling around her. Then she saw a man she knew was Alex, his smile stretching his face as if it were made of rubber, floating in front of her holding a bouquet of white flowers. He was nude from the waist down, his erection enormous. Just before she woke up, he bowed before her. When he raised his head, he was pointing a sawed-off shotgun at her face and laughing loud and abrasively. She screamed for him to stop but he fired, the bullets flying past her like rocks.

Even in sleep, Lily couldn't escape this awful man who had tried to steal her daughter from her. Alex had crawled inside her brain.

Turning on her side, she curled up next to Chris and tried to go back to sleep. All she could think about was Alex. Was he alive or dead? Where was he right now? Had he left, given up on Shana, moved on to someone new? She had to find a way to disentangle his insanity and find the string of bread crumbs that would lead her to him. Alex may not have stabbed Shana or shattered her bones, but he had almost stolen her sanity.

She got up to go to the bathroom. As she walked down the small hallway lined with closets, her eyes caught the green light on the alarm panel. She stopped and stared at it in a sleepy daze. She remembered setting the alarm before she went to bed.

"Chris," she said, tapping him gently on the shoulder.

"What? What time is it?"

"Did you turn off the alarm?"

"No," he mumbled, turning back on his side and pulling the covers up over his shoulders.

"The alarm was set when I went to bed and it's off now."

"God, Lily, set it and go back to sleep. You probably forgot."

In seconds, she heard him snoring. She started to walk away but she had a horrid feeling that something was wrong. "No," she said, shaking him again. "I didn't forget."

Now he was awake and grumpy. He reached over and turned on the light. "Why do you have to wake me up? Now I won't be able to go back to sleep and my calendar is jammed tight tomorrow."

Lily didn't want to hear anymore. She tossed on her robe and rushed to the other side of the house, where the guest room was located.

The bed was empty!

Where had Shana gone at this time of night? She went to the garage, but both cars were there.

Returning to Shana's room, she sat down in a chair and stared into the darkness. Why would she do this to her? She wanted to scream, throw her body on the ground and thrash around in anguish. Her daughter was gone, possibly abducted. A maniac who was supposed to be dead was stalking her, maybe with the intention of killing her. Lily was responsible because she had taken Shana to Whitehall. If she had not overreacted, Shana would have never crossed paths with this lunatic. What she refused to accept, even though she knew it was possible, was that her daughter might already be dead.

The room was suddenly flooded with light. Chris was standing in the doorway in his robe. "I had a feeling she might run off. She may not act like it, Lily, but Shana has to be furious that you put her in a mental hospital. Maybe this is her payback."

"You're wrong," Lily said. "Something terrible has happened. Shana told me how much she loved me today. It was the first time in years that we really connected. She wanted to go back to Palo Alto and get a job to help with her expenses. She didn't run off, Chris. Where would she go on foot? She doesn't even know anyone around here anymore and I'm almost certain she doesn't have any money."

"I have no idea where she went, Lily. Most girls with Shana's background would be terrified to go out alone at night." His eyes filled with concern. "Come on, honey, come back to bed. I bet you a hundred bucks she'll be here in the morning. You can't let this drive you crazy. I called her a girl, but she isn't a girl. She's a twenty-eight-year-old woman."

Lily walked over and placed her palm in the center of his chest. "We have to find her. She could be in terrible danger."

"Not the dead guy again."

"When did you stop trusting me?"

"I trust you, Lily. I just think you're overwrought right now. I might be overwrought too if I'd gone through what you have, but you need to calm down and think rationally."

Lily started down the hall to get her coat when he stopped her. "Go back to bed and try to rest. I'll drive around and see if I can find Shana."

"I can't sleep until we find her. I'll go with you."

"No, honey, I want you back in bed. Let me handle this. I have a different perspective."

"And what is that?"

"Shana's been locked up at Whitehall. Being here with us watching her every move isn't exactly freedom. So she went for a walk." He leveled a finger at her. "You relax and I'll find her, but I'm warning you now, Lily, I refuse to drag her back like an escaped prisoner.

If she wants to see the sun rise over the ocean, she has every right to do so. Do you agree?"

Lily nodded and then followed Chris to the bedroom, leaning back against the wall as she watched him throw on a T-shirt and a pair of jeans. He pointed to the bed and Lily quickly got in and pulled the covers over her. She had never seen him so commanding, but she liked it, even found it sexy as long as he didn't go overboard.

If she'd taken the time to visit his courtroom, Lily thought, she would have seen this side of him before now. They were both judges, and their salaries were similar except Lily made slightly more. She wouldn't have a case to try without municipal court judges like Chris. He handled arraignments, various motions, plea agreements, misdemeanor crimes, and most important, preliminary hearings. A preliminary hearing was basically a mini trial, and at the end, the judge hearing the case decided if a crime had been committed and if there was substantial evidence that led to the belief that the defendant had committed it. The judge's official ruling was that the defendant should be held to answer in superior court, which was Lily's domain.

She had failed to treat Chris with the appropriate respect, the same mistake she had made with both of her husbands. She would have to correct herself immediately or she might lose a man she truly loved.

She jumped when Chris bent down and kissed her. "You seem more relaxed. I'm proud of you."

"I was thinking how much I love you and what a wonderful judge you are. Before I go back to work, I'm going to come to your court and watch you in action."

"I'd like that," Chris said, scooping his car keys off the dresser. "Try to get some rest. I'll call you the moment I find her."

Lily's concern returned, causing her to shiver. "What if you don't find her?"

"Then we'll call the police, the FBI, and notify every law enforcement agency in the state. Now rest and try your best to remain positive."

Shana regained consciousness in the trunk of the car. Inside a flash-ing second, she experienced complete and utter terror, so intense and horrifying that she was certain nothing could ever surpass it. Death was squeezing the breath out of her like a boa constrictor. She knew without a doubt that her entire life had been leading to this one moment. The rape could not compare. Whitehall could not compare. Nothing could compare.

Her internal organs were working desperately to keep her alive. Her heart was beating in tachycardia and placing her at risk of cardiac arrest. The human defense mechanism, sensing imminent danger, was flooding her body with adrenaline, coursing like a raging river inside her veins. Her brain, short-circuiting on fear, knew it must es-cape the reality of her predicament.

It could not.

Shana plunged into a dark well of thoughtlessness. Her mind took this avenue as the only solution.

When she awoke, she was in a twin bed. She tried to move but met resistance. A white canvas tarp with metal holes at the ends, such as the type you might find on a tent, was strapped tightly over her body, ending only a few inches under her chin. She could turn her head from side to side. Other than that, she couldn't move.

"Shana," Alex said, "you took a long nap." He had a chair pulled to the edge of the bed and was peering down at her face, a cigarette dangling from his mouth and the smoke swirling above his head like a dirty halo. He tossed the butt in an ashtray and then pressed it out with his thumb. "Sorry, Shana, I know you hate cigarettes. Nicotine is a terrible addiction."

"Where . . . where am . . . I?" Shana stammered, her mind dull and confused.

Alex stood and walked to a window a few feet away, his back to Shana. "You're only a short distance from your mother. She's right across the street. See." He turned around to make certain she was watching and then pointed out the window. "That's your house right over there."

Shana's mind was now alert and racing. She looked around the dark room and tried to figure out where they were. If they were near her mother's house, they had to be in the apartment complex outside the back gate. She had to find a way to escape. Alex was insane. She could see it as well as smell it. There was a putrid odor emanating from his body, as if he hadn't bathed in months. If Shana didn't get away, she would die.

She discovered she could move her hands if she sucked all her breath inside her and pressed her abdomen to her backbone. But moving her hands a few inches wasn't going to help. Somehow, she had to talk him into removing the tarp. "Why are you doing this to me? I thought you cared for me, loved me. I thought we were going to run away together and start a new life."

Alex spun around, his eyes darting all over the room and then landing on Shana. "I'm going to get your mother soon." He waited until he saw the agony on her face and then he smiled. "Don't worry. We're all going to be together. You don't have to worry about your mother. You look so much alike. I was stunned when I saw you both on the beach. I had trouble telling you apart."

Shana started to say something but Alex was approaching her. He took a seat in the chair next to her bed and lit another cigarette. "Sorry, I can't help it. The smoking, you know." He followed her eyes to the dresser, where a disposable syringe, a small glass vial, and a package of cotton balls were sitting. "That, well, that's Demerol. It's a narcotic. It's always been one of my favorite drugs. Unfortunately, it's addictive. Everything good is bad for you these days. Life's a bitch, huh?"

Shana was staring at him with wide, stark eyes. He continued speaking. "It gives you a sense of well-being. Trust me. You're going to love it."

"I . . . no . . . let me up. Please, let me go." Tears gathered in Shana's eyes. She began thrashing inside the tarp. Her nose began running. Panicked inside the tight canvas, she felt like a sniveling baby. Why had she gone out alone at night when she knew Alex was looking for her? But this, this was a nightmare come to life.

"Your mother should have come to visit you at the hospital," Alex told her, going to the bathroom and returning with a tissue. He wiped her nose and then tossed the tissue in the trash can. "I know you've patched things up because I saw you embracing each other at the beach. I could have taken both of you then, but there were too many people around and I wasn't set up yet." He glanced around the apartment. "I had to get approved for this place. They made such a big deal you would have thought I was renting a palace." He bent down and picked up a large box. "I want you to see your daughter. She'll look better after we go on our journey. On the other side, we'll all have glorified bodies."

"My daughter?" Shana tried to pick her head up to see what he was talking about, but her range of motion was too limited. Alex saw this and tilted the box so she could see the contents. Some kind of strange object was arranged on what appeared to be a satin pillow. She was too far away to identify the object but to her, the outside resembled a miniature coffin. When Alex brought the box closer, she saw it and had to suppress the urge to vomit.

Alex was holding a real coffin!

There was something inside that looked liked sticks attached to a round object about the size of a baseball. Finally she figured it out.

A head! It was a skeleton, a baby's skeleton!

Shana opened her mouth and screamed like a banshee. Alex pounced on her and placed his hand over her mouth. "Stop that, Shana. You're acting childish. People will hear you. We don't want that, do we?"

Shana shook her head from side to side.

"If I take my hand off, you have to promise you won't scream. Do you promise?"

She nodded and Alex removed his hand. "What scared you? That?" he said, glancing at the gruesome contents of the box, now on the floor by his feet. "That's just the remnants of what your daughter used to be. Your name in your former life was Jennifer Rondini. You died and then you were born again into your present body. I know there's a time difference, but they say your former soul doesn't enter your new body until you're older, somewhere around puberty. Before I found you, this was the only thing I had left of our baby. I removed it from the earth. I didn't want my only child in the dirt where animals could eat her."

"Please let me up or at least loosen this thing over me," Shana told him. "I can't breathe, Alex. It's cutting off my air. If you don't take it off, I'm going to suffocate. Do you want me to die now, right now? I thought you wanted us to cross over together."

Alex didn't answer. He appeared to be lost in his thoughts. For an unknown period of time, he just sat there in the chair next to the bed, smoking one cigarette after another and rocking his chair back on its rear legs. Then a curtain of darkness fell over his eyes. He grimaced and stood, walking to the dresser and filling the syringe.

"What are you doing?" Shana shouted. "Don't stick that in me, Alex. Please, I won't make any more noise."

Shana watched as Alex rolled up his sleeve, slapped his arm several times, and then plunged the needle into his vein. His head fell back and his mouth opened as the narcotic entered his bloodstream. He removed the needle from his arm and refilled it, walking over to the edge of the bed and untying one corner of the canvas tarp. He picked up Shana's arm. She jerked it away, but Alex seized it. He was too strong. She tried to escape through the opening in the tarp, but Alex's body blocked her. He whipped his belt off and tied it around Shana's arm, then plunged the needle in, hitting the vein on the first try. After he finished, he tossed the disposable needle in the trash can by the bed and retied the tarp tightly around Shana's body.

She was flooded with warmth and contentment, a welcome relief from the previous terror. She smiled and Alex smiled back.

"Good stuff, isn't it? You'll sleep now." Alex's words were thick and slurred by the drug. "I used to be fascinated by death, the process of dying. I never understood why I wanted to kill things and study them as they died. I was only seeking answers like any scientist or researcher. Death, I determined, is going backward through the evolutionary pond. The life essence that makes you what you are, well, it can be freed to join with the universe or what people refer to as the Godhead, or it can become trapped in another worthless body. So many people hate their lives. I know because they have clubs . . . suicide clubs. They want to die and trade their body in for a new one. I know you want that, too, so I'm going to help you do it, just like I'm going to help your mother." He exhaled a stream of cigarette smoke. "I know you're probably still harboring resentment over what your mother did, but on the other side, everyone loves each other. There's no anger, no resentment, no depression, no violence. It's paradise, just what we're all seeking, even if we don't realize it."

Shana was giggling, her eyes closed, her head rolling from side to side. The implications in Alex's words slipped past on a cloud of narcotic-induced delusions. She was back in time, hanging out with her teenage girlfriends, completely and mercifully unaware that her life hung in the balance.

A few blocks away, Chris traveled the dark streets, up one and then down another, searching the lawns, the sidewalks, between the houses. He steered the car into the narrow alleys and caused all the neighborhood dogs to begin barking and howling. The gas gauge on the Volkswagen was on empty. He had planned on filling it up that morning. He couldn't drive around any longer on fumes. He would have to give up or find a service station that was open at three o'clock in the morning.

As Chris figured it, Shana had made contact with one of her friends and they had picked her up. They could have gone out to a dance club, and nothing happened at those places until late. But she could have left a note. That is, unless she had connected with her friend after they had gone to bed. Now that made sense, he told himself, a heck of a lot more than an alleged dead guy snatching Shana from her bed.

He rubbed his eyes and tried to see the road in front of him. Here he was, bone tired, a hectic day ahead of him, searching the city for someone who more than likely didn't want to be found.

Good luck on finding a gas station that was open. Ventura was a bedroom community and they rolled up the sidewalks around ten at night. He was heading down the Pacific Coast Highway to find a gas station when the Volkswagen sputtered and died. He had never run out of gas before in his life. You weren't supposed to run out of gas in a Volkswagen. He'd known he was low on fuel and felt like an idiot. He should have taken Lily's Volvo.

"Damn it," he said, getting out and lifting the hood to raise the chances of someone stopping to help him. He was at least seven miles from the house, and in his rush to leave, he had forgotten to bring his cell phone. Cars zipped past him, but no one stopped. No one would stop at this hour. After waiting beside the road for at least thirty minutes, he locked up the car and began walking.

# THIRTY-FIVE

After Chris left, Lily sat up in bed and tried reading, but she kept falling asleep. She reassured herself that everything was okay, that Chris would come home any minute with her daughter in tow. Shana's insomnia might be to blame. Since the hospital hadn't sent her home with any medicine, she would have to take her to their family doctor and get her on one of the new sleep medications such as Lunesta or Ambien. Lily had suffered from insomnia until she had become involved with Chris. He had chased her demons away, and without the past haunting her, she slept through the night without a problem.

She tried to call Chris on his cell phone and became concerned when he didn't answer. Then she heard a ringing sound in the bathroom and realized he'd forgotten to take his phone. Since someone had to stay at the house in case Shana returned, she finally turned off the light and fell asleep.

When she awoke sometime later, she was snuggled up against Chris's back. He must have found Shana, she thought, feeling her body go limp in relief. Because of the blackout drapes in the bedroom, she couldn't tell if it was morning or still dark out. Everything had to be okay or Chris would have never come home. She felt hot and tossed the covers off. Chris's body was so hot, she wondered if he was coming down with something. Poor man, she thought, he'd become embroiled with her life and her life was never easy. She reached over his shoulder and placed her hand on his forehead, finding it warm and clammy.

Lily suddenly smelled something disgusting and foul. Was it body odor? Chris had never smelled like this before, not in their entire time together. He was meticulously clean.

"Chris," she whispered, fearful now that he was really ill. Odors were sometimes linked to serious illnesses. He moaned but didn't move or speak. She lightly touched his shoulder. "Honey, are you all right?"

He turned over, only inches from her face, his breath as disgustingly sour as his body odor. She could only see the faint outline of his face in the dark. "What's wrong, baby? Did you have to chase Shana down or something?"

All she could hear was his breathing, heavy, labored.

Suddenly it was as if a huge animal was squeezing her insides. Bile rose in her throat and she began pushing the thing next to her away, certain it wasn't her beloved Chris.

"Lily," the voice said softly. "It's time to go now. Everything is ready."

It wasn't Chris's voice. She screamed, scooting off the edge of the bed as fast as she could and frantically trying to find the newspaper rack where she kept a revolver. It had to be the man who'd been stalking Shana—Alex, the man who was supposed to be dead. He certainly wasn't a ghost. He was a flesh-and-blood human and she had to find the gun so she could defend herself.

In a flurry of movement, he was on top of her, pinning her to the floor, his naked body pressing into her. The gun was so close, just a few feet away. She pushed and kicked with all her strength but he was too strong.

"Stop fighting me," he said. "I'm here to protect you. I'll never let anyone hurt you again. I already have Shana. She's waiting for us. You're both so beautiful. You must be angels."

Lily continued to struggle, but his body was fueled by the abnormal strength of madness. He stood and she lunged for the newspaper rack. Before she could reach it, he placed his foot on her neck.

He was going to kill her!

She was choking, clawing at the carpet with her fingernails. He picked up what had to be his clothes and dressed, his foot still on her throat, alternating his feet so fast, she didn't have a chance to get away.

He picked her up and tossed her over his shoulder. She grabbed on to the door frame as he passed underneath, but he continued walking and she lost her grip. He carried her into the living room, out the open front door, and then darted outside.

Lily screamed, "Call the police! Someone help me! He's going to kill me!"

They were in the front yard, and Alex threw her to the grass and fell on top of her, sealing her mouth with his sweaty palm. Now she could see him clearly in the light from the neighbor's house. His appearance was shocking. An insane look shot from his eyes. He was unshaven, and his hair was filthy and uncombed.

"Why are you fighting me?" he said. "I've planned this for years, searched all over the world for Shana. This is what we want, what Shana and I want. She wanted her mother to go with us, so I had to come and get you. You don't want to be left behind, do you?"

Holding her tightly around her neck, he removed his T-shirt and stuffed it in her mouth as a gag. Then he picked her up again and tossed her over his shoulder, continuing on in the dew-covered grass. The sky was a dusty gray, but Lily could tell the sun was rising. The pain in her back was so excruciating, she feared she might have broken it.

Alex moved faster now, weaving through the houses, oblivious to the barking dogs. They walked past one window and Lily saw a

man at a table drinking a cup of coffee. She started kicking and
tried to scream inside the gag. With her head upside down and her
body raging on fear, she vomited inside the gag and tasted the bitter contents of her stomach.

The man in the window was gone now and they were passing
another yard. How could this happen? How could she be carried
like a dead body through a heavily populated area, without anyone
coming to her rescue?

Alex had to cross another street. Lily looked down at the asphalt.
Out of the corner of her eye, she saw a boy on a bicycle riding toward them, his basket filled with newspapers. He was looking right
at her. He had to see her, had to see she was in trouble. He rode right
past them, turning to glance over his shoulder at the odd sight and
then turning the corner and disappearing.

Everywhere she could see signs of life: cars, televisions, children laughing. Someone had to see her. Alex was traversing a parking lot of an apartment complex. He stopped and laid her on the
ground beside a Dumpster, reaching into his pocket and removing
a syringe. She tried to pry his fingers off her neck. "This is the best
part, the part you'll like. Shana loves it. You'll see when we get to
our temporary housing."

Shana? God help her, he had Shana!

Up until now, she had thought he was bluffing, that Shana was
safe somewhere with Chris, maybe having breakfast at the local
Denny's. Pinning Alex with her eyes, she felt on the ground for something she could use as a weapon: a rock, a coat hanger, a bottle. Alex
put a knee on her forearm and inserted the needle into her vein. She
watched in a dreamy fog as he then plunged the needle into his own
arm. A few minutes later, he removed the gag, caked with her vomit,
propping her up against the metal trash container like a rag doll.

Somewhere far away Lily heard voices. Alex was talking to an
older woman who had walked up to the Dumpster carrying a heavy
plastic garbage bag. "Let me do that for you," he said, taking the bag
out of her hand and placing it in the Dumpster.

"Thanks, that was very nice of you." The woman glanced at Lily and then returned her attention to Alex. "Oh, my, is something wrong? Is she hurt?"

"She's an addict," Alex told her, speaking in a controlled voice. He reached inside his pants and pulled out a tin badge in a plastic case, flashing it at the woman. "I'm an undercover police detective. Maybe it's better if you move on now. We have a big narcotics bust about to go down and I wouldn't want you to get hurt."

"These drug people," she said, shooting Lily a disgusted look. "They're all over the place these days. Thank you, officer."

"You have a nice day now," Alex called out as the woman walked off.

Through the fog, Lily tried to focus, remain awake. The drug was pulling her down and she knew she would soon be unconscious. She forced out a pathetic plea, but it was only a whisper. "Help me . . . do something . . . please."

As soon as the woman was out of sight, Alex pulled Lily to a standing position and tugged her along behind him like an errant child, her nightgown ripped and dirty, the sun streaking through the thin fabric of her gown and revealing her breasts, legs, and genitals. She stumbled and fell, but Alex jerked her back to her feet. He swept her up in his arms just as she lost consciousness.

When Chris finally reached the house, the sun was up and the door was standing wide open. "Good lord," he said, rushing in and racing up the stairs to the bedroom.

Lily was gone and the bedding was tossed on the floor. He ran back downstairs and checked the guest room. He went to the garage to see if Lily had gone out looking for Shana, but the Volvo was still there. Chris was gripped with fear. As he passed the alarm panel, he knew it was his fault. Lily had tried to tell him about the alarm but he had refused to listen.

Picking up the phone in the kitchen, he called 911 and told the operator his fiancée and her daughter had been kidnapped. A few minutes later, he recalled Lily having lunch recently with an FBI agent named Mary Stevens, and that she had promised to check

Whitehall out. Like a wild man, he began opening drawers and throwing everything on the floor, trying to find Lily's address book. "Idiot," he said, realizing that Lily kept all her contacts in her iPhone. Finding Stevens's number, he quickly dialed it.

"Special Agent Stevens," a woman said in a husky voice. "This better be good."

Chris told her what had transpired along with what he suspected.

"I hate to tell you this," Mary said, "but Lily and Shana are in great danger. I just returned from Whitehall Psychiatric Hospital in San Francisco. We believe the man who called himself Alex is a serial killer. The only good news is that they don't fit the profile of his other victims. Give me your address and my partner and I will be there in five minutes." Once she scribbled down the address, she added, "Don't leave the house. Stay there and work with the local police. I'll check to see if we got a match on the fingerprints Shana sent us. We need a picture of this guy ASAP."

Chris braced himself against the door. "Tell me what to do. This is my fault. I didn't believe them. I left Lily alone in the house with the alarm off. I didn't think to check the front door when I went out looking for Shana."

"Spare me," Mary told him. "Talking isn't going to solve anything. I'll check in with you once I'm on the road."

Chris hung up the phone, put his head in his hands, and sobbed. Once again, he had made a mistake. All he could pray for now was that his failure to take Lily and Shana seriously wouldn't lead to their deaths.

The response was overwhelming. The narrow block where Lily and Chris lived was now lined with black-and-whites, county vehicles, two K9 units, and three motorcycle officers.

Chris dumped out all the photos he could find of Shana and Lily on the dining room table. An officer made copies to hand out to the search team.

Coupled with information provided by Agent Stevens, the local PD determined they were dealing with a dangerous individual and called in every officer they could find. The police helicopter was up and searching. They knocked on doors and questioned as many people as possible.

By nightfall, they had nothing.

Mary Stevens dropped by the house and was drinking coffee in the kitchen with Chris and one of the detectives from the Ventura PD named Hank Sawyer. She told him that Sawyer had been her supervisor before she transferred to the Bureau.

Chris's hands were shaking and dark circles were etched under his eyes. "She's dead, isn't she? They're never going to find them. They're both dead." He knew people sometimes waited months, even years, only to find out their loved ones had been murdered. He had already lost his wife and daughter. How could it happen again?

Stevens was leaning back against the kitchen counter. "Lily's tough. She'll make it. I know it's no consolation right now, but these things take time."

Chris watched as a team of technicians began stringing cable and wires to set up a command post in the dining room. "Do they think he's going to ask for a ransom?"

"We're covering all the bases," Mary said, taking a slug of her coffee.

"Do they know anything, anything at all?"

"We know Shana wasn't imagining things. We matched the prints from the items she gave us. Let me tell you, this is one scary fucker." Mary tossed the Styrofoam cup in the trash and then went to the sink to splash water on her face. "His real name is Adam Pounder, but he has three aliases in addition to Alex Purcell, the name he used at Whitehall. For clarity, we're referring to him as Alex. He did his first stint in a mental institution for throwing acid in a girl's face." She stopped speaking and dried her face with a paper towel. "He murdered another young girl a day after he was released from Camarillo State Hospital. He's allegedly involved in a suicide club that the Bureau and numerous PDs have been investigating. Five people have died and we believe Alex may have killed them. We decided a suicide club was the perfect place for a serial killer to solicit victims. These people want to die and Alex is more than happy to oblige them. He's also a suspect in a homicide in Oklahoma."

"A serial killer?" Chris said, collapsing in a chair. "Are you seriously saying the man who kidnapped Shana and Lily is a serial killer?"

Mary walked out the door without answering, stepping over the wires and cables. Chris watched through the windows until she got in her car and drove off.

The small room was dark, illuminated only from the light in the bathroom. With the shutters closed, it felt as if there was no air in the room. Shana heard a key turn in the lock and stiffened.

Alex's appearance sent shockwaves of fear through her. His navy blue blazer was now wrinkled and stained, and the white T-shirt he had been wearing had disappeared. His face was agitated and his eyes sunken in his head. He didn't look like the same man. The last injection had been hours ago, maybe days. Shana was beginning to lose track of time. The room was littered with fast-food sacks and ashtrays were overflowing with cigarette butts. The stench alone was unbearable.

"It didn't have to be this way. Now it's all wrong. Look at this place, it's disgusting." Alex was spitting out his words in a rapid manic fashion. "I have your mother in another apartment, but they're out there now . . . the police. They're everywhere. They have helicopters and dogs. We have to get to the pond." He was pacing and suddenly stopped, turning and facing Shana. His eyes softened somewhat but he was so out of control he couldn't stand still.

"It's almost time," Alex said, walking to one side of the room and slapping the walls. "Morrow said the planets would be aligned perfectly for us now. The universe is ready. We have to go now, damn it." He looked accusingly at Shana. "This is your fault. If you'd stayed in the hospital, everything would have been great. We could have gone with Norman."

"Listen, Alex . . ."

"Shut the fuck up. Alex is dead. We're all dead. Life is an illusion.

My mother didn't have to tell Jennifer's parents to take her away. We loved each other. She was like me. We're a different species. People don't understand us. When she killed our baby, I had to help her escape."

"Alex, please listen to me," Shana pleaded. "You've got to get out of this room. You're going stir-crazy. Let's go out. We'll get something to eat, maybe go somewhere."

Alex stopped walking and sat down in the chair.

"We can go on a roller-coaster ride if you want," Shana continued, making up things as she spoke, trying to determine what he would react to in a positive way. "You said you'd never been on a roller coaster. We could go to Disneyland or Knott's Berry Farm. We're not that far from those places, Alex. We could have fun."

"We're going soon," Alex said, standing and untying the canvas tarp. "We don't have time for amusement parks."

Shana sat up in the bed, rubbing her hands and then reaching down and massaging her legs. Her legs were so numb, she wasn't sure she could walk.

Alex had moved to the back of the room. Shana didn't see him coming until she felt his hands around her throat and heard her own skull crack as it collided with the wood headboard. Then everything turned black and her body fell limp and lifeless to the floor.

Sunlight flooded the room. Lily opened her eyes to the light itself, the mystery, watching as the dust particles danced in the air. Her tongue felt thick and fuzzy and her back was throbbing. She didn't remember anything other than a vague sense of something amiss. Then she saw Shana and her heart almost jumped out of her chest.

Shana was stretched out on a small bed beside her, nude except for a white sheet draped over the lower section of her body. Her eyes were closed and her arms crossed over her chest. She looked as if she were on a slab in a morgue. Until a person saw their child with the pallor of death, they could never comprehend the meaning of the word heartbreak.

Alex was backed into a corner in the back of the room, a

large-caliber revolver dangling in his hand. Almost casually, he pointed it at Lily. "Don't move or I'll shoot."

Lily didn't care if he killed her. Finding herself unrestrained, she stood up. "You murdered my daughter! Shoot me, you bastard. Go ahead. You're going to rot in Hell for what you did. I'd kill you myself if I could, and don't think for a minute that I wouldn't. I'll track you down and blow your fucking head off. I've done it before and I'll do it again."

Instead of firing at her, Alex simply knocked her to the ground with his arm. Lily felt as if she'd been struck by a machine instead of a human. She hit the floor hard, losing consciousness. A few moments later, she got back on her feet and lunged at him again, this time raking her fingernails down his cheeks. This time he kicked her, then placed his foot in the center of her chest.

"Stop this," he said, swiping at his mouth with the back of his hand. "I never thought you'd act this way. You're being foolish. Shana isn't dead. She's sleeping." His eyes drifted downward as he removed a cigarette from his pocket.

Lily turned her head to Shana. She had to be dead. She was too still to be alive. Tears streamed down her face. In her mind, she saw Shana clucking at her from her playpen, an adorable smile on her round face. Then she saw her in her softball uniform sliding into first base. Only memories, she thought. Alex was going to leave her with nothing but memories. She couldn't live if her daughter was dead. She couldn't be a wife to Chris; she couldn't do her job as a judge. Her life was over.

"Kill me," she told Alex, the look on her face almost as crazed as his. "Go ahead. I don't want to live. Shoot me. Do it."

Something changed in his eyes. He bent down and picked Lily up in his arms, carrying her to the bed. She couldn't see the gun but she knew he had it in his hand. Kneeling down beside the bed, he placed his face close to hers.

"I'm insane," he said, a pitiful testimony. "I can't control the things I do. I can't make the noises in my head go away."

"I know," Lily said, measuring her voice as she desperately tried to formulate a plan. What if Shana was alive? If she was, Lily had to save her.

"I can't take the pain anymore. Don't you understand? I can't take the pain and the loneliness. If they catch me, they'll send me to prison this time. I can't survive in prison. I'm too weak, too insane. The inmates will kill me."

"I know . . . I understand . . . Come to me, Alex. Let me hold you in my arms. I care about you. I really do."

"No," he said, the darkness leaping back into his eyes. "You're trying to trick me. I'm not an idiot." A tentative hand reached out and touched a strand of her hair.

"I know, you're brilliant," Lily told him. "And you're wrong, Alex. I would never try to trick you. What did you do to Shana? What's wrong with my daughter?"

"I told you, she's sleeping."

Lily was praying, begging God to help her, believing against reason that Shana was still alive. She remembered the day she graduated from junior high and how beautiful she had looked, how she stood at least a head taller than her other classmates. It couldn't end this way, her young life, her future, stolen. "Alex," she said, "come to me, baby. Get in the bed with me and hold me. I'm afraid."

"I have to get ready now," he said, reaching for her gown. "We have to go to the pond. If we can't get to the pond because of the police, we'll have to do it here."

He pulled her gown over her head and placed it on the nightstand. She didn't move or struggle. Her eyes were glued to the gun, tracking it like a target, waiting for the right moment to appear. She had to wait, maintain control, not say or do anything that would upset him.

Alex picked up a damp washcloth from a bowl of water by the bed and began moving it slowly over her breasts and stomach. He washed the tears off her face, then lifted each foot and washed it. "When they take you to a funeral home, they clean and prepare your body. I've already prepared Shana."

Lily was beyond fear now, in another range of emotion that was pure intent. Even when he was moving the washcloth over her body, he kept the gun at his side.

Now, she told herself, go for it now. He was distracted, lost in his thoughts. Just as she was about to grab the gun, Alex stepped back and the opportunity was gone. He pulled something out of his pocket.

"Sit up so I can put this necklace on you. When we leave, I want you to look like a queen. I already have my princess, but I needed a queen."

She still had to find a way to get her hands on the gun, so she sat there like a mannequin as he put the necklace on her, then a bracelet, and finally a diamond ring that he placed on her left hand. The jewelry couldn't be real as the stones were too large and would have cost a fortune. Regardless, she might be able to use the ring as a weapon. When he finished, it was a macabre spectacle. She was completely exposed and decked out with jewelry while her daughter's partially naked body was only an arm's reach away.

This was a dream, she told herself, another nightmare. Any minute she would wake up and find herself in her bed with Chris beside her. She always had nightmares when she was under stress.

Alex was slipping another ring on her finger, pushing it past her knuckle. He had dropped down to his knees beside the bed. She tried to lie down, thinking she would have a better chance of getting the gun, but Alex placed a hand behind her and lifted her back up.

He stood and leveled the gun at her. "I never had a bride, a wedding, or a family of my own. Now Shana's going to be my bride and you can be my second bride. In paradise, you can have as many wives as you want."

"There's still time, Alex," Lily said. "I can leave Chris and marry you. Then we'll all be a family. We can run away somewhere where no one will find us. Everyone thinks you're dead so no one will be looking for you."

"No," he said. "You're lying. You don't care about me. We have to go now before the police find us."

Lily made the sign of the cross over her chest. "As I walk through the valley of death," she said, squeezing her eyes closed, "I will fear no evil. Thy rod and thy staff will comfort me, my cup . . ."

She waited for the bullet to tear into her flesh, waited for the darkness, prayed that Shana would somehow be waiting for her on the other side.

Nothing happened and her eyes sprang open.

Alex's hand was trembling. A line of perspiration appeared on his forehead. She remembered the newspaper article Shana had shown her and the statements Alex had made to the police about not being able to follow through on his end of the suicide pact. "Give me the gun," she said firmly. "You can't do it. You didn't kill yourself before and you can't now. To make it up to Jennifer, you have to go first."

He stared at her, the gun jumping as he tried to steady it.

If Shana was alive, Lily knew of only one way to save her. She had to talk Alex into killing himself. If she wasn't successful, she had to find another way to make certain her daughter was the last person standing. As long as she knew Shana had a chance to survive, she would willingly die. Her primary objective, however, was to shame Alex into taking his own life.

"You let Jennifer down, Alex. You shot her and then went back on your word. Killing either me or Shana won't absolve you. I'm a Catholic and we know about these things. You won't even make it to purgatory, let alone paradise." He was listening. She had his full attention. "Do you know what Hell is? Hell is repetition. How would you like to relive the worst day of your life through all eternity? Maybe that's what you've been doing. The reason you keep returning to that day with Jennifer is because you murdered her, Alex. When you didn't follow through with your end of the bargain, what you did to Jennifer changed from mercy to homicide. In the eyes of God, taking a human life is a grave sin, a sin punishable by eternal damnation."

"I have to die first?" he said, blinking rapidly. "But I want us to go together. I don't want to die alone. Once I kill myself, you'll just call the police."

"You're wrong, Alex," she told him, her voice soft and consoling.

"I'm afraid the police will send me back to prison. I went to prison for killing a man. Shana would never tell you, of course, but it's true. I'm the one who should have gone to Whitehall, not Shana. Everyone thinks I'm crazy, even Shana. I was delusional when I let them commit Shana. Don't you understand? I'm schizophrenic. I hear voices. I want to die every bit as much as you do."

"Will you hold me?"

"Yes," Lily said, her eyes brimming with tears. "I promise, Alex." Overwhelmed by sadness, she couldn't help but pity him for his tortured life. Shifting her gaze to Shana, she knew if she was already dead, killing Alex wouldn't bring her back. But she couldn't worry about that now. If Alex killed himself, his death would be on her conscience and she would have to carry that burden the rest of her life, just like she had Bobby Hernandez. If she waited, stalled him, the police might find them and take him into custody. But she couldn't take that chance, not when her daughter's life was at stake.

Turning his back to her, Alex crossed the room. Lily watched as he picked up a syringe and the same drug he had injected her with earlier. She could run, try to escape. What if he was preparing the shot for her or for Shana? Her question was answered when she saw him stab the needle into a vein in his arm. He quickly refilled the syringe and injected himself again. Glancing back over his shoulder at Lily, his lips curled in a weak smile of satisfaction. He continued injecting himself until the vial was empty and he clumsily reached for another small bottle on the dresser and repeated the process until that vial was empty as well.

Alex's left arm was smeared with his own blood. Already weaving and stumbling, his eyelids turned into slits, he tried to make it to the bed but collapsed on the floor. "Hold me. Please hold me. It will be fast."

Lily got out of the bed and placed her hand under his head, bringing it to her chest. He was harmless now. She started to get up to check on Shana but something held her in place. She felt as if she had somehow slipped inside his mind, become a part of him. They were engulfed in silence.

Time stood still.

She held him and stroked his hair, gazing at his face. She didn't move or speak. Her mind was filled to capacity with the event she was witnessing. When his hand opened and the gun fell out, she made no attempt to retrieve it.

"Please," he said, his voice just above a whisper, "tell me you love me."

"I love you, Alex." Her chest was rising and falling with emotion. She glanced at Shana and then back at Alex. Never in her life had she felt such pain, such pathos, and it wasn't just for Shana, it was for the man in her arms.

His eyes closed. The anguish disappeared from his face and he looked peaceful. She rocked him in her arms until it was over, until his body was still and he was no longer breathing.

Before her eyes, Lily saw something, a flash of light so bright that it took her breath away. Her body was flooded with a sense of serenity and exquisite beauty. As fast as it had come, it left. She wrapped a sheet around her body and rushed to her daughter's side.

Shana opened her eyes to her mother's face and a room full of people: police officers, paramedics, two FBI agents, along with several detectives with their badges hooked to their belts.

Before Lily had a chance to dial 911, the police had burst through the doors with their weapons drawn. They made an attempt to resuscitate Alex but it proved futile. The narcotics had suppressed his respiratory system and he was pronounced dead at the scene.

The paramedics had given Shana a shot of adrenaline, bringing her out of the narcotics-induced stupor. "Mom," she said weakly, looking around the room. "Where am I?"

"You're safe, sweetheart." Lily was wearing her nightgown and Chris had given her his jacket. She had a sheet wrapped around her lower body. "It's over. We're in an apartment down the street from our house. Alex is gone. I was so afraid. You'll never know."

Shana tried to sit up but one of paramedics insisted she remain prone. "Just rest," he said. "You've had a rough time." The man turned to Lily. "I think she suffered a mild concussion because she has an abrasion on the back of her head. From the tracks on her arm, the suspect must have been injecting her either with the Demerol or the morphine we found. We want to transport her to the ER and have her checked, but she'll be fine."

Chris looked down at Shana and stroked her arm. "We had every cop in L.A. looking for you and your mother. I'm glad you're all right. I was worried about you."

"Where is Alex?" Shana said, looking around the room.

"He's gone, honey," Lily told her, exchanging glances with Chris. "He'll never hurt you again."

"He's dead, isn't he?"

"Yes, but that's what he wanted. He didn't suffer."

Shana turned away. Lily moved to the other side of the bed and saw she was crying. "I-I feel stupid," she stammered. "I don't know why I'm crying. It's sad, you know? He wasn't really that bad a person. When I was at Whitehall, he took care of me, kept me from going nuts. He was just fucked up, Mom. He got messed up with the drugs, I guess."

"I know," Lily said, bending down close to her face. "It's sad, but Alex hurt a lot of people. The drugs were only a fraction of the problem. He was going to kill you, kill both of us. He would have never been normal, and he would have spent the rest of his life in prison for the crimes he committed." She brought Shana's hand to her mouth and tenderly kissed it, trying not to cry. "I wouldn't have been able to bear it if he'd hurt you. Thank God you're all right."

Shana blinked back the tears. "I want to go home. I don't want to go to the hospital. Can't we go home?"

"Not until they check you out." Lily turned to Chris and he stepped up beside her, placing his arm around her waist. "From now on, everything's going to be fine. Chris and I are going to be with you every step of the way, helping you get your life back on track."

"I'm down for the count, kid," Chris said. "Just don't sneak out of the house anymore or I might have to spank you."

Lily glared at him but Shana was smiling. "Are you kidding? I'm never going out at night alone again. You don't have to threaten me. I'm not an idiot. If I can't sleep, I'll read a book or something. I was scared shitless."

The police officers stepped out of the room so the paramedics could lift Shana onto a stretcher and carry her to the ambulance. Once she was strapped onto the gurney, she gestured for her mother to come closer. "You saved me again, didn't you? Don't tell me you didn't because I know better. I couldn't move, but toward the end, I was going in and out of consciousness and I could hear. You talked Alex into killing himself. He finally got what he wanted. Think of all the lives you may have saved. If they had awards for mothers, you'd win every one of them."

"You're imagining you heard something but you didn't," Lily lied. "The only thing that matters is that you're all right." She leaned even closer and whispered something else in her ear. Shana looked up at the paramedic and smiled, then turned back to Lily. "I agree. I'll get right on it."

Once the paramedics loaded Shana into the ambulance, Chris asked, "What did you tell her?"

"I told her the paramedic was gorgeous and that she should give him her number. She agreed. Now that I think of it, that would make Shana a real ambulance chaser."

Both of them laughed and then Chris hugged her, lifting her feet off the ground. "After all this, you got me to laugh. You're amazing, Lily."

"Of course I am," she said. "If I wasn't, I would have never caught you."

The window in the apartment was open and Lily walked over to it, staring out over the ocean. There was no breeze and the water was perfectly still, shimmering in the morning sunlight. Paradise, Alex had said. Like most people, whether they admitted it or not, Lily wanted to believe as much as Alex. She wanted to believe there was a second chance, a paradise, something waiting for them on the other side. Maybe he had made it, she thought, and was right that minute standing in a green celestial garden with Jennifer, the only person he'd ever loved.

"Lily," Chris called to her from the door. "We need to go. We told Shana we'd meet her at the hospital. If we don't get down there fast, she might hitch a ride with an ax murderer."

Although she'd heard him, Lily couldn't pull herself away from the window. She was watching the water, focusing on one enormous wave as it gathered far out at sea and rolled rapidly toward the shore. On the beach, a flock of seagulls circled and then landed. While the rest of the gulls searched for crumbs left by sunbathers, one gull took flight and soared straight up. Her eyes followed it until it disappeared on the horizon.

"I was just thinking about Alex," she said, walking over to Chris. "I think his death was the easiest thing he'd ever done and at the same time, his greatest achievement."

Chris waited as Lily walked through the door of the small apartment and then followed her. "The way I see it, the maniac got what he deserved. I'm just thankful it's over and that you and Shana are safe."

"He believed in paradise." Lily stopped and glanced back at the apartment. "For just a moment, I think I was actually there."

"Where?" he said, anxious to leave.

"The other side."

They stood outside, Lily taking a deep breath of fresh air. Chris kissed the top of her head. They stood there for a few moments longer, letting the warm sun wash over them before they headed to the car.

# EPILOGUE

Subsequent to Alex Purcell's death, the FBI and other law enforcement agencies across the nation credited him with more than twelve separate unsolved homicides. The police determined that the crusty substance Shana had seen on the window in Alex's room at Whitehall was human blood, human blood with the same DNA as Norman Richardson.

Lily remained skeptical about the other crimes. When a law enforcement agency learned that a killer like Alex had been apprehended, they had a tendency to dig out all their cold cases in an attempt to clear them. They were convinced Alex had killed a woman as far away as Alaska. Most of the evidence was circumstantial and could never be proven in a court of law. Even if Alex didn't actually perpetrate all the crimes attributed to him, Lily knew it provided solace to grieving relatives who wanted to believe their loved ones' deaths had been avenged.

The FBI tracked down Alex's family in Arizona, where they were living under another assumed name. They were prosecuted for tax evasion, harboring a fugitive, perpetrating a fraud, and numerous other violations.

Alex's estate was valued at six million dollars and the jewelry he had placed on Lily was genuine and worth over two hundred thousand dollars. The majority of his wealth came from the three hundred patents he held on his various inventions, which ranged from computer components to lasers and robots now used in a wide range of surgical procedures.

While watching the news one day, Shana clapped when she saw Nadine being handcuffed and placed in the back of a police car. After piecing together the tragic events of Alex's life, Shana felt Alex's mother had heavily contributed to his mental illness.

Due to her mother's relationship with Special Agent Mary Stevens, Shana had been allowed access to Alex's school records, court records, and other documents and files from the various institutions he'd been housed in throughout the years. During his hospitalizations, he was brutally sodomized by another patient, stabbed, and subjected to dangerous mind-altering chemicals, some with long-range permanent side effects. She also discovered that Alex had been administered electric shock treatments on ninety-three separate occasions.

It was inside the state facility, the place designed to care for and treat the mentally ill, that Alex became acquainted with genuine madness.

His grave was exhumed and the coffin found to be empty. Dr. Charles Morrow had signed the death certificate for a fee of twenty thousand dollars. Morrow had been supplying Alex with narcotics for as long as four years. His license to practice psychiatry was revoked and he was sentenced to five years in prison for falsifying a death certificate for profit, two counts of kidnapping, one which involved Ruth Hopkins, the woman who had been singing "Amazing Grace" in the emergency room. Ms. Hopkins, as it turned out, was a well-known gospel singer who had recorded more than six albums.

Morrow was also charged with altering patients' files, illegally dispensing narcotics, and administering psychotropic medications such as Thorazine without written consent from the patient or their court-appointed guardian. He was found innocent of harboring a fugitive.

Peggy Campbell was found guilty of striking a patient, exposing a female patient in front of a male attendant, and other misdemeanor violations. In addition, it was discovered that Peggy, as well as Betsy, had no nursing or medical credentials whatsoever. Peggy served five days in jail and was placed on thirty-six months probation, with the specific stipulation that she was restricted from seeking employment in a psychiatric or medical facility.

Lee had resigned by the time the California Attorney General began his investigation and was questioned and released. She became a witness for the State and was cleared of any wrongdoing.

The following year, Shana graduated from Stanford with honors. Six months later, she passed the bar on the first try.

Sixty days after Alex's death, Whitehall psychiatric hospital was closed by the California Attorney General. This sparked a major investigation of institutions throughout the country that were found to have committed similar unscrupulous practices.

One particular chain of hospitals, a multibillion-dollar publicly owned corporation, even had what they referred to as a PET team, a psychiatric emergency team. This so-called team loitered in emergency rooms attempting to snag insured clients, and another went so far as to visit city shelters in Colorado, Oregon, and Washington during the winter months, showing the occupants pictures of sunny beaches and plush landscaping as a tool to entice them into signing themselves in to their institution, which they falsely claimed was a state-run retirement community. Their hospital fees were paid for by Medicare as the majority of these individuals were indigent. Instead of referring to these practices as *patient snatching*, as Shana had, the media labeled it *bounty hunting*.

In one appalling scenario uncovered during the investigation, hospital representatives went so far as to frequent AA meetings, afterward taking some of the participants to a bar and plying them with alcohol until they convinced them to sign voluntary commitment forms.

Lily and Shana formed a foundation to lobby in the state capital in Sacramento for reform of existing laws involving the troubled psychiatric industry.